CAPTIVATED

A Deep in Your Veins Anthology

SUZANNE WRIGHT

The characters and events portrayed in this book are fictitious. Any similarity to real persons, living or dead, is coincidental and not intended by the author.

Copyright © 2021 Suzanne Wright

All rights reserved. This book or any portion thereof may not be reproduced or used in any manner whatsoever without the express written permission of the publisher except for the use of brief quotations in a book review.

Cover design: J Wright

ISBN: 9798754332171

Imprint: Independently Published

CAPTIVATED

To the readers of the series, who've all so patiently waited for the next instalments.

SHATTERED

(Max and Paige)

If there was one thing Paige West thought she knew for sure, it was that Max Kincaid did not like her. So when an argument between them ends in an explosive kiss, she's more than stunned. Even more shocking? He proposes a deal—she'll spend three nights in his bed, they'll burn off the relentless sexual chemistry, and then they'll each go their own way. Sounds simple. What could go wrong? Nothing, providing she can walk away emotionally unscathed. The trouble is … she's not so certain she can.

CHAPTER ONE

(Paige)

I paused in bopping my head to the music as my friend sidled up to me, looking rather red in the face. "You're blushing," I said. "Why are you blushing?"

Ava glanced around, ensuring no one at the afterparty was close enough to overhear. "You can't tell anyone. I mean, the guys probably wouldn't care, but they are kind of shy and likely wouldn't be making out in a dark corner if they were happy to go public." She twiddled her fingers. "What do you think?"

I turned to fully face her, now the height of intrigued. "I think you need to tell me who's getting it on." But the small brunette hesitated. I groaned. "Come on, Ava, you can't let something like that slip and then clamp those lips shut. Tell me who you saw making out."

She leaned toward me and whispered, "David and Denny."

My brows flew up. "Really? My, my, my."

She smiled. "I know, right? I'm kind of excited, because they really suit each—Dude, no, you can't go look."

"Oh, I only want a little peek. Guy-on-guy action can be hot."

"Don't be a perve."

I snorted. "Like you don't want to go watch more of the show."

Ava tried stifling an impish smile but failed. "Okay, I kind of do. We can't, though. It would be wrong."

"So very, very wrong. Which makes it hotter."

"Girl, you're in dire need of getting laid, aren't you?"

Undeniably, but ... "We're not talking about me. We're talking about David and Denny." The two males were part of the Grand High Vampires' legion made up of over a hundred vamps. There was only one female squad—Ava and I were both part of it. "I'm not really surprised that this happened. Something's been brewing between them for a while."

"I know. I hope it's serious. They're so cute together." She let out a dreamy sigh. "Let's not say anything about it to anyone else. It's their news to tell. I know it's hard keeping secrets on such a tiny island, but we can at least let them be the ones to spread the news—or not."

I nodded. "Agreed. We say nothing." The aforementioned tiny island was privately owned by the Grand High Pair and set in the Caribbean on which our gated community known as The Hollow had been built. There was no way to get bored here, because there was plenty of entertainment, including a nightclub, cinema, and bowling alley.

Hearing a loud laugh, I looked over to see another of my squad members, Alora, leaning into her mate, Evan, while chuckling at something one of the many party guests was saying. I nudged Ava and tipped my chin in Alora's direction. "She looks so happy. And Evan looks so smug."

Ava snickered. "Well of course he does. He's been pressuring Alora to Bind herself to him for a while now."

I understood why Alora had hesitated to rush into anything with Evan. It was no small thing to enter into a Binding considering a psychic link formed between the couple that was so invasive your partner would feel your emotions, hunger, mood, and even be able to sense your location.

For a long time, it was believed that such connections could only be broken by death, but my best friend and fellow squad member, Imani, had the ability to sever such links, including blood ties. Still, no one would ever make such a commitment lightly.

Bindings were week-long celebrations that culminated in a beautiful ceremony. The festivities featured everything from fancy dinners to paintballing, depending on the couple. And as Evan was the Grand High Pair's Heir, master vampires had come from far and wide to attend.

The grand garden was decorated beautifully with butterfly lights, torches, and candles. Many tables circled the man-made dance floor, which was currently far from empty. Most of the dancers were vampires, but a few were intoxicated humans—feeding from them was the only way our kind could get drunk. Many vampires were blitzed at this point. And since such celebrations could go on past dawn, most would be absolutely hammered when the afterparty came to an end. It wasn't unusual for some to crash on the beach and sleep the day away after such events. Contrary to popular belief, sunlight didn't hurt us.

I was ever so slightly on the tipsy side, but I hadn't fed from more than one drunken human tonight. Mostly because I was still bloated from the Binding feast. Vampires didn't need solid food to survive, but we certainly indulged.

"Evan's looking mighty fine in that tux," Ava commented. She slid me a mischievous look before tipping her chin toward a particular cluster of guys. "Max is looking rather dashing, too."

I ignored the flutter in my stomach. It didn't matter what the male in question was wearing—he always looked like he'd just stepped right out of a 'Sexiest Men Alive' article. Long and lean and muscled, Max Kincaid was all kinds of delicious. His watchful eyes made me think of a mountain lake—cool, calm, startingly blue. His mouth was nothing short of carnal; it could curve into a warm, sexy as shit smile just as easily as a cruel, you're-so-fucking-dead grin.

He'd recently traded his military haircut for a classic short back and sides … and damn if I didn't have the occasional urge to run my fingers through the rich brown strands he'd allowed to grow. I also wouldn't mind doing a personal inspection of his rock-hard abs, or maybe giving that epic ass of his a little squeeze.

At Ava's expectant look, I sniffed and said, "He scrubs up well."

She gave me a look that said she was not buying my apparent disinterest. And so she shouldn't. It wasn't *my* fault that he was so alarmingly seductive. He possessed the kind of appeal that any woman would be susceptible to. Especially with that air of complete control that held just a hint of wildness—it was *totally* bad boy.

More, he walked with the smooth stride and undauntable composure of any apex predator, like a jungle cat prowling through the underbrush. My hormones honestly didn't know what to do with themselves around him.

"He's not sleeping with Ursula anymore," said Ava.

Yes, I'd heard. The female had apparently thought he intended to commit to her. It seemed that she was wrong. And I'd be lying if I said a part of me wasn't relieved about it. Which was a little unfair of me, but there was no changing it. "Hmm."

"Ooh, are we pretending you're totally unaffected by the news and, more, that you don't want to jump his bones?"

"Yes, that's exactly what we're doing. So glad you're on board."

She sighed. "Fine. Just know you're not fooling me. I see how much you like him, and I'm thinking it's a two-way street."

Okay, now she was just confusing me. "Perhaps you haven't noticed that he actively avoids me."

Ava's brow creased. "No, I have. While he never really sought you out in the past, he also never went out of his way to not be around you … until recently. There's this weird, thick, crackly tension between you now."

There was. It felt unstable and precarious and filled with things left unsaid. I had the feeling that was why Sam and Jared—a couple who were not only the Grand High Pair, but also the commanders of our squads—had forced Max and me to train together several times. They were probably worried that the aforementioned tension would somehow translate into something bad on a battlefield.

"I thought you guys had a disagreement or something," Ava added.

"That would require us to actually talk to each other, and we don't do that outside of legion situations. He might occasionally say hi to me in passing, but I usually just get a nod or half-smile." He was uber social with everyone else, though.

All charm and confidence, Max was the kind of guy who could walk into a room and talk to anyone about anything. He had a way of sucking people in, putting them at ease, and making them feel good about themselves.

"He's not rude to me," I went on. "Just indifferent." Which kind of hurt.

"I'm not so sure he *is* truly indifferent to you."

"Give me one good reason why he'd fake aloofness towards me. He doesn't play mind games with women. If he's interested in a woman, he has no problems letting her know. But he's never once flirted with me. Not even when drunk off his ass."

"But he *did* defend you when Stuart badmouthed you."

"If Max hadn't, one of his other squad members would have. They look out for our squad, just as we look out for theirs."

"Stuart accused him of having a thing for you. Max didn't deny it."

"He also didn't confirm it, and he's never done anything that would suggest Stuart was right."

Ava's shoulders drooped, and her face set into a mask of disappointment. "I can't deny that. But don't be so sure Max isn't interested or that you have him all figured out. He isn't quite as one-dimensional as he seems."

Oh, I already knew that. He came across as so open and outgoing that it was easy to miss that he held back parts of himself and never fully let down his guard. "Did you know he never feeds from his bedpartners? I'm not just talking during sex, I'm talking *at all*. He doesn't let them drink from him either." I wondered if it felt too intimate to him; if he felt that he needed to keep something of himself back and, in turn, wouldn't take too much from them.

"It's unusual, but some vampires are like that. Ursula didn't seem pleased that Max is one of them. Speaking of Ursula, she keeps casting you very unfriendly looks."

I tracked Ava's gaze and sighed inwardly. Ursula stood with a few of her friends, muttering to them angrily. I'd caught her glaring at me a few times, but I'd ignored it. I was *not* going to start shit at my friend's party. "Before you ask, I have no clue what her problem is. She's never been all that nice to me, but she's never been uncivil or downright hostile either."

"Weird, huh?" Ava pursed her lips. "I never got the impression that Max was serious about her. Did you?"

"I've never gotten the impression that he's been serious about anyone. I don't think he wants to be. He seems out to have fun. That's why I wouldn't have made any moves of my own even if he had shown interest in me. I want a *partner*. I want what you and Salem have," I added, referring to a member of Max's squad.

"You'll find it."

"Given we live on an island where the ratio of men to women is like 60:1, you'd think it wouldn't be too hard for me to find a guy. But once they realise I'm not just looking for something sweet and shallow, they get wary."

"Because you're not just *any* woman. You're part of Sam's personal female squad. They're terrified she'll kick their ass if they hurt you. Also, you're a total badass yourself. Some guys find that intimidating." Deadpanned, she added, "Max doesn't."

No, he didn't, but … "Max isn't an option."

"Well, is there anyone you have your eye on? Personally, I'd turn my attention to Damien. He's a total hottie."

I hummed in agreement. "He also keeps staring at that cute little human waitress. Reuben and Ian seem to be teasing him about it." While Reuben was a member of Max's squad, Ian belonged to another. He and Reuben had been dating for a while now. "Ah, your very own hottie is heading this way."

Salem was big and badass and gruff. But then, most Pagori vampires were moody. They were also the strongest and fastest of the three breeds, but I didn't envy them. For one thing, as a Keja, I was only slightly weaker in those areas anyway. For another, their bloodlust was more intense, and the poor bastards had a red tint to their irises—a tint that often glowed when they were pissed, horny, or thirsty. Keja irises held an amber tint, which was far less noticeable. Unfortunately, we also had fangs, but they only descended when we willed them to.

Sventés were the weakest breed in terms of strength, they didn't have the Keja hypnotic beauty, and their gifts tended to be defensive rather than offensive—though, in cases such as Ava, not always. But they had different strengths. For instance, their bloodlust wasn't overpowering, and they had no tints to their irises. This enabled them to better blend with and live among humans, which was no small thing in my opinion.

Reaching Ava, Salem drew her close and dipped his head to kiss her. "I've been looking for you."

"You say it like I've been missing for hours." She leaned into him. "I've only been gone, like, twenty minutes."

"Twenty minutes too long," he said. Yeah, he didn't like being away from her much. It was pretty cute. He'd Bound himself to Ava, which I thought showed good judgement on his part, because she was freaking ace.

I lightly touched her shoulder. "Gotta use the restroom, I'll be right back."

I strode through the crowd, exchanging smiles and hellos. Sam and Jared's adorable assistant, Fletcher, tried dragging me onto the dance floor.

Laughing, I pulled free of his grip as I backed away … and crashed right into a wall.

I quickly turned. Not a wall. A person so tall, solid, and tough he hadn't even flinched. *Max*. I forced a smile. "Sorry, didn't see you there."

"No worries," he said in that low, deep voice that flustered my hormones. His vampiric scent—something our kind developed on Turning—was just as compelling. The guy smelled like dark chocolate and fresh mint … just like my favourite candy bar. How was that even fair?

His brow knitted. "You haven't seen David or Denny, have you?"

Unfortunately, no, I'd been deprived of what surely would have been a scorching scene. I shook my head. "Nope. But if I see them, I'll tell them you're looking for them."

"No need. I just wondered if—" He cut off, his hand flying out to grip my arm and steady me. Why? Because Ava accidentally-on-purpose stumbled into me, forcing me to almost fall into him.

Her gaze glinting with mischief, she apologised profusely. I narrowed my eyes at the little minx, who then blew me a kiss and walked away with Salem.

Oh, I'd get her back for that. I stepped away from Max, felt heat boring into me from across the room … and saw that Ursula was glaring at me again. I exhaled heavily. "Your ex really needs to stop snarling at me," I told him. "I don't know what her deal is, but this isn't the time or place for her to act on it."

He sighed. "She's a little pissed at me right now."

"But it's *me* she's snarling at. And while I get that that's not something that'll really bother you—"

"Whoa, why wouldn't it bother me?"

"Well because … you know … you don't like me."

His brows snapped together. "When did I say that I don't like you?"

"You don't have to say it. It's easy enough to sense." But there was really no point to this conversation, was there? "Just have a word with her if you get a chance."

I shrugged past him and headed into the mansion that was once solely the residence of the prior Grand High Master. Sam and Jared hadn't wanted to live here; they felt it was too much Antonio's home. So the ex-ruler, along with some other vampires, now only occupied half the building. The other half was office space.

Inside the restroom, I quickly went into a stall and did my business. I was washing my hands when Ursula sauntered inside, *all* attitude. Well wasn't this just excellent.

Glaring at me, she flapped her arms. "I don't get you."

I blinked. "Excuse me?"

"You want him. Max. I see it. So why not be with him or—better still, in my opinion—be clear to him that it isn't going to happen so he can move forward?"

Uh, what? I puffed out a breath. "Okay, I have no idea what you're talking about."

Her lips flattened. "Max is a good guy. Only a bitch or a fool would play him. Which are you?"

"Play him?" I echoed, drying my hands with paper towels.

"You give off just enough of a signal to make it clear that you want him, but then you act all aloof and chilly toward him. Why? Are you playing hard to get? Do you just get off on being a hot and cold bitch to keep him off-balance? I'm honestly confused."

"That makes two of us, because I *still* have no idea what you're talking about. But you know what, none of this needs to be discussed here and now. This is Alora and Evan's night."

I went to walk away, but she slid into my path. I felt my eyelid twitch. If there was one thing I did not do well with, it was having someone try to keep me somewhere I didn't want to be. It reminded me of a period in my life that I most hated.

Ursula set her hands on her hips. "If you don't want him, be straight with him and tell him that."

"I really don't need to," I said slowly, like I was speaking to a clueless child. "He isn't interested in me. Never has been. Ask anyone. They'll confirm it. If what you're looking for is a person to blame for why he hasn't committed to you, you're looking in the wrong place."

She snorted. "Oh, I don't think so. You have him all messed up."

I frowned. "Are you high?" It would explain a few things. I gave my head a quick shake, absolutely done here. "Let's just drop it. Like I said, it's Alora and Evan's night."

I made a move to skirt around her but, *again*, she blocked my path. Feeling my agitation build, I let out a humourless chuckle and flexed my fingers. "You need to step aside. Now."

"What I *need* is for you to stop acting like you don't know what I'm talking about," she countered, her eyes hard as ice. "You know exactly what I mean. You know exactly what you're doing to Max. You know it's cruel and shitty, and *that's* why you won't just admit to it."

My eyelid twitched again, because now she was all up in my space—*another* thing I hated. "You need to back up, sweetie. There's a good girl. Now, I'm going to go enjoy the rest of my evening. I suggest you do the same."

Again, I went to leave. Again, she got in my face.

Worse, she grabbed my bare arm, digging her nails hard into my skin, and sneered, "Well you can shove your suggestion right up your ass."

I snapped my hand around her throat, liking the choking sound that rattled in her throat. "You're pushing me a little too hard."

Her eyelids flickered. "Let me go." It was a shaky order.

"But I don't wanna. Besides, it seems like you want me to stay." And if I walked out, she'd only follow me to continue this. It was better all round to keep the situation contained here, where it couldn't taint the party.

She curled both her hands around my arm but didn't retaliate. Well of course she didn't. Because my gift? Well, I could transfer a wound from one person to another. If she injured me, I would only slap that injury onto her, and it would hit her three-fold.

Ursula gave me an imperious look that fell flat. "If you hurt me, I will go right to Sam—"

"And get laughed at," I finished. "Which sounds like it could be fun. How about we go together? We can even link arms and stuff. You can tell her how you tried starting shit at Alora and Evan's party, and how I tried walking away several times but you kept getting in my way. I'm sure she'll *totally* side with you."

Hinges creaked as the door opened.

Max poked his head through the gap. He took in the scene and cursed. "What's going on?" he asked, stalking inside.

"Please help me, Max, she won't let me leave," whined Ursula, feigning terror. "*Please* do something. She's crazy."

I snickered. Like he'd fall for that act or ever side with her over one of the legion.

Max looked at me, his face blank. "Paige, let her go."

The fuck?

A wheezing sound left Ursula, and I realised I'd tightened my grip on her throat. Oops.

"Come on, just let her go," he said, a soothing edge to his voice … like I needed to be talked down from a major meltdown or something.

People often accused me of having a Berserk button. Which was not true. But yes, I had a temper. And yes, if someone went too far, I did tumble all over their shit. But it was downright insulting that he'd think I'd lost it— Ursula would be *unconscious* if that was the case. I could easily take her down. He should know that.

"You can't keep her here against her will," he said.

Well of course I could. It was only fair, since she'd tried to hold me here when *I'd* tried to leave.

Exasperation swiftly crossed his face. "Dammit, Paige."

He said that to me a lot. In that very tone. Far too often, really. Because Max here, well, he had control issues. I didn't always fall in line with what he wanted. And apparently, what he most wanted right then was for his itty, bitty she-vamp to be safe.

I pouted at her. "Well would you look at that, Ursula, it seems like he's a little protective of you. Isn't that sweet? Hey Max, while you're here tainting my air, maybe you could spell out that I had nothing to do with why you two are no longer together."

"He can't say that," she said. "Not without lying."

I narrowed my eyes at him, because he was looking shifty all of a sudden. "Did you use me as an excuse as to why you wouldn't commit to her or something?"

He frowned, his head drawing back slightly. "What? No."

"So if you didn't mention me at all—"

"Oh, he mentioned you," Ursula cut in, glaring at him. But then, as if remembering she was supposed to be playing the terrified damsel, she morphed her glare into a mask of fright. "Please, Max, do something. *Help me.*"

I rolled my eyes. "Such a diva."

He took a careful step toward me. "Come on, Paige, let her go."

He was *seriously* not only buying her crap but pretty much jumping to her defence? He really believed I had so little control that I might snap her neck?

Irritation flared through me yet again. And I could think of the perfect way to get it all out of my system. Namely, knocking him on his ass.

I flicked up my eyebrow. "You want her, come get her."

CHAPTER TWO

(Max)

Did I know that Paige hadn't truly lost her temper? Of course I did. But if I'd sided with her, Ursula would have attacked her in a fury. Then Paige would have beaten the shit out of her—something Paige would have later regretted due to it being Alora and Evan's Binding celebration. I didn't want that.

Plus, Ursula didn't truly deserve to get her ass handed to her. She was wrong to direct her anger and hurt at Paige, but she *did* have a right to that anger. It was my fault she was hurting, so I'd deal with the consequences and, in doing so, stop Paige from doing something she'd later regret. That meant switching her irritation from Ursula to me—something I'd clearly succeeded in doing. A little too well, by the looks of it.

I'd noticed Ursula follow Paige, so I'd figured there would be a confrontation of some kind. When neither exited the restroom, I'd suspected some shit was going down. Paige would not engage in a public smackdown during her friend's celebration. But play with Ursula just a little in a contained environment? Yeah, she'd do that if for no other reason than she'd be pissed at Ursula for pulling this shit during the party.

"Beating *her* ass would do nothing for me—she'll be too easy to take down," Paige added. "But you? Yeah, I'd get a kick out of duelling with you."

I didn't doubt it, but I hadn't expected her to issue such a challenge. I'd figured she'd toss Ursula aside and then verbally rip me another ass hole. Paige and I had duelled many times in the arena, but that was different. That had been about improving our combat skills. It hadn't been about hurting each other. "You know I'd never lay a finger on you in anger."

Something flashed on Paige's face. Something ... vulnerable. But then she lifted her chin a notch. "Then I guess I'll be keeping your dainty princess with me a little longer."

Ursula turned wide eyes my way. "*Help me,*" she pled, forcing her voice to shake.

I bit back a snort. I wasn't buying her act. She might be wary of Paige, but she wasn't terrified for the simple reason that she knew Paige wouldn't go *too* far.

"Oh, I don't think she wants to stay with me, Max." Paige shook her head sadly. "She's waiting for you to come rescue her. That's what princes do. You clearly want to be hers, so don the shining armour and get moving."

I had no interest in being anything to Ursula, let alone her damn prince. Paige was utterly mistaken if she thought I was protective of the other female. The only woman in this room I was protective of was Paige. And not just because she was a member of the legion.

I'd wanted Paige West since the moment I first laid eyes on her. Wanted to explore that tall, slender body. Wanted to taste that fleshy mouth. Wanted to see those blazing green eyes glaze over as she came. Wanted to know how her coconut-and-cream scent would smell when spiced with arousal.

I'd had far too many fantasies about her. About stripping her, touching her, burying myself balls deep inside her. She had fucking great hair—thick, sleek, wavy, with streaks of purple running through it. I'd imagined bunching that dark mass in my hands while she sucked me off.

I hadn't once acted on what I wanted, though. It wouldn't have been fair to her. She was the last person in the world who should have to deal with my personal baggage. I owed her more than I could ever repay, though I doubted she'd see it that way.

Paige hadn't hidden that the attraction was mutual. She wasn't afraid to approach a guy she liked. And since I'd doubted I'd have the will to turn down any move she made, I'd allowed her to think she didn't hold any interest for me. I'd done my best to ensure she'd see no point in making any such move. It had worked. But it had also caused her to have little time or patience for me, which I hated.

I also hated that the longer I fought her pull, the harder it had gotten to keep my hands off her. It was just as hard seeing her with other men. I couldn't even stand seeing her drink from human donors. Jealousy had near blinded me when I saw her feed from a drunken male human earlier.

I'd spent most of the night watching her. It was hard not to. That goddamn sexy little dress wasn't helping matters. It was black and sleeveless and tight, and I wanted nothing more than to see it hiked up around her waist while I took her. Those heels could stay on—

"Max," whined Ursula. "*Do something.*"

"Yeah, Max, do something," urged Paige.

I sighed, my shoulders lowering, because the steely glint in Paige's eyes told me she was not going to back down. "We'll duel, if that's what you want.

But put her out of the room first." There was no way I was going to try wrestling Ursula from Paige's grip. Mostly because it was near impossible to make Paige release *anything* she wanted to keep—something that had quickly become apparent during training sessions.

Paige licked the front of her teeth. "If I shove her out, I won't be gentle about it," she warned.

Given how Ursula had acted … "I wouldn't expect you to be."

Surprise flickered in Paige's eyes.

Ursula gaped at me, her fake fear quickly replaced by anger. "You bastard. I can't believe you—" She gurgled as Paige dragged her toward the door while humming a tune.

Paige roughly shoved her out of the restroom, locked the door, and turned to face me.

"Is there any chance you'll drop this so we can go back to the party?" I asked.

She kicked off her shoes and planted her feet, every inch of her battle-ready.

Hell. "I'll take that as a no."

"We don't use our gifts."

I inclined my head, planning to disable her as fast as possible. Because I did not want to have a full-on duel with her. I certainly wasn't going to go at her full-throttle, but I doubted she was planning to return that favour. I couldn't blame her. "Well, who's—"

She exploded into action, all fists and feet and elbows. I blocked and ducked and sidestepped. Still, she landed a fair amount of blows, and they all hurt like a son of a bitch.

I'd fought an endless number of opponents. I knew to study their technique so I could predict and counter their moves. There were only two things that Paige was ever guaranteed to do during each fight. One, she never telegraphed her intentions. Two, she never set a pattern. Both of which made it hard to pre-empt and block her.

I retaliated, but not hard. I mainly focused on trying to subdue her. There was nothing easy about it. Trying to pin Paige in place … fuck, you'd have better luck nailing a blob of ice-cream to a tree. She was as quick and slippery as a goddamn cat.

Pausing, she glared. "If I wanted a spar, I'd have said so. Fight. Me."

"I'm not going to hurt—*motherfucker.*" I didn't have time to rub at the jaw she'd just slammed with a fist, because she flew into action again.

I put a little more *oomph* behind my strikes, determined to neutralise her so we could put a stop to this duel. As a Pagori, I was faster and stronger than her. The problem was … she'd been trained to fight people who were faster and stronger; trained to use that strength and speed against them. And she did that very thing right then.

We kept on exchanging blows, though mine were mostly defensive. I'd hoped to wait her out, but she showed no signs of tiring or calming. Then one of her fists rammed right into my Adam's Apple, and I was absolutely done with this ridiculous shit. So I did what I'd agreed not to do—I used my gift of sensory paralysis.

With the simple action of balling up my hand, I took away her eyesight and hearing. She froze with an enraged gasp. I slammed her against the wall, secured her arms above her head, and used the weight of my lower body to pin hers in place. Satisfied that she was going nowhere, I returned her senses to her.

Paige's beautiful eyes narrowed. "You motherfucking son of a fucker." She struggled. *Hard.*

My blood shouldn't have heated. Shouldn't have pooled low. But seeing her trapped, feeling her buck against my cock, having her breasts brush against my chest, knowing she was completely at my fucking mercy ... yeah, I got hard. And she felt it. Stiffened. Swallowed. Went from angry to cautious in a second flat.

She didn't tell me to free her, didn't move an inch ... as if worried that anything she did or said would come across as some sort of sexual challenge.

I *should* let her go. *Should* back away. But I didn't. Maybe it was the adrenaline, maybe it was the alcohol in my system, maybe it was that fucking dress ... but I snapped. "Fuck." I slammed my mouth down on hers.

Jesus, she tasted like sin. And I had to have more. There was no stopping, no resisting, no pulling back. All the need I'd bottled up for too long bubbled to the surface and shattered my control.

I took her mouth in a hot, bruising kiss, so fucking greedy for her. That greed was raw and violent and edged with possessiveness.

I licked and nipped and explored every corner of her mouth, wanting to imprint my own on it. She kissed me back, bold and sure and just as hungry. I swallowed every moan as I roughly ground against her, oblivious to everything but her.

My heartbeat thrashed in my ears, and my lungs burned for air. But I didn't free her mouth. Couldn't. Not when I'd craved this moment for *so fucking long.*

She sucked on my tongue, and a growl rattled my chest. I kissed her harder. Deeper. Hungrier. Fucking intoxicated by her.

A little whimper slipped out of her. A sound so hoarse and ragged and desperate that it was like fingertips ghosting over the head of my cock.

I freed one of her wrists only to transfer it to my other hand because, yeah, I liked having her caged against the wall like this. I snaked my free hand under her dress, snapped off her thong, and shoved it in my pocket.

She gasped, her eyes glassy. "Max."

I cupped her hard. "Need you nice and slick." I plunged two fingers inside her. She was blazing hot. Exquisitely tight. So fucking wet.

I wanted her wetter.

I pumped my fingers in and out of her, keeping my mouth pressed to hers so I could taste every moan and whimper and gasp. "I'm going to fuck you so hard you'll feel me all night," I snarled. "You're going to spend the rest of this party with my come in you."

She snarled right back. "Like that idea, do you?"

"Yeah, I do. And so do you." I took her mouth again, addicted to her taste. My dick was so full and heavy it ached. But I wanted her to explode around my fingers before I fucked her, so I growled in satisfaction when I felt her inner walls begin to quake and tighten. "That's it, come all over my hand."

I licked a line up her throat and breathed deep, fighting the urge to sink my teeth into that soft flesh. I wanted her blood in my mouth. Wanted to drink it down. Wanted to keep some part of her in me. More, I wanted her teeth in my—

She came. And it was a gorgeous sight. Her eyes went wide, her swollen lips parted, a loud cry burst out of her. Her inner walls clamped around my fingers, squeezing and rippling. My cock twitched in envy.

Done waiting to take her, I withdrew my fingers, snapped open my fly ... and froze as a fist began pounding on the door.

"Just assure me that neither of you have killed the other," Sam called out, effectively throwing a bucket of water over us.

There was another voice. It was muffled but familiar. *Ursula*. Apparently she'd alerted Sam.

Paige blinked hard, the sex-drunk glaze fading from her eyes.

Hell. I didn't look away from her as I replied, "We're fine."

"Yeah, fine," said Paige, her voice as thick and hoarse as mine.

"There, told you they were probably all right," said Sam in her British accent. "Now bugger off."

Ursula's muffled voice came again, and then I heard two sets of footfalls as both females walked away.

Paige planted her hand on my chest and pushed.

Cursing in my head, I backed away and redid my fly. She didn't once look my way as she straightened her dress and then slipped on her shoes. She glanced around as if searching for something—no doubt her thong. She obviously hadn't noticed I'd pocketed it. And I didn't care to tell her.

Clearing her throat, she pointed at the door, still refusing to meet my gaze. "I'm going to go."

"And carry on like this never happened?"

She shrugged. "I would think you'd prefer it that way. You might not have the most indiscriminate of dicks, but you don't get involved with women you don't like."

"I like you just fine."

Her eyes finally snapped to mine, now flaring with annoyance. "Bull*shit*. Something about me rubs you up the wrong way. Which isn't your fault. But nor is it mine. So I say we just keep doing what we've always done and give each other plenty of space. Oh, and since you seem to be so protective of Ursula, do ensure she gives me that same space."

I frowned. "I'm not in the least bit protective of her."

"You practically begged me not to hurt her."

"Because she's not a bad person, she's just pissed at me."

"She's also pissed at me, and I don't even know why. I have a feeling you do. But I'm hoping you weren't lying when you said you didn't use me as an excuse for why you ended things with her."

"I wasn't lying. And I didn't end things. She did."

Paige's brow furrowed. "*She* did? No way am I buying that. She was all bitter and spiteful and acting like a woman scorned." She perched her hands on her hips. "Look, if you don't want to tell me what happened between you two, fine. You don't need to. It isn't my business anyway. But don't lie to me."

"I'm not fucking lying. She declared it was over, so it's over."

"Why the hell would she do that when she clearly cares about you?"

I closed the space between us and dipped my face to hers. "Because I said your name while I was fucking her."

Paige blinked, and then her arms slipped to her sides. "Wait, what?"

(Paige)

He was … He couldn't mean … I didn't … "No, seriously, what?"

"You heard me. I said your name. I'm not proud of it. I'm pissed that it happened. But there's no way for me to take it back, so she's rightfully livid."

Struggling to make sense of what he was saying, I just stared at him for a long moment. "But … why would you … I don't understand."

"It's not obvious? I want you." His eyes briefly dipped to my mouth. "I want you so much you pop into my head when I'm with other women. I try pushing you back out, but it doesn't work. You're all I can see. I don't like that it happens, I don't like how unfair it is to whoever I'm with at that moment, but fuck if I've been able to stop it happening."

I went back to simply staring at him, feeling … lost. "But you're, like, Flirty McFlirterson, and you've never once come onto me."

"Two minutes ago, I had my fingers buried inside you."

"Before tonight, I mean."

He lifted his hand as if to stroke my hair, but then he dropped it. "You saved my life the first time we met. I don't remember that part. But I remember what came before it. I'd seen the other vampires who were tainted by The Reaper's Call, so I'd known what would become of me, and I'd felt myself fading, weakening, fracturing."

I could still remember the horrible state he'd been in. The Reaper's Call was a sort of incorporeal venom that contaminated and tainted blood, leaving its victims in a frenzied, zombie-like frame of mind. They attacked mindlessly, spreading the taint of The Call with a mere bite. There was thought to be no cure or counteragent, but I'd discovered that I could use my gift to rid him of the bite he'd received from an infected vampire, thus also ridding Max's system of the taint … healing him in the process.

"It's one thing to know you'll die," Max went on. "It's another thing to know that you'll lose all sense of who you are before you do; that you'll become a monster. I hadn't thought I'd be saved, so the whole thing had felt like a slow death. I don't just owe you my life, Paige. I owe you my fucking sanity."

The fuck he did. "You don't owe me anything. All I did was use my gift."

"And, in doing so, brought me back. In my books, you don't repay something like that by coming onto the person who saved you when you have so little to offer. No, you protect them, you look out for them, you respect them enough not to muddy their life with your personal shit. So I told myself I wouldn't touch you. And despite wanting you with every breath I took, I held out. Until tonight." His eyes darkened. "I swear I can still feel you squeezing my fingers."

I swallowed, mentally scrambling to process his words. The guy had been resolved to never touch me because he felt that he owed me? I didn't even know what to think of that. It was sort of noble. But it also seemed senseless, because there was no debt. Not really. And I was *no* saviour.

Oh sure, my gift *could* help people. But it wasn't exactly a 'good' power. I didn't so much heal as *steal* an injury—sometimes from myself, sometimes from others—so I could then slap that wound onto another. My power was a weapon, especially on the battlefield. Healing injuries was more like a side effect of it.

Max wasn't the only person I'd helped who'd been tainted by The Call. None of the others appeared to feel they owed me. Hell, we'd all aided each other countless times when in the field anyway. So this … no, I didn't see why Max should feel indebted to me.

One thing I understood was that if he *had* fucked me tonight, he would have regretted it because of this deal he'd made with himself. Hell, he was probably regretting the very little we *did* do. And that knowledge was enough to make me back away.

Ignoring the sinking sensation in my stomach, I smoothed out a non-existent wrinkle in my dress. I could forget this happened. Totally. I could forget he kissed like a master. I could forget how his fingers felt inside me. I could forget the intense orgasm that whipped through me. Really. Easily. Totally.

His eyes narrowed at my retreat. "What's going on in that head of yours?"

I forced a casual shrug. "I don't agree that you owe me anything, but I respect your decision to keep things platonic." It wasn't like I had a choice, was it? "We'll just put what happened here out of our minds." I crossed to the door, cool and composed. "Enjoy the rest of your night." Then I left.

CHAPTER THREE

(Paige)

With a slice of toast in one hand and a drink in the other, I stepped out onto my balcony the following evening. It was fairly dark, but my vampiric eyesight picked up everything just fine as I watched the activity below. Most people in this particular Residence Hall—which was exclusive to legion members—preferred the beach-view rooms, but I liked being able to look out upon The Hollow as it came to life each evening when the sun set.

People walked along the paths, wandered in and out of buildings, or crossed the bridge that had been built over the man-made, white-sanded beach. Several buildings bordered the beach, including bars, stores, cafes, restaurants, and Residence Halls. Antonio had once described the community as a world within a world. It was a pretty accurate description.

Settling on the patio chair, I alternated between eating my toast and sipping my vanilla-flavoured NST. A mix of blood and vitamins, the Nutritional Supplemental Tonics did a good job of answering our cravings, but they never *truly* quenched our thirst the way pure blood did.

I watched as several people filed out of the Guest House near the mansion. The vampires who'd come to witness Alora and Evan's ceremony would be heading home this evening. Many of them were pretty hoity toity, so I wouldn't miss having them around.

Thinking of the afterparty made my stomach roll. After the restroom scene with Max, it had been tempting to slip away and head home. But that would have been noticed, not to mention selfish—it would have offended Alora. So I'd strolled out of the restroom casual as you please and sought out my BFF, Imani.

Word had gotten around that Max and I had some sort of tiff in the restroom. I'd explained what happened to Imani—minus the finger-fucking incident and his 'I want you' confession. Imani had laughed and expressed surprise over his apparent protectiveness toward Ursula. I hadn't corrected her.

She'd also given me a 'you're not telling me everything' look, but I'd ignored it. I'd also ignored the occasional feeling of Max's gaze boring into my skin throughout the rest of the party. I hadn't been sure I could meet his eyes without blushing. I still wasn't. Nor was I certain he wouldn't sense that, to my absolute annoyance, I wanted more.

Draining my bottle, I looked beyond the gated community to the vast tropical rainforest that surrounded it. It was beautiful and almost otherworldly with its—

Sorry to bother you so early, Jared telepathically began, startling me, *but Sam and I need you. Would it be okay for me to teleport to your home now to collect you?*

Setting my empty bottle on the table, I blinked, surprised by his request. *Yes, of course. I'm on my balcony.*

Moments later, a tall, broad-shouldered advertisement for sex materialised in front of me. Yeah, Jared was hot as hell.

"What's up?" I asked, standing.

"We're in need of your healing skills." He teleported us both to the infirmary, where Sam and Antonio waited, their gazes locked on the male lying in one of the beds.

My mouth dropped open. "Jesus." His face was grotesquely swollen, he had thick oozing lumps all over his body, his skin was chalk white, and his heartbeat was worryingly weak. "If I didn't recognise his scent, I'm not sure I'd know it was Quinlan." He was one of the legion's commanders and had recently lost two squad members during an assignment that went to shit.

Sam's aquamarine eyes fixed on mine. "He was sliced here." She pointed at rake wounds on his chest. "The poison did the rest."

"Wait, *Lenox* did this?" As far as I knew, he was the only vampire at The Hollow who could sprout poisonous claws. He was also part of Quinlan's squad.

"Yes, and I'll expand on that once Quinlan is healed. You can give his injury to that piece of shit over there." She jerked her chin toward the unconscious male on the neighbouring bed. "The guards are constantly complaining about all the whining he does from his cell, so they were glad to hear his number was up."

That was the thing about my gift. Unless there was someone I could transfer an injury to, it would return to the person from whom I'd taken it—even if that person was me. Which was why The Hollow's prisoners often came in handy.

I splayed my hand over Quinlan's chest and let out a *call* I couldn't quite explain. Then it was like a magnetic energy shot out of my palm and locked on the wound. There was a rippling under my skin that circled my lower arm as it shot from my palm to my elbow. I swiftly turned and slapped my hand on the unconscious prisoner's arm. The rippling started again, descending my arm as I transferred Quinlan's injury to him. That fast, his body became *ravaged* by poison, since it had hit him three-fold.

Jared lifted his hand, sparks of electricity dancing along his fingertips, and I figured he meant to kill the vampire with a fatal electric strike. There was no need. The poison did the trick, and the prisoner exploded into ashes.

"I do like your gift, Paige," said Antonio, as elegant and calming as ever.

"So do I." I looked down at Quinlan. Although he was still pale and unconscious, he was no longer on death's door. And the drip of blood he'd been hooked up to would certainly help.

Sam looked at Mary Jane, who'd been a nurse in her human life and so liked to work at the infirmary. "Call Jared when Quinlan wakes. And don't worry about Lenox. There'll be guards both inside and outside the room. He won't get in here."

Seeming reassured, Mary Jane gave a short nod.

I followed Sam, Jared, and Antonio out of the infirmary and into the hall. "What happened between Lenox and Quinlan?" I asked no one in particular.

Sam scratched at her nape. "Lenox, the tosser, has gone AWOL."

I blinked. "AWOL?"

"He took the news of Brook's death *beyond* badly," she said, referring to a member of Quinlan's squad who'd recently died. "Lenox kept an emotional distance from everyone but still regarded Brook as his bloody bestie. They were paired up when on the field. *Except* for the most recent mission, since Quinlan refused to let Lenox go with them."

I frowned. "Why did Quinlan refuse?"

Jared explained, "Lenox seemed to be having problems. He wasn't giving it his all during training. He was acting reckless on missions and avoiding any form of socialising—even with Brook. Quinlan gave him time, but Lenox got worse rather than better. Quinlan left him behind because he didn't trust that Lenox would follow orders and be mindful of his own safety."

"And Brook died," I said.

Sam nodded. "Lenox blames Quinlan and obviously decided to dish out some karma. We have people tracking him, but it's not going to be easy."

"I awarded him with additional power years ago, and Lenox then developed the gift to 'jump' from one place to another in a blink," Antonio added. "It is not quite teleporting, because he cannot travel further than a kilometre each time."

"But it means that any time we get close to him, he's going to blink his arse somewhere else," said Sam. "I don't think he'll try to leave the island, though. Not until he's killed the two people he holds responsible for Brook's death—which won't happen."

I felt my brow furrow. "Who's the other?"

"Ivan," replied Jared. "He partnered with Brook during the mission."

"Where is Ivan?" I asked.

"He *was* at his bed-buddy's home, which is what saved his life," said Jared. "Lenox went looking for him this evening and tore his apartment up. Luckily we got to Ivan first and hid him. Lenox won't stop looking for him, though."

Antonio let out a sigh loaded with sorrow. "This is why I am always glad to see vampires Bind. None of the vampires who have emotionally broken like this had a mate."

I felt my brows raise. "Huh. I didn't know that."

"I do not believe vampires are built to be alone," Antonio went on. "We still have some human needs. We are also susceptible to the same emotional struggles. Death, loss, constant killing—all those things put a strain on us, especially legion members, as such things are a big part of their lives. Immortality itself adds to that strain.

"There are some who remain detached from others to spare themselves the pain that comes with loss. I suppose they believe this will be what saves them in the long-run. It never does. For the soul, it is best to grab what pieces of happiness you can."

I'd have to agree with that. And what was the point in living forever if you had no one to share your life with anyway? Being alone certainly hadn't helped Lenox or any of the other vampires who had broken in the past.

"Lenox will probably come for Quinlan again," I hedged.

The mercury tint to Sam's irises—something she hadn't developed until she mysteriously became a hybrid—flared brightly. "The guards will end the wanker if he does."

"Will you be asking Maya to track him while in her jaguar form?" I asked.

"Your squad as a whole will be searching for him," replied Sam. "Many squads will be sent out. Our best tracker is Sebastian. But, as you know, he's currently accompanying Ryder on his trip."

A relatively new vampire, Ryder had been forced to stay at The Hollow for a long period of time while he got a grip on his bloodlust—something which had taken longer than usual, because he'd used his notable gift many times to aid the Grand High Pair, and that had repeatedly caused his control to waver. As he now had a firm hold on his bloodlust and no longer needed to be confined, he'd been allowed to enjoy a round-the-world trip while also learning tracking skills from Sebastian.

"I don't want to call Sebastian home unless it's absolutely necessary," Sam went on. "There are plenty of people on this island. Lenox is one man. We'll find him. But it'll be a case of all hands on deck, because there's a lot of ground to cover both inside and outside the gates of The Hollow. We need Lenox caught, and we need it to happen bloody yesterday."

Later that night, my squad and I followed Sam as we traipsed through the rainforest in search of Lenox. Jared was leading Max's squad and stayed reasonably close, exchanging the occasional frustrated look with Sam. We'd been out here for hours and had spotted no sign of our prey. But then, it wasn't exactly difficult to stay hidden out here. There was plenty of plant life to conceal you, plenty of trees to climb, and plenty of potent scents to cover your own—animal musk, wet earth, rotten fruit, swampy water, floral scents.

There was also a whole cacophony of noise to override any sounds you might make. Crickets chirped. Wings fluttered. Insects buzzed. Monkeys howled. Waterfalls roared.

The rainforest truly was magnificent. Ropy vines looped around thick trunks. Bamboo trees stood tall and proud. A beautiful canopy of leaves hung over us.

The wildlife tended to go still and quiet when we approached, recognising us for the predators we were. But I still managed to glimpse a few hiding in the trees.

Alora, who had the ability to talk to animals, had recruited some birds and larger predators to help us search for Lenox. But the rainforest was so expansive that it was no easy feat.

Still, we kept searching, making as little noise as possible. It wasn't always easy, given that the ground was littered with dead leaves, half-eaten rotten fruit, and dry plant pods. Then there were the pools of muddy water that lay here and there.

In her jaguar form, Maya was in her element out here. But she soon began to tire, chuffing and coughing in complaint. I suspected she was exasperated that their search was coming to nothing.

Walking alongside me, Imani nudged me. "Is there a reason Max keeps staring at you?" she asked, her voice too low to carry to others.

I'd felt his gaze on me more than once, but I hadn't looked his way. Hopping over a twisted tree root, I lifted a brow. "You don't think I'm stare-worthy?"

"I think you're keeping something from me, and that is not fair. My curiosity needs to be fed."

I snorted. "I've noticed. But since I'm just as nosy, I can't even give you shit for it."

"Did something happen between you two?"

Sensory memories assaulted me—his hot mouth on mine, his fingers curving and stabbing, his cock grinding against my clit. "It's nothing I care to talk about here and now."

"Later, then," she said, sidestepping a prickly pineapple bush.

I nodded. "Later."

Another hour went by before Sam and Jared declared it was time to return to The Hollow. Once we'd eaten lunch at the canteen, we headed to another part of the rainforest to do a second search. It was just as fruitless as the first. By the end of it, we were all seriously tired. We were vampires, not machines.

Due to said fatigue, I asked Imani to postpone her visit until the following evening. Not for my sake, but for her own. Although she was a Keja, she'd once been injected by a serum that was supposed to reverse vampirism. Instead, it had changed her in various ways—both strengthening and weakening her. She tended to tire faster now, but she still often stupidly overexerted herself. So both myself and her mate, Butch, worked on ensuring she got enough rest. As such, I was both surprised and miffed when a knock came at the front door shortly after I'd finished my late dinner. *Awkward minx*, I thought as I made my way to the door.

(Max)

Hearing muffled voices, I glanced over at the guys in the hall who were eying me curiously while talking among themselves. And I knew it would quickly circulate around The Hollow that I'd come to Paige's apartment. The legion were like gossipy old women.

I inched up a brow, daring them to comment. They quickly looked away, but not fast enough to hide their smiles.

Not everyone bought that Paige and I had simply had a disagreement in the restroom. Some were sure that something a little more interesting had happened, and I wondered if that number included these two vampires here.

Just then, Paige's front door opened. Surprise flashed in her eyes, and her expression then went vacant. Well at least her gaze was finally meeting mine. She'd refused to acknowledge me since walking out of the restroom last night.

"We need to talk," I told her.

She looked about to blow me off, which I couldn't allow—this was too important. Knowing she wouldn't want her neighbours to overhear anything they might repeat, I slid the vampires down the hall a quick glance to show her we weren't alone. She tracked my gaze, and her mouth tightened.

"Fine." She stepped back, allowing me to enter, and then closed the door. That easily, the air crackled with awareness. An awareness that we were alone, that we'd crossed a line last night, that she'd have been fucked raw if Sam hadn't interrupted.

Paige cleared her throat. "You said we needed to talk," she prompted, folding her arms.

"We can't go on like this."

"What?"

I walked toward her. "You know what," I said, my voice even. "You pretend I'm not nearby. You avoid looking at me. You greet everyone but me." I thought she might go on the defensive, but she let her arms fall to her sides and conceded my point with a tilt of her head.

"I know. I just felt … awkward and I let that get in the way, which I can't afford to do, considering we have to work together. It won't happen again."

That was one of the things I liked about Paige. She might have a lot of pride, but she never failed to admit to her mistakes, no matter how big or small they were. I wondered if she considered last night a mistake. Probably. Which bothered me a lot more than it should have. But it hadn't been a mistake to me, no, the mistake had been in me believing I could forever ignore how much I wanted her. Hence why I was there.

She bit her lip. Such a simple act, but it made my cock jerk. Made me wonder how it would feel to have those teeth biting my neck. Her tongue swiped over her lower lip as her gaze held mine. The flare of heat there made the memories of last night flash through the forefront of my mind.

I stared into those gorgeous pools of green as I stepped closer. "You're thinking about it, aren't you?"

Her eyelids flickered. "About what?"

"Last night. Do you regret it?"

She exhaled a shaky sigh. "No."

A knot in my gut unravelled. A knot I hadn't even realised was there until just now.

"Do you?" she asked.

"The only thing I regret is not burying my dick inside you. I always knew if I touched you even once, it'd be a point of no return for me; that I'd only want more."

She swallowed. "I'm not looking for a fling, Max."

"I know. But you want me. I want you. If that was going to go away, it would have happened by now." I'd spent years hoping it would, but it never had. "Seventy-two hours."

Her brows inched together. "Huh?"

"Give me seventy-two hours."

"To do what?"

"Make you come over and over and over, until we're both wrung dry."

Her pupils swallowed the colour of her eyes.

"You might not want to admit it, but part of the reason you wouldn't look at me was that you worried I'd sense what you'd rather I never knew." I lowered my face to hers. "You don't want last night to be a one-off. I know I don't. It wasn't enough." It had only made everything worse, because now I knew how things *could* be between us.

She spluttered. "We can't just hole up somewhere for seventy-two hours."

"I know that. We'd do whatever shit we needed to do around The Hollow, as usual. But then you'd come back to my bed each night." And I'd take her in every imaginable way as many times as I could. Because it had become abundantly clear to me that I wouldn't manage to keep my hands off her. Not unless I finally explored the chemistry that pulsed between us. Not unless I got to act out the many fantasies that rattled around my brain and made it impossible for me to see any woman but her.

Paige didn't respond. She just stared at me, her lips parted, her expression utterly unreadable.

When she finally went to speak, I put my finger to her lips and said, "I'm not looking for you to give me an answer here and now. I know I've probably taken you off-guard. I know this isn't a typical suggestion. But I also know that both of us will struggle with pretending last night didn't happen."

She didn't deny it, which I was glad of.

"I don't want to pretend," I went on. "I don't want to keep obsessing over how good it might have felt if we'd finished what we started. And I don't see why either of us should have to. We're adults, we're single, and forever is a long fucking time to spend having what you want so close yet so out of reach. So I say we just take it." I cupped her chin and swept my thumb over her mouth. "Seventy-two hours. Think about it. You can give me your answer tomorrow night."

With that, I left … knowing if she gave me a 'no,' I wouldn't behave and just walk away. I wouldn't let it drop so easily. No, I was too fucking far gone for that.

CHAPTER FOUR

(Paige)

The following evening, Imani stared at me, gaping. "Make you come over and over and over until you're both wrung dry? He actually said that?"

"Yup," I replied, shifting slightly on my rug.

Cassie used the end of her wheat-blonde braid to fan her face. "I wish someone would make me an offer like that."

It hadn't been only Imani who turned up at my door to 'get the gossip.' It had been my entire squad. They'd all noticed the odd looks Max and I had exchanged earlier while patrolling the rainforest, and they all wanted answers. Since I could really do with having some advice, I had no issues with giving them said answers. Especially since Max would be here in a matter of hours, and I'd have to give him a yes or no.

So now, all seven of my squad were spread around my living room. Some sat on the half-moon leather sofa. Others sat on dining chairs they'd dragged in from the kitchen. All were drinking vodka-flavoured NSTs—well, aside from Imani, who could only stomach vampire blood since the serum she'd been injected with messed with her system. The vodka-flavoured drinks never gave vamps an alcoholic buzz, but they tasted pretty good.

Ava let out a soft sigh. "It's kind of sweet that he kept his distance out of respect for how you'd saved his life."

"He doesn't owe me anything," I insisted.

"Maybe not, but he *feels* like he does," said Ava. "It's just super sweet that he reacted by basically depriving himself of what he most wants."

Sipping her NST, Alora narrowed her eyes at me. "He really said you'd keep going back to *his* bed? His specifically, not yours?"

I felt my brow crease. "Yes, his. Why? What am I missing?"

"He doesn't take women to his apartment, sweetie," the redhead replied. "Like *ever*. It's a no-no for him."

Jude nodded, making some of her rich brown hair tumble over her shoulder. "I've heard a few females complain about it. Apparently, he's willing to make an exception for you."

Ava's eyes lit up. "Ooh, how interesting."

"Don't go reading anything into that," I said. "He asked for seventy-two hours, which makes it pretty clear he isn't looking for anything serious."

"True." Ava pouted, setting her empty bottle on the coffee table. "Bummer. I had hopes that you two would get together. You might not seem like an obvious couple, given he's a little … domineering while you're not the type to tolerate such shit. But Salem and I aren't an obvious couple either. I'm chirpy and giggly and full of energy. He's surly and growly and more homicidal than most. But we work."

"Yeah," I agreed. "But that's because you both want the same thing. Max and I don't. Hence why he suggested three nights—he knows I have no interest in a fling, and he's probably worried I'd get attached if we were involved with each other for too long." I couldn't even say he'd be wrong. He was the kind of guy a girl could easily fall for.

"What are you going to do?" Maya asked.

I hesitated, biting my lip. "I want to say yes to his suggestion."

"So say yes," Ava blurted out, leaning forward in her seat.

"*But*," I went on, "I don't want to be one of the multitude, you know?"

Keeley's nose wrinkled. "Yeah, I get that. But I don't think he views you as one of the multitude, or he wouldn't want to break this personal rule he seems to have about not having women in his apartment."

Her eyes on me, Imani pointed at Keeley. "That's a good point. Another good point? He said he'd make you come over and over and over."

"That is a noteworthy point," agreed Alora.

"Definitely goes in the 'Why you should totally do it' column," said Cassie.

Maya nodded. "Orgasm Central is a wondrous place to be."

Keeley sighed, tilting her head. "I kind of miss it."

Jude gave Keeley's hand a comforting pat as she said to me, "You should also consider that the rumours of him being a man-slut might be just that—rumours. I know a lot of guys resent how much female attention Max gets purely because there are far fewer women than men around here. It wouldn't surprise me if some of them spread disparaging rumours about Max to put women off. I mean, that's what's happening with you, right? So I wouldn't let the stuff you've heard factor into your decision. Especially when we're only talking three nights."

The rest of my squad nodded or murmured their agreement.

I swept my gaze over everyone, taking in their expressions. "You all think

I should say yes, don't you?"

"You *are* going to say yes," said Imani. "We know it. You know it."

Yeah, I did know it. I'd done nothing but think long and hard over his proposal ever since he made it. While a few issues had made me hesitate, none had carried enough weight to drown out his statement that forever was a long time to spend having what you want so close yet so out of reach. I didn't want to carry on like this—imagining, wondering, fantasising.

It made more sense to finally satisfy all our … sexual curiosities, for lack of a better term. Fantasies were never better than reality. There was no way sex between us would live up to what my imagination had conjured. It would definitely be fun, though. And like he'd said, we were single adults. We knew the score. Knew it would just be three nights of pleasure that carried no strings. By the end of it, the sexual tension between us would be a thing of the past, and we could move forward as colleagues. Hell, we might even become friends one day.

"I tell ya," began Keeley, twirling a strand of her blonde hair around her finger, "it's gonna be an intense seventy-two hours—minus the parts where you're not inside his apartment, of course. You can just tell that he'll be a rock star in bed."

Imani smiled. "Our girl's gonna get so supremely laid."

"And then she's going to give us every detail." Ava did a little clap. "I can't wait."

I snorted. "Now I think we should move off the subject of me and Max. In fact, I think maybe we could ask Maya if she's looking forward to Ryder returning home."

The shapeshifting vampire tensed. "Why would I?"

"Well, the fling you guys indulged in before he left seemed pretty intense," I said.

"It was," said Maya. "But he made it very clear that it would be short-lived. He ended it two nights before he left The Hollow. Or did you forget all that?"

"I didn't forget, I just wasn't so sure he truly *wanted* to end it. He seemed really into you."

"He was distant and kind of closed-off," said Maya.

"But looked at you like you were the only thing *worth* looking at."

"Yeah, well, he couldn't have been *that* interested. The night before he left for his trip … well, he spent it with one of the vamps who works at the bowling alley, Krista. She said he asked her to 'wait' for him."

I felt my brows snap together. "Really? Who told you that?"

Maya clipped her dark hair behind her ear. "She did."

"I never heard even a whisper about that." I looked at the others, who all shook their heads and said no such news had reached them. "It might not be true, Maya."

Cassie nodded. "Krista has been known to tell little tales. Don't be so quick to believe her."

Maya just shrugged, her expression declaring she was done talking about it. I knew better than to push her—it would get me nowhere. The others knew it, too. So we changed the subject again, choosing a lighter topic this time.

A short time later, everyone made moves to leave. Some wished to get back to their mates to have dinner, while the single women headed to the Mexican restaurant. I would have accompanied them if Max wasn't due to turn up at my apartment soon. So, instead, I ate a quick dinner—which wasn't easy, given that my stomach was fluttery with nerves. It couldn't have been more than an hour later when a knock came at the door.

It didn't matter that I'd been braced for the sheer impact of him. My body nonetheless stirred to life when I opened the door to find Max stood there, still and watchful and spectacularly masculine. I moved aside, silently inviting him to enter.

He prowled inside, each step fluid and purposeful. When I closed the door, he lifted a brow. "Well?"

I took a subtle, fortifying breath. "Okay."

His blue eyes heated, and the tension in the air thickened. He crossed the space between us and loomed over me, his gaze searching mine. "Let's make sure we have this straight. For seventy-two whole hours, you'll belong to me."

I felt my head jerk back. "Whoa, *belong*?"

"Yes, belong," he said, his voice dropping to bedroom territory. "There won't be a single part of you I haven't touched. I'm going to know your body better than anyone else ever has—even you. I'm going to fuck you every which way I can have you." He trailed his finger down my neck, adding, "I'm even going to come down this pretty throat, just like I've imagined doing a thousand times."

I gave him an imperious look and sniffed. "We'll see how it goes."

His mouth quirked. "You'd better pack a bag. You won't be coming back here until the seventy-two hours are up, and they're going to begin the moment we step into my apartment."

"Look at you getting all forceful."

Max lowered his face to mine. "You have no idea how forceful I can be. But you'll soon find out." He took a slow step back. "Get whatever you need."

Anticipation whirred in my blood as I tossed clothes and other items into my duffel. I'd no sooner zipped it up than he grabbed it—not so much playing the gentleman as being his typical alpha-self.

We passed many people as we made our way to his apartment, which was a few floors above mine. All were quick to give us conspiratorial, knowing looks. *Bastards*. It was a shame that neither I nor Max could teleport.

Finally, we arrived at his place. Stepping inside, I saw that it was pretty much a mirror image of my own. Of course, he had none of the feminine touches I'd added to my apartment.

Glancing around, I said, "Wow, your place is pretty tidy for a bachelor pad." I turned to him ... and almost sucked in a breath. His eyes were alive with a raw need that was carved into every line of his face.

He dropped my duffel near the door and then prowled toward me. "One thing: I don't mix sex and feeding."

Disappointing, but ... "Noted."

He palmed the side of my face and brushed his thumb over my lips. "I really hope you like hard and fast, because there's not a fucking chance I can go slow right now."

The hand on my face dived into my hair, fisted it tight, and snatched my head back. Then his mouth was on mine. No, *ravaging* mine. The kiss was all greed and hunger and urgency. And I absolutely revelled in it.

We pretty much yanked off each other's clothes as years' worth of suppressed need finally found its outlet. There was nothing gentle or playful about his touch or mine. No, we grabbed and squeezed and pulled, desperate for more.

He hoisted me up, walked me further into the room, and dumped me on the sofa. In vampire speed, he was kneeling between my spread thighs and hooking my legs over his shoulders. Then his mouth was on me and, sweet Jesus, it would not be long before I came. Nope. Because he feasted on me like he wouldn't last another moment if he didn't.

He drove me up hard and fast into an orgasm, his tongue swiping, licking, probing, lashing, and swirling. But he didn't stop when I came. He kept going, adding his teeth and fingers to his arsenal. And I was just ... gone. Gone. It was a full-on sensual assault, and I stood no chance of holding out. I came hard a second time, my head thrown back, my thighs trembling.

He let my legs slip off his shoulders as he sat back on his haunches. With a snarl, he gripped my thighs tight. "Fucking have to be in you." He dragged me off the sofa and planted me on his cock.

My back bowing, I cried out in shock and just a little bit of pain. He was thick and hard inside me. Longer than I was used to. "Jesus, Max."

He slowly lifted me until only the head of his dick was inside. "You can take it." He roughly impaled me on his shaft once more. "And you will."

(Max)

Gripping her ass, I slammed her up and down on my cock over and over. Christ, she was tight. Better than anything I'd ever felt. Fit me so damn perfectly it was almost scary.

She clutched my shoulders, letting out the sexiest fucking sounds, taking what I gave her even though I was being far too rough. I couldn't ease up, couldn't slow down. I'd needed this for too long; dreamed about it too many times.

I slid one hand up her body to palm her breast, wanting to feel it bounce in my grip. *So damn soft.* "Take over. Ride me."

She did. *Fuck* she did. Moving just as hard and fast as I had.

"Good girl." I filled my hands with her breasts, loving how silky soft and round they were. I squeezed, shaped, and moulded, memorising every inch.

Each pinch or twist of her nipples made her scorching hot inner muscles spasm around my cock. I wanted the taut little buds in my mouth. Now.

I turned and none-too-gently splayed her out on the floor. "Love these tits." I sucked a nipple into my mouth and started powering into her.

She arched into me, digging her nails into my back as I licked, nipped, sucked, and tugged on her nipples with my teeth. She was as delightfully sensitive as she was responsive. Her little moans and whimpers went straight to my cock. I swear I could play with her breasts for hours and not get bored.

"Max," she breathed. "I'm gonna come."

I released her nipple. "Not yet."

Her eyes narrowed, and she stabbed her nails harder into my back. "If I want to come, I'll come."

"That so?" I slowed the pace of my thrusts until they were nice and easy and shallow. "Hmm, then feel free to come," I invited, knowing this wouldn't be enough to get her off.

She bared her teeth. "Don't be an ass."

I swivelled my hips, making her gasp. "Remember what we talked about before we came here? I told you that you'd belong to me. That means your orgasms belong to me, too. So you'll have one when I say you can, not before."

She raised her head from the floor. "Oh my God, I will fucking end you!"

Loving how easy she was to rile, I bit back a smile and kept thrusting soft and slow. "No, you'll be a good girl for me. Good girls get what they want." I flicked up a brow. "Now … do you want to be fucked or not?"

"Obviously," she gritted out, looking delightfully feral in that moment.

"Then do what I told you to do, because I really don't think orgasm denial will turn out to be your thing." I gave her my weight and began slamming into her again. All red and swollen, her lips parted on a gasp. "Your mouth would look so fucking pretty covered in my come."

She angled her hips to meet each slam of my cock. "Shit, you're so deep."

Growling, I pounded harder. The pulse thumping in her neck drew my eye, and my mouth watered. I grazed it with my teeth, so fucking tempted to bite down and drink. My stomach actually twisted at the thought. Instead, I snapped my hand around her throat and hammered into her even harder.

"You're going to come for me now," I said. "I want to feel it. Come on, baby, give me what … fuck, yeah." I groaned as her hot inner muscles clamped around my cock.

I rode her through her orgasm, loving the throaty scream that erupted from her throat, and then my own release swept over me. Hard. Fast. So fucking intense I felt it in my teeth. It seemed to go on and on and on, and then the strength left my body in a rush.

I collapsed over her, tucking my face into the crook of her neck. Her arm weakly flopped over my back while the rest of her all but sank into the floor. We stayed like that for long minutes, panting and shaking.

She let out a shuddery breath. "Wow. Just wow."

Lifting my head to meet her gaze, I hummed. "'Wow' works."

She blinked, and I got the sense that she hadn't realised she'd spoken aloud.

In all honesty, I wasn't comfortable with the fact that I'd just had the best fuck of my life. It wasn't supposed to be that good. I wasn't supposed to have come that goddamn hard. But it had been amazing. Mind-blowing. Dangerously addictive. And already, as I slowly glided in and out of her, I felt my cock thicken again.

Her brows inched up. "Hmm, someone's ready for round two. I do like a man with a quick recovery time."

I felt one corner of my mouth twitch. "Hope you got plenty of sleep yesterday, because you won't get much of it today."

CHAPTER FIVE

(Max)

"You going to tell us what's going on between you and Paige?"

I slid Stuart a sideways glance as I replied, "I wasn't intending to, no." It was no one else's business. And I really had no interest in discussing it with her ex-boyfriend, especially since he'd once talked badly about her. So I went back to scanning the labyrinth of trees around us. I narrowed my eyes each time I saw movement, but it was always an animal of some sort—a snake twining itself around a branch, a bird hiding in a tree, a spider scrambling to avoid us, a boar taking cover behind a bush.

During the short period in which Paige and Stuart had dated, I'd come close to punching him too many times to count ... for no other reason than that I'd been blinded by fucking jealousy. Until then, I'd honestly had no idea I had it in me to experience a jealousy so black and deep, but it had hounded me for months.

Even now, despite that her relationship with Stuart ended a long time ago, I still couldn't think of it without grinding my teeth. It was even worse now that I'd touched her, kissed her, been inside her. Because, as much as I goddamn hated it, I felt a little too territorial where she was concerned. Hence why I'd wanted her in my bed. A place I had indeed fucked her after we gravitated from the living room to my bedroom.

I'd never actually slept beside a woman before. I'd thought it would feel at least a little strange. It hadn't. I'd liked it. Liked waking to find her there. Liked having that instant, easy access to her body.

"If you two were hoping to keep it on the down low, you've failed," said Stuart. "Anyone can see something's going on."

While I really did not want to have this conversation, I didn't bother to deny that she and I had crossed the platonic line—it was too obvious in the looks we exchanged and how the tension between us no longer held a hum of sexual frustration.

"I'm guessing that 'something' started in the restroom at the party," Stuart added.

"And I'm sensing you have a problem with it. What, are you regretting you let her go?" Because if the guy expected me to step aside to clear the path for him, that wasn't going to happen. Well ... not until after the seventy-two hours were up. Then she was free to do whatever she wanted with whoever she wanted. Which had me grinding my teeth yet again.

Stuart shook his head. "No. Paige was right in what she once said to me—we aren't what the other needs. We would never have worked as a couple. That doesn't mean I don't look out for her."

"How is quizzing me looking out for her?"

"Max ... look, you're a good friend. A great fucking friend. A man I'll always trust to watch my back. A man I know is loyal to the bone. But you make a shit ... hell, I can't even say 'boyfriend.' When you're involved with someone, you're never anything more than a bed-buddy. And hey, that's not bad. *As long as* the woman you're bedding is good with that."

"Paige and I have an understanding. She knows where we both stand."

"But is she *good* with it? I once heard her tell Jude she's looking for a partner. And you, well, you avoid attachments."

I sighed. "Look, I get it—you don't want her to get hurt. You don't want *any* of the women to get hurt. I'm with you on that. Like you, I look out for them. But I can assure you I have no intention of hurting Paige. We won't be involved with each other long enough for that to happen anyway."

"So you two are just going to have a brief fling?"

"Something like that." Catching the way Stuart's brow pinched in disapproval, I added, "I know she deserves better. I do. Which is why I kept my distance for a long time. I meant to keep on doing that, but it didn't work. It was wishful thinking on my part to believe it would. There's only so long you can resist someone who's right in front of you every night."

Stuart exhaled heavily. "Yeah, I get it. Just ... be careful with her. I wasn't careful. I was a shithead, to be exact. Don't make my mistake."

"I don't intend to. Never would." I frowned when Maya's jaguar came to an abrupt stop.

She swung her head toward Alora, who instantly stiffened and then looked at Jared. She must have telepathically passed on a message, because then Jared's voice was in my head.

Lenox is here. Pair up. Be ready.

I glanced around but saw no sign of any—*there*. A burly, salt-and-pepper haired male appeared a dozen feet away from Sam, but he was gone in a fucking flash only to reappear elsewhere.

We attacked in an instant. The jaguar sprang with a roar. Stuart exploded into molecules and zoomed Lenox's way. Damien's astral form disappeared, no doubt in pursuit. The night was suddenly alive with electric strikes, ripples of psychic energy, telekinetic blows, the jaguar's roars, Chico's darts, psionic blasts, crackling energy balls, and the shrieks of the tropical birds that Alora had recruited.

I spared a moment to check on Paige. She stood near Imani, on guard and highly alert. Satisfied, I switched my attention back to Lenox. The fucker was doing a good job of evading our attacks, because he kept blinking from spot to spot, and there was no way for us to anticipate where he'd next appear.

I couldn't paralyse his senses. Not when he moved so fast. If the fucker would just stay in place *for a few seconds* … but he never did.

And why would he?

He didn't have a gift that allowed him to attack from afar, so he would not waste precious seconds standing in one spot. Plus, as a member of the legion, Lenox knew our gifts; knew how we fought in battle; knew to move fast in order to dodge our every attack. He also knew not to get too close—many of us could take him out, but not all could do it from afar.

Jared began teleporting from one place to another, doing his best to catch Lenox, but he was always a few seconds behind the bastard.

Again, I spared Paige a quick glance to check on her. She must have felt my gaze, because she looked my way for a brief moment.

Everyone form a circle but face outwards, Jared ordered. *Cover all directions. Attack if you see movement.*

So that was what we did.

I noticed Jared and Damien's astral form pop into view here and there, but none were ever close enough to grab Lenox. Shooting yellowy-green ooze from his hands, Denny repeatedly tried catching the motherfucker. But Lenox evaded him every time.

Keep attacking, Jared ordered. *With any luck, we'll tire him out.*

But there was no such luck. And, really, there was every chance Lenox would simply disappear if he felt he was even close to tiring. What I kept wondering was … why would he bother exposing himself this way? What did he have to gain?

I growled. "Can anyone work out what the fuck he's doing?"

"It's like he's playing with us," David replied, letting out yet another psionic blast.

I frowned. "What, he gets off on pitting himself against the Grand High Pair and their personal squads?"

David shrugged. "Possibly."

A loud hiss of pain. "*Motherfucker.*"

I stiffened. *Paige.* I turned to see her staring at the back of her shoulder.

No, at the fucking claw marks now spanning the back of her shoulder.

"Shit, Paige!" Imani called out, her eyes wide.

"Get her out of here, Jared, we have this!" Sam yelled.

I tried hurrying over to Paige, but she was gone in a flash. *Son of a bitch.*

(Paige)

I suddenly found myself standing outside the rows of containment cells beneath the mansion—all of which were constructed of indestructible glass. I wasn't sure if Jared picked the one nearest to us out of convenience or because he was ready for the captive inside it to die, but he pressed his thumb to the sensor beside the door. The moment it opened, Jared barged inside. Electricity shot from his fingertips and crashed into the captive. The vampire shook, his eyes rolling back in his head as the electricity whipped through his system and held him immobile.

Jared glanced at me as I entered the cell. "Give him the wound."

Gladly. God, the poison stung like a bitch. I'd gotten the goddamn shock of my life when claws raked me from behind—they'd felt like hot slices of pain.

It took mere seconds for me to transfer my wound to the captive. Jared didn't give the poison a chance to do its job. He ended the vampire with an electric bolt, making the captive explode into ashes.

Panting, I rolled back my now healed shoulder. "Lenox appeared behind me just long enough to do damage. Then he was gone. Either he purposely tried manipulating us into forming that circle so he could get behind us, or he just took advantage of the move. Personally, I don't know why he bothered. He had to know I could transfer the wound to someone else."

Jared twisted his lips. "My opinion? It was a punishment. He's *all* about punishments right now. He tried making Quinlan pay, but then you healed him. More, we relocated Quinlan once the guy was conscious and at full strength."

"You hid him like you did Ivan?" I asked, following Jared out of the cell.

"Yes. Lenox has no doubt been looking for them, and he's no doubt frustrated that he can't find them. Come on, let's get back to the others."

"Wait, I need to remove this tee. It has residue of the poison on it."

Jared went quiet for a moment, his eyes going out of focus. Then they were clear again. "Lenox has apparently disappeared or, at the very least, is having a rest. I'll teleport you to your apartment so you can change your tee. But if he reappears before you're ready to go, I may have to leave you at home so I can get back to Sam and the squads."

I nodded. "Understood."

At my apartment, I trashed my ruined top before pulling on another. The moment Jared teleported us both back to the rainforest, my squad members rushed to my side to check that I was fine, despite my assurances that I was healed.

I caught Max staring at me, his fists clenched, his eyes glinting with … something.

"The wanker did a Houdini right after you left," Sam told Jared. "So his aim wasn't to separate you and me in the hope that he'd then be able to take one of us out." She swore. "We were stupid to give him an opening like that. It just never occurred to me that he'd be so bloody ballsy as to turn up in the middle of the circle and attack someone from behind."

"Same here," said Jared. "Especially since I was starting to think he was just hopping around for shits and giggles."

"That or, as David suggested, he was pitting himself against all of us," said Max.

"It was probably a bit of both," mused Jared. "Throw in that he'll be pissed at how his plot to kill Quinlan and Ivan isn't working so well and, yeah, I'd say he wanted to vent."

Max looked at me again. "*And* get back at Paige for saving Quinlan."

"That, too," agreed Sam. "And the prick will bloody suffer for it."

We figured that Lenox would be long gone, but we stayed out there for another hour just in case. When our search came to nothing, we returned to The Hollow. Again, we were all dog tired.

Outside our Residence Hall, I briefly talked with my squad members— or, more accurately, I hushed them when they started bombarding me with whispered questions …

Did you agree to Max's suggestion?
Is he good in bed?
Did he feed from you?
Are you really staying at his place?
Did he live up to his word and make you come several times?
How likely is it that we could convince you to record him talking dirty, because I just love his voice?

The latter question came from Cassie.

I held up a hand to stave off any further questions. "This isn't the time or place for us to have this conversation. For now, all I will say is that he's a man of his word." He hadn't just made me come more than once during the first round, he'd done it *every* round. And he hadn't been kidding when he'd said I wouldn't get much sleep. He'd woken me three times throughout the day. Not that I was complaining.

"But I want every detail," Ava whined.

"Well you may have to wait until the seventy-two hours are up," I told her, "because he and I agreed that I'd spend my free time at his place until then." We'd both be heading up to his apartment once he was done speaking with Sam. I cast them a quick look, wondering what they were talking about.

Ava heaved a sigh. "Fine. But maybe take notes so you don't forget anything."

Her mouth twitching, Keeley shook her head at the small brunette. "Do you not get sex regularly from Salem or something?"

Ava frowned. "Of course I do. I'm just all about the details, but Paige prefers to only ever deliver the abridged version."

I shrugged. "It's just quicker." Again, I slid Sam and Max a curious look. What the hell was so important that they had to talk about it *now*?

(Max)

Folding her arms, Sam gave me an 'are you high?' look. "You do know Paige, right?"

I gritted my teeth. "Of course I know her."

"Then you know she'd never agree to this."

"You're her superior, she follows your orders."

"But this isn't an order I'd ever give her. I have no reason to, and she'd be ticked off at me for so much as suggesting it. I wouldn't blame her. Come on, Max, you're not dense. You have to see that for me to ask that of her would be an insult, pure and simple. It would be me saying I have no faith in her abilities, which is bollocks. Paige is perfectly capable of protecting herself."

I felt my mouth tighten. Apparently Sam had forgotten, but … "Lenox hurt her tonight." My voice was like gravel.

"I know. I was there. And I'm still well and truly pissed about it. But it's not like she had a near death experience, is it? He clawed her. She healed herself."

Not the point. "Only because Jared was able to teleport her to someone who she could transfer the wound to. If he hadn't been right there to take her away—"

"But he was there, and he will be each time we try tracking Lenox. So, no, I won't ask her to remain behind just on the off-chance that Lenox might target her again."

"We both know he will." The guy had nothing but vengeance on his mind. He wanted to make Quinlan and Ivan pay. If that meant removing Paige from the equation, he'd do it. "Tonight was both a warning and a punishment. He was letting her know he was pissed she'd interfered, and he was cautioning her not to do it again. But she *will* do it again."

"And we'll be ready for however he chooses to handle that. He will not find it so easy to touch her a second time. I'll make sure of it. You can't honestly think I'll tell *a member of the legion* to sit this one out because, hey, she'll be in danger. This is kind of what being part of the legion is all about. There's always risk involved. And before you ask, no, I won't pair you two up when we're on the field so that you can be at her side."

Fuck, I *had* been about to ask that.

"It wouldn't work. Your gifts don't complement each other's. And you might be used to sparring with each other, but not with working together as a team. Plus, she'd never agree to partner with you over Imani anyway—Paige is way too protective of her. You know all this. I really don't know why we're having this conversation."

"Coach, just—"

"No, Max, I won't baby her. I certainly won't hide her away until all this crap blows over. The other girls would stage a protest if I did, because they'd see it as unfair to her, which it would be. And you're not really in a position to ask something like this of me, no matter how concerned you are for her. You might be sleeping with Paige—yeah, I heard she's staying at your place—but you're not her mate or even her boyfriend. Unless there's something I don't know?"

There was plenty Sam didn't—*couldn't*—know. Like that my heart stopped when I heard Paige's hiss of pain earlier. Like that a ball of anxiety had sat in the pit of my stomach right up until Paige reappeared in the rainforest, healed. Like that my gut kept twisting at the thought that Lenox would for sure target her again. But I held all that in and said simply, "She and I are friends."

"That's all? Disappointing. But not surprising, given you don't do relationships."

I forced my back teeth to unlock. "Just because you're happy Bound to Jared doesn't mean that being Bound is the only way someone can *be* happy."

"Of course it doesn't," she easily agreed, no sarcasm. "And, yeah, you're happy as you are. That's good. It means you won't react like a wanker when Paige eventually takes a mate. It *will* happen at some point. She's not a person who'll be content with spending forever on her lonesome."

I was well-aware of that. I pretty much shoved the thought aside every time it popped into my head.

"Don't worry, she won't pressure you to step out of your comfort zone and give her what she needs. That's not Paige. She'll want a bloke who *wants* what she wants, and she'll accept nothing less. One day, she'll have that. And you'll have no choice but to see it all play out in front of you. So it really is good that you're happy as you are, Max, or that shit would fucking *burn*. And I don't want to see one of my boys get hurt." With that, Sam walked off.

CHAPTER SIX

(Max)

Leaning back in my seat, I hooked my foot around the leg of Paige's chair and pulled her closer, so she was situated between my spread thighs. "What happened with you and Stuart?"

She blinked, pausing in chewing her pizza.

Well it could be said that my question had come out of left-field. Especially since we'd just been pondering over whether the colour orange was named because of the colour of the fruit or vice versa. But while Stuart had convinced me earlier that he wasn't holding a candle for Paige, I couldn't help wondering whether that went both ways.

"You don't know?" she asked, crossing one bare leg over the other. At my request, she was wearing only my tee, which hit her mid-thigh.

"I know the basics. I know you dated for a short time. I know that you being so independent bothered him. Or, more specifically, that it hurt his pride that you didn't *need* him. But I don't know *your* side of the story."

She shrugged. "There's not much to tell. Stuart's a pretty likeable guy. Very different from the assholes in my past. I'd hoped it would go somewhere. But he likes to be needed. Which is fine, but I don't need or want someone to be my rock. I depend on me, and I like it that way. I've always been highly independent—it's just part of my nature. But he wanted me to change, to tone down my self-reliance. That wasn't going to happen, so I broke things off."

"He was pissed. Said some pretty shitty stuff about you." I watched her face carefully, searching for any signs of hurt. There were none.

"I know, I heard. He later apologised to me. It was easy enough to forgive him and move on, because … well, I *liked* him, but I hadn't *cared* about him, so his snarky comments hadn't really bothered me all that much."

And my system took a long, relieved breath. Which was ridiculous, because I shouldn't give that much of a shit one way or the other.

Sipping her cola-flavoured NST, she eyed me curiously. "You're pretty self-reliant yourself. To the point of pushing other people away, actually."

I instinctively bristled, feeling defensive, but nonetheless admitted, "I suppose I am."

"Have you always been that way?"

I went to blow off the question. It was a reflex since, in my experience, 'sharing' with a woman gave her the wrong idea, and I didn't like to mislead people. But, as I'd told Stuart, Paige knew where we both stood. She wouldn't read anything into it. Plus, well, I wanted her to know me better—an urge I didn't bother to question, because I probably wouldn't like the answer.

"No," I replied. "It's sort of a by-product of my upbringing. Not that I had neglectful parents. They were great." I took another bite of my pizza. "I was an army brat, so we travelled a lot. I'd lived in fourteen different places and attended eleven schools before graduating."

Her eyes went wide. "Wow."

"I don't wish my childhood had been different. I got to see so many places, and I wouldn't trade a single minute of it. But it had it's bad points. I was always the new kid and couldn't really form lasting friendships. It's also hard to leave friends behind over and over, so after a while you stop truly connecting with people. You keep your friendships and relationships shallow. It just makes things easier."

She twisted her mouth. "And that childhood survival habit sort of followed you into adulthood?"

"Something like that." I tilted my head. "What was your childhood like?"

"Normal. Utterly normal. Doctors for parents. One sibling, who's now also a doctor. Though I got the feeling Serena only followed in their footsteps because they pressured her to. Imani reminds me of her a little. Her parents were just as opinionated about how their children's futures should go. But whereas Imani went her own way, Serena broke her back trying to make our parents proud. She grew to believe it was what *she* wanted too. She may even still believe it."

"Did they pile that same pressure on you?"

"No. They let me be. As a kid, I thought it meant they didn't care. But as I got older, I came to realise they felt that they'd made a mistake in trying to dictate my sister's future—it had pushed her away. They didn't want to do the same to me."

Having finished my slice of pizza, I grabbed my beer-flavoured NST. "Were you close to your sister?"

"No. We're just so different, and there's a huge age gap between us, so we never connected. I was a surprise baby, you see. She was sixteen when I was born." Paige let out a wistful sigh. "I would have liked it if we had been close. But she didn't make time for anyone, let alone me. She put her job before everything and everyone, including herself. After our parents died, she pretty much *buried* herself in her work."

"They died?"

She nodded. "When I was twenty-one. Boating accident. Of course, that was when Serena and I found out that our father had a whole other family."

"*What?*"

"Yep. A woman he'd been with for fifteen years. They had two sons, three cats, and a freaking holiday home in Spain."

For a long moment, I could only stare at her. "Jesus Christ." I squeezed her hand. "I'm sorry, baby. It had to have been a huge fucking blow."

"It was." She stared off into space. "You think you know someone. All of them—inside and out. But people have a way of surprising you."

As she took a long swig of her drink, avoiding eye-contact, I could see she regretted saying as much as she had. I didn't like that. So I decided to return honesty with honesty.

"I know what it's like to realise you don't know someone as well as you thought you did," I said. "When I was ten, I walked in on my mom having sex with one of my dad's closest friends."

Paige's jaw dropped. "Shitting hell."

"Yeah. It made no fucking sense to me, Paige. Still doesn't. My parents always seemed so happy. She loved my dad. I know she did. I don't get how she could have done what she did. Maybe she was just lonely—I don't know. That might be a reason, but it's not an excuse."

"No, it's not. I don't understand how my dad could have done what he did either. Did you tell your dad what you saw?"

My stomach dropped as a familiar guilt swarmed me. "No. I kept meaning to, but then I'd freeze. My mom had tried convincing me that he didn't need to know; that it would only hurt him; that she'd never do it again. It was easier to go along with it, because then things wouldn't have to change. It was a selfish decision on my part."

Her face softened. "Max, you were ten years old. Also, it was a catch twenty-two situation. And *of course* you wouldn't want your parents to separate. Very few children would."

I shrugged, though I was feeling anything but nonchalant. "Maybe I made the right decision. Maybe I didn't." I'd never know, and that haunted me. "It was hard seeing how he doted on her, completely oblivious to what she'd done and so sure she'd never betray him."

"I'm kind of glad my mom never knew my dad led a double life. It would have killed her. His other woman knew nothing of us—or so she claimed. The whole thing was just ... fucked up. Serena distanced herself even more from me after that. Retreated within herself. I can't say I blame her. The whole thing messed with my head, too. I had some major trust issues for a long time. I feel like I worked past them."

I'd developed some trust issues of my own. But unlike Paige, I hadn't been able to shake them off. Or maybe I just hadn't tried hard enough.

"I still have some hot buttons, though. I guess that's unavoidable, really."

There was a sort of click in my brain as I realised … "That's why you reacted so badly when Imani kept her relationship with Butch a secret from you at first. Secrets are a hot button for you."

She rolled back her shoulders, looking a little awkward. "I can be extra sensitive when people I care about keep things from me. It's stupid, and I'm working on it. I was unfair to both Imani and Butch."

"It wasn't just you. Most of the girls were. So was I and the majority of my squad at first."

"It wasn't just that she'd been so secretive. I didn't want Imani to be hurt again. Which is no excuse. I was out of line." Paige sipped at her drink again. "Butch is good for her, deranged killer or not."

A smile tugged at my mouth. "He's so far gone for her it's almost embarrassing to see."

"Most Bound couples are like that. It would be stupid if they weren't. I mean, it's pretty much the ultimate commitment for a vampire."

I felt my smile falter. "Is that what you want for yourself?"

"Eventually, yes. But I'm in no rush. It's more of a long-term goal."

"You got any others?"

She set down her bottle. "To not resent immortality. It worries me that I might. That I could grow bored or jaded or even a little crazy. Like Lenox. I mean, he's been part of the legion for years, but he's turned on some of his own people because he broke under the strain of everything. I have a pretty destructive ability, and it would be hard for someone to kill me if I went AWOL. I could hurt a lot of people before I'm taken down. And there'd be no one to heal them because, well, I'm the only sort-of-healer here."

The thought of her fracturing like that, of her losing part of herself and being hunted by the legion, made my stomach curdle. "I've heard of other vampires breaking. I've never seen it happen before."

"None were mated, and Antonio thinks that played a big part in why they broke. They were alone for so long—they had no one to lean on, confide in, or ground them. He said some stay detached like that, as if it will save them from one day snapping. But Antonio believes we're better off not alone; that we should grab some happiness for ourselves. I happen to agree with him. But like I said, I'm in no rush to Bind myself to someone."

She *would* do it, though. And Sam was right. I'd have to watch it happen. I'd have to pretend I was happy for Paige and whoever she chose as her mate. Would have to pretend I didn't want to beat the piss out of him.

Feeling my blood begin to boil, I shook off the matter. I didn't want to think about the future, I wanted to concentrate on the now. Because at this moment in time, she was here with *me*. She was sitting in my kitchen, wearing nothing but my tee, and she was wholly mine for another thirty-six hours. I'd be a fool not to make the most of it.

(Paige)

"Come here."

The low, deeply spoken order was so unexpected, I almost jumped. "Will I get another orgasm if I do?" I asked.

His eyes flared. "Yes."

"Then I'm game." I slipped off my seat and set my hands on his bare shoulders while I straddled him. The gorgeous bastard was wearing only his jeans. We'd shed most of our clothes earlier when we first arrived. He'd no sooner closed the front door behind us than he'd slammed me against it and fucked me right there. He'd also eaten me out before we got to the whole 'fucking' part.

He smoothed his hands up my thighs. "I like seeing you in my tee. But I like you naked more." He tugged on the material. "Take it off. Hmm, that's better. Now undo my jeans for me."

Oh, I was more than happy to do that. His cock sprang out, hard and thick and ready. I curled my hand around it, and he hissed out a breath.

"Take me in you. That's my girl."

I bore down on him, taking him inside me inch by slow inch. He didn't help me. Just watched, the red tinge to his irises glowing slightly. Once I was finally impaled on him, I teasingly squeezed my inner muscles around him.

His jaw went tight, and a groan slid between his clenched teeth. "Lean back and put your elbows on the table. Very good. Now stay still for me."

To my surprise, he didn't cup and shape and squeeze. No, he skimmed his hands over me—stroking, indulging, exploring. His touch was both soft and blatantly proprietary. I shouldn't have liked it, but I did.

"Perfect," he said.

"Do I get to touch now?"

"No."

Motherfucker.

"But you will get to come in about, hmm, five minutes."

Oh, well then he wasn't a motherfucker.

"It might take a while before you do actually come, though."

"Why is that?"

His eyes danced with humour. "Because I've noticed that wickedly slow fucks tend to irritate you."

"Then why, pray tell, will there be another wickedly slow fuck?"

"Maybe I *like* to irritate you."

"You know, I was thinking the same thing." In which case, he *was* a motherfucker.

Soon enough, he had me spread over the table while he stood between my legs, fucking me with excruciatingly lazy thrusts. But I didn't get snippy or snarly. I didn't complain or whine or beg. Nor did I play him at his own game, no, I played my own. And my game? Well, it basically consisted of me stomping all over his patience.

I feigned disinterest in what we were doing—idly tapping my fingers on the table, whistling a merry tune, commenting on the décor, saying the alphabet backwards, singing the *Ghostbusters* theme song.

At first, he was amused. But it wasn't long before annoyance crept into his expression. That was when he started trying to distract me by pinching my nipples, playing with my clit, and moulding my breasts ... which did make it a lot harder for me to fake indifference.

The singing, of course, became impossible when he shoved a finger in my mouth and ordered me to suck it. So I bit it. Not hard enough to break the skin, but enough for it to hurt. What I hadn't expected was for his cock to flex inside me. The dude might not be willing to admit it, but he wanted to mix sex and feeding—he just wouldn't.

So, me being me, I withdrew his finger and—moving so fast he had no chance to react—I reared up and lightly clamped my teeth around the lifegiving vein in his throat but without biting down to feed from him. And Jesus Christ the man lost it. He fucked me like I was the first woman he'd seen in decades.

He didn't ask me to bite him, but he also didn't ask me to release the vein. So I didn't. I just stayed like that, clutching his shoulders tight, while he rammed in and out of me until, finally, we both came long and loud.

I woke the next evening to a cock plunging inside me from behind as I lay on my side. Which was never a bad way to wake up. Ever.

It was no slow fuck. No, Max pounded into me with hard, feral thrusts, his hand gripping my thigh a little too tight. All the while, he whispered all kinds of stuff in my ear—that he loved being inside me, that I was born to take his cock, that he loved filling me with his come.

He dug his teeth into my shoulder, making me think he just might bite down, but he didn't. Just as he hadn't when he took me in the shower before we settled into bed, or when he fucked me during the day while I was still half-asleep. Yeah, using his teeth in an almost-bite had become a 'thing' now. I wasn't sure who he was teasing—me, or himself. Hell, maybe he was teasing us both.

Whatever the case, it was working its magic on me. Which might have been why my orgasm crashed into me out of nowhere. It swept him under, too. And then we were both trembling and struggling to catch our breaths.

When my brain switched back on, I realised he was still half-hard inside me. I went to get up, but he splayed a hand on my stomach.

"Not yet," he said, nuzzling my nape. "I want to feel you a little longer."

Having no issues with that, I relaxed into him again. I ignored that I was liking this a little too much. Ignored that I could easily imagine us doing this evening after evening for a long time to come. Maybe Max would one day want that with someone, but he didn't want it with me.

Having learned about his upbringing, I understood him better now. Understood that he didn't have commitment issues. No, he had issues trusting and connecting with others. The brain sought patterns, especially during hard times. He'd been forced to repeatedly leave behind people who he connected with and, thus, he'd come to associate 'bonding' with 'loss.' And his mother's betrayal was no doubt the icing on the top of the cake—it would have felt like yet another example of how getting close to people only led to pain.

On an intellectual level, he would of course know that forming a connection to someone wouldn't always result in hurt. But that wouldn't negate him reflexively avoiding true attachments. *Especially* if the person in question lived a life of risk and constant danger, because it could be too easy to lose someone to that danger.

Still, Max—being the determined, tenacious man he was—would for sure power past all that when he found a woman who made him *want* to. That woman simply wasn't me.

Which was fine. Really. I didn't want it to be me. At all. Nope.

God, I was such a fucking liar.

CHAPTER SEVEN

(Paige)

Just like the past couple of nights, both my squad and Max's tried tracking Lenox as a team. This time, we didn't spread out too much as we trekked through the rainforest. Sam and Jared wanted us all to stay close together. Or, more specifically, they wanted me surrounded by people so that Lenox would have a low chance of attacking me again.

Personally, I found it unlikely that he'd even try. Seeing me so well protected would surely discourage him from acting again. Maybe that was what happened, or maybe he just wasn't in the areas we searched, but we found no sign of the bastard anywhere.

When lunch time came around, we all returned to The Hollow. My squad and I ate lunch at the café. Afterward, Imani wanted to stop by the store to grab a bottle of water—now that she didn't drink NSTs throughout the night, she had to up her water intake to stay hydrated. I offered to go to the store with her while the other girls went on ahead of us to meet up with Sam, Jared, and the guys.

Imani and I were just crossing the bridge that had been built over the man-made beach when she spoke. "So … tonight will be your last night with Max."

My stomach sank, just as it did whenever that none-too-cheery thought floated through my brain. But I couldn't admit that to Imani. She'd only get angry with Max for 'hurting' me when, in fact, he'd set out not to from the get-go. So, keeping my expression blank, I merely said, "Yup."

Her eyes narrowed on my face. "You have no hope that he'll put an extension on this, do you?"

"Not a one. He told me some stuff. Enough for me to understand why he is the way he is. And no, I'm not expanding on that. He told me those things in private."

"True, but did he *say* that he didn't want you to repeat them?"

"No, but he also didn't give me the green light to share them, so I won't. All I will say is that I can see why he shies away from getting deeply involved with women."

Imani hummed. "So, like, he was betrayed by a fiancée or something?"

"You can throw as many theories at me as you want—I'm not going to confirm or deny anything. And in my position, you wouldn't do it either."

Her shoulders lowered in defeat. "You're right, I wouldn't. You know, I'm kind of surprised that you two got round to talking about whatever issues he has. I didn't expect to hear that you've been having deep conversations."

"Max can talk to anyone about anything—he keeps very few things private."

"Well, yeah. But this is one of the subjects he never touches. Maybe he feels like he owes you an explanation as to why he's not offering you anything real. Or maybe he just thinks that if he can make you understand why he's this way, you two can become friends after the sexytimes are over."

It seemed more likely to me that he'd felt comfortable sharing because he'd known I'd be able to relate to some of his personal issues. But I didn't say that, because if Imani heard 'personal issues,' she'd start tossing more theories at me. It seemed better to distract her. "Do you still not find human blood the least bit appetising?"

She threw me a sour look for changing the subject. "No. I still can't consume NSTs either, but Butch has no problems with me feeding from him all the time. I just don't like that he's constantly having to replenish his hunger for blood, though." She paused as she pushed open the front door of the store. "It still feels weird not having fangs anymore. I mean, I never actually liked having them. I used to complain about them. But it still feels odd."

"I'd find it kind of strange, too," I said as we headed to the refrigerator, where she snatched a bottle of water. "But I can't say I'd perceive it as a terrible loss."

We both rounded the aisle, and then I inwardly cursed. Because behind the counter stood Ursula. Apparently she'd switched jobs, because she normally worked at one of the other stores.

"Wonderful," Imani muttered under her breath.

Ursula's gaze slammed on us as we crossed to the counter. What could only be described as pure scorn rippled across her face as her eyes met mine. "I was sure you were bullshitting me, and I was right," she said to me, all sass. "Well, congrats. Whatever game you were playing with Max paid off, didn't it?"

Imani turned to me, her face lighting up. "Ooh, was it like a sex game? Because I'm fond of those." Yeah, Imani was like me—she enjoyed fucking with annoying people, too.

Ursula sniffed at me. "It won't last, you know. What's going on with you and Max won't go the distance."

"I appreciate the heads-up." I waved my hand, adding, "Could you maybe speed things along?"

Instead, she folded her arms. "What, you think I'm wrong?"

"No, it's just that I'm in a rush here—gotta go feed my velociraptor. Benji gets seriously cranky when he's hungry."

Someone snickered behind me. Glancing over my shoulder, I saw the cute waitress I'd caught Damien ogling at the Binding ceremony. There was a glint of amusement in the human's eyes. I gave her a quick smile and then turned back to Ursula just in time to see her take payment for Imani's water.

Ursula then shook her head at me. "I don't know what Max sees in you. I just don't."

I shrugged. "That's okay. Not all people have good taste."

"Well, just so you know, I intend to file a complaint about the restroom incident. You laid your hands on me, you refused to let me leave, you threatened to harm me. And if it hadn't been for Max, I'm quite sure you *would* have hurt me. I'd expect better from a member of the legion."

"That's nice, dear."

Imani smiled at me. "She's sort of adorable, isn't she? 'File a complaint.' Like it'll be a blip on your radar when we have *so* much more important things going on."

"Don't think saying shit like that will make me think it's not worth it." Ursula's eyes sliced back to me. "No, I *will* file it. It *will* be taken seriously. You *will* be held accountable. Sam and Jared will make sure of it, because your behaviour reflects on the legion. And being part of it doesn't give you the right to do whatever the hell you want. So be prepared for a temporary suspension, bitch."

Imani leaned into me, observing the other vampire with a detached look on her face. "It's like she wants you to hurt her, isn't it, Paige?"

"I was thinking the same thing," I said. "She wants me to do something that can support her 'Paige is a very bad girl' case."

"There might be more to it than that." Imani lifted her shoulders. "I mean, some people are into pain. It's not really my thing, but I don't judge. To each their own."

"I'm not into pain either. Although I do like a few spanks now and then."

"Same here."

"Not as a punishment, though. Just because I like it."

We both turned to leave.

"Hey, I'm not done," snapped Ursula.

What, like she held some sort of authority over me or something? Feeling my face harden, I leaned toward her, satisfied when apprehension flickered in her eyes. "Be very, very careful," I told her, a dark note in my voice. "I know why you're pissed. Yeah, Max told me what he did. You have every right to be angry, but not at *me*. I haven't done shit, and I won't be your personal punch bag. Nor will I pounce on you so you can go spread tales. To be frank, you just don't matter enough. You are *nothing* to me. Nothing." With that, I headed for the door with Imani at my side.

Just as we were about to leave, I heard the waitress say, "So, Ursula … apparently making an enemy of a powerful vampire who's part of Sam's personal squad seemed like a good idea to you. How's that working out for you?"

Outside, Imani puffed out a breath. "God, that woman is a pain in the padded ass. What did Max do that put both you and him on her shit list?"

Clearing my throat, I scratched the side of my head. "He kind of said my name when he was fucking her," I said, my voice uber low.

Imani gaped at me for a long moment. "I'm without words."

"Not really, because you just spoke, but I get what you mean. Now let's change the subject."

She shook her head madly. "Oh no, this is too juicy. Tell me more."

"You really need to rein in your nosiness."

"Where would be the fun in that?"

I stumbled to a halt as Jared materialised in front of us. "Oh, hi." I tensed as I took in his sombre expression. "Lenox struck again?"

"I'm afraid so." Jared gave Imani a quick nod and then teleported himself and me to the infirmary. Like last time, Sam was waiting there. Also like last time, a person lay on one of the beds, their system riddled with poison. But in this instance, it was a woman. A woman who also happened to be human, and Lenox's poison appeared to have had a far worse effect on her—there were more red lumps, more open sores, even some patches of decaying skin.

I crossed to the bed. "Oh, hell."

"I'll go grab us a prisoner," said Jared, and then he was gone.

I looked at Sam. "Who is this? I don't recognise her scent." And her face was just one big swelling.

"Ivan's bed-buddy, Elise, who also happens to be his vessel," Sam replied, her mouth tight. When a human agreed to only feed one particular vampire, they were known as their vessel. "My guess is that Lenox tried bugging Elise for info on Ivan's whereabouts—info she doesn't possess, so it was pointless. Lenox either hurt her because he didn't believe her or because he quite simply felt like it."

Either way, it made him an absolute bastard. "He might even have hurt her in lieu of Ivan. Or in the hope of making Ivan come out of hiding to face him."

"We won't be telling Ivan about this for that very reason. At least not until Lenox has been caught. I don't think Ivan is close to Elise, but he'll still feel the need to avenge his vessel—he gave her his protection; that's not something a vampire takes lightly unless he's an asshole. Ivan's uptight and far too misogynistic for my liking, but he isn't a complete arsehole."

Jared returned holding an unconscious vampire, who he then unceremoniously dumped on the floor. "He'll do."

After I'd transferred Elise's wound to the unconscious prisoner, Jared quickly dispatched him with a lethal electric bolt.

Once Mary Jane assured Sam that she'd take care of Elise—who hadn't yet woken—Sam arranged for some vampires to guard both the interior and exterior of the infirmary. Neither she nor Jared were worried that Lenox would return to finish off Elise, since she wasn't actually on his kill list, but the pair didn't wish to take chances.

As we walked along the corridor away from the infirmary, I slid the couple a quick look as I said, "Just so you know, there's a distinct possibility that Ursula is going to file a complaint about me. She might have only said it to rile me up, but I thought I'd let you know just in case she's serious."

Sam frowned. "What kind of complaint? That you're shagging Max when she's not? Because that's her actual problem."

Jared snickered, sliding his arm around his mate's shoulders.

"I know," I said, stifling a smile. "But she's still stewing over what happened in the restroom."

"What exactly *did* happen?" asked Sam.

I gave her a quick rundown of the incident, excluding the finger-fucking part of the story of course.

Sam let out a low whistle. "If Jared said another woman's name in bed, I would slice off his balls and force-feed them to him."

He winced. "I'd like to think you're kidding and you'd never do such a thing to me under any circumstances, but that would be wishful thinking, wouldn't it?"

Sam sniffed. "More like delusional. But you have no room to whine—you knew you were mating a crazy bitch."

He grinned. "You're right, I did."

"I'd be just as mad if Max had done to me what he did to Ursula," I said. "I'd feel seriously humiliated, too. I can see why Ursula created this big 'it's Paige's fault for playing Max' story in her head—she needed to justify confronting me because she knows that, in truth, this wasn't my fault. And maybe I should have handled it differently, but I was pissed that she'd taint Alora and Evan's party that way. I was hoping to keep the whole thing confined to the restroom. And yeah, okay, I played with her a little. But I didn't hurt her. I just held her by the throat a little too tight."

"I'd have done worse," Sam readily admitted.

"As part of the crazy bitch thing yeah, baby, you would have." Jared slid his gaze to me. "We take any complaints seriously, but this one won't go anywhere. I'm not sure why Ursula thinks that your being part of the legion means we'll feel that you shouldn't have retaliated. If someone gave her that impression, they were wrong to. We don't believe that just because someone's a member of the legion they should have to walk away from confrontations. And if we created such a rule, people would take advantage of it."

"Much like Ursula thought she could do," said Sam. "That was her fuck up. She doesn't have a case, Paige. You tried walking away. She blocked you each time. She also grabbed you, so it's no wonder you grabbed her right back. *None* of which she mentioned that night when she came running over to me saying that you and Max were fighting in the restroom."

I felt my brow crease. "She didn't tell you that she and I had argued?"

"Nope. She made it seem like she'd just stumbled upon you and him duelling. Who won?"

My lips flattened. "He managed to restrain me, but not until he'd cheated and used his gift—we agreed we wouldn't do that."

An impish twinkle danced in Sam's eyes. "I got the feeling I interrupted … something when I knocked on the door. Your voices sounded kind of strange."

I fought to keep my expression neutral. "It was a duel."

"Of tongues, maybe."

"No, it was an actual duel."

"It was bloody foreplay. Me and Jared still do it sometimes."

He frowned at her. "You always whip the tips of my ears. Hurts like a son of a bitch."

Sam tossed him a sideways glance. "Just be glad I don't whip your balls."

He winced at the mere idea of it.

Sam looked at me. "Anyway, I'm sorry for interrupting the foreplay session. I hope you at least had *one* happy ending before I knocked on the door. If not, I'm sure you've had plenty of them since then. You know, I was surprised you'd agreed to a fling with Max. I got the impression you were looking for more than that."

Not wishing to go into detail, I merely said, "It's not so much a fling as a temporary arrangement with a super short expiry date."

Sam gave a slow nod. "Ah. Well that's crushed my hope that something serious might come out of this."

"He's not looking for 'serious.'"

"Most blokes aren't. Jared wasn't. He wanted to add me to his collection of consorts when I first arrived. He actually set the three women up in a nice apartment—yeah, they lived together, if you can believe that."

Looking incredibly uncomfortable, Jared cricked his neck. "I got rid of them for you, remember?"

"You did, even though you only wanted sex from me." Sam cut her gaze back to me. "That's the point I'm making. Just because a bloke isn't hoping for more than a few jumps in the sack doesn't mean he won't change his mind."

She had the right of it there. But after all Max had revealed to me so far about his past ... "I don't think Max will oh so suddenly come round to the idea of a real relationship."

"I'd like to disagree, but he's a stubborn little shit. And old habits die hard, don't they? We can get used to being alone and convince ourselves we're happier that way when, really, we just don't want to step out of our comfort zone. Ain't that right, Jared?"

He only sighed at the verbal jab.

"So there's a good chance that Max won't offer you more. If that happens, I think he'll come to regret it. Maybe not so much straight away, but eventually he will. I'm just hoping it won't be a case of 'too little, too late' for you."

I doubted it would be, because I doubted he'd ever have any regrets. But I did think Sam was correct in believing that the right person might make Max step out of his comfort zone—I'd had the same thought myself earlier.

I couldn't lie, it would be hard for me to see him with aforementioned right person. He deserved to be happy, though. So I'd be happy for him. Eventually. To some degree. Deep, deep, *deep* down. Or so I told myself anyway.

God, this whole thing sucked.

CHAPTER EIGHT

(Paige)

Feeling Max's gaze on my face, I kept my eyes closed. Not faking sleep, just ... well, hiding. Hiding that I was way too comfortable lying here on his bed as his fingertips ghosted over my bare back.

We weren't snuggled together. There were a few inches between us—inches we'd both put there as we rolled onto our sides to face each other. That small space was always there, and it always felt like a massive gulf. The only time we ever closed the distance was when we were getting hot and heavy.

"How did you become a vampire?"

Surprised by the question, I opened my eyes.

"I know about your Sire, Langley," Max added. "And I'm glad the fucker's dead. But I don't know how you came to be Turned."

I twisted my mouth. "When I was twenty-five, I was diagnosed with cervical cancer. The doctors said there was nothing they could do. I blurted it out to a bartender that night, finding it easier to talk to a perfect stranger. Turns out he was one of Langley's vampires. Langley came to me with an offer. Of course, I didn't believe he was a vamp at first. Not until he lowered his fangs and let his irises glow. Then I near pissed my pants."

Max's lips twitched. "I can imagine."

"He made it sound like vampirism was the best thing ever. He didn't tell me about a lot of things—the intense bloodlust in the early days, the struggle for control, the work he'd want me to do for him, the control he exerted over his nest, or the psychic blood-link that would prevent me from escaping him. I also hadn't known that Langley would set it up to look like I'd taken off with a guy. I didn't have anyone around who'd care to question that. I doubt my sister even batted an eyelid at hearing I was going away."

Pausing, I swallowed as an ache began to build in my chest. "I fled countless times. One of his flunkies would always find me and bring me back. Then I'd be punished before the entire nest, but not because Langley was angry. He didn't care when anyone fled. He thought it was amusing, and it gave him an excuse to do what he liked to do most: hurt people."

The hand on my back flexed, and then Max was dancing his fingers over my skin again. "Asshole. Why did he send you to retrieve Imani when he knew you were a flight risk?"

"He'd promised me that he'd free me from his hold if I brought her to him. But I couldn't do it. I didn't know why he wanted her, I just knew I couldn't subject her to whatever fate he had in mind. So I warned her about him, gave her money, and told her to run. She asked me to come with her. I pointed out that I couldn't; that Langley could use the blood-link to find me. She then told me that she could snap the link. You can imagine how quick I was to accept her offer." I doodled a circle on the bedsheet with my fingertip. "How did you become a vamp?"

"A woman Made me. Her plan was to build a line big enough to overthrow her nest in retaliation for banishing her. I didn't stick around to help her. After I'd learned to control both my bloodlust and my gift, I left. She never tried to find me. I'd merely been a tool that didn't work well enough to do the job she wanted, so she went and found herself another."

What a bitch. "Sadly, until Sam and Jared made it punishable by death, it wasn't uncommon for vampires to randomly Turn people." There were some who stupidly still did it, and they always paid for that. "Do you wish you'd never been Made?"

"I did for a while. But I'm not the type to have a pity party. I figured this was my new reality and that I'd just have to deal with it. So I did. I came to like being what I am. I like the added strength and speed and my gift. I feel more comfortable in the legion than I ever did anywhere as a human."

"It's the same for me. Being part of the legion is tough at times. And life at The Hollow … it can be like living in a bubble—your life is so free of every day shit like rent and bills and all that stuff. But that bubble isn't exactly protective, since it includes a truck load of danger. It's way scarier than my years on the run. And yet, I've never felt safer. Is that weird?"

"No. Not weird at all. I know exactly what you mean."

That little moment of total understanding must have made him feel as uncomfortable as it did me, because we both briefly looked away. "Have you seen anything of your parents since you Turned?" I asked.

"No. If I was a Sventé, I guess I could have. But with these red irises? No. Both my parents are gone now anyway. My dad died in action. And my mother then drank herself to death." He moved his hand from my back to my waist and settled it there, tracing my hipbone with his thumb. "I hate that

I had to go 'missing' and let them believe I might be dead—I'd gone missing from their lives once before. They didn't deserve to have it happen twice."

I blinked. "Twice?"

"I was abducted as a baby by some fucking weirdo who couldn't have a kid of her own and so decided that I'd be hers."

I felt my jaw drop. "What? No way."

"Way. The police tracked me down after three weeks, but it must have felt like years to my parents. I don't remember any of it, obviously. But I remember my parents were seriously overprotective for a long time. I can hardly blame them for that, though."

I lightly touched his chest. "I'm sorry that happened," I said, not really knowing what else to say to something like that. What a head wrecker it would be to know you'd been kidnapped as a baby.

The hand on my hip slipped down to palm my butt. "Love this ass," he said.

Apparently we were done with the heavy stuff. Good. Because our talks made it hard to remember that we were only about sex.

He squeezed my butt. "Has anyone ever taken you here?"

"No. And you won't be doing it either."

His mouth kicked up into a smile, and his eyes then dropped to my chest. "Hmm, such pretty breasts." He dipped down and sucked one nipple into his mouth.

My eyes fluttered closed, and I palmed the back of his head. The whole time he toyed with my breasts with his tongue, his hands roamed over me, sure and bold. Every little touch felt … more. Because I was conscious of how little time we had left.

Once the sun set, this would be over, I'd be gone, and we'd move forward as colleagues. The thought made my heart squeeze and my nose sting. But I wasn't going to spoil this with tears or complaints. I wasn't going to have an internal pity party. No, I was going to make the most of what time we had left.

I was also going to make damn sure he remembered me.

(Max)

I suddenly found myself flat on my back with Paige hovering over me. Damn, the woman was fast. And a lot fucking stronger than she looked.

I frowned when she began shuffling backwards. "Where are you going?"

The look she gave me was wicked.

I hissed as she dragged her tongue up my shaft from root to tip. My thigh muscles jumped. "Jesus."

Fisting the base of my dick, she took me into her mouth—no preamble, no warning, no hesitation. Just closed her lips around the broad head and then sucked me deep.

I drew in a sharp breath and bunched my hands in all that gorgeous hair. "Yeah, that's it. Fuck, your mouth looks even prettier when it's full of my cock."

She couldn't know how many times I'd imagined her sucking me off. The reality was better than those imaginings. It was like being surrounded in a hot, silken fist. She wasn't gentle or tentative. She sucked hard, kept the suction tight, let out these goddamn moans that went straight to my balls.

I groaned as I hit the back of her throat. "Take more, baby." She did, swallowing again and again. I cursed as the muscles of her throat contracted around me. "Yes, like that, good girl." Watching those lips slide up and down my shaft and feeling her tongue rub the underside just right ... shit, I was currently feeling far too possessive of that mouth.

Hell, I was feeling far too possessive of *her*.

Since our 'arrangement' began, I'd explored every inch of her. I'd taken her in every way possible—soft, slow, hard, fast, rough. I'd taken her in practically every position. I'd fucked her on nearly every available surface in my apartment.

And it wasn't enough.

I only wanted more. Which meant I was royally fucked.

Meeting my eyes, she pulled her mouth off my cock and lowered her fangs. My pulse jumped. She let her fangs lightly graze the head of my dick and then soothed the sting with a swipe of her tongue. I knew she wouldn't draw blood; that this was only a tease. But fuck if I didn't want her to just do it.

Instead, she retracted her fangs. Disappointment flooded me. But then she swallowed me down again. And again. And again. My balls drew up tight, and my thighs trembled.

I fisted her hair tighter. "Swallow it. I want my come in your belly."

She didn't pull back. She sucked harder, humming ... and my release hit me so hard I swear I saw goddamn spots.

Finally, my orgasm eased off, and I pretty much slumped to the bed, panting and sated.

But I wasn't done with her yet.

Once I could move, I hauled her up my body and kissed her hard as I rolled her onto her back. "Stay." Then I took away her sight.

She tensed. "What the fuck?"

"Shh, you'll like this." I licked at the pulse beating in her neck. It was like a damn siren's call, and I couldn't even say why. I'd never had a problem resisting the urge to feed during sex. Until Paige.

"This is so weird," she said, blinking hard.

"No different than being blindfolded. And it has the same effect." It'd make everything more intense for her.

I could also take away her hearing. She would then really have little clue what was coming. But I knew that taking two of her senses away at once would be a bit much when she'd never done this before. Maybe next time. Drowning out the voice that reminded me there wouldn't be a *next time*, I settled between her thighs and nuzzled her slick folds. "Come whenever you're ready." I licked at her slit, and she sucked in a breath.

There was something almost addictive about going down on her. Her taste, her moans, her raspy demands, how shamelessly she arched into my mouth and scratched at the back of my head—all of it shot straight to my cock.

I loved teasing the hell out of her by driving her up hard and fast but then backing off right before her orgasm could hit her. It was something I did over and over, and it was no surprise that she bitched at me each time without fail.

"There's no point in saying 'come whenever you're ready' if you're gonna take for-fucking-ever to get me there!"

"You hate me, don't you? That's what it is. You actually hate me."

"Oh my God, I will kill you! Seriously! I will murder the shit *out of you!"*

"Right, that's it, I'm killing you! I am. Sam will understand."

Chuckling, I shoved two fingers inside her, distracting her that easily. "You know, if I didn't like the noises you make as much as I do, I'd take away your ability to talk so I didn't have to listen to you bitch at me. Good girls don't threaten to kill people. But since you deserve a reward for how hard you made me come earlier …" I roughly pumped my fingers in and out of her while working her clit with my tongue.

I knew her body well, so I knew exactly where and how to touch her to make her come fast. I pushed those hot buttons right then, groaning when her inner walls heated and tightened. Yeah, she was close.

"Come on, baby, let go for me." I drove a third finger inside her, and she imploded with a choked cry—her head thrown back, her spine snapping straight, one hand fisting the bedsheet while the other gripped my head tight. Then she sagged, boneless.

Hard as a rock once more, I crawled up her body and returned her sight. I wanted to be looking right into her eyes as I took her. I lodged the head of my dick in her opening and then planted my lower arms either side of her head. "Wrap me up."

She curled her arms and legs around me. "I suppose it's going to be another wickedly slow fuck, isn't it?" Her voice was dry as a bone and thick with need.

I smiled. "How did you guess?"

"You seem to get off on seeing me all riled up."

"I do like pushing your Berserk button, yes."

"I do *not* have a Berserk button."

"She says while digging her nails into my back and baring her teeth. Not that I'm complaining. You're cute when you get all feral."

Paige narrowed her eyes. "Cute? *Bunnies* are cute. I—"

"Talk too much." I slammed deep inside her, knocking the breath out of her lungs. I groaned, feeling my eyelids drift closed. God, she was soaking wet and so hot it almost burned. It was a tight fit but perfect all the same. Too perfect.

Opening my eyes, I saw that hers were shut. "Look at me."

She did, and the hunger there punched me right in the gut and made my balls tighten.

I sipped from her mouth as I slowly thrust in and out of her, driving deep each time, wanting her to really *feel* every inch. Wanting to imprint it all on her memory. Wanting to fucking possess her. "Love knowing your belly is full of my come right now."

After long minutes, I got to my knees, tossed her legs over my shoulders, and gripped her thighs. I saw the glint of anticipation in her eyes; knew she thought I meant to up my pace. But I didn't, so that glint rapidly faded. She actually folded her arms and glared at me.

I failed to bite back a smile. "Something wrong?"

"What could possibly be wrong?" She began humming to herself while staring at the ceiling, and I felt one of the ankles over my shoulder start idly twirling.

I knew she thought it pissed me off when she did this shit, but I liked it. Liked that we … played. It was different. Intimate. Something I'd only ever done with her.

I also liked shocking a curse out of her by abruptly ramming my cock deep inside her, taking her off-guard. I did it right then.

Her eyes went wide, and her hands flew out to grip the bedsheet. "Jesus *fuck.*"

I slowly reared back but then slammed deep again. And again. And again. Dragging the whole thing out, not wanting it to end.

My cock throbbed when one of those little whimpers I loved slipped out of her. "Want me deeper, baby?" At her nod, I curled over her, tilting her hips, and planted one hand either side of her head. The new angle made my cock slide even deeper inside her, and we both groaned.

I resumed taking her slow and hard, doing my best to block out the little voice in my head reminding me that after the sun set, I'd never have this again. Would never again taste or touch her. Never again feel her hands or mouth on me. Never again fill her body with my cock and come. But the voice just kept on whispering, and those whispers got harder and harder to pretend away.

"Fuck," I bit out. Then I was powering into her, unapologetically brutal.

Her brow creased in pleasure/pain, but she arched into every savage lunge, digging her nails into my arms. I was thankful she didn't ask me to stop, because I wasn't sure I could.

So many sounds rung through the air—her moans and whimpers, my groans and grunts, flesh smacking wet flesh, the headboard slamming into the wall. There was another sound. A sound that seemed louder than every other, one that called to the predator in me.

The frantic beat of the pulse in her neck.

My eyes dropped to it. My mouth watered. And I found myself circling it with the tip of my tongue.

Maybe it was the delicious stutter in her breath. Maybe it was the way her pulse erratically spiked. Maybe it was just that I quite simply no longer wished to fight myself on this, but I sank my teeth down hard. Her blood flowed into my mouth, her body arched into mine, her hand grabbed at my hair. And I rutted on her like a fucking animal.

She tasted so insanely good. Sweet and rich and addictive. And I knew I'd messed up. I shouldn't have tasted her, because now I'd always crave her. But that didn't stop me from drinking deep again and again.

I pulled back for one reason only. I needed something from her. Still roughly pounding into her, I snatched her gaze. "Feed from me."

Wariness glimmered in those glassy eyes. "You don't really want that."

I snarled. "Do it."

"You already partly broke your rule by taking my blood. You might want to leave it at that."

"Fucking do it, Paige."

"You sure?"

"Now. I need it," I admitted.

She lowered her fangs, watching my reaction closely. She must have been satisfied with whatever she saw, because she reared up and bit into the crook of my neck. The slash of pain and suction of her mouth felt so fucking good and then … I couldn't even be sure what exactly happened, but my control seriously just vanished.

I didn't bear in mind the relative differences in our strength. Didn't even fuck her at human speed. No, I hammered into her at vampiric speed, absolutely lost in her, in the moment, in the feel of her drinking from me.

A part of me was *in* her now, just as a part of her was in me. That thought alone was enough to make an orgasm whip through me—there was no stopping it, no having the presence of mind to make sure she came as well. The release was too violent, too intense, too blinding. So I was relieved when I heard her scream and felt her explode around my cock.

All hollowed out, I slumped on top of her. *Jesus goddamn Christ.*

CHAPTER NINE

(Paige)

Plonking the last of my clothes into my duffel, I swallowed around the tightness in my throat. I wanted to feel numb, or maybe angry. I usually did subconsciously reach for anger when I was hurting, but the habit failed me right then. So I was stuck feeling like shit. My heart ached, my stomach kept rolling, and a weird pressure was building in my chest.

Shit, this sucked balls.

I'd woken to find myself alone and a NST waiting for me on the nightstand. Max was pottering around the apartment, and he'd no doubt heard me moving around, but he hadn't even so much as popped his head through the doorway.

We hadn't showered together the way we usually did on waking. Well of course we hadn't. Our time was up now. And he was no doubt waiting for me to get back to my own apartment.

Although it kind of stung that he was clearly avoiding me, I was glad he was giving me space. I didn't want him hovering over my shoulder while I packed, because I wasn't sure I'd have been able to hide just how hard this was. Not the packing part, but the knowledge that I'd never be back here. I was now simply one of his fellow legion members again—no more, no less.

My stomach flipped once more. I had no one to blame for this but myself. I'd sensed that I could totally fall for this man. It had scared the shit out of me, because he wouldn't welcome that love. But I hadn't walked away. Hadn't ended our arrangement early. Nor had I refused to take his blood, which had been seriously dumb.

I was still kind of shocked that he'd fed from me. He hadn't only done it the one time. No, I'd woken to the feel of his teeth slicing into my shoulder at one point. He'd also bitten my inner thigh while finger-fucking me during a later session. Each time, he'd pressured me to bite him in return, and I'd put up no resistance. Like a dumbass.

Finished packing my clothes, I began grabbing my other bits and bobs. I was searching for my hair tie when Max finally appeared. He didn't enter the room, though. He leaned against the doorjamb, his expression unreadable.

God, he was gorgeous. Sexy. Hotter than hot. And waiting for me to get gone.

I cleared my throat. "Hey. I'll, um, be out of here in just a sec. I can't find my hair tie. Have you seen it anywhere?"

He slowly shook his head, uncharacteristically quiet and remote.

"If you find it at any point, pass it to me when you get a chance." I zipped up my duffel, snatched it off the bed, and crossed to him. "Well, I guess I'll see you around."

He lazily pushed away from the doorjamb but didn't step aside. "Paige." He didn't say more. He sighed, scrubbing a hand down his face.

And I got it. He was worried I might have read something into him breaking one of his personal rules. That was why he'd stayed out of my way and was now acting so distant. It was a message, plain and simple, that nothing had changed. Since I hadn't actually needed that reminder, the whole thing was a slap in the face.

"You don't have to say anything, Max." I would seriously rather he didn't.

"Feels like I do," he said, his voice pitched lower than usual.

"You really don't. I'm quite aware that nothing has changed for you. There's no need for you to spell it out. I get it. I'm good. *We're* good. If you're worried that things are going to be weird or awkward, don't. We'll work together just fine. Hey, maybe we'll even be friends."

A hardness slid into his eyes. "I could never be platonic friends with you, Paige," he stated, his tone flat. "I don't say it to be an asshole, I just ... I couldn't do it."

Well it *would* be tricky, given the sexual tension between us was still as acute as ever, but it would dissolve eventually. And since, unlike me, he didn't have any none-too-platonic feelings dancing around his system, he wouldn't have that shit to contend with. "You won't always feel that way."

"You'll find it so easy for us to be friends, will you?" He said 'friends' like it was a dirty word.

"I didn't say that. I just mean that, well, we'll both be living at The Hollow for centuries and centuries to come. The law of probability says you'll get past this feeling at some point. We both will."

"Centuries," he echoed quietly, an edge to his voice.

Yeah, centuries of seeing him pretty much every night but never being able to touch him outside of sparring. It was going to be hard as hell at first for sure. But it would get easier. And it was kind of annoying that he was being all surly about this when he wasn't the one hurting. He just didn't like that he hadn't fully worked me out of his system. Nice.

"This isn't easy for me either, you know," I said, though I didn't dare admit exactly how difficult it was. "But I'm not being a bitch and making you pay for that, am I? No. Because we both knew what this was, and what it wasn't. So there's no need to be a dick, Max. Besides, you're the one with all the rules and boundaries." Oh shit, my voice broke.

His face softened. "Come here."

I went rigid. "No."

The bastard pulled me into his arms anyway and held me tight. "Hug me back."

"No." Because if we crossed any kind of line now after the seventy-two hours were up—if we hugged, kissed, acted as *anything* other than colleagues—it would probably happen again. Maybe only at sporadic moments when we were both feeling a little weak, but it would happen. It was better to just make a clean break here and now; to underline that our time was up and just move forward.

I pushed out of his arms and straightened my shoulders. "Bye," I said, the word unintentionally soft. I shrugged past him and walked through the apartment, hating the way my chest twisted and tightened.

"Paige," he called out as I put my hand on the doorknob.

I stiffened but didn't turn to face him. I just glanced over my shoulder. He stood a few feet away, his face again an impassive mask, his mouth open as if to speak. But he clamped his lips shut.

I forced a smile, but it was weak. "Like I said, you don't have to say anything." I left the apartment, softly closing the door behind me. The *snick* carried such a finality that it made my throat ache all the more.

Dammit, I would *not* cry.

But the backs of my eyes burned, and my nose began to sting like hell. Cursing inwardly, I hurried to my apartment at vampire speed. Inside, I slammed the door shut and let my head fall back, as if it might stop the tears from falling. My breath hitched, to my utter fucking horror and—

My instincts screamed at me, and I froze as every inch of my skin prickled. *I wasn't alone.*

Straightening my head, I pivoted to face my intruder.

Lenox grinned. "I've been waiting for you."

Hell.

(Max)

Clenching my fists, I swore long and loud as the front door closed behind Paige. I wanted to go after her. Wanted to call her back.

Wanted to tell her ... what? What could I possibly say?

I couldn't ask her to stay, because I couldn't give her a good reason to do so. She wouldn't agree to prolong our arrangement. Wouldn't agree to a full-on fling. Wouldn't settle for anything less than a real relationship.

I didn't balk at the idea of the latter the way I normally would, but I had no intention of offering her anything serious. Paige didn't need to be saddled with my shit. When it came to flings, I could hold back, because it was just sex. In a relationship, I'd have to give it my all. I wasn't sure I could. I trusted Paige, but I had no trust in happily ever afters, so I couldn't honestly enter into a Binding with her.

I scrubbed a hand over my head. Fuck, watching her leave had been so much harder than I ever could have thought it would be. Why had I thought seventy-two hours would be enough? Or had I known it wouldn't? Had I subconsciously pushed myself into a situation where I'd be so set on keeping her that I'd even try a relationship?

Surely it wasn't the latter. Surely I wasn't *that* fucking selfish when it came to her that I'd put my wants before what was best for her.

Of course I was. Or I never would have touched her. I never would have pushed her to feed from me out of some dark need to make sure she always carried a part of me.

Closing my eyes, I cursed myself to hell and back ... because I knew myself well. Knew I wouldn't manage to stay away from her. Knew I'd try seducing her at every given opportunity, try to make her consider letting a simple fling be enough.

It wouldn't have to be a *shallow* fling. We wouldn't need to put a time-limit on it. We could be exclusive. I'd agree not to feed from anyone other than her, if she wanted that. I'd certainly ask her not to feed from anyone but me. Surely I could convince her that Binding wasn't the be all and end all.

She'd want someone who cared for her, true, but ... well, I did. She was important to me. Had been for a long time. She mattered to me more than I was comfortable with, in all honesty. That would surely make a difference to her. It had to. Because she'd only been gone a few minutes, and already being apart from her wasn't working for me at all.

I rolled back my shoulders, determination snaking through me. I'd go after her. Talk to her. Plead my case to her. And if she turned me down, well, I'd just keep at her until she agreed. There was no other option, because I wasn't ready to give her up.

Paying zero attention to the voice that told me I'd never be ready for that, I stalked out of my apartment and headed for hers.

(Paige)

Well this wasn't good. At all.

Any other time, I would have telepathed Jared to ask for assistance. But right then, I didn't bother, because I would have failed. Why? Well, Lenox wasn't alone. He had a hostage. A female vampire who possessed the ability to block telepathic contact—hence the low hum of static in the air.

A female vampire who also happened to be Ursula. And she looked damn terrified.

Considering Lenox held the tips of his poisonous claws to her throat, I couldn't really blame her for that. Not even I could heal a fatal slit to the throat.

Keeping my expression blank, I focused on him as I said, "A lot of people are looking for you."

"Yes, I know." His mouth twisted. "I always liked you Paige, but you've become a problem for me."

"A problem, huh?" I could say the same to him. Though it would be an understatement.

"I need some people to die. You keep saving them. You can see how I might have an issue with that."

"Killing them wouldn't change anything."

"But it is necessary. They lost their right to live. Now let's not delay matters. Ursula here is counting on you. Oh yes, I'm quite aware that you two aren't terribly fond of each other. That's what makes this all the better. She won't sacrifice herself for you, nor care much that she'll have to watch you die. But you, being a good soldier, would never sacrifice a hostage to save yourself, no matter who they were." He tossed a syringe onto the carpet at my feet. "I took it from the infirmary when I went looking for Elise, but she's been moved. I've filled it up for you."

I didn't pick it up. "What's in it?"

"You already know."

I did. Because that yellow substance was very familiar. He'd filled the syringe with his own damn poison.

"Inject yourself with it."

"Why not just claw me?"

"I need to be over here with Ursula to ensure you behave yourself. There's a lot of poison in that. Enough to kill you in under a minute. She and I will watch you die. Then I'll let her go."

I snorted. "You expect her to believe that?"

"She had no hand in Brook's death, so I have no reason to harm her."

"Elise didn't have a hand in it either."

He shrugged. "I knew you'd heal her. I just hoped to flush Ivan out. The coward won't face me, though." He tipped his chin at the syringe on the carpet. "Stop stalling and pick it up. This is nothing personal, Paige. I truly would never otherwise wish to hurt you. Particularly since you saved Brook's life once. But you leave me no choice."

A knock came at the door, causing us all to tense. Hope leaped in my chest. I couldn't cry out for help as it would only get Ursula killed, and then Lenox would jump his ass out of here. But just maybe I could somehow get this person to—

"Ignore them," said Lenox. "Pick up the syringe. My patience is waning fast."

Another knock came at the door. "Paige, open up!"

My heart skipped a beat. *Max.*

"We need to talk!" Max quickly added. "I'm not leaving until we do!"

And I knew he meant it. He wouldn't be put off by my not answering. He'd keep on knocking until I did. Right then, I was so damn thankful for his tenacious streak.

"Paige, let me in!"

Lenox swore beneath his breath.

"He's not going to go away," I told Lenox. "He's also going to draw attention. People will see him pounding on my door and wonder why I'm not opening it. You've attacked me once, so it won't take much for people to wonder if you're here."

Again, Lenox cursed. "Answer the door. Make him leave. But don't be so stupid as to tell him I'm here. And stay in my line of sight. I will know if you signal for help. I'll snap this one's neck and be gone before anyone can even try to touch me."

I believed him. I crossed to the door, pasted a calm expression on my face, and then opened it wide.

Max stood there, his fist poised to knock again. He lowered his arm, pinning me with a determined look. "We need—"

"To talk, right," I finished. "But that can't happen right now."

"Sure it can," he said, utterly unfazed by my objection. "You'll only be eating breakfast. I'll talk while you eat."

"Not without missing your meeting with Sam and Jared." Before he could point out that there was no meeting, I added, "Go see them and get that out of the way. I should still be here when you're done, but only if you don't take too long." I closed the door, hoping he'd read between the lines, and turned to face Lenox. "There."

The asshole gave me a faint smirk. "Excellent. Now ... inject the poison into you."

Not likely. "What happened to Brook was awful, Lenox. Tragic. And I know you must be—"

"You know nothing," he spat, his eyes flaring. "He would have been mine, you know. But he wanted more than the occasional bedroom companion, and I didn't wish to complicate things. So we ended."

I almost gaped. Shit, I had *not* seen that coming.

"I couldn't give him—no, that's not true, I *wouldn't*—give him the things he wanted," Lenox went on, his tone clipped. "But I resolved that I would watch over him. I swore I would keep him safe. It was all I could do. And if I'd been on that mission, he *would* be alive. But Quinlan wouldn't allow me to go, and Ivan didn't watch Brook's back as he should have. Now Brook is dead because of *them*. So no, it was not a tragic accident. They are at fault, and they will pay. But that's not going to happen until you're out of the picture, because you keep ruining my plans. Now, *pick up the fucking syringe*."

I slowly raised my hands in a gesture of peace. "Okay." I slowly padded over to it, naturally in no rush, and lifted it from the carpet.

Lenox grunted in what might have been approval. "Now get it over with."

Jared materialised a few feet behind Lenox. Relief damn near felled me. Jared wasn't alone. Sam and Cassie were with him.

Lenox stiffened, his eyes going wide in both shock and horror. "W-what's happening?"

Well if I had to guess, I'd say Cassie was inside his head, because he'd otherwise have slit Ursula's throat and bolted. Instead, he retracted his claws.

He watched, his eyes still gleaming with horror, as his arms released Ursula, who darted away from him and plastered herself to the wall.

The others then closed in on him, and he swallowed hard.

I smiled at my friend and squad member. "Thanks, Cass."

Her mouth curved. "Never a problem, sweetie."

Sam cocked her head at Lenox. "Well this wasn't the best idea you've ever had, was it? That's the thing about being AWOL. You don't consider everything. Like that one of my squad would for sure outsmart you."

He began ranting at her, demanding to be released, calling her every name under the sun.

Catching sight of the syringe in my hand, Sam frowned. "What's with the needle?"

"He filled it with his poison," I explained. "He wanted me to inject it into my system."

"Ah, I see." Sam took it from me and moved to stand directly in front of him. "I know you're immune to the effects of the poison, I'm just gonna do this for the fun of it." She stabbed the syringe right into his eyeball, and Lenox let out a guttural cry of pain.

I recoiled because *ew*. The needle bopped from side to side as he frantically moved his eye as if he could dislodge it.

Sam nodded, as if satisfied with the spectacle. "I can't tell you how warm and fuzzy your pain is making me feel right now."

Jared snickered, shaking his head.

A fist pounded on the front door. "Paige! Open up!"

"I let him know you're fine," Jared told me, no doubt meaning he'd telepathed Max. "He needs to see that for himself, though."

Sam sighed at me. "You'd better let him in before he has a hernia."

The moment I opened the door, Max barged inside and cupped my head. "You all right?"

"Of course," I replied. And then his arms were tight around me, his face buried in my neck, his body all but humming with relief, rage, and a lingering panic. He was hugging me like he hadn't seen me in years, and all I could do was hug him back.

"Fucking prick needs to die." Max lifted his head. "Where did he—What the fuck, Coach?"

I felt my mouth quirk at his reaction to the sight of a still whining Lenox, whose eye still sported a syringe.

"I think it suits him," said Sam. "Some might say I should have a little sympathy for you, Lenox. I heard a little of what you said about Brook, so I can understand why you lost the plot, but it's *no* excuse for anything you've recently done."

I frowned, wondering *how* they could have heard. Jared must have noticed, because he then spoke.

"We teleported to your balcony first, not sure where you'd be and worried he'd spot us and get away before Cassie could thrust into his mind. When we realised where exactly you were and that his back was to us, we made our move."

Lenox once more began ranting and raving at Sam.

She slid her gaze to Max. "Do me a cheesy quaver and shut him up, will you?"

I smiled, having learned 'cheesy quaver' was slang for 'favour' in Sam's vocabulary.

Releasing me, Max closed his fist, and then Lenox's curses were totally silent.

Sam turned to a very pale Ursula, tilting her head. "I'm wondering why *you're* here."

Her voice shaky, Ursula explained how Lenox had snatched her as she'd been on her way to work. She and I both then gave our accounts of what happened here. All the while, Lenox stood unnaturally still thanks to Cassie, and utterly quiet thanks to Max.

Sam beamed at Lenox. "Well, let's take you to your new home. Just think how ironic it is that Paige has been healing your victims by transferring their injuries onto prisoners … and one night in the future she'll use you in the same way to save someone else. I think they call that karma. I call it fucking fabulous."

She, Jared, and Lenox then disappeared.

Ursula made a beeline for the still-open front door and darted out of the apartment. Cassie moved at a slower pace, expressing her relief that I was fine.

Max and I were then alone.

CHAPTER TEN

(Paige)

Blowing out a breath, he sank onto the sofa as if the life had been sucked out of him.

Not sure what to think of that, I tipped my head to the side and asked. "Are you okay?"

His gaze met mine, alive with chaotic emotions. "You could have been fucking killed so, no, I'm not. When I realised you were in danger … Shit, Paige. You don't know how hard it was for me to let you shut that door in my face. But I knew I had to. I knew I couldn't barge in here, because I didn't know what kind of scene I'd be dealing with. It fucking killed me to stand out there and trust the others to help you. *Killed* me."

Bowled over by the sheer anguish in his voice, I just stared at him, not knowing what to say. Not knowing what to do. I wasn't good at comforting people, and I was beyond shocked that he seemed to need said comfort.

Feeling unable to just *stand there,* I slowly moved toward him. But even as I then stood before him, I was still uncertain about what to say or do.

Max exhaled heavily. "The things you told us Lenox said to you … Fuck if I'm not him."

I almost jerked back. "What? No. Why would you even think that?"

"He held back from the person he most wanted, didn't he? He swore that he'd simply keep them safe instead. That's what I did with you."

I crouched in front of him and rested a hand on his leg. "That doesn't mean you're like Lenox. Or that you'll end up like him, if that's your worry. You would *never* do the shit he did. Ever."

Max scoffed. "Do you know why I came here?"

I felt my brow furrow. "No, why?"

"I was going to ask you to agree to a fling. Not a shallow, meaningless one. More of a casual but exclusive relationship."

I sighed and shook my head. "Max, I—"

"Then I realised you were in danger, and my world fucking tipped over."

"What?"

"When I stood out there in that hallway waiting for news from Jared that you were okay, safe, *alive* … every second that went by felt like a goddamn hour. And during those seconds that turned into minutes, I realised a few things. Mostly that I'd been lying to myself."

Refusing to let hope build inside me, I asked, "About what?"

"A few things. Do you remember I once told you that forever was a long time to have what you want just out of your reach?"

I nodded. "I remember."

"I had it in my head that what I felt for you was mostly sexual. I told myself we could fuck each other out of our systems. Told myself I could walk away afterwards without a problem. But subconsciously, I knew none of that was true. Knew I didn't just want you in my bed; that I wanted you smack bam in the middle of my world."

I felt my pulse quicken. "What are you saying? That you want to try a relationship?"

He leaned forward and drifted his fingers through my hair. "Sam said something to me a few nights ago. She pointed out that I'd have to watch you Bind with someone eventually. That I'd get to watch it all play out in front of me, so it was good that I was 'happy' alone. The thing is … it would eat me up, Paige. Eat me up to see you with someone else, which isn't the right reason to ask you to give me a shot. So I wouldn't, if that was the only reason I wanted to try a relationship with you."

Still reeling from the fact that there was *one* reason he was up for this, I raised my brows. "There's another?"

"Yeah, although I didn't realise it until I was stood in that hallway." He palmed my face with both hands, his eyes all soft and warm. "I love the shit out of you."

Utterly stunned, I didn't breathe for a moment. "What?"

"I pretended it away. Not because I didn't want something with you, but because I don't have a lot of faith in relationships. My parents … they were solid. Tight. So fucking happy. What my mother did rocked me. But I think you can understand that, because hearing about your dad's other family rocked you. It's enough to disillusion a person, isn't it? It makes you think you can't *really* know people. That you can't trust happiness, so you don't go looking for it. And I guess a part of me felt that I had no *right* to look for it, because I can't quite shake off the guilt I feel for not telling my dad about my mother's betrayal, even though I'm not sure if telling him would have been the right decision."

I gave his leg a comforting squeeze. "That guilt is senseless, but I do understand why you're torn up about that. And you're right, I do understand why your mother's actions rocked you. I can see why your upbringing caused you to avoid relationships. I did that for a long time, though I didn't realise it back then. It was a while before I saw that my pattern of picking one asshole after another was my way of avoiding real commitment. I subconsciously knew I'd never be happy with those men, knew I'd end things at some point, and that was why I picked them."

"The difference between you and me is that you confronted your issues and worked on them. I didn't do that. I kept on fucking up. Convinced myself I was fine the way I was."

"And now?"

"Now I'm done with that shit. Fair warning: I've never been in a relationship before, and I get the feeling I'm going to mess up. Often. But I'm asking you to give me a shot anyway. And if you say no, well, I'll just ignore it on the grounds that that answer doesn't work for me."

I felt my mouth curve. "I'm not going to say no."

"You're not?"

"No. I can't promise I'll be much good at the relationship thing. My past ones didn't really count, and none ended well. I figure this will be a learning experience for both of us. I'm up for it, though."

He flashed me a blinding smile. "Exactly what I want to hear."

(Max)

Wicked fast, I lifted her from the floor, dropped her on my lap, and then closed my mouth over hers. It wasn't a kiss. It was an all-out explosion. We ate at each other's mouths, ravenous and frantic.

I slid my hands all over her, unable to get enough. Stroked her face. Squeezed her breasts. Pulled on her hair. Clutched her ass.

So many emotions fired through me—relief, hunger, desperation, a longing to reconnect. I'd thought she might turn me away, might find it too hard to believe I'd meant all I'd said. But she'd trusted that I wouldn't make such a declaration unless I was one hundred percent certain, and that meant fucking everything.

We yanked at each other's clothes. My tee disappeared. Hers was gone next. But I didn't have it in me to wait until we were fully naked. I couldn't even pause to whip off her bra. I fucking *had* to be inside her.

In a millisecond, I had her flat on her back on the sofa. I snapped open my fly to free my dick, managed to get one leg out of her jeans, yanked her panties aside, and shoved my cock into her.

Paige gasped as her entire body jerked. She grabbed my shoulders. "Max." It was a demand for me to move. A demand I was happy to answer.

I bit her lower lip. "All mine."

I rode her hard, plunging deep into her body. It was fast. It was intense. It was goddamn feral.

She scratched at my arms, tilting her hips to meet every heavy slam of my cock. And just when I sensed she was close to coming, she sank her teeth into my shoulder. It was pain, it was pleasure, it was more than I could take.

I spat out a curse and hammered into her harder, feeling my cock swell and throb. The moment she pulled back, I bit into her neck. Her blood flooded my mouth, and my release barrelled into me right then.

Slumped over her, I kissed her head, my breaths ragged. "Love you, baby."

Her fingers danced over my nape. "And I love you."

My head shot up. "Fucking good."

She chuckled. "Yeah, I guess it is."

I pressed a soft kiss to her mouth. "Mine," I repeated.

She nodded. "Yup."

I brushed her hair away from her face as I stared into her eyes. "You know I want to Bond with you one day, right?"

"I was hoping that was the case, yes. But it isn't something either of us is ready for. We need time, and that's okay. Like I've told you before, I'm in no rush. For now, it's enough to know that you love me. Enough to know that this thing we have is as serious as serious can get."

"Oh, it's definitely serious." I kissed her again, loving that she now belonged solely to me. Loving that I could kiss this mouth whenever I wanted. Loving that I could touch her any time any place anywhere. "I want you to think about moving in with me. Don't give me a human answer like 'it's too soon' or some shit like that. We're immortal. When time isn't running out, it's not a driving factor. Just think about it. Like you said, what we have is serious. Permanent. I like having you in my space. I like waking up and seeing you right there. I like showering with you every evening before we head off." I put a finger to her lips when she parted them to speak. "No, don't give me an answer now. Just think about it."

She playfully snapped her teeth at my finger. "Okay, I'll think about it."

I grunted, satisfied. "From here on out, you don't feed from anyone but me. *Only* me. Unless it's an emergency—then you can drink from others."

She gave me an imperious look. "How very gracious of you."

"I think so," I said, ignoring her sarcasm. "Also, no one but me will be feeding from you."

"So many demands," Paige complained, though her eyes danced with humour. She gently poked my shoulder. "I just have one demand of you."

"Shoot."

"No secrets. We always be open and honest with each other, even when it's hard."

"No secrets, baby. I promise you."

She hummed. "Some people seal promises with kisses, you know. Or so I've heard."

I smiled. "Really? I can get behind that." I took her mouth with mine yet again.

ENTICED

(Lexi and Damien)

None of Lexi Solomon's life plans had included living on an island filled with supposedly mythical creatures. Being inexplicably drawn to one of them isn't so great, considering relationships between humans and vampires have no future, but Damien Addams compels her like nothing else. He also wants her in his bed. More, he wants to claim her as his vessel, meaning no vampire but him will be allowed to feed from her. Tempting. But it would also be reckless … because she's falling too fast and too hard for a man she can't keep.

CHAPTER ONE

(Lexi)

Maisy placed her empty tray beside mine on the long bar and side-eyed me. "So, how's your ass?"

I shot my friend and fellow waitress a put-out look. "Fine." Such a lie. It ached like a champ.

"I still can't believe …" She trailed off as a silent laugh shook her shoulders.

My mouth went tight. Being chased by an anteater was one of those things that only sounded funny until it actually happened to you.

I went on weekly wanders through the rainforest, which were often led by one of the many vampires who resided on the island. Everyone in my group, including the vampire guide, had laughed their tits off when an anteater—probably guarding its young or something—darted onto the path and charged right at me like I'd fucked its mother. It apparently hadn't chased me for more than a few seconds, but I'd ran away in a blind panic. That run had ended when I slipped and fell flat on my ass.

I sighed at my *still* laughing friend. "We agreed to never talk about it."

"I'm sorry," she pretty much wheezed out. "I just can't stop seeing it in my head."

"I don't appreciate just how much this amuses you. I could have been killed. Anteaters have the biggest claws in the animal kingdom, you know."

"I just think it's crazy that you'll run from an anteater while letting out a girly squeal—"

"There was *no* squealing."

"—yet you can stand up to any vamp who tries pressuring you to offer them a vein." She shook her head, trying to stifle a smile. "I wouldn't have expected you to be so easily spooked by a wild animal. You're surrounded by predators *every* moment."

Why yes, I was. But it was sometimes easy to forget that. Mostly because so many of the vampires here at The Hollow were very human-like in several ways.

When I'd first arrived on the island five months ago, I'd been freaked the fuck out. I mean, I'd literally *just* discovered that vampires existed, and then I was whisked away. I'd always figured I'd be buzzed to hear that there were in fact supernatural creatures out there. Particularly since the human race was just a load of shit and would destroy the world for sure if left to its own devices. But it was different when you realised that, hey, you weren't on the top of the food chain after all.

Settling at The Hollow had taken some getting used to. Accepting that preternatural beings roamed the Earth wasn't so hard. But living among a species that could drain me dry and had all kinds of powers? That was a *whole* other thing.

It made me feel seriously vulnerable and at a *major* disadvantage. Particularly since a full freaking army of them—known as the legion—lived right here. But with the exception of a few, they weren't otherworldly or creepy. They were just … people. So, yeah, it was all too easy to forget the danger they presented.

I snapped out of my thoughts as the bartender began placing bottles and glasses of NSTs on my tray. They often smelled of whatever flavour they were as opposed to blood itself. Which was good, or I'd otherwise be nauseous as hell at the end of every shift.

Hearing a booming laugh, I turned slightly toward the sound. Feeling a smile tug at my mouth, I looked at Maisy. "Harvey's here again," I said, referring to one of the legion.

"Hmm, I noticed," she said. "A few of his squad members are with him." Her eyes twinkled with mischief. "Including Damien."

"Hmm, I noticed." But I tried not to look his way too often because my stomach insisted on fluttering each time our eyes met. "You going to talk to Harvey this time or scurry away like a scared doe again?"

Maisy narrowed her eyes. "I don't scurry, I just walk fast. And I *do* talk to Harvey. Until he starts flirting. I'm still not entirely sure I want to get involved with a vamp again."

"You do remember that you *are* a vampire, right?"

"How can I freaking forget?" she grumbled.

"You don't like *anything* about being one?"

"Sure I do. I love my gift. I always wanted to be a witch when I was a kid. Being telekinetic is close enough. But I guess I can't help resenting my new reality because I didn't fully choose it for *me*. I Turned to be with Compton. But then we split. And being forever linked to your ex is not fun."

"I can imagine. You know, the Grand High Pair might grant you freedom from Compton's hold. You could ask."

"I could. But he hasn't done anything wrong. Couples separate all the time. I'm sure Sam and Jared would understand that I don't like being psychically linked to my ex, but they'd probably also see it as my problem to deal with. There are no doubt plenty of vamps out there who made the mistake I did."

"And, just like you will, I bet they all moved on and found someone worthy of them." Now that my tray was full, I carefully lifted it. "Maybe Harvey will make your new reality more enjoyable. Come on, he's cute. Fun. Doesn't take himself too seriously. And he likes you enough to persevere, despite how often you shoot him down."

She sniffed. "If there were more available women on the island, I'm not so sure he'd be so tenacious."

"I am. He likes *you*. Just give him a chance. What have you got to lose?"

"And if Damien finally makes his move, are *you* going to give *him* a chance? No, don't tell me he's not interested. You know he is. And why wouldn't he be? You've got the little heart-shaped face, the pouty mouth, all that blonde hair that's almost silver, and your eyes are a gorgeous blue-grey. Hell, I'd do you if I was gay."

I laughed. "Well thanks."

"Seriously, he watches you like he could just gobble you all up."

"Well, to him, I sort of *am* food."

She snickered. "That you are. And if he asks to take a bite, you should absolutely let him. There's nothing quite like having a vamp feed from you."

So I'd often been told. "I doubt he'll ask. He never does anything other than look. Which tells me he might like what he sees but not enough to act on it. And it's not like we'd have anything other than a one-night stand anyway, given we're not the same species. Relationships between the two rarely end well."

Maisy sobered slightly. "Yeah, I can attest to that. But there ain't nothing wrong with a one-night stand. And he'd be a mighty fine way to break your dry spell."

Without a doubt. But I'd rather put him out of my mind. The guy had a way of making me nervous, so I'd prefer to pretend that his eyes weren't on me.

Holding my tray above my head, I walked to the area of the club that I covered. I winded my way through bodies, set bottles and glasses on tables, and took yet more orders.

People danced, laughed, talked, and drank. Most were vampires, but there were some humans too. A few strolled around offering themselves up as blood donors … like walking, talking Cosmos or something. And *many* took them up on their offer, since vampires could only get buzzed if they drank the blood of intoxicated humans.

No doubt due to the vampiric enhanced senses, the music here wasn't as loud as it would be in a human nightclub. It didn't pound at my ears and beat through the floor. Just the same, the neon strobe lights that slashed through the dark space weren't overbright or harsh on a person's eyes. All of which made it easier to work here night after night.

Waitressing might not be the most thrilling of jobs, but I liked it. Especially since, despite that the club was always crowded, it wasn't a fast-paced work environment. There was a very relaxed atmosphere in pretty much every corner of The Hollow. Plus, the pay was fair, the hours were reasonable, and I got to work alongside a woman who'd fast become my best friend. I'd never really had a best friend until I came here.

Noticing that a fight seemed about to break out between two vamps, I sighed. It once would have unnerved me. Now it just exasperated me, because they never failed to break shit. So I was sincerely grateful when others intervened and calmed them down. Particularly since the two posturing males were the naturally aggressive Pagori vamps.

Really, you'd think that the red tint to their irises would be seriously off-putting, but they were actually easy to overlook. Though I suspected that was because all vamps had a preternatural allure that drew humans in. Quite a few were close to mesmerising, but it was Damien who stood out most to me.

It wasn't so much about his physical appearance, though he was most certainly scorching hot—a broad-shouldered, long-legged tower of roped muscle, sleek dark skin, and alpha energy. He had this ... way about him. He wasn't a typical dark, dominant, broody alpha. No, Damien's full mouth always wore a ghost of a smile. He didn't prowl like a leopard on the hunt. He *cruised* along—calm, cool, smooth, steady, relaxed ... as if he'd done and seen it all before, and nothing in the world could surprise or faze him.

He oozed the kind of confidence that came not from your satisfaction with your appearance but from your total acceptance of yourself, flaws and all. He didn't give off a false bravado. Wasn't out to impress, no, he was out to enjoy life. But he *did* impress—as was evidenced by the amount of females who, to my sincere annoyance, flirted with him relentlessly.

He also happened to smell *amazing*. Every vampire had their own unique scent. Damien smelled of sandalwood, leather, and musk. I was far too susceptible to it for my liking.

After filling my tray with empty glasses and bottles, I returned to the bar and called out the next set of orders. The empties were quickly swiped from my tray, and one of the bartenders then began to prep the next drinks.

Maisy appeared beside me with her own tray, a smug little curve to her mouth that made my eyes narrow.

I touched her arm. "You talked to Harvey, didn't you?"

She shrugged, going for nonchalant, and called out more orders before replying, "He asked me out again."

"And?"

"And I said I'd think about it. He grinned like it was a yes."

"Because he knows he's wearing you down."

"He really is, the bastard," she muttered.

I chuckled, delighted. "I think he'll be good for you." Harvey was the life and soul of every party; he'd force Maisy to really *live*. She needed that.

"Hmm, we'll see. And just so you know, Damien's still watching you."

"You say that like I should do something about it. Like I said before, he can't be that interested if he hasn't made any moves. The guy's not exactly shy." And me? I didn't make moves. I always got nervous and fidgety and … gah, no, I would not put myself through the embarrassment. "Now, what kind of date does Harvey have in mind?"

Grinning, Maisy gave me a rundown of her rather flirty conversation with him. I laughed and fanned myself and teased her. Soon enough, we were both heading off in different directions to again hand out drinks and take more orders. Having set down my very last glass, I was able to lower the tray as I turned. I almost collided with the burly Old-World-mannered Pagori that just *appeared* in front of me. Shit, the vamps could move seriously damn fast.

He gave me a smile that was all charm and grace yet impersonal, just as he always did. "Lexi. So good to see you."

Ugh, I did *not* like this dude even a little. All vamps were predatory, but some more than others. Vamps like Castor didn't seem to *see* people when they looked at humans. They saw faceless, interchangeable food supplies. And they looked down on humans so had no problem being assholes toward us. There were dicks in every species, I supposed. "Thanks. Excuse me."

He tutted. *Tutted.* "Always in such a hurry."

To get away from him, yeah. "I'm working, so I can't take the time to chat."

"The manager isn't going to give you trouble for taking a small break."

If Maeve thought part of my break would involve feeding a vamp, no, she wouldn't give me trouble at all. She was something of a vampire groupie—addicted, on some level, to being fed from.

Castor licked his gleaming white teeth. "Why don't we go somewhere more private?"

I gave him a polite but distant smile. "I'd prefer not to, thanks."

He stepped into my space like it was totally his right. Or, more to the point, like I *had* no rights to the space. He inhaled deeply. "You smell good. I'll bet you taste better than you smell."

I couldn't help rolling my eyes. "I cannot count the number of vamps who've said that to me. It's like the ultimate donor-pick-up line. Now if you'll excuse me …" I tried to skirt around him, but he easily glided into my path.

He glared down at me. "I see how it is. You think you're too good for my kind. You're too high and mighty to *lower* yourself to be fed from."

Right then, he made me think of guys who branded any woman who rejected them 'frigid' or 'stuck up.' I lifted my chin, refusing to be intimidated. "You really need to get out of my way."

"And you need to understand that you have no power here. Like it or not, you are the inferior race. It is a privilege to feed a vampire. You should be grateful for the honour I'm offering you."

Honour my ass. It was impossible to see someone as 'superior' when they were clearly a bully down to their core. Oh, he'd physically overpower me in an instant. He might even have an ability that could reduce me to ashes here and now—I wasn't sure. But he was still too pathetic to be at all frightening.

I met his glare with my own. "You're still blocking my path. I'm not sure why that is, but I do know I don't like it. Now *move*."

Another familiar male materialised at Castor's side, sneering at me. "I wouldn't waste my time on this one, Castor," said Dion, who was part of his nest. "She refuses to feed anyone."

I sniffed. "No, I just have high standards. Neither of you meet them."

The red glint to Castor's irises flared. He snapped a hand around my arm and yanked me close. "Condescending little—" He let out an animal cry of pain as I grabbed his balls and roughly twisted them.

"Let go of me," I clipped. He did, so I released him fast, having no freaking wish to touch that asshole's junk for longer than it took to—

"What the fuck is going on here?"

We all froze. The question wasn't loud. Wasn't spoken like a whip. It was low. Calm. But edged with a dark, deadly menace that made my skin prickle. And I didn't need to glance behind me to know that the deep, rumbly voice belonged to none other than Damien.

Dion flashed him a jovial grin that was somewhat shaky. "Oh nothing, nothing. Everything is fine. Isn't it, Lexi?"

I snorted. "No." If he'd thought I'd cover for Castor, he was out of his mind.

Damien sidled up to me, blanketing me with that damn scent that drove my hormones crazy. "What happened here?" he asked me, his dark eyes focused on me like lasers.

Distantly noting that a few of Damien's squad members had gathered behind him, I replied, "Castor grabbed me. I didn't like it. He also won't just accept that I won't let him taste me. I didn't like that either. I asked him to get out of my way. He didn't. In fact, he grabbed my arm instead. So I went for his balls."

His eyes rock hard, Damien cut his gaze to Castor. "You've been warned about pushing humans to provide you with blood, haven't you? Twice, as it happens."

His face flushed and his brow pinched with pain, Castor let out an unrepentant huff. "She should not be a resident here. She is prejudiced against our kind. Considers it beneath her to feed us."

I went still. That was a super serious accusation, and I just hoped to hell that no one bought it.

"Just because she doesn't want *you* feeding from her doesn't mean she has anything against vampires in general," Damien said to him, and my insides relaxed. "She has the right to say no. She said no. Deal with it."

Castor's face reddened even further, and he shot me a withering look. He went to leave with Dion.

"Not so fast," said Damien, his voice soft. "You got off with warnings in the past, Castor. Sam and Jared made it clear that you would be punished if you attempted to bully another human or laid a finger on them in anger. We don't tolerate that shit here." And then, well, Damien fisted the asshole's shirt and hauled him out of the club, his squad members in tow.

Maisy came to my side and let out a low whistle. "And Hero of the Hour shall be awarded to … Damien Addams. See how he rushed to your rescue? I'd say the man is done with merely 'watching.'" She crossed two of her fingers. "Here's to hoping."

CHAPTER TWO

(Damien)

Walking back into the club, I cursed beneath my breath.
Christ, that woman.

The thought floated through my head far too often—and always with a note of exasperation. Irrational, yes, because it wasn't Lexi's fault that my body tightened each time I even *thought* of her. It wasn't her fault that she made me feel so greedy it bordered on possessive. It wasn't her fault that I struggled to keep my damn eyes off her … or that I'd developed an obsession with her ass.

Well, it was one perfect, tight little ass. And I was an ass man through and through. Eying hers as she walked around the club was a pleasure I indulged in often.

I'd held off on approaching her so far, because I'd known she needed time to settle here and get used to my kind. She'd naturally been a little unsure of vampires in the beginning. All newbies were. They saw us for the predators we were; recognised that they were effectively in a jungle filled with creatures against whom they stood no chance.

I needed her to understand I was no threat to her. I wanted her to see me as a man, not simply a vampire. I was both. Talking to her occasionally might have helped with getting that across, but I knew myself well. Knew that if I got too close too often, I'd lose my resolve to give her time.

It had seemed better to simply hang back. So I had. But there had been nothing simple about it, because I wanted her with every breath I fucking took.

I'd nearly swallowed my tongue the first time I saw her. I'd known plenty of stunning women, but Lexi Solomon … Christ, she was a pretty picture. All that hair. Big, hooded eyes. Fucking killer smile. Perky breasts that made my hands itch to palm and squeeze. And, of course, that phenomenal ass. Then there was her confident, casual, devil-may-care attitude that I found hot as hell.

She seemed more at ease around my kind these days. A good thing, because I was done hanging in the shadows. I'd waited long enough, and I'd been planning to approach her tonight. What I *hadn't* been planning was for her to get harassed by fucking Castor. That could be enough to set my plans back, to make her hesitant around vampires again.

Silently cursing Castor, I walked through the club in search of her. I found her at the bar, where she stood talking with the waitress who Harvey had set his sights on.

Lexi's striking eyes flicked to mine, and there was no stopping my body from reacting. Not when, that fast, a furious need surged through me. My heartbeat stuttered, my blood heated, my cock thickened.

Christ, that woman.

I moved to her and curled my hand around her wrist, feeling her pulse jump. I liked that. I also liked the flash of sexual awareness in her eyes. "Let's talk a second." I slid my gaze to Maeve. "Lexi is taking a break."

Nodding, Maeve smiled. "Not a problem." She waved a hand behind her. "Feel free to use the break room."

Not a bad idea. It meant that Lexi and I could have privacy. Cupping her elbow, I led her behind the bar and down a small, thin hallway.

Inside the empty break room, I closed the door. Maybe it was because we were both aware of how very alone we now were that the air immediately began to thicken. I let my gaze drift over her face as I asked, "First of all, are you all right?"

Lexi shrugged, her lips pursed. "Yeah, fine."

She genuinely seemed it, but it was possible she was just putting on a brave face. "No one would expect you to be okay. Being pushed around like that by anyone can be unsettling. That unsettling shit gets magnified when you're dealing with a preternatural being who is far stronger than you are."

"And if he was anything other than a pussy, I probably would have been terrified."

I felt my mouth quirk. "Fair enough."

"He'll really be punished?"

"Oh yeah." I slowly closed the distance between us. "Humans aren't second rate citizens here, despite what Castor seems to believe. Neither are women, but he also seems to hold that mistaken view as well. He'll soon learn that vampires don't get special treatment round here if they fuck up. He already has two strikes against him. He was warned he'd face serious consequences if he pulled that crap again."

"I don't think he believed anyone would follow through on it."

"Maybe not. If so, he's stupid. Sam and Jared run a tight ship. It's necessary for rules to be enforced consistently if you're going to keep an island full of vampires under control."

"I guess so." Lexi cleared her throat. "I want to be clear that Castor was wrong in what he said. I'm not prejudiced against vampires."

"I never thought you were," I assured her. She'd shown wariness in the beginning, but never disgust or bigotry. "You can like vampires and still not want to be a donor. A lot of old school vampires hold a very disparaging view of humans. Consider them fodder, not people. Castor is one of them." The number of his nest who'd come with him to live at The Hollow were just as bad. "But we don't all think that way."

"I know."

Good, because I didn't want her thinking *I* was anything like Castor or the rest of his ilk. "Has he given you problems before?"

"He's rude to all the humans. It isn't just me. I don't know what his deal is, but you'd think he wasn't once human himself."

"Rude how?"

"Just dismissive and cold. Until he wants something. Like to feed from one of us. Then he turns on the fake charm."

"How many times has he approached you in the past?"

She narrowed her eyes as she thought on it. "I don't know. Four, maybe five. He was very forward and even a little sleazy, but not snotty and physical until tonight."

Just thinking about the bastard grabbing her made my blood boil. But then her tongue flicked out to nervously touch her lower lip, and I was officially distracted. She had a mouth that was nothing short of sinful. I wanted to taste it, bite it, feel it sliding up and down my cock.

Forcing my gaze back to hers, I said, "If it happens again, you have to report it. Humans have failed to do so in the past, thinking they'll be cast out of The Hollow if they're complaining or 'making waves.' That's not how it works here."

She gave a hard nod. "Okay."

"Have any other vampires acted in a similar fashion?"

"One or two can be pretty forward, but usually only when they're drunk. They never take it too far, and they never get ugly. Just a little pushy. Dion is worse than most. He seems determined to drink from every human on this island—why he thinks it'll be a point of pride, I don't know. With Castor, he just seems to be one of those people who feels they should be able to have whatever they want whenever they want. Or something. I don't know." She bit her lower lip. "Thank you for stepping in. I appreciate it."

I edged closer, leaving mere inches between us, and pinned her gaze with mine. The tension between us ramped up, making the air fairly crackle. "Maybe I wasn't doing it to be noble," I said, pitching my voice low. "Maybe I want something."

The warmth in her eyes faded. "Ah," she said, and I knew she suspected I wanted to drink from her. Oh, I did. But I wouldn't manipulate her that way. Plus, I wanted her to *want* my teeth in her skin.

"A kiss," I said.

She blinked, visibly surprised. "A what?"

"You heard me." I curled my hand around her nape. "You can handle a little kiss, can't you?"

Her pupils dilated, and she licked her lips. "Seems like a fair payment."

"Hmm, I agree." I dipped my head and brushed my mouth over hers. Her lips parted, I swept my tongue inside … and a brutal need seemed to *slam* into us both.

Fuck.

I greedily ate at her mouth, and she gave as good as she got. The kiss was hot, bruising, ravenous. Jesus, she tasted good. Too good.

Possessiveness settled into every bone, and a growl that was nothing short of territorial rattled my chest. I thrust my fingers into her hair and fisted. Her hands flew up to my shoulders and held tight. The kiss went on and on and on as we licked, nipped, and feasted. She sucked on my tongue, the little witch, and—

A loud laugh came from outside the room, reminding me where we were. I broke the kiss, but I couldn't quite let her go yet. Shit, I fucking ached to take her right then. It was a real, honest to God's ache. But I wouldn't do that. Not here, not *anyplace* tonight. I wasn't going to ask her to invite me to her bed when it was possible that, despite what she'd said, she was shaken by Castor's behaviour.

I hummed, swiping my thumb over her mouth. "I was right in what I suspected."

She swallowed, her eyes deliciously dazed. "And what was it you suspected?"

"That if I ever tasted you, I'd want more. I'll *have* more. Just not tonight."

She bristled and flicked up a brow. "Cocky."

"But right. Aren't I?"

"We'll see. But don't hold your breath."

I had to smile. "You think you'll stop me from having you? That's cute."

"Cute?" she echoed, a little edge to her voice.

"Yeah. I gave you time to see past the vampirism and settle in at The Hollow. That time is up. Thank fuck. I want you. You want me. And yeah, I'll have you. You won't be able to move by the time I'm done with you, and there'll be only one thing you want."

Her eyes glimmered with both need and uncertainty. "What?"

I dipped my head again and replied, "More."

Standing opposite me the following evening, Maya blew out a preparatory breath and rolled back her shoulders. She slid Sam a brief look and declared, "I'm ready."

My squad didn't always train with Sam's all-female squad. In fact, the two trained separately more often than not. But Sam and Jared liked us to mix occasionally because some of the females were in relationships with guys from mine. The Grand High Pair thought it best that the couples got used to fighting while close to each other so that it wouldn't feel so foreign on a battlefield. None of us could afford to be distracted.

Sometimes we trained out in the rainforest, but mostly we used this indoor arena near the mansion. With the sand on the ground, it resembled a large horse paddock, and the main sides of the building were marked with the letters A, B, C, and D—representing north, east, south and west respectively. The stands were currently empty, as was the VIP box.

Tonight, Sam insisted that Maya work on her shapeshifting speed. In her jaguar form, Maya was fast and vicious and explosive. But Sam wanted her to be able to shift mid-lunge so that she could dive on an enemy as a jaguar. Due to my gift, I was an ideal person for Maya to practice on.

Sam moved into our peripheral vision. "Go!"

Maya took a run and jump. She shifted shape while in the air, but not quite fast enough, so she wasn't fully jaguar when she landed on me. I grunted as I hit the ground hard, her claws digging into my shoulders deep enough to draw blood. But she didn't draw blood, and I felt no pain. Because it was my astral form she'd taken down.

I quickly leaped to my feet. Astral projection wasn't a common vampiric gift, and it was incredibly rare for someone's astral form to be solid. I couldn't *keep* it solid for long periods of time, so Sam didn't have me take hits for others during battle unless truly necessary, because my squad could otherwise subconsciously begin to depend on me to shield them. Just because I *looked* solid didn't mean I always was.

Back in her human form, Maya swore beneath her breath. "I can do better, I know," she said to Sam.

"Yes, you can," Sam easily agreed. "So let's see you do it."

Over and over, Maya charged at me and shifted shape while lunging. Over and over, I hit the ground. She shifted faster each time. But then she began to slow again, obviously tiring.

The training session soon reached its end, and everyone began filing out of the arena. I was almost at the door when Sam called out my name. Turning to her, I lifted my brow in question.

"Can we have a quick word?" she asked, standing beside Jared.

"Sure, Coach." I headed over to the pair. "What's up?"

"I was just hoping you could give me the full story about what happened last night between Castor and the human waitress, Lexi," replied Sam.

Folding my arms, I relayed what I'd seen and heard.

Sam's nostrils flared. "That bloke is a bloody prick."

"No argument there," said Jared. "The rest of his nest are no better in terms of attitude, but they at least follow the rules. Castor doesn't seem to think any rules apply to him, or he just doesn't care about the consequences."

"He seemed shocked when Harvey and I took him to the containment area last night," I said. "As if it really hadn't occurred to him that he'd be held accountable for his actions. He might have thought you'd never take the side of a human over a fellow vampire."

"Maybe," agreed Jared.

"Has Castor received his punishment yet?" I asked.

Sam shook her head. "We left him in a cell during the day to sweat about what's coming. I like it when they sweat. Plus, I wanted all the details before I went apeshit on his arse tonight."

Jared sighed, scrubbing at his jaw. "I thought the warnings we gave him after his previous missteps would be enough. It's not as if it isn't well known that Sam is a little too fond of torture and maiming."

She shrugged. "I find it relaxing."

His mouth curved. "I've noticed." He looked at me. "How's Lexi?"

"She claimed she was fine," I replied. "But I think the incident with Castor shook her up a little."

"I like that she twisted his balls," said Sam with a grin. "My kind of girl."

Jared snorted.

"She said Castor approached her a few times in the past but never took it this far before," I informed them. "He has a *real* problem with the word no. Plus, he just doesn't seem to think that the rights of a human will ever come before his own."

Sam's grin faded. "I had a feeling the first time I met him that he was gonna give us problems. He whined like a brat because he wasn't allowed to have consorts on the island. He even asked me to lift the ban just for him. I told him to shove his request up his uptight arse, which didn't go down well." She puffed out a breath. "I'll speak with Lexi and make it clear that she needs to report any further incidences."

"I already did that," I said.

"Really?" Sam tilted her head, eying me curiously. "Very attentive of you."

I forced a casual shrug. "I don't want her thinking that her being human means she doesn't have rights equal to our kind."

"Hmm." Sam crossed her arms over her chest. "You know, I noticed you watching her at Alora and Evan's Binding ceremony. You have a little thing for Lexi?"

I had a little thing for keeping my private business exactly that—private. "You never used to be so nosy, Coach."

"Oh, you're batting away my question with a breezy comment?

Interesting. You know, I like Lexi. When humans first arrive here, they're usually *proper* Nervous Nellies. They shake and stammer and can't meet my eyes. Not Lexi. I could tell she was uneasy—and why wouldn't she be, especially since she'd *only minutes ago* found out our kind exists?—but she kept her cool. Looked me right in the eye while I spoke to her. And she didn't ogle Jared, which earned her more points. All in all, I was impressed."

I wrestled down the urge to ask how Lexi had discovered we existed—there was much I didn't know about her. And I could tell by the knowing glint in Sam's eyes that she'd sensed my struggle. My blasé act wasn't working so well apparently.

"If you're trying your hand at matchmaking again, you need to stop," I said.

She blinked. "I matchmake?"

"All the fucking time. Don't think none of us knows that you're the one behind David and Denny recently getting together. And Harvey told me you've been urging him not to give up on Maisy. Which he hasn't, and she's folding under the pressure, if that makes you feel good."

"It does, thanks."

I smiled. "You're shameless, Coach."

"It's one of my finer qualities. And I actually *wasn't* trying to matchmake in this case purely because Lexi's human. Realistically, you two can't have a serious relationship—she ages every night, and you'll always remain the same. But there's nothing wrong with having a tumble, is there? I think she'd be up for it."

"Why is that?"

"Because I also noticed *her* watching *you*."

CHAPTER THREE

(Lexi)

Crossing the bridge that would take me to the club, I looked down at the man-made beach below. All white sand and turquoise water, it was unbelievably inviting. Some people who clearly had a night off work were sprawled on loungers or towels, chatting and laughing or just plain relaxing.

I'd likely do the same when my next night off work came round. Of course, there were other things to do around The Hollow, and I did enjoy going to the movies with Maisy. But I was a water baby, so I'd spent a lot of time on that beach over the past five months—sometimes of an evening, sometimes during the day while the vampires slept. I never lasted long on a lounger, though, as I got restless far too fast. Swimming was more my thing.

I would truly *love* to use the beach behind the mansion so I could scuba dive in the ocean. But only the important vamps had access to that beach, such as the legion. I'd only stepped foot on it while at special events, during which I'd often waitressed. Many of said events took place on—

"I hope you're pleased with yourself."

Gah. I came to an abrupt halt as Dion and one of his buddies, Colm, appeared out of motherfucking nowhere, so apparently one of them could teleport. "I usually am," was all I said.

Dion's jaw tightened. "No one has seen Castor since he was frog-marched out of the club. I have been refused access to him, as he is apparently 'occupied.' Sam and Jared are not merciful people."

"Which is why I find it kind of baffling that your friend risked their wrath. Personally, I wouldn't go there."

"Castor was in a foul mood and took that out on you. It was wrong, yes, but not deserving of the sort of punishment he will no doubt receive at the hands of the Grand High Pair. Sam herself is particularly bloodthirsty."

She was, if the rumours were true. I found that kind of delightful, really. "I'm not entirely sure why you're talking to me about this."

Dion's nostrils flared. "All you had to do last night was agree that everything was fine when Damien approached. Instead, you threw Castor right under the bus."

Ignoring the way my stomach twisted at the mere mention of Damien, I snorted. "If you think I'll ever protect someone who clearly has no issue being rough with women, you're seriously freaking mistaken."

"It would not be wise of you to make enemies here. Especially if you like being a waitress at the club. I am quite sure the manager would dislike having a waitress with such a bad attitude. You could be very easily replaced, you know. There are many humans who long for a different position—particularly the maids who clean the Residence Halls. Do keep that in mind."

"In other words, I should stay quiet if vamps give me problems or you'll pressure Maeve into finding another human to take my place as a waitress? Go for it," I invited. "See how far it gets you."

I was pretty certain no one would fire me—it would come across as a punishment, which would give the wrong impression to humans and vampires alike. I didn't believe Sam and Jared would want that. Plus, Damien assured me that humans would never be seen as 'making waves' if they filed any complaints. I believed him over this asshole.

"I thought you were intelligent," said Dion, which was literally the nicest thing he'd ever said to me. "Clearly I was wrong. You underestimate my influence here."

"Or you overestimate your own merely because one of your nest was once a commander within the legion."

Dion looked as though he might say something else, but then his gaze wandered to something over my shoulder. Snapping his mouth shut, he took a step back.

Wondering what had spooked him, I glanced over my shoulder to see one of Damien's squad members, Salem, standing a few feet away glaring at Dion. Yeah, I'd have backed up, too. Salem was a scary motherfucker and only ever smiled around his tiny mate, Ava.

"We'll talk another time," Dion said to me. He then looked at his friend. "My apartment." Nodding, Colm teleported them both away.

Finally. I looked behind me again, intending to give Salem a grateful nod—purposely or not, he'd scared Dion away. But Salem was already gone.

Pulling in a breath through my nose, I rolled my shoulders and headed to the club.

He was back. And he was watching me. Again.

Usually, Damien's stare was all heat and intense focus. Tonight, there was a knowing glint there, reminding me he knew exactly how I tasted. That gaze also held a promise. It wasn't just a promise of sexual satisfaction. No, it was a promise that he'd have more, just as he'd vowed.

His words drifted through my mind, unbidden …

You won't be able to move by the time I'm done with you.

My cheeks heated. Fuck, it was hot in here.

It had surprised me when he asked for a kiss last night. I'd truly expected him to request blood in payment when he'd declared he wanted something. And, well, I'd had no qualms at all with finding out if a kiss would be as hot and electric as the sexual tension between us hinted at. It hadn't been that intense, though. It had been even fucking *more* intense. Wild. Thrilling. Intoxicating.

His cocky 'I'll *have* more' comment had indeed made me bristle, but it hadn't annoyed me half as much as I would have liked. Because all that confidence and dominance pushed my best buttons whether I was good with it or not.

Did I want more? Hell, yeah. If a kiss between us could be that explosive, sex would be off-the-charts hot. And I had no hang-ups about one-night stands.

The only thing tainting the situation was the knowledge that once we'd had our night of fun, his attention would shift to someone else. He wouldn't watch me like this anymore. That shouldn't bother me, and it unnerved me that it would. There was little I could do about that, though. The situation was what it was.

Needing a reprieve from him, I was super glad when my break began. I retreated quickly to the breakroom, where I gulped down some water as I sat at the table. Damn the scorching hot bastard for getting me all flustered and tingly. It seriously wasn't fair.

I'd tried putting him out of my mind, but it wasn't as easy as I'd hoped. Concentrating on simply doing my job didn't help either. The club might be busier than usual due to it being a Friday night, but it was also as relaxed as usual, so I wasn't rushed off my feet.

Not even Dion's presence here proved to be distracting, despite that he occasionally offered me little snarls and kept coming to the bar to whisper shit to Maeve while also staring at me. I wasn't sure whether he was doing what he'd hinted at earlier or just trying to make me *think* he was. Maeve was acting just as warmly as usual towards me, so if she *did* think it was better for me to be replaced she sure as shit wasn't showing it.

Joining me in the breakroom, Maisy took the seat opposite me and twisted off the cap of her cola-flavoured NST. "Just so we're clear, are we pretending Damien's not eye-fucking you?"

I chugged down more water. "Yes, we are."

She gave me a curt nod. "Got it." She took a swig of her own drink and then pointed a finger at me. "But don't think I'm buying that you didn't kiss him last night. You came out of this room with your eyes all glassy and your face all flushed. *And* your mouth was swollen, so you definitely kissed him."

"Or maybe I sucked him off."

She almost choked on her NST. "You did that on purpose."

I smiled. "Of course I did."

Setting her bottle on the table, she leaned forward, her eyes dancing. "You kissed him. We both know you did. And he must have enjoyed it, because it would seem he's back for more."

"Or he's here to have a drink with his friends."

"Nope. He isn't really talking to them much, and he waves off any women who try flirting with him, which I'm sure you've noticed."

I had noticed, and I could admit that I liked it.

"Face it, Lexi, he's here for you. And I am *loving* it. You need to get laid, and I need to hear how he is in the sack, so this will work for both of us."

I could only snicker.

"He also found a seat in *your* area tonight."

He had, which was new. It was also one of the reasons why putting him out of my mind wasn't working. I'd been going back and forth from his table all night. Each time I approached, he was sure to smile or greet me or toss out some compliment.

"So," I began, "has Harvey been turning on the charm again?"

"Changing the subject are we? Fine. It's probably best that you're not thinking too much about sex while you're working anyway. Damien will scent it if you're turned on. As for Harvey, well, he did ask me out again. I told him I was still thinking about it, but after the bastard followed me around the club for fifteen minutes straight while singing some weird-ass song that I'm pretty sure he made up, I said okay."

I grinned. "Best news I've heard all night."

"Hmm, I have a feeling it'll become second best once Damien declares he intends to fuck your brains out, but we won't talk about that."

I snickered again. "Well, thanks."

Our break seemed to end all too soon. We went back to the club floor, and I headed off to take orders and collect empty glasses and bottles. When I arrived at Damien's table, his mouth curved into a sexy as shit smile.

"Hello again, Lexi," he said.

I felt my lips tip up. "Hey yourself." I didn't miss the way his gaze honed in on my ass when I bent over to grab the empties. One of his squad members, Stuart, helped me set them on my tray, all graciousness. He held up his hands in a gesture of innocence as his eyes—now lit with amusement—slid to Damien, who was now glaring at him. And I realised Stuart was just poking at him.

Shaking my head, I walked to the next table. And on and on it went, until my shift was finally over. By then, all the patrons had left, including Damien. Dion had been one of the last to leave, so I'd thought he might try to get me alone to continue his little rant, but he thankfully didn't.

Ready to head home, I stepped outside ... and almost staggered to a halt. "What are you doing out here?" I asked Damien, who was leaning against the lamppost.

"Waiting for you," he replied. "Salem told me that Dion spoke to you earlier but that the conversation didn't seem to be pretty. I didn't trust that Dion wouldn't try to get you alone after work." Pushing away from the lamppost, Damien glanced around. "He didn't linger, so it doesn't look like he intends to. Still, I'd prefer to walk you home."

I felt my brows rise. "Oh. Okay." But I wasn't buying that was the *entire* reason he wanted to walk me home, I wasn't naïve. "I don't think he's hiding in the shadows or anything," I said as we began to walk. "He left with Maeve. She spends a lot of time with him. I think she's hoping he'll Turn her. Though it may just be that she's a ... well, that she's fond of being a blood donor."

"A vampire groupie, you mean. And yes, I suppose she is."

"I heard that some humans get addicted to being fed from." It came out sounding like a question.

Damien twisted his lips. "I don't know if it's really an addiction in the truest sense of the word. But those humans like Maeve are constantly chasing that first high and never quite finding it, so maybe." He cast me a sideways glance as we reached the bridge. "I've heard you haven't allowed any vampires to feed from you. You're not curious about what it's like?"

I shrugged. "A little."

"But?"

"There isn't a 'but.' It's like with kissing, though. Just because I like kisses doesn't mean I'm good with being kissed by just anyone."

"I understand. Most vampires will relate to that. Just as you don't want to be seen as food, *we* don't want to be seen as convenient fangs for humans who want the 'high.' Not all of us have fangs, of course, but you get my point."

I did, and it made sense.

"But there are some vampires, like Dion, who aren't so discriminating."

We chatted about inconsequential things as we walked across the bridge and made our way to my Residence Hall. "This is me," I said when we reached it.

"I'll walk you to your apartment. It's best to be sure that Dion isn't waiting for you there."

I gave him a look that said I didn't buy that his intentions were so noble, but Damien only chuckled. Damn, that rumbly laugh did all sorts of things to my hormones. "Fine." So inside the building we went.

Would I brush him off when we reached my apartment? No. Playing hard to get wasn't my thing. And though it wouldn't feel too good when his focus abruptly shifted to someone else, it wasn't like I could hold that against him. I was human. He was a vampire. A one-night stand was the wise way to go.

Maisy's situation was a perfect example of how a serious relationship with a vamp could go wrong. She'd Turned for Compton so that they could be together forever … and then they'd separated, and now she was facing immortality without the person she'd given up her human life for.

The thing was … Maisy hadn't originally been looking for anything serious with him. It was all about casual sex in the beginning. But feelings came into play, and they'd had two choices—go their separate ways or bring her fully into the world of vampires. Countless immortal vs. mortal couples had found themselves in the same boat over the years. In that sense, it was really too easy for humans and vamps to get hurt if casual sex between them became more, which was why it was best for the two species to stick with one-night stands. So, yeah, I was good with just enjoying one night—or day, depending on how long he stayed over—with Damien. It seemed better than nothing at all.

Plus, in a way, it was sort of liberating to know that this was all about *the now*, not the future. I knew in advance that this would be a one off. I knew it wouldn't go anywhere. I knew it was only about sex. For me, there was a strange kind of … comfort in knowing exactly how something would go. Plus, there was no pressure for me to impress or open up or anything like that. It would be light and fun and uncomplicated.

After a short elevator ride and a brief walk down a long hallway, we arrived at my front door. And then he was towering over me, his body heat beating at me, his eyes drinking me in. "I want another kiss," he said, lowering his head. He didn't wait for me to okay it. He just took my mouth. Plundered and consumed and demanded.

I clung to his upper arms, moaning as he angled our heads to deepen the kiss. My body—already a mess of racing chemicals and edgy nerve-endings—reached for him. Ached for him. Melted into him.

He broke the kiss. "I've wanted to do that since the first time I saw you." He rested his forehead on mine, his hands in my hair. "Invite me in, Lexi," he coaxed, his voice low and deep and so gravelly with need it gave me goosebumps. "Invite me in."

I swallowed hard and nodded.

Satisfaction bloomed in his eyes. He stepped back, letting me unlock my door and push it open. I walked inside, flicked on the light, and turned to face him.

He mule kicked the door, shutting it. "Come here."

I did, but I was slow about it, not quite as submissive as he probably expected.

He ghosted his fingers down the column of my throat. "This is how it's going to go."

If he gave me some speech about how this would only be a one-time thing, as if there was some risk of me getting all clingy afterwards, I would *totally* kick him in the junk.

His eyes blazed into mine. "I'm going to fuck you. And I *mean* fuck you. It won't be slow. It won't be gentle. There'll be nothing sweet about it. I'm going to take you hard. Harder than anyone else has ever taken you. And while my cock is slamming so deep you can barely handle it, I'm going to drink from you. I want the taste of your blood in my mouth when I fill you up with my come. You got a problem with any of that?"

For endless seconds, I could only stare at him. "Nu-uh." I was really too tongue-tied to say anything else.

His gaze darkened to flint. "Good." Then he was on me.

CHAPTER FOUR

(Damien)

Thrusting my hands into her hair, I closed my mouth over hers and sank my tongue inside. Need bubbled up fast, hot and explosive. It raged in my blood, scorched my skin, thickened my cock, and stole my breath.

Lexi grabbed at my shirt as I took total possession of her mouth. This was no mere simple kiss. It was a forty-car pile-up that inflamed us both.

An aggressive hunger beating at my insides, I backed her through the small apartment, stripping her clothes along the way, stroking everywhere I could reach. Her skin was so fucking soft, so fucking biteable.

She was wearing only panties by the time we reached her bedroom. I sharply tugged at the scrap of lace, ripping it from her body. Drinking in her naked form, I felt the breath whoosh out of me. She was all delicate curves and smooth muscle, soft in all the right places. A surge of possessiveness hit me hard, its intensity taking me off-guard.

"Jesus, Lex. You're fucking beautiful, do you know that?" I didn't wait for a response, I wasn't looking for one. All I wanted right then was to fuck her with my tongue.

I tossed her on the bed, careful to bear in mind the relative differences in our strength. She was so fragile compared to me. So vulnerable. So very much at my mercy. And that hit my prey drive big time.

"You're gonna come hard for me." Kneeling on the bed, I shoved her thighs apart and put my mouth on her.

She arched with a gasp and gripped the bedsheet. "Oh, fuck."

I didn't go easy on her. I ate her out like I was starved for her, gripping that delectable ass tight, digging my fingers into the firm globes.

Five months. Five months I'd imagined this, wondering how she tasted; what she looked like when she came; whether I was right in thinking that her ass would fit perfectly in my hands—it did.

Everything about her enticed and spurred me on—her hoarse moans, her floral perfume, her sweet and spicy taste, and how goddamn beautifully responsive she was. There were so many things I wanted to do to her, and I had so little time to do them all.

It wasn't long before she came—apparently, she had a quick trigger—but I didn't stop. Not until she'd come a second time, while I was pumping my fingers in and out of her.

She slumped on the bed, trembling, breathing hard, watching me through hooded, glazed eyes as I sucked my fingers clean. "That was some seriously dark oral magic you just did."

I felt a chuckle bubble up. "Dark oral magic, huh? I can go with that." She made such a gorgeous picture, all flushed and needy and ready for me. Fuck, I had to have her.

Not wanting a single thing between my skin and hers, I quickly shed my clothes, moving at vampiric speed. "Spread your legs wider. Good girl."

Kneeling between her thighs once more, I curled over her and sucked one taut, dusky nipple into my mouth as I palmed her breast. "Tilt your hips up for me, baby. That's it." Locking my eyes with hers, I inched the broad head of my cock inside her and *shit* that was a tight fit.

Her breath hitched slightly, and she balled up her hands. "Fuck me, Damien."

Like I had any other plan. I draped myself over her and gave her my weight, wanting her to feel trapped, surrounded, helpless. Even owned.

I gripped her jaw, feeling a little feral in my need to possess and take and use. "You'll feel me for days, Lex." I slammed home hard enough to shake the bed, ramming every inch of my dick inside her in one smooth and undeniably brutal thrust.

She sucked in a breath, her eyes going wide, and dug her nails into my shoulders as her body clamped down on my cock. "Shit, Damien."

Growling, I savagely powered into her, moving faster than any human could, careful not to cause her pain. "Christ, baby, you're so tight." It was like thrusting into a hot, wet fist, the pleasure so intense it was almost excruciating. As she arched her body into mine, taking what I gave her and demanding more, I growled. "That's it, let me have you."

I took her mouth again as I rode her hard, tasting every moan and whimper. Her hands stroked and scratched at my back. Her heels dug into the base of my spine. Her inner muscles squeezed and sucked at my cock. And her pulse … it fucking called to me.

I could hear her blood thrashing in her veins—fast, steady, rhythmic … like a damn song. It was hypnotic and haunting and drowned out the growls, moans, and smacks of flesh.

Hunger rose up inside me, sharp and fierce, and twisted my gut. "Offer me your throat, Lex. Yes, like that. Such a good girl." I sank my teeth down hard and groaned as her blood poured into my mouth—warm and sweet.

I drank and drank as I violently pounded into her body like I was trying to punch a hole through it. Her hand flew to the back of my head and held it there as her slick inner walls became tighter and hotter. Then she came. Imploded beneath me with a scream, her core rippling around my dick and shoving me over the edge. I growled against her throat as I hammered into her once, twice, and then blew my load deep inside her.

Jesus, it wasn't often that I was out of breath. In fact, I'd fought in battle and kept my breathing reasonably steady. But at that moment, I was actually panting like a goddamn racehorse.

I licked over the bite on her neck, sealing the small wound, and lifted my head. Her eyes were shut, her cheeks were flushed, her swollen lips were parted, and there wasn't a single line of strain on her face.

I nipped at her chin, watching as her eyelids fluttered open. "I want to stay."

She smoothed her hands over my back. "Then stay," she said, her voice soft and raspy.

"You won't get much sleep if I do."

She gave me a lazy smile. "Well I should hope not."

(Lexi)

I'd half-expected to find him gone when I woke, but he was sleeping peacefully beside me, his arm tossed over my waist, every muscle in his face relaxed. He'd certainly earned that deep rest, considering how many times he'd taken me through the day. The man was a goddamn machine.

That whole 'I'll fuck you harder than any other man ever has' thing? Not an empty boast. So it was little wonder I ached in so very many places right now.

It would be fair to say we'd fucked like animals. Seriously. It had been wild and savage and urgent. We hadn't only made use of the bed. He'd taken me against the wall. In front of the mirror. On the floor while I was on my hands and knees. He'd even bent me over the vanity unit at one point.

I'd probably be aching a lot more if he hadn't run me a bath at the end of what could only be described as a sex marathon. I'd tried waving him off, too tired to move even as I'd known the Epsom salts would help, so he'd pretty much bathed me himself.

Had any man ever done anything that considerate for me before? No, I was pretty sure they hadn't.

I was also pretty sure none of them had ever made me come that damn hard before. Or that many times in one night—well, day. He'd been so focused on me and my pleasure. He'd never once asked me to touch or suck his cock, but I'd done both, determined to make the most of what time we had.

I could honestly say that no other man had suited me so well in bed. He'd certainly become a benchmark against which I'd measure all future guys … which was a problem, because it was unlikely that they'd outmatch him. It was genuinely a shame that there would be no repeats, but still for the best. *Dammit.*

I edged out of bed, pulled on my satin robe—a 'welcome to The Hollow' gift from Sam and Jared's fabulous assistant, Fletcher—and padded into the bathroom. I didn't need to take a shower since I'd soaked in the tub before I fell asleep that final time. So after I'd done my business and brushed my teeth, I returned to the bedroom.

Damien was sitting on the edge of the bed, slipping on his shoes. He looked at me, his usual ghost of a smile present on his face. "Hey," he said simply.

"Evening," I greeted as I began pulling clothes from drawers. Pleasantly surprised that I didn't feel at all awkward, I said, "Thanks for insisting I take that salt bath."

His mouth curved into a cocky grin that was far too sexy to make me bristle. "You gave me all kinds of shit when I put you in that water."

"I did? Sorry. In my defence, I was drained. But you *did* warn me I wouldn't be able to move once you were done with me. It was good of you to keep your word."

He chuckled. "I'm a good guy that way." He braced his elbows on his thighs and watched as I dragged on my clothes … like it was a fashion show or something. I saw no point in getting all shy and asking him to look away. He'd seen all there was to see. *Touched* pretty much all there was to see. Bitten quite a few of those places as well.

I'd heard many times that there was something seriously erotic about having a vampire feed from you, but I truly hadn't expected to like it much. It had actually been a *lot* hotter than I'd anticipated.

I'd thought it would hurt more than it had. But there'd only been a brief slash of pain, and then nothing but pure bliss—a bliss so intensely euphoric that it sent my orgasm forcefully barrelling toward me each time. I could see why some might get addicted to that high.

"Are you working tonight?" he asked once I was fully dressed.

I didn't mistake the question for him wondering if I was free this evening. I could sense it was an idle enquiry. Knew he was making small talk and ensuring things were good between us before he headed home.

"No," I replied. "It's my night off. I wanted to go to the beach, but Maisy hounded me until I agreed to go see a movie with her instead." I started dragging a brush through my hair. "What are you doing with your evening?"

"I have poker night with the guys."

"Really? I had no idea you were all into strip poker."

His brow furrowed. "I never said *strip* poker."

"You did in my head. And the images I'm now seeing are blowing my mind. Do you touch each other too? Please say yes."

A rumbly laugh bubbled out of him and, predictably, here came the goosebumps.

Smiling, he rose from the bed and crossed to me. "I like you, Lexi Solomon."

My chest did *not* just go all warm. "I like you, Damien Addams." I placed my brush on the dresser. "And now I have to eat. You hungry?"

"Not really. I'm sort of tanked up on your blood right now." His pupils dilated. "You taste like heaven, you know."

"I didn't know. Thanks for telling me."

His brow pinched. "You don't feel weak or anything, do you? I was careful not to take too much blood, but …"

"I'm fine. Honestly." But we truly needed to stop talking about him feeding from me, because the memories were making my body tingle in all kinds of wonderful places. "Right. Breakfast."

I walked out of my room, down the small hallway, and into my kitchen. I thought Damien would make his excuses to leave, but he trailed after me, his mouth twisted. And I sensed … "You want to ask me something."

He blinked. "I do, yeah. Do you mind me asking how you came to be at The Hollow? Sam made a vague reference to it last night but didn't expand. And, well, I'm nosy."

I shrugged. "It's not an interesting story, but I'll tell you if you want to know." Although I was genuinely surprised he'd care to ask.

He slid onto one of the breakfast stools. "I do."

"Okay." I popped two slices of bread into the toaster. "Basically, I saw something I shouldn't have seen. I stumbled upon Hoyt battling with a vampire he'd tracked," I said, referring to one of Sam and Jared's trackers. "I saw enough to know they weren't human. I know I should have run or screamed or something, but I just froze. It wasn't out of fear, I didn't really feel anything other than … I don't know, it was like I was caught up in a dream or something."

Pausing, I grabbed the carton of orange juice from the fridge and then a glass from the cupboard. "Hoyt subdued the vamp, knocked him out, and then came over to me. He moved slowly, carefully, trying not to scare me I guess. But I'd known he could pounce on me in a second—I'd seen how fast he moved—so I wasn't reassured. Still, I didn't run. Felt rooted to the spot. He tried to erase my memories but couldn't."

Damien's brows flew up. "Really?"

"Yeah." I poured juice into my glass and took a sip. "Apparently that happens sometimes with humans, though no one's quite sure why." Hearing my toast pop up, I put the two slices on a plate and began to butter them. "Hoyt said I had two choices—I could die, or I could go with him."

"And you agreed to come here."

"Nope. I chose 'death.'"

"Death?" echoed Damien, his mouth kicking up.

"Oh yeah." I returned the juice carton to the fridge. "I had no wish to go anywhere with goddamn vampires. But Hoyt wasn't down with that. He tried to explain that the place where he'd take me was beautiful. That I'd be safe there, safer than I'd ever been before. But, yeah, I was like 'dude, just kill me.'"

"I guess I can understand why you'd be sceptical."

Setting my plate and glass on the small island, I sat on the stool opposite Damien. "Hoyt rolled his eyes and declared I was going with him, and that he could just as easily kill me at The Hollow if I genuinely didn't want to be there. I was shocked when I first arrived. I never expected to learn that vampires lived in the damn Caribbean."

"It came as a surprise to me as well. Though not quite as shocking as learning they exist. What happened next?"

I bit into my toast. "One of the humans gave me a tour and explained everything—about the place itself, about vampires, about the legion, about how it was optional for us to let vamps feed from us. She promised I could leave anytime, *providing* I allowed one of the more powerful vamps to erase my memories of the place." I took another bite of my toast. "The idea of having my mind messed with bugged me more than the idea of staying. It sounds dumb, I know—"

"No, it doesn't. I've had a vampire walk through my mind. I didn't much like it. I'd rather have my memories and deal with the fall-out of a situation than live a life of ignorance, so I get it."

Having finished one slice of toast, I moved onto the next. "I think what *really* put me at ease and made me consider staying was Sam. I imagined the ruling vamps to be ancient and otherworldly and super scary. But Sam and Jared … well, I don't know if I'd call them mentally stable, but they're very genuine. Especially Sam. She's real. Blunt without being cold. I kind of needed 'blunt and real' right then, because I was dizzy from realising I didn't know as much about the world as I'd thought I did."

Damien nodded. "Considering how much paranormal fiction is out there, you'd think it'd be a lot easier to accept that there's truth in some of that fiction, but it can be a fuck of a shock."

"It can, and I'm surprised I held it together. But I did, and I chose to stay, thinking it would be a fresh—albeit sort of weird—start for me."

"Any regrets?"

"No. None." I bit into my toast again. "The life I have now is better than my old situation in many ways."

He cocked his head. "Your human life wasn't so great?"

I took a long swig of my juice. "That's another story."

He looked about to push for more info—typical alpha. But he apparently decided to rein in his curiosity, because he changed the subject to something lighter.

We chatted about mundane things as I finished my breakfast. I was glad he hadn't just cut and run earlier, but I supposed it was stupid of me to have thought he would. Damien wasn't *that guy*. He wouldn't make a woman feel used.

Once I'd eaten, I walked him to the front door.

His long fingers curling around the handle, he stared at me for a short moment. "I'm glad you invited me in, Lexi."

I felt my mouth tip up. "I'm glad I did, too."

He tucked my hair behind my ear, a faint smile on his face. "See ya." With that, he left.

Closing the door, I flicked the lock and puffed out a breath. His presence alone took up so much space that the apartment suddenly seemed so much emptier. And as it hit me that he'd never be back here, I felt a twinge of pain in my chest. "Fuck."

CHAPTER FIVE

(Lexi)

"What a way to break your dry spell." Maisy fanned her face. "Seriously, we should pull out the pompoms because, *damn*, Damien really did us proud."

Taking a step forward in the line of customers leading to the concession counter, I frowned. "What's with the 'us'? You weren't there."

"No, but I was hoping he'd make it super good for you. And he did. Like on a *whole* other level than what I'd anticipated. You deserved that, so I'm *all* for expressing my appreciation in some way."

"I don't think he'll be expecting a thank-you from you, so the pompoms can stay in your closet."

"As you like."

I shook my head, smiling. The cinema's brightly lit foyer was loud, thanks to the patrons talking, the rattling of the popping popcorn, the gurgling of drinks as they poured out of dispensers, and the movie trailer playing on the monitors above the counter. The smells of nachos, butter, salt, and popcorn laced the air, making me hungrier than I already was.

"You know, I'm kind of jealous," Maisy went on as we took another step forward in the line. "I've never had an evening like that. Where a guy took me that many times in that many ways, I mean."

"Neither have I." If Damien had deliberately set out to ensure I'd never forget him, he'd damn well succeeded. There was no way for the memories of a night—or day, in this instance—like that to just ... fade or fracture so that you were left with only the highlights.

"It's almost like Damien had all these fantasies stored up and was determined to make them a reality, isn't it?" Maisy put her hand on my arm.

"Oh, and the salt bath thing? That was so sweet. And the way he stuck around and talked to you earlier to be sure you didn't feel used and discarded was just as sweet. Not many guys would do that. He's a keeper."

"I know, thanks for reminding me that I won't be the one who keeps him," I said, my voice dry.

She winced. "Sorry, sorry, I spoke without thinking." She let out a wistful sigh. "It's a damn shame that he isn't human."

It was, but there was no sense in dwelling about it.

Finally at the front of the line, we bought popcorn and drinks. Then we were walking down a shadowy hallway as we headed to the theatre where our movie would soon play. Inside, we claimed seats on the back row and settled in to watch the previews.

It wasn't long before the movie began, and I had to repeatedly stifle a smile as Maisy jumped and softly cursed during each intense scene. Zombies always freaked her out.

Halfway through the movie, I leaned into her and quietly said, "I need to use the restroom. I'll be right back."

She didn't look away from the screen as she said, her shoulders hunched up, "Okay, but hurry, because this movie is *way* too fucking scary for me to watch it on my lonesome."

I snickered, resisting the urge to point out that—as a vampire—she could surely take out a few zombies if life ever deemed it necessary.

I quietly padded out of the dark theatre and walked to the restroom. A few people were inside, talking or washing their hands. Recognising them but not knowing them well—on an island this small, it was impossible not to have met pretty much everyone—I gave them each a brief hi before finding a stall.

Once I'd done my business and all that jazz, I dried my hands with some paper towels and then dumped them in the trash can on my way out of the restroom. I turned the corner and stepped into the dimly lit hallway—

There was a blur of movement as someone darted toward me at vampiric momentum, and then Castor was towering over me. "You bitch," he spat, backing me into the wall.

Taken off-guard, I blinked. "Excuse me?"

His upper lip curled. "Hours. I was punished for fucking *hours* because of you."

I gave him a once over. "You look okay to me."

He hissed. "Because I've *healed* since then."

Well, yeah, I figured that.

"I had broken bones, blisters on my face, cuts all over my body from Sam's fucking whip."

Sounds like it was quite the party. "She really doesn't like it when men get rough with women. It's pretty common knowledge. Now I'd like to get back to my friend, so …" I tried to skirt around him, but he slammed a palm on the wall each side of my head. I sighed. "Well this is cosy."

"You have no sense of self-preservation, do you?"

"I could say the same to you, dear Nosferatu. What is it you want?"

His brow inched up. "What do I want? I want to have not suffered hours of pain. But I did, because of *you*."

I folded my arms. "Your mommy didn't hold you responsible for much when you were a kid, did she? Silly of her. That shit tends to breed entitlement. You're kind of stuck at that emotional age where your own wants and needs come before everyone else's. So sad. It's what made you act like an ass and break the rules. It's what makes you blame *me* as opposed to *yourself* for the pain you went through. I've known quite a few people like you. They all manage to fuck up their lives, and they never seem to realise they're doing it. Weird. And highly pathetic."

He put his face closer to mine. "You dare look down your nose at me? You are *nothing*."

"And you are testing my fucking patience."

"I could end your life right here at this very moment. And yes, I would probably be punished for it. But you would still be dead."

"Your point holds merit. But I'm confused as to why you think this makes you scary or powerful. *Anyone* can hurt someone weaker than them—it's not a sign of strength."

"Do you think that being Damien's toy for one evening makes you special and gives you the right to speak to me this way? I can smell him on you. Did you let him feed from you?"

I lifted my chin. "What's it to you?"

"You did, didn't you? Is that what it takes to make you give it up? You won't do it unless you get to also spread your legs like a good little whore?"

"I prefer 'slut.' Sounds sexier." I jumped as his hand snapped around my throat. I snarled. "Let fucking go of—" He was gone. *Dragged* away from me. And then he was a few feet away wrapped in a yellowy-green goo that oozed out of Denny's fingers. David and Stuart were also there, glaring at the piece of shit.

"That was a *huge* mistake, Castor," said Denny.

"Release me this instant!" the asshole demanded, struggling against the goo.

"Uh, no." Denny glanced at me. "Are you okay?"

I pushed away from the wall. "I'm good."

"Can you tell me exactly what happened?" asked Stuart.

I did so, and then added, "Considering he's so pissed about being punished, I'm not understanding why he'd risk receiving another one."

"Some people don't respond to physical punishments," said Stuart. "They feel the pain, but it doesn't motivate them to back down. It simply riles them up even more." He exchanged a look with Denny, nodded, and then burst into molecules. Molecules which then swept out of the hallway and disappeared around the corner. Cool gift.

"Sam and Jared are currently away from the island, but we'll get Castor to a cell," David told me. "They'll deal with him later."

Castor froze, his eyes flaring. "I am *not* going back to a cell."

"Now that's where you're wrong," said Denny before sliding his gaze to me. "We'll take care of this. David will walk you home."

The vampire in question nodded and gestured for me to get moving.

"I'm here with a friend, Maisy," I said.

"If she wants to stay here without you, she can," said David. "If not, I'll escort you both to your apartments."

"Does no one care that she struck me?" Castor burst out. "Do humans not receive their own punishments?"

I whirled to face him. "I didn't strike you. I didn't even *touch*—" And then it hit me. "Is that what this was about? You wanted to provoke me into doing something that would earn me a punishment of my own? You were hoping for a little revenge?"

Denny snorted. "Bad plan, Castor. We saw you cornering her. We heard you insulting her. We witnessed you grab her by the throat. If she *had* retaliated, not one person would have claimed that you didn't have it coming."

Castor sneered. "So women get special treatment round here?"

"No, they get equal treatment," replied Denny. He then looked at me again. "Go on, Lexi. Head home. We got this."

Nodding, I turned and walked away with David at my side. Damn, what a night.

(Damien)

Having lost yet another hand, I slapped my cards on Reuben's dining room table. A gloating Chico greedily grabbed his winnings while Harvey and Reuben mumbled complaints. Rubbing my temple, I lifted my bourbon-flavoured NST and took a long swig.

Harvey glared at Chico, who'd won five times in a row. "Won't your mate be looking for you? Max, Butch, and Salem headed off to their girls. I'm thinking Jude will be upset that she's waiting on you."

Chico snorted. "You'd like it if I upped and left, wouldn't you?"

"I'd fucking love it," said Harvey.

"Jude went bowling with a few of her squad, so she ain't waiting on me." Chico glanced at Reuben. "Is Ian expecting you at his place any time soon?"

Reuben shook his head. "He's reading a new book that came out tonight—one he's been waiting on for a whole year—so he currently doesn't care I even exist."

"Excellent," said Chico, gathering the cards together. "It means I can squeeze more cash out of you before I head home." Pausing, he eyed me closely. "You seem a little distracted tonight."

I was. Hence why I'd been playing atrociously. I hadn't won a single hand. To be honest, my mind just wasn't in the game.

"It wouldn't have anything to do with that waitress you've been ogling for months, would it?" Chico tilted his head. "Her name's Lexi, right? A little birdie told me you came strolling out of her apartment earlier."

Setting down my bottle, I felt my lips flatten. That was the thing about living at The Hollow. It was practically impossible to keep secrets among a population so small.

Not that I'd hoped to keep what happened between me and Lexi a secret, but I didn't plan to talk much about it either. The last thing I had any interest in doing was telling anyone how insanely good the sex fest had been, or there'd be dozens of males sniffing around her in no time at all. I found myself clenching my fists at the mere idea of it.

Harvey looked at me, his brows lifting. "You spent the entire day with her, huh? I figured you'd make your move soon. I suppose it was a long time coming."

It was, and it had been a million times better than I'd expected. I hadn't been able to get enough of her. She excited every one of my senses. Evoked a depth of need in me that was close to feverish. Stirred up a vicious and alien possessiveness in me that compelled me to chain her to my side. Something which I absolutely could not do.

Leaving her at sunset had been … well, I hadn't liked it. At all. I'd wanted to stay a while longer. I'd wanted to fire more questions at her. Wanted to learn more about her. Wanted to get inside her pretty little head.

I'd also wanted to tumble her back into bed.

I'd actually woken before her, but I hadn't moved an inch. I'd been way too comfortable where I was. If I hadn't known that fucking her once more would have given her mixed signals, I would have draped my body over hers and buried my cock inside her. But our day together had reached its end, and the next evening had already began, so I'd kept my hands to myself.

Reuben frowned at me. "It's not like you to be so tight-lipped. Not that you brag about the women you bed, but you don't usually give us a death stare for asking questions."

Well I didn't usually crave women like they were a fucking drug. "We playing another round or what?"

Harvey leaned forward, all nosiness. "I know you're not purposely trying to intrigue me, Damien, but the more you avoid talking about her, the more I want to know *why*."

Oh for fuck's sake.

"Same here," said Chico, his mouth curved. "I'm not getting the sense that she pissed you off or anything, Day." He studied me for a few moments. "You like this girl, don't you?"

Perceptive motherfucker. "If you'd rather I dealt out the cards, hand them over."

"Yeah, you like this girl." Harvey sank back in his seat. "I gotta wonder why you're here with us, then, instead of rolling around the sheets with her."

It wasn't obvious? "She's human," I reminded him.

"Yeah, but if you're going to struggle to keep away from her, going cold turkey is the worst thing you can do. You'll just make her forbidden fruit, and that'll make her even *more* tempting. And that temptation will be in your face pretty much every night, which'll make the whole thing even harder."

The man wasn't wrong. But I knew better than to touch her again. I instinctively knew I'd never be able to fuck her out of my system. That wouldn't work with Lexi. The more I touched her, the more I'd want her. "This is one of those situations where keeping your distance is best," I explained, purposely vague.

"Fair enough," said Harvey." But do you think you *can*?"

"Yes." Probably.

"That right there was a lie, my friend. Look, I agree it's best for you not to get seriously involved with her, given she's human. But here's the thing. You're not the only guy who had his eye on Lexi. The others resisted making a move because, like you, they knew she needed time to get used to our kind. I think some also noticed you were clearly into her, and they didn't want to piss you off so hung back. Once it becomes known that you had your taste of her and you're done, all those guys will make their own play."

My gut twisted, and I barely bit back a growl.

"Yeah, I can see you're not good with that idea. Well, if you're not sure you could handle seeing her with anyone else so soon, you need to do something about it." Harvey clicked his fingers. "Ooh, claim her as your vessel."

My heart leaped. I'd never asked a human to be exclusively mine to feed from, but plenty of other vampires had claimed vessels at one time or another. It wasn't always sexual. People mostly did it when they didn't want an impersonal feeding arrangement.

"Then you'd have rights to her," Harvey went on. "No other guy on the island would dare touch her. And you could walk away when you were ready."

It was a fucking brilliant idea.

It was also a terrible idea.

Brilliant, because her blood was goddamn addictive, and I was a little too possessive where she was concerned to deal well with other men crowding her.

Terrible, because there was every chance I'd just become more and more territorial of her. That couldn't end well at all.

"Is she one of the humans who hope to be Turned?" asked Reuben.

I pursed my lips. "I doubt it." She hadn't said or done anything to give me the impression that vampirism appealed to her. She hadn't asked about the transformation, the lifestyle, my gift, or anything else vampire-related. She *had* asked if some humans became addicted to being fed from, but that didn't hint at her hoping to be Turned.

"Unless you ask her, you won't know," Reuben pointed out.

"She hangs with a vampire," said Harvey. "She and Maisy are tight. It could be that Lexi so easily befriended her because she wants to be Turned at some point in the future. It might not be the *near* future. Some humans want to enjoy their 'best years' before having their genetic makeup frozen in place."

Chico nodded, idly shuffling the cards. "You could ask Coach or Jared if Lexi has put in an application to be Turned. They'd tell you."

I scratched my temple. "I don't know if—" I cut off as a gust of molecules rushed into the room and then reformed into Stuart. I tensed at the hard look on his face. "What's wrong?" I asked, unease pricking at me.

"I figured you'd want to know what just went down at the movie theatre." Stuart set his fists on his hips. "It's Lexi."

I was out of my seat in an instant. "What about her?"

"Castor pulled another stunt. She's okay," Stuart hurried to add, raising one hand. "He didn't hurt her, though he did grab her by the throat—"

My blood boiling, I didn't hang around to hear more. I rushed out of the apartment in vampiric speed and headed right for the movie theatre.

CHAPTER SIX

(Damien)

Rage a live wire inside me, I skidded to a halt in front of Castor, who was tangled in ooze and being dragged along the floor of one of the theatre's dark hallways by Denny.

"Where's Lexi?" I asked, my tone clipped, aware that Harvey, Stuart, Chico, and Reuben had fanned out behind me.

"David walked her and Maisy home," replied Denny.

Harvey appeared at my side. "*Maisy* was involved?"

Denny shook his head. "She was just here to see a movie with Lexi. They're both fine."

I flexed my fingers, glaring at Castor even as I asked Denny, "What the fuck happened here?" My voice sounded like crushed rock.

"According to Lexi, Castor basically blamed her for the punishment he received, wouldn't let her walk away, and then called her a whore for sleeping with you. He also grabbed her by the throat."

A growl rattling my chest, I towered over the motherfucker, balling up my hands. "You called her a whore?" The question was calm. Soft. Low. Menacing.

"She slapped me!" the asshole insisted, curling in on himself.

Denny snorted. "No, she didn't. But I think she's right in believing that you *wanted* her to do it so she'd receive a punishment like you did. It would explain why you did your best to provoke her."

"Not just provoke her," I said, still glaring at Castor. "*Scare* her. You get off on intimidating women? On *grabbing* them? Because that's fucking twice you've touched her. Once was one time too many."

Castor fruitlessly struggled against the ooze. "Protective of her, are you?"

He let out a derisive sound. "Women are good at messing with a man's mind and making him irrational. Take you, for example. You are taking the side of a human over one of your own kind." A smirk crept onto his face. "But I doubt you would have done so if she hadn't spread her thighs for you. Was she good? I would think not. Humans are far too delicate to be much fun." His smirk faded when I didn't react.

"I see what you're doing," I told him. "You want me to challenge you to a duel so that Denny would have to release you. You think it's your best chance of escape." I gave a slow shake of the head. "I'm not inclined to give you a single thing that you want."

Castor's eyes flickered. "I will not return to a cell."

"You're right, you won't." I briefly tipped my head to the side. "At least not yet."

Castor tried edging backwards on his elbows only to bump into Stuart, who'd made his way behind him.

My jaw hard, I closed the distance between us in one fluid stride and yanked Castor up off the floor. "You should have stayed away from Lexi. You definitely shouldn't have touched or insulted her. You shouldn't have even made the mistake of *breathing her air*. In sum, you brought this shit on yourself." I slammed my fist into his jaw.

(Lexi)

My head snapped up at the hard knock on my front door. I wondered if Sam and Jared had returned to the island and now wished to question me about what happened with Castor. Probably.

Leaving my mug of hot chocolate on the kitchen island, I slid off my stool and padded through my apartment. Reaching the front door, I pulled it open. My pulse leapt at the sight of Damien, his hands plastered on the wall either side of my doorway. Instantly, the air snapped taut and something flared between us that caused my stomach to flip.

"Hey," he said simply.

I cleared my throat. "Hi."

"I wanted to check on you." He glanced over my shoulder. "Can I come in?"

Considering the chemistry between us was still as strong as ever, that didn't seem wise. And yet, I found myself opening the door wide. "Sure."

My heartbeat stuttered when he brushed past me as he stepped inside. If my body could just calm the fuck down and not be so easy for him, that would be great. I closed the door and folded my arms. "I take it you heard about what happened at the theatre."

A muscle ticked in his cheek. "I heard. Stuart gave me a heads-up. You were gone by the time I got there. Denny assured me you were fine, but I wanted to see that for myself."

I was genuinely surprised that Damien had bothered to get involved. Then again, he was part of Sam and Jared's squad, so he no doubt made this kind of stuff his business. "I really am okay."

He slipped his hands into the pockets of his jeans. "I'm not certain all women would be in your position."

"He wasn't really there to assault me. It was more of a mind game than anything else." Otherwise, I probably *would* have been a little shaken up by the whole thing. "He meant to provoke me. When it didn't work, he went too far—"

"He went too fucking far the moment he caged you against the wall," Damien all but growled.

I wasn't gonna lie, the note of protectiveness in that growl got me all tingly.

"He's being taken to a containment cell as we speak," Damien added. "Sam and Jared will most likely banish him after once more punishing him."

I felt my brow furrow. "Really? But he didn't hurt me or anything—"

"He might have done if he'd had the chance. As you said, he was trying to provoke you. But that wasn't happening, so there's every chance he'd have gotten so pissed that he did something very, very, *very* stupid. Besides, if he can't follow the rules here, he won't be allowed to stay. Simple."

"I can't say I'll be sorry to see him gone. I've known too many guys like him. Pushy men who treat women like shit … as if they're objects to be used, abused, and then dumped. My mom was unfortunately very fond of such assholes. For her, the more dangerous a man was, the better. She mistook abusive for strong. Which was *way* too much information, I'm sorry." I shook my head, annoyed I'd revealed so much.

"Don't be. I like these sneak peeks I get of you."

I parted my lips to speak, but no words came. I didn't really know what to make of his comment, and it didn't seem smart to ask him to elaborate. Maybe we could become friends—or, at the very least, friend*ly*—at some point in the future. But I didn't feel that I could manage that right now.

"Well, thanks for checking up on me," I said. "I really am okay. I think Maisy's madder than I am."

"Harvey's gone to check on her."

"She'll be glad to see him."

"You sure?" Damien cocked his head. "I didn't get the impression that she likes him as much as he does her. She kept him hanging for a while."

"Not out of disinterest. She's still struggling with being a vampire."

"She applied to be Turned," he pointed out.

"Yeah, to have forever with the guy who is now her Sire—they were a couple at the time. Now that they're not, she resents how much she gave up to be with him, which means she's finding it hard not to resent what she is."

"Vampirism has its perks, but it requires a lot of sacrifices. People are often good with it. But give it a few centuries, and they start regretting that there are certain things they'll miss out on, like having children." He paused, watching me closely. "Do you think you'd handle life as a vampire well?"

I felt my nose wrinkle. "I don't know if I could truly get behind drinking blood—I get nauseous just thinking about it. And the ways of your world are scary at times. Some things about vampirism are appealing, though. You'd never get sick, for one thing. Having a gift would be cool, and if that makes me childish then whatever."

"Not childish. It is awesome having a preternatural gift—no one will claim differently. Although some are disappointed that their ability isn't more offensive or notable."

"Do you like yours?"

"Yeah. It comes in useful, and it got me a place in the legion, so I'm grateful to have it." His eyes drifted over my face. "You sure you're all right?"

"I'm positive. Castor doesn't scare me. He's too petty to be frightening, though he doesn't seem to see that."

"No, he doesn't." Damien's gaze locked on my mouth and, shit, my lower stomach clenched.

He needed to leave. He really did. Because my hormones were a hot mess, and it would be all too easy to close the distance between us. I still wanted him far too much. Knowing how good it felt to have him inside me only made it worse.

Without thought, I licked my lips. "Thanks for stopping by." It was a clear *you should go now*.

He drew in a breath through his nose and gave a curt nod. He slowly reached out and grabbed the door handle. He paused. Closed his eyes. Cursed beneath his breath. Then his hand snagged my nape, yanked me close, and he slammed his mouth on mine. That easily, I went up in flames.

He took my mouth in an urgent, heart-pounding, hotly sexual kiss that burned away any objections I might have made. This was a bad idea. A really, really bad idea. But I had no intention of putting a stop to it. I wasn't sure I even could.

He dragged off my tee, whipped off my bra, and shoved down my jeans and panties. I didn't get a chance to strip his own clothes, I only got as far as snapping open his fly before he hoisted me up and kissed me again.

I grunted as my back met the wall, and then my legs were hooked over the crooks of his elbows. "We shouldn't be doing this." But I curled my arms around him and tilted my hips toward the thick head of his dick as it bumped my slick folds.

"I know, but I gotta have you again." He rammed his cock inside me.

A gasp got stuck in my throat. Jesus, the dude packed some *serious* heat.

There was no way for it not to burn as my inner muscles stretched around his long, thick shaft, so I couldn't bite back the little whimper that slipped out of me.

"Shh, baby, I got you." Then he was pounding into me like he just couldn't wait any longer. He drove so deep, so hard, so fast—aggressive and unrestrained. "Yeah, that's what I needed." He groaned. "You feel so fucking good."

So did he. I'd never felt so utterly *filled*. There didn't seem to be a spot he didn't touch. I felt every ridge and vein as he dragged his cock over supersensitive nerve-endings. And there was something about knowing we absolutely should *not* be doing this that made it all even hotter, so I was obviously whacked in the head.

"You needed this, too," he gritted out. "You like having my dick in you, don't you?"

I squeezed my eyes shut. "I don't want to like it."

"But you do. You can't help it." He claimed my mouth again. Possessed it. Imprinted his fucking self on it, the bastard. "I want my come filling you up again, Lex. Make that happen for me." He sank his teeth into my throat.

The slice of pain, the pull of his mouth, the feral slams of his cock … it all became too much. My release crashed into me, stealing my breath, bowing my back, and making my inner walls clamp around his shaft. It was blissful, it was explosive, it was devastating. I only absently noted Damien jamming his dick deep as jets of come burst out of him.

I collapsed forward, resting my head on his shoulder as my breaths sawed at my dry throat. *Jesus holy Christ.*

He nuzzled my hair, his own breathing not quite steady. "I'm staying here again."

I didn't lift my head to look at him. I couldn't. Because if he looked in my eyes right then while my defences were down, he'd see how much I wanted that. Probably see far more.

I swallowed. "I don't think that's a good idea."

"You're right, it isn't." He pressed a kiss to my hair. "But I'm still staying."

And because I apparently had no willpower when it came to him, I didn't protest when he carried me to bed.

As we lay facing each other a few hours later, shortly after another round of non-wise sex, we quietly talked about inconsequential things—nothing deep, nothing serious, nothing too personal. So I was more than a little surprised when he abruptly blurted out, "You hinted that your old life wasn't great. Will you tell me about it?"

I bit my lip, hesitant. We shouldn't be getting to know each other, we should be giving each other a little space until the chemistry died off. But apparently I was *all* into doing unwise shit tonight, because instead of blowing off his question, I warned, "Much like how I came to be at The Hollow, it's not really an interesting story."

"I'd still like to hear it."

"Do I get to ask you a question afterward?" I asked, expecting him to say something like 'It depends on the question.'

He shrugged one shoulder. "Sure, if you want."

Fair enough. I took a slow breath. "Back then, I wasn't in a good place. Mentally or physically. I kind of messed up. Big time."

His brow creased. "In what sense?"

"I had a plan, but it didn't work out. And then I was just lost."

"What kind of plan?"

"It was really pretty simple. A family, a steady job, a home in a nice neighbourhood."

"You wanted what you didn't have growing up," he guessed, the observant bastard.

"Yes. My mom isn't a terrible person. Just very self-centred, and she could never handle being alone, so she'd drift from one loser to another and drag me with her. I never really had a home. Or a family. I never knew my dad. And my mom's family wanted nothing to do with her, and she wanted nothing to do with them, so they had no interest in me either."

"Then they were stupid."

I let out a short chuckle. "Anyway, what I wanted more than anything was kids. So I was, like, over the moon when I got pregnant. But then I was in a car accident. I miscarried, and there was a lot of internal damage. I couldn't have kids after that." I swallowed around the lump that built in my throat. "So my whole life plan suddenly got derailed. Especially since my boyfriend left me soon after."

"He *left* you?"

"The miscarriage hit him hard, too. Some things can bring a couple closer while other situations lead them to drift apart. I guess we weren't as solid as I thought, because we did the latter. I went through a self-destructive phase. Partied too hard. Lost my job. I was two months away from being evicted when Hoyt brought me here."

Damien took my hand and gave it a little squeeze. "That's what you meant when you said this was a fresh start for you."

"Yup. I'm not missing out on anything while being here. I can't have kids, I don't have anyone who'll miss me, I was jobless, and I would have lost my home anyway. Maybe it's crazy, but I feel happier and more settled living on an island full of vampires than I did in my old life. This is completely different from my initial plan. But I needed 'different.'"

His dark eyes, unusually soft, roamed over my face. "I'm sorry about the miscarriage, Lex."

"Yeah, me too." I exhaled a shaky breath. God, I needed to change the subject fast or I'd be blubbering all over him. "So … what was your old life like?"

"Nothing to write home about. My dad died before I was born, and then my mom married his brother. I think she was just afraid of being alone because she didn't love Austin. He was a rich motherfucker and that definitely appealed to her . She 'lunched' and socialised and shopped like it was her job. She couldn't spend Austin's money fast enough. He was good with that because it meant she was dependent on him."

"You didn't like him," I sensed.

"No. He didn't like me either. Mostly because he hadn't liked my dad, and he resented that my dad was the love of my mother's life. Whenever Austin looked at me, he was reminded that he was second choice."

"So he wasn't a great step dad, then?"

"He demanded perfection, and I wasn't interested in pleasing him. Most of the time, an insistence on perfection is really just an excuse to criticise someone or hurt them. So, as I didn't long for his approval or meet his standards, he was content to overlook me, and I was happy to be overlooked. Austin gave most of his attention to his biological son—my younger half-brother, Kaiden."

"You didn't like him any more than you liked his father, did you?"

"Kaiden and me were like oil and water. He's a self-entitled little shit. He did everything he could to earn his daddy's approval, including treating me as an outsider and trying to make me feel like I didn't measure up."

"They both sound like complete assholes."

"Accurate description. As I'm sure you can imagine, I don't miss them. Or my mother—she wasn't really there anyway. She emotionally checked out after she lost my dad, which devastates him."

I frowned. "How can you know it devastates him? You talk to his ghost or something?"

"No, I talk to *him*. It turns out that he hadn't actually died. He'd become a vampire. He couldn't be in our lives, but he'd stayed close and watched over us. So when he found out I'd been the victim of a racial attack and was on life support, he took my body out of the hospital and Turned me to save my life, hoping I wouldn't hate him for it. I didn't. Still don't."

"Wow," I breathed. "Shit, it must have been so hard for him to be so close yet so far from you all those years."

"It was. He was lonely as hell back then. He later met a woman, which made it easier for me to accept Sebastian's offer and attend try-outs for the legion. I'm still in touch with my dad. He's happy."

"Are you?"

"Yeah." Damien smoothed his hand down my body and cupped me hard. "Especially right now." He thrust one finger inside me and groaned. "Life is good."

CHAPTER SEVEN

(Damien)

While Lexi puttered around the kitchen shortly after breakfast, I sat quietly at the island. I liked watching her move. She was efficient. Purposeful. Sensual. Every sway of her hips drew my attention to that delectable ass. It cried out to be spanked, which I hadn't gotten around to yet.

Yet? No, scrap that word. This wouldn't be happening again. I couldn't come back here—not even for a quick visit. Because I didn't think I'd manage to leave again without first burying my dick inside her once more.

Christ, that woman.

She'd kept a physical space between us since waking, much as she had on the previous sunset. It was for the best. But I fucking hated it.

Harvey's words from last night kept drifting around my head. If I followed his advice, it might well come back to bite me on the ass. If I didn't, well, I'd be kicking the shit out of any man who made a move on her. It really felt like I was fucked either way.

Fighting her pull would have been a lot damn easier if the attraction was purely physical. But there was a lot to like about Lexi Solomon. She was genuine. Accepting. Gutsy. Cautious and guarded, but still open to letting people into her life; open to giving them a chance to earn her trust.

And fuck, she could be funny. We'd talked a lot between sex sessions yesterday, and she'd had me laughing so hard when doing impressions of people. She was brilliant at accents, and her impersonation of Sam was perfect.

I couldn't help but find it crazy that she wasn't the least bit scared of Castor but almost had a major freak out when we spotted a spider on her bedroom wall. Oh, she'd dismissed it at first. Even as her shoulders went stiff, she'd acted all aloof and uncaring, clearly determined to ignore how its presence creeped her out—Lexi didn't give into fear easily, I'd learned. But the closer it had crawled toward the headboard, the edgier she'd become until eventually she'd flown off the bed and done a full-on body shiver while insisting I throw the spider out of the window.

We'd exchanged more stories about our lives, and I'd learned just how damn useless her mother was. She and Lexi had ended up in homeless shelters on several occasions. But Lexi had never once tried to trivialise any of my own childhood shit; never been all, 'oh, the poor little rich boy.' That just wasn't the way she operated.

"It's not like you to sit in silence," she said, wiping her hands on a kitchen towel.

I met her eyes. "I was just admiring the view." She didn't look as though she believed me. "I don't regret coming here, or staying with you, if that's what you're wondering."

"You should regret it." She chucked the towel onto the counter. "So should I."

"But you don't," I sensed.

She straightened, all defensive. "Well you make me come really hard."

A chuckle burst out of me. "I love your honesty." I patted my thigh in invitation.

"Oh no. Keeping space between us is best."

In a blur of movement, I was stood directly in front of her. "I don't like space." I *did* like that she never seemed spooked by how fast I could move. No reminders of the fact that, hey, I wasn't human appeared to bother her.

I palmed one side of her face and swept my thumb over her cheekbone. "Do you like it when I feed from you?"

She swallowed. "You know I do."

"Then I'm going to give you something to think about."

"Huh?"

"I want you to consider being my vessel." I needed to keep her at my side a little longer. Needed to have some claim on her. Needed time to get over my obsession with her.

She narrowed her eyes. "What exactly would that entail?"

"Nothing complicated," I assured her. "In a nutshell, no one else but me would feed from you, and you'd officially be under my protection. That means anyone who harmed you by word or deed would deal with me."

"But you would feed from others?"

"Would you rather I didn't? Why are you scowling at me?"

"Because I *would* rather you didn't, and that bothers me. Feeding just seems so intimate. Even without sex."

I curled an arm around her and drew her close. "Then I'll drink from only you."

"Just like that? It wouldn't bug you to restrict yourself?"

"Fuck, no. Your blood is addictive." I brushed my lips over the pulse in her neck. "And now it's mine."

"Whoa there, I didn't agree to be your vessel."

I lifted my head. "But you're going to. I can tell."

"I don't think we'd manage to keep it … nonsexual."

"You mean we'd end up fucking? Yeah. We would." There was no sense in lying to ourselves about that.

She rubbed at her forehead. "It was only supposed to be a one-time thing."

I kissed one side of her mouth. "I know."

"We did it twice."

I pressed a kiss to the other corner of her mouth. "I know."

"Making it a regular thing wouldn't be smart."

"I know that, too." I palmed her face with both hands. "But I see you, and I *want*." The reaction was as basic as it was powerful. "I've never wanted anything the way I want you. And your blood, fuck, there's nothing like it." I licked and nipped at her neck. "Say yes."

She cursed when I teased the hollow beneath her ear with my tongue. "Dammit, Damien, that's my goddamn weak spot."

I knew that. "Say yes."

"I'll think about it."

Good enough for now. "Make sure that you do." Righting my head again, I nipped her lower lip. "I'll find you later."

She frowned. "You say that like it will be super simple."

"When one of my kind regularly feeds from a human and has much of their blood in our system, we can find them very easily—providing they're not too far away. We feel them. It's like a tug in our blood that draws us their way. But *only* if we've fed from them recently. I suppose it's nature's way of ensuring we don't lose our food."

"Huh. I didn't know any of that."

"Now you do. See you later." I gave her one last hard kiss and then left her apartment, feeling remarkably lighter.

Okay, so she hadn't agreed to my request yet, but I believed she would. I'd seen the flare of interest in her eyes. And I got the sense that she was no more eager for us to part ways yet than I was.

Outside, I walked toward my own Residence Hall, feeling the cool evening air on my skin. I nodded or tipped my chin at the people I passed, most of whom appeared to be on their way to work.

Jared's voice suddenly flowed into my head. *You're not going to like this,* he warned.

I felt my eyes narrow slightly. *What is it?*

A telepathic sigh. *Castor is in the wind.*

My step faltered. *Say that again.*

He got away.

I cursed a blue streak. *You are fucking kidding me. How?*

He got into a fight with the guards as they were taking him down to a cell. He got free and scampered.

I ground my teeth. *Shit.*

Sam and I are at his apartment right now. It doesn't look like he's been back there.

I instantly altered my course and headed for Castor's building in vampiric speed. I reached his floor mere moments later.

We also have people searching both The Hollow and rainforest for him as we speak, but it's more than probable that he's already fled the island, Jared added.

Seeing that Castor's front door was open, I stalked inside and found the Grand High Pair in the living area. "I do not fucking believe this shit," I clipped.

"Believe me, we're just as pissed as you are," said Jared.

No, they weren't. They couldn't be. Because Castor hadn't targeted someone who belonged to *them*. Lexi might not be wholly mine, but I still had rights to her. Or I would when she agreed to be my vessel. Which she'd definitely do. I had plans to hound her until she did. "What did the guards have to say?"

"Nothing," said Sam. "They're ashes. Going by the scorch marks on the floor, he lit up the poor sods and burned them alive."

"Fuck." I scrubbed a hand down my face.

Jared glanced around us. "If he's been back here, he hasn't taken anything."

"He'll have known it wouldn't be long before the ashes of the guards were discovered," I said, digging deep for a calm I had no chance of feeling. "I can't see him caring to come back here to grab his shit. If he has any sense, he'll have split."

"We share that view, but we don't take chances," Sam told me. "I want to speak to Dion. I say we three be the first to tell him about Castor and see what he has to say."

Pleased that she was good with me coming along, I nodded. Dion lived two floors down, so it wasn't long before we stood outside his apartment. It was Sam who knocked on the door.

Whipping it open, Dion double-blinked. "Oh, I wasn't expecting ..." He tensed, studying our faces. "What is wrong?"

"Let us in," said Sam. "We have news you're not going to like."

Dion stepped aside and invited us into the apartment with an impatient sweep of his arm. "What is it?" he asked the instant the front door was closed behind us.

Sam tipped her head to the side. "When did you last speak to Castor?"

"Castor?" Dion looked off to the side, his eyes narrowed in thought. "He stopped by my apartment a short time after you released him."

"You haven't seen or spoken to him since then?"

"No. Why?"

"It would appear that he's done a runner. But not before burning two prison guards alive."

"Prison guards?" Dion gave a fast shake of his head. "I don't understand."

So Sam told him the full story and *made* him understand.

Exhaling heavily, Dion walked over to the sofa and sank onto it. "I knew he was furious with the human, but I did not expect him to approach her again."

"Why furious?" asked Jared. "All she did was say no when he asked to feed from her. Which she's fully entitled to do."

Dion rubbed at his nape. "He feels that she looks down on him."

Sam snorted. "She probably does. I know I do. Why did he hone in on Lexi?"

"Castor doesn't have a high opinion of women in general," said Dion.

"That's not ground-breaking news," said Sam. "But there's something else. Something that made him particularly sensitive to her rejection. There has to be. Because he can't seem to let it go."

I agreed with Sam. There had to be more. And if Dion's expression was anything to go by, it was true, but he was clearly hesitant to discuss it. Sam, Jared, and I simply stared at him.

Dion sighed long and loud. "She looks so very much like our deceased Maker, it is uncanny. If you were to research Chanel, you would no doubt be shocked at how close the resemblance is."

Sam frowned. "And, what, he didn't like Chanel or something?"

"On the contrary, he adored her," replied Dion. "He thought her 'different' from the women in his past—all of whom had betrayed him in some sense. He wanted to Bind himself to her. She promised it would happen one day. Others could see she was toying with him, but Castor was blind to it. Until he caught her in bed with another man. It took a few more betrayals on her part before he left her. He found another woman. A good one. But, as Chanel did not like to share her toys, she had his woman killed. In short, Chanel ruined him. She ruined many vampires in such a way, so it was no surprise that one eventually turned on her. Castor mourned her even while he hated her."

"And when he looks at Lexi, he remembers a woman who put him through hell?" asked Sam.

"A woman who never saw his worth, who didn't see him as good enough to rule the nest alongside her, who—with the exception of the time she Turned him—never allowed him to feed from her."

Which might shed some light on the situation, but ... "It doesn't excuse that he's been treating Lexi like a piece of shit," I cut in. "He's essentially making her pay for what another woman did to him." I hissed out a breath. "I should have done worse than slap him around a little last night."

"Slap him around a little?" echoed Sam, her mouth curved, her voice ringing with disbelief. "From what I heard, you broke four of his ribs and dislocated his jaw."

I shrugged. "I didn't say they were light slaps."

Dion blinked at me. "You did what?"

Rather than answer his question, I fired one of my own at him. "Where would Castor go?"

Dion thought on it for long moments and then shrugged. "I am not sure where he will choose to lay low. I only know that you will find it difficult to locate him. He is most adept at hiding."

"But not as adept as our trackers are at hunting," Jared pointed out.

Dion sighed. "No, not that adept."

The Grand High Pair asked him a few more questions before we filed out of the apartment.

"I didn't want to say this in front of Dion," Jared began. "But Evan telepathed me a minute ago. He found evidence of a trail on the eastern side of the rainforest. The trail stops near a river that isn't far from the edge of a cliff. It seems likely that Castor swam across the river, jumped over the cliff, and hightailed it to the nearest island."

"Likely, yes," said Sam. "Even probable. But not for certain. And that bugs me." She bit the inside of her cheek. "We need to talk with Lexi."

Um, we did?

"She's probably at work," Sam mused. She turned to Jared. "Can you bring her to our office at the Command Centre?"

"Sure," replied Jared, who then teleported away.

Before I could ask Sam why she wanted to speak with Lexi, she was rushing off in a blur. Knowing where she was heading, I followed her to the Command Centre at vampire momentum. Fletcher usually sat outside the office, but his desk was currently empty. Sam didn't comment on it, so I guessed that his shift hadn't yet begun.

Following her into the office after she'd unlocked the door, I asked, "Why are you summoning Lexi?"

"I would have thought it was obvious. We have to warn her what's happening."

I felt my brows dip. "She probably already knows that Castor's gone. News travels fast on the island and …" I squinted as realisation dawned on me. "Wait, you think he might come for her, don't you?"

Sam gave me a grim look. "It's a possibility."

It hadn't occurred to me until then, but Sam was right. *Motherfucker.*

Just then, Jared appeared in the middle of the room with Lexi. Just looking at her made my chest tighten. I wanted to yank her to me, hold her tight, and kiss the breath from her lungs.

"Don't worry, you're not in the shit," Sam assured her, taking the seat behind her desk. "We just need to talk to you."

"Should I take it that you haven't found Castor yet?" asked Lexi. "Because you don't appear happy."

"A trail was found, but it ended near a river that's pretty close to a cliff-face," Sam told her. "It looks like Castor did one of two things. Either he crossed the river, went over the cliff, and then swam off. Or he used the river to help hide his tracks and is still on the island somewhere. The first scenario seems the likeliest, so we'll be sending trackers to find and retrieve him. But we need to be prepared for both possibilities. He'd be a fool to stick around but, well, Castor's kind of a fool. We'd like you to agree to a twenty-four/seven guard until we can confirm Castor is gone."

Lexi's brow creased. "You're expecting him to come after me if he's still here?"

"I don't expect him to. But I've noticed that he blames other people for his fuck-ups. It's sort of his thing. In his mind, you're probably the person who's responsible for the situation he's currently in. Also, it turns out that you look a lot like someone he has serious beef with, which could give him added reason to turn all his anger onto you. On the other hand, it might not. But I like to err on the side of caution, so I'd prefer that you have someone close by."

"I'll do it," I quickly declared, making Sam and Jared's head whip round to face me. I explained, "Lexi's my vessel. She's under my protection. I'll be the one who watches over her."

Sam's brows lifted slightly. "I see." She slid her gaze back to Lexi. "I'm assuming, then, that it's okay with you if Damien acts as your guard."

I went still inside, expecting Lexi to make it clear that she hadn't yet agreed to be my vessel and perhaps even call me a presumptuous bastard. She wouldn't be wrong.

"I'm fine with it," Lexi replied, making relief blow through me. "I'm not sure I'll truly need a guard, but I won't object to having one."

"Then it's done." Sam leaned back in her seat. "I'm going to suggest that you skip work tonight. Castor's nest will be all stirred up. They'll be worried that his actions will have them all banished from here. They might get the bright idea to talk to you and have you appeal to me and Jared to let them stay. I don't want any of them bothering you. So rather than have a bunch of people watching your back at the club, it would be better to simply take you out of the equation. You have an issue with that?"

Lexi shook her head. "Do you need me to let Maeve know?"

"Jared and I will do that. You head to your place with Damien, or even to his place—whichever. Once we've pinned down Castor, we'll let you know."

CHAPTER EIGHT

(Lexi)

Dumping my purse on the sofa, I puffed out a breath. "Well that took me off-guard. It never even occurred to me to wonder if Castor would stick around, let alone head my way."

Damien stalked toward me, his gaze intent on mine. "I won't let him get to you if he does."

"I believe you."

"Do you?"

"I wouldn't say it if I didn't."

"Good." He combed his fingers through my hair. "You hungry?"

"I could eat a quick snack. I was about to go on my break when Jared came for me."

Damien took my hand and led me into the kitchen. "Sit. I'll make you a sandwich."

I frowned. "You don't have to do that."

"You're my vessel, remember? That means I've got to make sure you're eating enough, or I can't feed from you. I've been careful not to take too much blood."

He *was* careful. He bit me often, but sometimes he did nothing more than take a quick lick and seal the wound. "I haven't said yes to being your vessel."

"Sure you have. You just didn't say it aloud."

I rolled my eyes, unable to truthfully claim that he was mistaken. "Whatever."

He gestured at the island. "Sit."

Perching myself on a stool, I watched as he pulled out ingredients and dishware. "Do you think Sam is right to worry that Castor could still be on the island?"

"I think she's right to cover all our bases. Plenty of unexpected things have happened during my time in the legion. I've seen things you wouldn't believe. I've known vampires to take unbelievably stupid risks just to get revenge or be spiteful. Humans seem to move on from things much faster, probably because they're always aware that any day can be their last. But immortal creatures? They don't have to worry about time passing them by. They don't have that subconscious sense of urgency to get things done, make their mark on the world, and make peace with those they've wronged or been wronged by. They don't have the 'life's too short' mentality."

"So they tend to cling to shit and hold grudges for long periods."

Nodding, Damien slathered butter on a slice of bread. "Think of small kids who have no awareness of their own mortality. It can make them fail to appreciate many things and get too emotionally wrapped up in matters that seem so minor or trivial. Vampires can sometimes be that way. Sure, we *can* die. But it's easy to forget that when you don't age or develop illnesses or in any other way physically deteriorate. Especially since we can heal from most injuries pretty quickly."

"I get it." I hadn't considered any of that before. It made me look at the current situation in a different light. "For me, Castor's behaviour is nothing short of petty. But I tend to blow trivial stuff off because it doesn't seem worth wasting my time on it. But if time isn't something you need to worry about wasting, I guess you could become someone who got too hung up on petty things—even if only for the drama factor out of sheer boredom." Watching as he slapped meat and condiments onto the bread, I added, "You're not like that."

"No. But I'm part of the legion, not someone like Castor who sits around all night never putting his ass in danger. When you take risks with your life often, you don't take your immortality for granted the way some vampires do."

My stomach curdled, and suddenly I didn't feel so peckish. There was indeed a lot of danger involved in being part of the legion. I'd heard of so many assignments. Heard of various injuries the members had suffered. Heard how some had even once been tainted by The Reaper's Call—something that could make a vampire ill and was highly contagious. The thought of Damien persistently being in danger … it just didn't sit well with me.

I snapped out of my thoughts at the sound of a plate sliding across the island. I blinked down at the sandwich now directly in front of me.

"What's wrong?" asked Damien.

"I just don't like that you take such risks, even though I know you do it for honourable reasons. I can admire it and also dislike it at the same time."

His face softened. "Eat, baby."

I lifted the sandwich and took a bite. "What did Sam mean when she said I look like someone who Castor has beef with?"

"We heard from Dion that their Maker was a woman who pretty much fucked Castor over—someone he'd initially believed was 'different' than those from his past. He's used to betrayal, apparently." Damien began giving me a brief rundown of Dion's story while pouring me a glass of orange juice. He placed the drink beside my plate. "It doesn't justify anything that Castor has done, obviously. But it does show why he seemed to take your rejection so personally. His emotions aren't really directed at you."

I bit into my sandwich again. "I can't really relate to what his Maker put him through, but it would be hard to believe someone is different from the others who've hurt you only to realise that, hey, you were wrong."

He gave a slow nod. "That shit is hard to swallow."

I tilted my head. "You sound like you know that from experience." When he didn't respond, I quickly assured him, "You don't have to tell me anything. I won't be offended." Especially since he'd already told me anecdotes from his past.

"It's not a secret. Just not terribly interesting."

"If you don't mind sharing it, I'd still like to hear it."

"All right." Still standing, he bent and braced his lower arms on the island. "My mother and stepfather were, in a word, snobs. Their friends were snobs, and the offspring of said friends were also snobs. I explained how my brother, Kaiden, was the golden boy, right?"

I swallowed my food before replying, "Yes."

"Well, it turns out that snobby girls often prefer the black sheep to the golden boy."

I felt my mouth quirk. "So you got plenty of pussy."

He returned my small smile. It was sheepish rather than arrogant, though. "To put it bluntly, yeah. But those girls were all the same—vapid, materialistic, out for what they could get. So when I met Bianca in a coffee shop, she was a breath of fresh air. Nice girl. Single mom. Worked two jobs to support her kid. She was motivated and independent and attentive."

Everything his own mother wasn't, I thought.

"Although she'd had a shitty start to life, she didn't hold my financially comfortable background against me. Some did that. Acted like I had no right to my own worries. Bianca didn't. Neither do you."

"Everyone has problems. Having money simply brings a different set of problems."

"You're right, it does. Anyway, back to Bianca ... I asked her to move in with me, but she hemmed and hawed. She didn't want to uproot her kid until she was sure that she and I were solid. I thought we were. Only we weren't. I learned that the day after Austin's funeral—he died of a heart attack. I went to see her, but she wouldn't let me in. She said we were over, and she asked me to leave. I was confused and hurt and pissed. I was also sick of arguing with her through the fucking front door, so I left. No matter how many times I tried talking to her after that, she stone-walled me."

"Really? That's shitty. And cowardly. She could have at least respected you enough to be straight with you."

"You'd think so, wouldn't you?" He sighed, shaking his head. "It made no sense to me at the time. None. But I respected her wishes and let her be."

"Did you eventually find out why she pulled that shit?"

"Oh yeah. The day I went to the reading of the will, I learned that Austin had left me nothing, but I'd expected that. I didn't care. Kaiden made a weird comment. Said Austin could have at least left me twenty grand. He then added, *'Bianca found it a pretty substantial amount.'* I froze, and my stomach dropped. When I asked what he'd done, he just smirked and said, *'Everyone has a price, big brother.'*"

I felt my jaw drop. "He paid her off? Son of a bitch."

"He told her I'd been disinherited and that she'd get no cash, but that he'd give her money in exchange for her cutting me out of her life."

"But … why do something so vindictive?"

"A couple of months before Austin's death, Kaiden caught his fiancée—a woman his father pretty much chose for him—coming onto me at a party when she was drunk. I don't think Kaiden loved her, but he was rightfully pissed at her. He was also pissed at me. I hadn't done a thing to lead her on, and I'd pushed her away when she tried kissing me—he knew all that. But his pride was hurt. It hit the low self-esteem that he likes to pretend he doesn't have."

"So the bastard struck out at you," I said, pushing aside my empty plate.

Damien nodded. "I beat the piss out of him. People heard about it and assumed I'd just been pissed that Austin left me nothing in his will. My dad knew different, but he gave Sam the false version when she contacted him."

"What? Why?"

"When I first joined the legion, I was a bit of a shit toward Sam. The entire squad was—at Jared's encouragement, I might add."

I smiled and took a swig of my juice. "Yeah, I heard about that. You were total dicks."

"We were. Sam wanted to give us all a metaphorical kick up the ass and bring us back down to Earth. So she found out something from each of our pasts to throw at us, to remind us what had given us our strengths in the first place. My dad didn't feel good about handing her info that could hurt me, so he told her the bullshit version instead, knowing it would slap me back down to reality just as effectively."

"Well, both Kaiden and Bianca need a few fucking bitch slaps."

Straightening, Damien came toward me. "It was years ago. I've long since passed caring." He looked at my plate. "You finished?"

I set down my glass. "Yup."

He took my hand and pulled me off the stool. "We done talking now?"

"I guess so."

"Good." He bit me. Sank his teeth into the crook of my neck. As always, it woke my body right up. Chemicals raced. My heart pounded. And I pretty much melted against him.

"Damien," I breathed. "Dammit, this should *not* count as foreplay." But I could feel myself growing damp. I pushed at his chest. "Maybe *I* want to be the one sucking on something this time."

He licked at the bite and met my gaze with a smile. "I'm not going to stop you."

So I went to my knees, fished his cock out of his jeans, and took him into my mouth.

He hissed out a breath. "Jesus, baby." It wasn't long before he exploded, his hand bunched in my hair, a curse on his lips. "Hmm, you deserve a reward for that."

Like I'd argue.

CHAPTER NINE

(Lexi)

Sitting in the club's breakroom the next evening as we ate our lunch, Maisy stared at me, her mouth open. "You agreed to be his vessel?" she asked.

I nodded, resisting the urge to squirm in my seat, suspecting she'd tell me what I didn't want to hear—that I'd messed up here. It wasn't like I'd undo what I'd done. I couldn't. If that made me a masochist, well, you learned something new about yourself every day, didn't you? Or night, as the case might be.

Her shoulders sagged, and she let out a tired groan. "You've learned nothing from the mistakes I've made, have you?"

"Maisy—"

"Really, did I not teach you anything at all?"

I flicked a hand her way. "*You're* the one who suggested I let him feed from me."

"I figured you'd do it once. Maybe twice. That it would just be some casual thing."

Personally, I didn't really see how anything that sensual could truly be entirely casual. But then, I probably wouldn't feel that way if it was any vampire other than Damien. Nothing I felt about or toward him was casual, but that was my little secret. I intended on keeping it to myself. Hopefully I'd done a good job of hiding it from the female squad members who'd been casually posing nosy questions at me all night as they tried to get a feel for where my head and heart was at.

Still my guard, Damien had come with me to the club and spent most of the evening just standing at the bar, watching my every move. But I'd seen him occasionally shake his head at the female squad, who all gave him bright, innocent smiles.

Maisy folded her arms. "You do understand that, as you're his vessel, he now has a claim on you, right?"

I felt my brow furrow. "It's more that he has a claim on my blood."

"True, but it might as well run deeper, because no one—man or woman—will make any sort of move on you while you're the property of a vampire. Yeah, I know 'property' sounds bad, but it's not meant in a disrespectful way. It doesn't mean you're considered a thing. It means you're valued, in vampire terms. My kind respects that sort of claim. So, basically, you're now considered off the market. Did he tell you that?"

"Well, no. But I wouldn't have dated someone else while being Damien's vessel anyway." Hell, I couldn't even *see* other men. It was like he'd swallowed up all my mental space. He was all I saw. All I wanted. All I couldn't permanently keep.

She tensed at my words. "Please don't tell me that you two are also still sleeping together."

Once more, I found myself fighting the need to squirm. "Well …"

She groaned again. "*Lexi.*"

"I don't know why you're making a big deal out of this." *Lie.* "Plenty of humans agree to be vessels."

"It would be no biggie if you didn't care about Damien—no, don't even deny that you do, Lexi, I see it in the way you look at him."

My pulse jumped. That didn't sound good. "*How* do I look at him?"

"Like he's yours," she said softly. "Having a fling with him wouldn't necessarily be a big deal if you weren't attached to him. But he means something to you."

Well it seemed that my feelings weren't so secret after all, dammit. I just hoped he hadn't sensed the truth for himself. No, he'd have backed right off if he had.

Sighing, I slumped in my seat. "I don't *want* to care about him." But how could I not? He was just so … so *Damien*. It wasn't about his individual qualities at all, it was about him as a person—the entire package. He was everything I'd want in a guy. Everything I'd never before had.

For me, trust was more important than love. I didn't find it easy to trust people, though. I wasn't sure I ever really had. And I didn't particularly like taking chances on people, because it rarely paid off in my experience. But Damien … I trusted him completely.

He was nothing like the assholes my mom used to date—deadbeats who thought 'strength' meant slapping around people who were weaker than them. He was nothing like any of my own exes, who'd had no real staying power and always put themselves first. Damien would never touch a woman in anger, never be cruel to a person he was supposed to care for, never neglect the people who mattered to him, never be anything but reliable and loyal and caring.

Her face softening, Maisy leaned forward and braced her elbows on the table. "If it makes you feel better, I think he has feelings for you, too. That's why I'm not feeling good about your agreeing to be his vessel rather than keeping distance between you and him. Essentially, you're playing with fire. But I think you know that." She shrugged. "I don't see a happy ending for you two unless you're prepared to Turn, sweetie. If it's something you would consider, fine. But don't repeat my mistake. Don't Turn for him. It's got to be something you'd want for you."

She was right. Unless I knew I could happily live as a vampire *alone*, I couldn't make that leap for someone else. I had to do this for me, or not at all.

I bit my lip. "Do you regret Turning?"

"These days? Not so much. Because I recently made the official decision to make the most of my new situation rather than whine about it. But I want to stay angry at Compton, and it's hard to do that when I have times where I think I could be happy."

"You can still be mad at him even while you're happy. You don't owe him for any happiness you feel. In fact, to move on and still find contentment despite what he did ... that's probably the best form of revenge, isn't it?"

Her brows inched up. "I guess so. He doesn't like that I'm officially dating Harvey. It's not jealousy. It's as if Compton just can't deal with one of his exes being with someone who's so much better than him."

"Harvey *is* so much better than him. More, he's way cuter."

She grinned. "That I can wholeheartedly agree—" Her eyes went wide. "Lexi!"

I'd barely had the chance to register that someone was behind me when an arm hooked itself around my neck ... and then my surroundings changed in a flash.

(Damien)

No other trails have been discovered around The Hollow, Jared told me, *but Sebastian hasn't found any sign of Castor either. He hasn't yet searched all the nearest islands, though.*

Leaning against the bar while I waited for Lexi to finish her break, I tapped my fingers on the scarred wooden surface. *Is it possible that Castor simply just drowned while trying to swim to safety?* I asked Jared. *It's not like we'd spot his ashes, is it?*

There was a beat of silence. *Maybe. But Sam will be disappointed if that's the case, because she's looking forward to maiming his ass.*

Think she'll let me watch?

A snicker. *Probably, if you ask nicely and promise not to interfere. How's Lexi?*

Okay. She'll be a lot better when Castor is found. She doesn't think he'll come for her, but she wants him out of the picture all the same.

We all do. Jared paused. *Gotta go. We'll keep you in the loop. You just concentrate on Lexi.*

Like I could do anything else. And not only because there was a potential danger out there to her. The woman had been on my mind since I first laid eyes on her.

The news that I'd claimed her as my vessel must have circulated quickly, because no males ogled or flirted with her. Vampires respected such claims. It was a language they understood. Only a goddamn fool would ignore it.

Knowing Lexi would have at least five more minutes before her break was over, I crossed to the table where the female squad sat. Flicking up my brow, I skimmed my gaze over each of them. "Is there a reason you've been pulling Lexi into conversation after conversation rather than letting her work? No, don't tell me you were just being social."

Sheepish, Imani raised her shoulders. "We wanted to meet your vessel." The others nodded.

"Now that you have, maybe you can all give her some space," I suggested.

Paige swirled her bottle, her eyes lit with humour. "Are you worried we'll scare her off?"

"There's eight of you," I said. "As a group, you can be a little overwhelming. Plus, you're all nosy as hell. I don't doubt that you tried quizzing her."

"We did try," Cassie admitted, "but she's ace at dodging questions or answering without *really* answering—it's a skill I lack and admire."

"I swear, Damien, our intention wasn't to put Lexi through a gauntlet or anything," Ava assured me. "We were just curious about this woman who has you all tied up in knots. Ooh, you're not even stuttering denials. I thought you'd try to play the whole thing down." Grinning, she gave a little clap. "This is awesome."

I frowned. "Is it?"

Ava gave me a *duh* look. "Well of course. You're one of our boys. We want you happy."

"Lexi's human, so I shouldn't have to point out that nothing serious can come of this," I said, my voice edged with impatience, my stomach twisting painfully.

"You're not walking away, though," said Jude.

"Because she's my vessel."

Maya snorted. "You claimed her as your vessel because you feel it's the only claim you can have over her. Also, it keeps other guys away from her. That suits you fine."

I shrugged. "Yeah, so?"

Keeley gave me a faint smile. "At least you're not denying it."

"This doesn't have to be as complicated as you're making it in your head," Cassie said to me. "Yes, Lexi's human. But we were all human once. We didn't stay that way. Who's to say she has to either?"

"I'm not going to ask her to Turn for me." The temptation was there, but I wasn't selfish enough to act on it.

Maya tilted her head. "You wouldn't want that?"

Of course I fucking would, but ... "Only if she felt that this life was right for her, with or without me. If something happened to me on an assignment, she *would* have to go on without me." And that could very well put her off.

Ava pursed her lips. "Well maybe you could try giving her reasons to *feel* that this life would work for her. Tell her more about vampirism. Use your gift to have some fun with her. Show her the positives of our way of life."

Imani nodded. "Instead of holding back and bracing yourself to lose her, give her your all. Reel her in. Make it so that she can't imagine not having you right there with her every night. I don't think that'll be hard. It's obvious by the way she talks about you that she's *totally* into you. More, I think she—"

"Damien!" Maisy grabbed my arm, having dashed to me in vampiric speed. "He took her," she burst out, her eyes flashing with fear. "Castor. He took her."

My heart literally fucking stopped, and every muscle in my body seemed to tighten. "What?"

"One of his nest, Colm, teleported him into the break room," said Maisy, her words tumbling out of her in a hurry. "They were there and gone too fast for me to do anything."

Heat rushed to my head as fury and dread pounded in my blood. I clenched my fists, needing to punch something. "*Fuck*." I would have rushed off—though where, I didn't know—if Paige hadn't come to me and laid a hand on my shoulder.

"Stay calm, Damien," said Paige, all business. "Lexi needs you to keep a clear head. You've drank from her plenty of times recently, you can find her."

And I had every intention of doing so. But the tug in my own blood that told me what direction she'd gone in was a very weak sensation, which meant she wasn't close by.

I was about to leave, having no thought in my head other than to search for Lexi, when Sam and Jared materialised beside me—both looking ready to shit fury on someone's ass.

"Ava gave me a heads-up," Jared explained. "We can find Lexi, Damien. I'll help you. Just tell me what direction she's in, and we'll take it from there. If that means teleporting from spot to spot until the tug you're feeling in your blood gets stronger, then we do it. Now, point me in a direction that will take us to her."

I drew in a breath. "North," I ground out.

Jared nodded. "Then we go North."

(Lexi)

I was released with a shove and almost tripped over a fallen tree. Wings fluttered rapidly as a bird shrieked in what seemed like surprise at our abrupt arrival. It disappeared into the canopy of one of the many, *many* trees.

I whirled around and found myself facing both Castor and Colm. Well no wonder Castor wasn't leaving trails all over the place. He had his very own personal teleporter. And they'd brought me to the fucking rainforest.

"Oh, feel free to run," Castor invited, his smile all teeth. "It will be most fun to hunt you."

Like I'd give him the satisfaction. If he'd been human, I'd have taken my chances. But it would be pointless to flee from one vampire, let alone two. I'd never outrun them. Just as I'd never overpower them. Calling out for help … well, that might do some good, considering there were people out here searching for signs of Castor.

"No one is around," said Castor. "This area has been searched. The hunting parties have moved on. And even if someone did come into view, Colm would teleport the three of us out of here so we can continue this in private. But scream if you'd like." His smile widened. "I do enjoy hearing a woman cry out in terror."

Colm chuckled, a cruel glint in his eyes.

Panic beat in my chest and made my stomach bottom out. Castor might not scare me, but the thought of breathing my last breath sure did. Dammit, I was *not* going to die here. No way. I would not lose my life to these two fucking assholes. I also wasn't going to let them see just how much I was pissing my pants right now. They'd no doubt get off on it.

Adrenaline pumped through me, readying me to … what? What could I do other than try to distract Castor from making my death a quick one?

Silently cursing, I made an effort to keep my breathing steady, digging deep for a calm that sadly eluded me. Someone would find me, right? Maisy would have told Damien that I'd been taken. He would have contacted Sam and Jared. They'd do their best to locate me, and they had plenty of people to help them with that. I just had to stay alive until they got here.

I folded my arms so that Castor wouldn't see how badly my hands were shaking. "What's your plan? To leave me here? To kill me? Or something else that's equally stupid?" I gave myself a mental pat on the back for managing to keep my voice steady.

"What makes you think it would be stupid to end your life?" asked Castor.

"Sam and Jared wouldn't exactly condone it, would they?"

"I suppose not, but they do not concern me," he said with a dismissive wave of his hand. "They may be experts at torture, but Colm and I will be gone from here very soon. The Grand High Pair will never find us." He genuinely seemed to believe that.

"They have trackers," I reminded him. "One in particular is good at what he does."

"Ah, Sebastian, yes. I don't doubt that he will search for me. But when that search comes to nothing, he will eventually give up and turn to tracking the other many vampires who are on Sam and Jared's hit list—many of whom have committed terrible crimes. Locating a vampire who killed one measly human will not be their priority."

"Maybe not." *Probably* not, actually. "But they also can't be seen to let such things slide—it would encourage others to pick off humans. It would also be seen as weakness on Sam and Jared's part if they fail to enforce their laws. The Grand High Pair can't afford to be weak, so don't be so sure they'll one day stop hunting you. Or your friend there."

Colm gave me a look that was *all* arrogance. "It is difficult to capture a teleporter."

"But not impossible," I said. "Hoyt subdued one the first time I saw him. And I would imagine he's subdued many other teleporters before that."

Colm's eyes flickered.

"We appreciate the warning," Castor said to me, his voice dry, "but we're prepared to take our chances."

"I see that. Or you wouldn't have taken me from the club. What I don't get is why you brought me *here*. You could have taken me anywhere in the world. Why here?" Why to a place where he'd have a better chance of being caught?

Castor lifted his chin. "To show the world that the Grand High Pair are not fit to hold their positions. If a man such as me—not a master vampire, not one with a terribly impressive ability—can end the life of one of their pets in their own backyard and then escape, my kind will realise that the pair are not strong enough to lead and protect. There will be an uprising. Someone more suited to being in power will take their place, and then things will go back to the way they were. The new laws will be gone. The old ones will return."

"Or you'll just get caught, and this will all have been a waste of time."

"I see you are banking on your disappearance leading to a search and rescue mission." He pursed his lips. "Perhaps it will. Damien *does* seem to be protective of you."

Hearing his name made my heart squeeze. If I did die here, he'd never know how much I cared for him. Why had it only minutes ago seemed so important that he didn't find out? And why had I only now realised that I didn't merely care for him, I loved the big bastard? Okay, so maybe I *had* known it before now, I just hadn't been comfortable admitting it to myself.

"Of course he is," I said, straining to keep my voice cool and even. "I'm his vessel. I'm under his protection. Another reason why killing me wouldn't be the greatest idea."

Castor gave me a pitying sigh. "My dear Lexi … how naïve you are. You give Damien too much credit. Oh, he would probably wish to avenge you if you were killed. But it is not because he *feels* anything for you. You are no more than a toy. One he appears to like playing with very much, but still just a toy."

Colm nodded with another of those callous smirks. I was *seriously* starting to despise this dude.

"There would likely be outrage if you were murdered, but it would not last," Castor went on. "You would quickly be forgotten. Humans pass on each and every day. They hold no real significance to us. In other words, you have left no mark on Damien, despite what you might think. His grief, however deep it might be, would be short-lived. We will not have to test that theory, however, as I do not intend to kill you."

I fought a frown. He'd earlier said something about ending my life in the backyard of the Grand High Pair, yet now he was declaring it wasn't his intention to kill me? The vamp was making no sense. But I didn't point that out, because if his plan to obliterate me had suddenly changed, that could only be a positive thing.

"If you don't want to kill me, what *do* you want?" I asked.

"Is it not obvious?" Castor was directly in front of me in the blink of an eye, his face hard as stone, his eyes two pools of scorn. "I intend to give you what you deserve before Colm and I disappear from this godforsaken place. You will pay in blood for the hours of pain I endured because of you."

"Because of me?" I echoed. "We're really back to that again? Do you always blame others for your fuck-ups, or am I just special that way? Come on, you can't possibly have thought that you could flout the rules and not face the consequences."

"*Ridiculous* rules," he muttered. "If I had thought they would be enforced, I wouldn't have bothered to even *apply* to reside at The Hollow. Sam and Jared are incredibly stupid if they think vampirekind as a whole will ever see humans as anything other than what they are—food." He roughly tangled his hands in my hair. "Let's get this done, shall we?"

My heart slammed against my ribs. "Punishing me won't punish Chanel," I blurted out.

He went so unnaturally still it was eerie. "Where did you hear that name?"

"Dion was in a chatty mood." I licked my lips. "It must be a bitch that you can't get closure, considering she's dead and all. But I'm not her." *Fuck, Damien, where are you?*

"You are so very like her, though. Isn't she, Colm?"

"*Too* like her," said Colm.

Castor licked the edge of his incisor as he stared at me. "I remember the first time I saw you. You smiled at me, but it was not real, just as her smiles never were. Again and again I approached you at the club. You were polite enough, but it was clear that you didn't consider me worthy of your time. She was much the same. People were expected to wait on her. No one was considered her equal. I should have snapped her pretty little neck, but I didn't. A woman much more precious than you or her could ever be died because of that. Chanel had her murdered."

Seeing all the emotions swirling in his eyes, I asked, "Who do you hate more? Chanel for killing that woman? Or yourself for still loving Chanel in spite of it?"

His nostrils flaring, his grip on my hair tightened until my scalp stung like a mother. "I am done talking about her. She no longer matters."

I shoved him hard, but he didn't budge an inch. It was like trying to push a damn wall. "Let go of me."

"No, that is not part of my plan."

Dread filling every part of me, I fought him hard, punching and kicking. The bastard only laughed, never once loosening his hold on my hair. Growling, I struggled harder, desperate to be free, and scratched at his face. He hissed long and loud—

My head whipped to the side as a hand came down hard on my cheekbone, shattering it. Pain rippled through my face, making it feel as though my eye had exploded. A little dazed, I blinked and swayed, a horrid ringing sound filling my ears.

Castor put his face closer to mine. "I told you I mean to end your life here. That is true. Your human life will soon be over. But you will then begin another life." He smirked. "You think you're too good for vampires? Let's see if your view changes after I've made you one."

CHAPTER TEN

(Damien)

I stilled as Jared teleported a large group of us to yet another part of the rainforest. Concentrating on the tug in my blood, I realised it was no longer pulling me in the same direction as it had before. "We've gone too far North this time," I told him. "Go back, but not too much."

Jared nodded and relocated us again.

Frustration beating at me, I shook my head. "We need to go back a little more."

It took two more tries before, finally, the *pull* I felt toward her was so fucking intense I knew Lexi was nearby. My pulse leapt. "Yes, here. She's close." Following that pull, I'd taken only a few steps forward when an almighty scream split the air. My heart stuttered. *Fuck.* I left my physical body, able to move faster in my astral form, and rocketed toward the sound of her cries … just in time to watch Castor toss her to the ground.

I skidded to a halt as shock slammed into me. She was convulsing violently, her back arched, cries of sheer agony erupting from her throat. Blood stained her tee, dripped from a bite wound on her throat, and was slathered around her lips. The bottom dropped out of my stomach. *Fuck, fuck, fuck.*

"Ah, Damien," said Castor. "How lovely of you to join us."

I didn't look at him. Going to her side, I dropped to my knees. "Lex." She didn't respond. Didn't even seem to hear or see me, lost in a sea of excruciating pain—the kind that was part and parcel of a vampiric conversion. He'd drained her to the point of near death and then force-fed her his own blood.

Anger roaring through me hot and fast, I snapped my head up to snarl at Castor. "You fucking bastard."

"It would not be a good idea to kill me," he said, lifting a hand to ward me off. "My blood-link with Lexi is already in place. If I die, it will break. She is too weak to survive that."

He wasn't wrong. She'd need the link to get her through the transformation. Plus, in this state, she'd never survive the torment of it breaking anyway. Fisting my hands, I spat out a curse.

He sniggered when I made no move toward him. "Right decision, Damien." He flicked a look at Colm. "Get us out of here before the others arrive. Sam and Jared will surely be close." But Colm didn't teleport them anywhere. Castor glared at him. "What are you waiting for? Get us away from here."

"I-I can't," Colm said through clenched teeth, his body unnaturally still.

Castor's brows snapped together. "What?"

Colm ground his teeth. "I c-can barely m-move."

There was a rustle of branches and then … "That's thanks to Cassie's grip on your mind," Sam said as she, Jared, and the female squad members stepped out of the trees.

Castor froze, his eyes darting from person to person, searching for a weakness in the circle they'd formed around him, Colm, Lexi and me.

"Don't do it, Castor," said Sam, the mercury glint to her eyes glowing. "I can see you're ready to flee, but just don't. I'm really not in the bloody mood to chase you."

I looked down at Lexi, my gut twisting as she convulsed yet again, her eyes unfocused and unseeing. I'd never felt so fucking helpless. So fucking useless. I glanced up at Paige. "Can you do something?"

Her face a mask of anguish, Paige slowly shook her head. "Even if I could take the bite and transfer it to someone else, I can't take his blood from her system," she said, an apology in her voice. "She's already changing. I'm sorry, Damien."

"There's nothing anyone can do," Castor proudly declared. "What is done is done."

I was *so* gonna obliterate that fucker. Not any time soon, though. He needed to suffer some first. And he would. We'd all make sure of it. But that brought me no satisfaction or comfort. How could it, when Lexi's cries of pain echoed through the rainforest? I swallowed around the lump in my throat, brushing her hair away from her face.

Sam tilted her head, studying Castor intently. "You know the penalty for taking someone's human life against their will. And yet, you took the risk of doing this here, where there was a better chance of someone tracking you. That's not making sense to me." A few moments later, a realisation appeared to dawn on her. "Oh, I get it. You thought you could do this right under our noses and then flee, right? You thought it would make me and Jared look weak."

Jared sighed, giving Castor a look of mock sympathy. "That's where people like you always fuck yourselves over. You care so much about avenging slights that it often overrides your sense of self-preservation."

Motherfucking *done* here, I scooped up a trembling Lexi and stood. "I want to get her out of here. And I want *him* to pay for this in ways he would never have seen coming."

"You cannot kill me," Castor insisted.

"Not right at this moment, no," agreed Sam. "But that's fine. I don't wish to kill you anyway. I have *way* bigger plans than that, and they all involve making you scream like a fucking banshee. Will that work for you, Damien?"

"It's a start," I replied.

Jared looked at Colm. "You'll be a guest of our fine accommodations as well."

The vampire's eyes flickered. "I just t-teleported—"

"There's no 'just' in the part you played," Jared told him, his red irises flaring.

Castor's breathing began to pick up. "If you hurt me, Lexi will feel my pain. You would put her through that?"

"Lexi won't feel a thing," said Jared. "Imani will sever the blood-link before we touch you. Of course, that won't be until after the conversion is complete. You're going to spend the rest of whatever years we allow you to live in a cell."

Castor suddenly charged at him in vampire speed, a battle cry on his lips. A cry that ended abruptly when Jared swept out his arm and wacked Castor, sending the asshole careening into a tree.

Sam snickered at him, conjuring her energy whip. "You think you can provoke us into killing you?" She shook her head sadly. "Oh Castor, Castor, Castor." She lashed out her whip, and it wrapped tight around his throat. She smiled. "We're going to have *so* much fun with you."

Hours later, I sat in the chair beside the bed on which a very pale Lexi lay, my elbows braced on my thighs. The convulsions had eased, and her cries had faded, but only because I'd had Chico use his poisonous thorns to make her unconscious so that she'd have a fucking break from the pain. That break wouldn't last long, though. She'd fed from me several times already, but she'd need more blood soon. That need would snap her awake.

Cursing beneath my breath, I swiped a hand down my face. The conversion generally took three days, though it could sometimes take four or five. I couldn't keep her unconscious throughout the entire conversion, because she needed to feed on blood to get through it. She needed to be awake for that part. Giving her blood through a drip wouldn't work, and the bloodlust was powerful enough to drag her out of unconsciousness anyway.

The transformation was rough as fuck. I didn't have vivid memories of my own, but I did remember the pain—there was nothing like it. Every part of you hurt from your teeth to your veins. Every breath seemed to burn your lungs. Every inch of your skin felt raw and hypersensitive, so that even the feel of the air dancing over your nerve-endings hurt like a mother.

There was no way to get comfortable, but still you slept every now and then ... as if your brain knocked you clean out to give you whatever brief escapes it could. You'd never otherwise psychologically survive the all-consuming agony. You'd just check out. Disconnect from what was happening. Disappear into a corner of your mind to hide. Yeah, it was that bad.

Right from the very beginning, the need to feed was always there. Always. It made your stomach burn and cramp and pang. And when the bloodlust kicked in, it reduced you to your animal instincts.

I didn't remember much about those times when I was somewhat feral and plagued by the drive to hunt. But I did remember when the need for sex crept in. Remembered the insanely intense arousal that never seemed to ease off, no matter how often I came. The sexual cravings didn't replace the bloodlust, they enhanced it. And through it all, the pain was ever present. Not quite as crippling by that point, but there all the same.

Another tremor wracked Lexi's body, and I winced. Fuck, I hated seeing her this way. If she'd chosen to Turn, it would have been one thing. I still would have detested seeing her in pain, but knowing she'd consented to endure it would have made a difference. But this ... she hadn't asked for this. The change had been thrust upon her. And even as I longed for it to be over, I dreaded finding out if she'd resent what she was.

I sensed more than saw Jared teleport into the bedroom. The apartment wasn't mine or Lexi's. It was one of several that were allocated to newborns. More like a spacious hotel suite, it had windows built to withstand vampiric strength so that there was no chance of a newborn breaking the glass and escaping while overcome by bloodlust. They could do a fair amount of damage when on a rampage, so it was important that they be contained. But no one wanted to put them in a cell, so this was the next best thing.

When moments of silence went by, I spared Jared a sideways glance. "If you're here to tell me to get my ass to training, don't bother. I'm not leaving Lexi's side."

"I'm not going to ask you to," he said. "Fuck knows I wouldn't have left Sam if the situation were reversed."

My shoulders lost some of their tension.

"Besides, you're actually an ideal person to be with Lexi throughout the conversion. Whenever she's feral from bloodlust, you can be with her in your astral form, keeping your physical body safe from attack. Plus, she knows and trusts you. Right now, she needs someone she trusts, so it's better that she'll see you here during those lucid periods."

"She shouldn't trust me," I said, shame curdling in my stomach. "I swore I'd protect her from Castor. Fuck, I never considered that he had someone teleporting him around. I should have."

"None of us thought he had help. Sure, we knew Colm could teleport. But he was good at seeming like a quiet little mouse who was content with trailing after Dion. I wouldn't have guessed he'd be so ballsy or so stupid as to support a man who had a target on his back. So, either we all failed Lexi, or the blame for her Turning belongs to Castor. I'm going with the latter."

"I know it's his fault that she's Turning, but I still let her down. I told her I wouldn't let him get to her. She believed me. Believed I'd keep her safe."

"But she had to also know that, despite how much you meant what you said, there was no way you could guarantee that he wouldn't reach her. Come on, Damien, Lexi is a logical woman. If she's angry with anyone once she's fully converted and thinking straight, I really can't see it being *you*."

I wanted him to be right. I really did. "Know what guts me?" I asked, my voice cracking. "I once told her I could find her anywhere because I'd taken her blood. While she stood in that rainforest with Castor, she would have banked on me finding her. She would have been waiting for me to show up and save her. But I didn't get to her fast enough."

Jared moved to stand in front of me and cocked his head. "What about me? Do you blame me for not getting you to her before he could Turn her?"

I frowned. "No. You worked hard and fast to find her, but we had a fuck of a lot of ground to cover—"

"Exactly. If I don't hold any blame, how can you?"

I snapped my mouth shut. She let out another whimper, and my heart squeezed. "The fucker had nothing to gain by doing this to her. Why do it?"

"Because he could, Damien. Sometimes, that's the only motivation a person needs. The belief that they're entitled to do whatever they want."

He was right. I'd seen that sort of behaviour over and over in Austin and Kaiden, hadn't I? Such people often destroyed many lives because they never thought of anyone but themselves. They were just so eager to strike out at everyone and avenge every bruise to their ego. They never thought beyond the gratification they'd get from their actions. Like tantrum-throwing toddlers.

"You're not responsible for any of this, and I don't believe Lexi will hold you responsible. I'm not saying she'll be thrilled. There's a good chance she'll resent that the choice was taken from her and that she was Turned by someone out of sheer spite—I know how that feels. But I only ever blamed that on my Maker. Lexi won't blame *you*."

Maybe not, but there was a possibility she'd be so utterly pissed that she just couldn't stand to be on the island any longer. Many newborns who'd been Turned against their will headed off alone, feeling lost and adrift. "She might ask to leave The Hollow once she's fully in control of her gift and her bloodlust."

Jared pursed his lips. "She might. And we can't force her to stay. But don't be so quick to assume she'll be casting blame and packing up her shit. Give her a little more credit, Damien. Like I said before, she's a logical person. I don't think you should be so sure you'll lose her."

"I never really had her."

"Because she was human, and that was an obstacle. That obstacle isn't there anymore."

The selfish part of me was glad of it, wondered what it could mean for me. God, I was such a fucking asshole. And although Jared could be right in claiming I might be worrying for nothing ... "I refuse to get my hopes up."

"It would hit you hard if those hopes came to nothing, I get it. But don't lose *all* hope, that's all I'm saying." He glanced back at Lexi, who whimpered as yet another tremor assailed her body. "I'll bring a donor here once a day. I know you might not like the idea of her feeding from others, but you'll have to deal with it. Your blood alone won't get her through this."

I gave a curt, begrudging nod, knowing he was right.

"Contact me if you need anything," he added. "We're all here for you as well as for Lexi."

Feeling my throat thicken, I nodded again. "Do one thing for me."

"What's that?"

"Don't let Sam get carried away and kill Castor. I want at him too." More to the point, I wanted to feed the fucker every single one of his own teeth. Then maybe his tongue. Possibly even his own dick.

Jared's mouth curved. "Consider it done. But you don't need to worry. She wouldn't rob you of that pleasure anyway."

CHAPTER ELEVEN

(Lexi)

Good God, I felt. Like. Absolute *shit*.
Like I had the flu, a hangover, and a migraine all at once. My eyes hurt, my lips were dry, my throat felt shredded, and my head felt like a lead weight. Awesome.

I didn't need to open my eyes to know that I wasn't alone. I could smell Damien. Hear every breath that left his lungs. Hear his heart beating steady in his chest. The sound made my stomach clench and my mouth water. Um ... okay.

I felt ... different. Weird. Alien, even.

Smells were stronger. Sounds were sharper. And I knew if I opened my eyes, colours would be more vivid.

There was a subtle, background pulse in my body and brain. A need for something that was currently satisfied. A need for blood.

Memories flashed through my mind, hazy and fractured. Castor. The rainforest. His teeth in my throat. His blood in my mouth. Pain. God, there'd been *so much pain* I'd thought I was dying. I'd *wanted* to die. Wanted it to all end—the agony, the need for sex, the thirst for blood, the urge to hunt. It all had ended, apparently.

And now I was a vampire. Yeah, it didn't take detective work to figure that out.

There was a rustle of material. Footfalls came my way. The mattress dipped slightly, and then Damien's scent blanketed me.

"Hey, baby," he said, his voice low and soft. "Brace yourself before you open your eyes. It might hurt."

"Feels like someone stabbed them with needles." The words were hoarse.

"It might be that you'd have preferred that over what really happened. I wouldn't blame you."

Oh, he was right to think I was pissed. I'd like to beat Castor to death with his own fucking leg for forcibly Turning me. He'd made sure it *hurt* when he bit into my throat, he'd made sure I was afraid and he'd damn well gotten off on it. In so ruthlessly ending my human existence, he'd robbed me of the right to choose this life.

But would I have preferred death? No. Having lived at The Hollow for so many months, I'd come to realise that, essentially, vampirism was just another state of being. It wasn't a form of afterlife. I hadn't lost my soul, I still had a pulse, I could still eat food, I wouldn't have to sleep in a coffin, and I wouldn't burn in the sunlight.

In other words, I was still *me*. I wasn't a monster. I wasn't a thing of nightmares. I was just a new and improved—and somewhat immortal—version of me. Not that all this wasn't scary or that I'd shake off my anger at Castor any time soon. But I wasn't going to hate myself or my existence the way he'd hoped. Really and truly speaking, there were worse fates.

I forced my heavy eyelids open. Light stabbed my eyes like white-hot pokers. I hissed out a breath and squeezed my eyes shut. Fuck, he hadn't been kidding when he said it'd hurt.

His hand rubbed my back. "Shh, keep them closed a little while longer if you need to." He pressed a soft kiss to both my eyelids, but there was a hesitance in the way he touched me. As if he wasn't sure his touch would be welcome. Maybe he thought my skin still hurt to the touch. Well, I hadn't exactly moved toward him, had I?

"I'd snuggle into you, but I feel like I'll vomit if I so much as lift my head," I said.

He went very still. "Snuggle?"

"I realise you're a macho man and may like to believe you don't snuggle, but you totally do when you're asleep. How long before the nausea and head pain passes?"

"A few minutes. Maybe longer."

I blinked a few times, letting my eyes slowly adjust to the light, and then fully opened them. I focused on his face, taking in the lines of strain. "Hey."

He rubbed my back again. "Hey."

I licked my dry lips. "I'm guessing Castor's dead." Because I couldn't feel the blood-link that Maisy had talked so much about.

"Not yet."

I frowned. "I don't feel connected to him."

"You're not. Imani severed the blood-link while you were out cold."

I felt my brows inch up. "Oh." Well that was definitely good. I glanced around, taking in my surroundings.

"You're in one of the small apartments they keep for newborns."

I'd suspected as much. Maisy had mentioned how she'd lived in one for a short while. She'd told me a lot about her early nights. She'd also told me about her conversion, but nothing could have prepared me for how intense it had been. Not just the pain, but the bloodlust and the maddening arousal.

Hazy though my memories were, I could recall hearing his voice so many times. I hadn't always known who he was, but I'd recognised his voice. I remembered feeding from him, remembered having him inside me over and over. Others had come and offered their blood, but never had he left me alone.

"You stayed with me," I said.

"Of course I fucking stayed with you. I'm …" Damien trailed off with a soft curse. "Jesus, Lex."

I frowned at the guilt that rippled across his features. "Don't you dare apologise. None of this is on you."

"I swore I wouldn't let him get to you."

"Oh well if you swore it …" Snorting, I shook my head. Pain lanced through my skull, and I winced. "Shit, shouldn't have moved."

He glided his fingers over my scalp, gently kneading and stroking. "Has the nausea passed yet?"

Not daring to nod for fear it would bring on another surge of pain, I replied, "Yes."

He grunted in what could have been satisfaction.

"You can't control other people's actions, Damien."

"You're giving me assurances when it should be the other way around." He cursed again. "There's nothing I can say that will make this easier on you."

I felt my brow furrow. "Do I look like I'm on the verge of a breakdown or something?"

"No. But I am waiting for you to go ape shit."

"Not my style."

Seconds ticked by as he stared at me. "Baby, just in case you haven't processed it yet, you're a fully-fledged vampire now."

"I know." It was quite a doozy.

"There's no reversing the transformation."

"Yep, I've heard that."

"Your life is now going to be *seriously* different. New laws, new strengths, new weaknesses, new *diet*."

"I have considered all that." I'd always thought the latter would bother me most, but the thought of drinking blood no longer made me queasy. It was too much a part of what I now was.

Frowning, he gave his head a little shake. "Why aren't you raging? Your human life was taken from you against your will."

"And I'm seriously pissed about that. Don't think I'm not. If I was going to Turn, it should have been my choice. It *might* have one day been my choice."

The line between his brows slipped away. "You considered Turning?"

"I thought about it."

"And?"

"And I wasn't opposed to it. I just wanted more time to think on it and be sure it was right for me. I'm not happy that I was robbed of that time, but I'm not devastated either. It is what it is."

"It is what it is," he repeated tonelessly, disbelief plain on his face.

"Yes, it ... Why are you burying your face in your hands?"

"This is just not how I expected this conversation to go."

"You thought I'd cry, rant, rage, maybe even attack you?"

He dropped his hands. "Pretty much, yeah. Don't get me wrong, I'm glad you're taking this so well, I'm glad you're not utterly devastated. I'm relieved you're not declaring that you hate what you are and wish to be killed—yeah, some newborns have done that."

"I'm not going to be one of them."

"I see that. And I'd like to believe you're truly processing it well as opposed to just being in shock, but—"

"I'm not in shock, and I'm not going to fall apart." And I would never let my anger at Castor make me hate what I was ... because that would have given him what he wanted. Plus, like I'd told Maisy when she'd mentioned wanting to cling to the anger she felt toward Compton, finding happiness was often the best form of revenge.

"So what now?" I asked. "I can't have full freedom yet, can I?"

"You need more time to get control of your bloodlust. Right now, you probably feel calm, but that can change in a split second."

"Everything inside me does feel sort of ... not quite unstable, but restless. Edgy." Like my mental state could alter at any moment.

"That will fade over the next few months, and then it'll be gone completely. You'll live here until then. It's not a prison. You can come and go whenever you please, just never alone."

"I'm good with that." I didn't exactly like the thought of being cooped up here or anywhere else, but ... "I don't want to accidentally hurt anyone." I'd heard stories where vampires had had to Turn humans purely because a newborn had drank so much of their blood that the only way to save them from death was to put them through the conversion.

"Ordinarily, your Sire would be at your side throughout however long it takes for you to gain control of your bloodlust and whatever gift you might develop," Damien went on. "But, as you know, you don't have a Sire. Still, you're part of Castor's nest, so Dion has offered to act as a sort of surrogate Sire."

I snorted. "Yeah, I'll pass. I don't really have any interest in being part of the nest."

Seeming pleased by that, Damien said, "Then maybe you'll consider letting me be at your side. I've been where you are. I know exactly what you're going through. I can help you in every way you need help."

It might have been *worded* like an offer, but it was a damn well declaration. He intended to be here, and that was that. "But you're part of the legion. You have training and—"

"Sam and Jared have already okayed it. If you'll agree to it, I'll be with you through your adjustment period. I'll live here with you so that you're never alone."

"Live here for months on end? Why would you want to do that?"

His face went all soft. "Because I'm yours, Lex. Where else would I be but with you?"

My heart jumped, and my breath caught in my throat. "Mine, huh?"

"Yours." He took my hand and pressed a kiss to my palm. "Only yours."

I swallowed hard. "Damien—"

"I thought you might blame me for not getting to you on time. I thought you might rage at me and want me out of your sight. It would have fucking gutted me. And I'd have understood, but I wouldn't have left you. Not even for a moment, no matter what you said or did. Because even if you'd hated me, you would still have fucking owned me. And I've got news for you, Lex, I own you just the same. You're mine. So yeah, I'll be here with you until Sam and Jared declare you're fit to move out. You'll be wasting your breath if you fight me on it."

I couldn't bite back a smile. "Do I look like I want to fight you on it?"

One side of his mouth kicked up. "No. No, you look kind of smug."

"I feel it."

He drew me closer, so my body was flush against his. "Not gonna lie, part of me is disappointed that I won't need to tie you to the bed and make you come over and over until you agree that you belong to me."

"Okay, now that *does* sound interesting."

"But most of me is plain fucking relieved. For the record, now that the conversion is over, the only person you'll drink from is me. That will go both ways. Unless one of us is ever in danger and needs blood, of course. Also, you'll come live with me."

My brows flew up. "I will, will I?"

"Well you can't stay in your current apartment. That Residence Hall is for humans. And since I don't intend to let you out of my sight much even when you're able to move out of this place, it only makes sense for you to come live with me." He shrugged, as if it were no biggie.

"Hmm, we'll see how it goes," I said to needle him.

He frowned. "You *know* how it's going to go, I just told you."

I chuckled and poked his chest. "You toned down your alpha ways when I was human. I'm sensing that's not going to be the case anymore."

"You sensed correctly." He rested his forehead on mine. "I'm sorry

Castor fucked you over and took this choice from you. But I'm not sorry you're a vampire. That makes me a selfish bastard, I know. It makes me feel like a sack of shit. But I can't be sorry that I'm able to keep you. Walking away from the only woman I've ever really loved would have been the hardest fucking thing I ever did."

Oh, my heart went and melted right there and then. I cleared my thickening throat. "Just in case you didn't know, she loves you right back."

He smiled. "Then she'd better kiss me."

"She would be very happy to."

(Damien)

I let her dominate the kiss. For all of three seconds. Then my hand was in her hair, fisting tight, while I ruthlessly devoured her mouth. I could let go with her now. I didn't have to hold back, didn't have to check my speed or strength, didn't have a voice in my head telling me I shouldn't be doing this. She could take everything I had to give as roughly as I wanted to give it.

And she was mine. All fucking mine.

A growl sawed at my throat. "I need to be in you."

"You say that like we haven't had sex in days," she said as I rolled her onto her back. "I'm pretty sure we've had plenty of sex lately."

I flipped up her long tee and freed my cock from my jeans. "But you were half out of it, so it wasn't the same. I want to fuck my Lexi." I thrust two fingers inside her. "Wet. You need to be wetter."

She shook her head. "I don't want to wait."

"And I don't want to hurt you."

"If I can't take it, I'll tell you to pull out." She curled her legs around my waist and nipped my jaw. "In me."

My mouth pressed to hers, I slammed home, breathing in the gasp that flew out of her. Trusting she'd tell me if it was too much, I fucked her hard. Harder than I ever had before.

She didn't complain. No, scratching at my nape and shoulder, she lifted her hips to meet every thrust. The new red tint to her irises began to flare, which called to the predator in me in a way I couldn't explain.

I was gonna fucking Bind myself to this girl. Not yet. It was too early for me to ask that of her—she'd only just been Turned. But there wasn't a doubt in my mind that we'd eventually have that Bond. Because there was no other woman for me.

Overwhelmed by so many emotions—love, relief, possessiveness, joy—I pounded into her again and again, feeling my release creep closer and closer. Watching her eyes dip to my throat, I said, "Take what you need from me."

"I don't know if I'd be able to stop when you tell me to," she admitted, her voice thick with so much hunger my cock twitched.

"I'll stop you if you don't pull back. Take what you need. Now, Lexi, don't—*Fuck*, yeah, good girl." Having her feed from me went to my cock every time whether we were having sex or not. I loved it. Loved that *she* loved it.

Once she'd taken enough, I said, "Pull back now, baby. Now, Lex." But she didn't. I tangled my hand in her hair and snatched her head to the side, smiling at her little snarl. "And you thought you'd struggle with drinking blood." Feeling my balls tighten, I mercilessly fucked in and out of her. "You're going to come for me now. Do it, Lex. Let go." I slipped one hand between us and thumbed her clit.

That easily, she broke apart.

That easily, so did I.

Recovering from my orgasm, I nuzzled her throat. "You smell amazing. Lavender and orange blossoms."

She loosely hooked her arms around my neck. "I wonder what my gift will be. I hope it's something cool. When will it surface?"

"It differs from person to person."

"I'll be grateful to have any ability, but I do hope it's nothing lame like shifting into a gerbil or something." She frowned when I shook with silent laughter. "Hey, it could happen."

"I've never heard of any vampire having that gift, if that makes you feel better."

"There's a first time for everything, though." She grimaced. "I'm starting to feel thirsty again. Is that normal?"

"The cravings will come and go, and you'll probably drink more than the average vampire over the next few months. Which is why I had Jared bring a whole crate of NSTs here. It's a sort of vampire starter kit, I suppose. There are different flavours for you to try. Once you've picked what ones you like, I'll have plenty of those flavours brought here for you."

"What about all our clothes and stuff?"

"They've already been brought here. I told you I had every intention of staying even if you didn't want me here." I couldn't have left her. No way.

"You're really going to live here with me until I can leave?"

I palmed her face with my hands. "Baby, there's nowhere else I'd want to be."

DARED

(Maya and Ryder)

Maya Duncan knows that moving on from Ryder Kingsley won't be easy, even if all they had was a brief fling before he left for a six-month-long trip. Well now he's back, and it's clear he has no interest in picking up where they left off. But after a group game of Truth or Dare forces them to put their hands on each other again, their resolve to keep their distance crumbles into nothing. But can the fling amount to more this time round, or are the rumours true? Is Ryder too deep in grief over a woman he lost to ever truly move forward?

CHAPTER ONE

(Maya)

Doing a double-take, I almost dropped the pile of dishware on Ava's kitchen floor. "Say that again."

Setting placemats on the long dining table, she replied, "I invited Ryder."

Yeah that was what I'd thought she said. *Hell.* "You … Why would you do that?"

"I was talking to him earlier while bringing up groceries, I casually mentioned the get-together, and then it seemed rude *not* to invite him." Taking the plates from me, she began putting them on the placemats. "I didn't actually expect him to say yes, but he did. Which is good. He hasn't mingled much since coming home from his trip last week. Everyone should have friends."

Oh, they should. Indeed they should. And despite that Ryder didn't seem interested in befriending me—well, to be fair, not many cared to socialise with people they'd once had a fling with—I'd still be fine with Ava inviting him … *if* it wasn't possible that she was up to something.

I folded my arms. "Please tell me you're not playing cupid."

Her head snapped up. "What? No. No, I'd never try to set you up with someone who isn't ready for a relationship. Just the same, I wouldn't mess with Ryder that way. Especially when it's possible he's still grieving. Sam doesn't seem to think he is. But we don't always know what's going on inside a person."

Very true. And when it came to someone as self-contained as Ryder, we *really* had no clue. But considering that he and his pregnant girlfriend had been attacked by a vampire and that he'd been the only survivor—a survival courtesy of vampirism—it was no wonder he had no wish to talk about it. I couldn't even begin to imagine how he must feel. My heart went out to him.

"There's no bad blood between you two," Ava went on, gathering cutlery from a drawer, "so I figured it would be no big deal if he was here. It's not, is it?"

I wouldn't exactly find it easy to spend an evening with a guy who had *way* too much power over my body, but I'd have to get used to it, considering we'd both spend eternity on such a small island together. There'd be no real way to avoid him. "No. No, it's fine. I was just surprised. *And* worried that you were going to try some matchmaking."

"That's not my intention, I swear. It's just that he hasn't mixed a lot with the people on the island."

"He did plenty of *mixing* during the first week he was released from isolation," I muttered.

"He hadn't had sex in months, so *of course* he went out and got himself laid a few times. But that's not socialising, it's just exchanging bodily fluids."

I wasn't sure it was simply a case that he'd missed sex. One of my brothers, Will, had lost his girlfriend in a house fire. For a while, he'd pulled away from everyone. Then he'd began bedding women like a dog with two dicks. To him, they'd all been faceless fucks—a way to quiet his mind for a while.

"Anyway, Ryder calmed down some after the first week," Ava added, nodding in satisfaction as she finished setting cutlery near each plate. "The little fling he had with you might have been casual, but he didn't sleep with others during that period. He insisted on exclusivity."

He had, but the sex had still been emotionless. Though ... there had been some angry sex on occasion, as if his demons sometimes got the better of him. I wouldn't be surprised to learn he'd fucked his way across the globe while on his trip.

"I didn't mention it before now because I wasn't sure you'd still come tonight," said Ava.

I frowned. "Why would you think that?"

"Since he got back, there's been this weird energy between you two. Not negative, just weird. I can't read it."

It was possibly the sort of energy that came from striving to pretend that neither of you knew each other in a biblical sense. We'd barely spoken, really. Not out of awkwardness. There simply wasn't anything to say.

Ava tilted her head. "Are you disappointed that he didn't ask to pick things up where they left off?"

"No. I didn't for a second think he would." I hadn't let myself hope, so there'd been no room for disappointment. "He was clear from minute one that our fling would end when he left, and he was just as clear that the ending would be permanent. He's not looking for emotional attachments, and I don't blame him. He's got some healing to do."

"Too true. I know it might be strange at first, but maybe you two could eventually become friends."

I wasn't sure he *wanted* friends. Not that he was antisocial or awkward. He could mingle just fine, and small talk seemed to come easy for him. Ryder was one of those solitary alphas, though—incredibly self-sufficient, preferred his own company, sought no validation from others, had zero interest in pleasing the masses, and didn't feel the need to have power over anyone other than himself.

"On a whole other subject," Ava began, "have you picked what you're wearing for your date tomorrow?"

Glad of the topic change, I replied, "No, not yet." Honestly, I hadn't thought much about it. I *wanted* to be excited. Coop, a personal assistant to one of the legion's commanders, was a sweet guy. He might not make my heart leap or pound, but I doubted he'd stomp all over it either.

"You know, I was stunned when you told me that Coop asked you out. I could tell he *wanted* to, but I didn't think he'd actually do it."

"Why not?"

"Well he's just so unassuming, and you're kind of scary."

I almost drew my head back. "What?"

"Not in a *bad* way. You have this innate, unshakable self-confidence that's as hot as it is intimidating. It makes you fierce in everything you do—how you have fun, how you fight, how you protect, how devoted a friend you are. And you're not easily impressed by, well, anything. I've seen super assertive guys flounder around you. So hearing that shy little Coop made a play took me by surprise."

I set my hands on my hips. "I don't think I'm scary. I'm very nice."

"Oh, you're both. Although you can be sweet as honey, your bark is *not* worse than your bite." Ava paused at the sound of a knock on the front door. "Salem will get it," she said.

The guy was in the living area with some of the other guests—Stuart, Paige, and Max. Only Cassie and Ryder hadn't yet arrived.

I heard footfalls, door hinges creak, and then Cassie's cheerful voice. She spent a minute or so talking with the others before padding into the kitchen, where she then gave both myself and Ava an enthusiastic hug.

Cassie's brow furrowed as she counted the placemats. "Who else is coming?"

And then came another knock at the door. My stomach did a slow roll.

"Ooh, that'll be Ryder," said Ava. "Now that we're all here, I can dish the food out."

Cassie looked at me, her brows flying up. "Ryder?"

I nodded, feigning casual. My friend gave me a look that said she wasn't fooled.

Cassie turned to Ava. "I thought Salem didn't like him."

Ava snorted. "He's got no issue with Ryder, he has an issue with the issue that he thinks I'm attracted to Ryder, which really should be a non-issue." She crossed her eyes.

Soon, everyone began filing into the kitchen. Butterflies took flight in my stomach as I caught sight of the man in question. Tall, dark, trim, tattooed, and *hot as fuck*, Ryder Kingsley was a man who drew the eye. He was cool, self-possessed, impossibly sexy. I'd never known a person who seemed to breathe so easily. It was like he was totally at peace with who he was and where he fit in the world.

Although he was incredibly composed, there was an edge of restlessness there. Like that of a lone wolf who felt the call of the wild. More, he exuded a powerful sexual energy that never failed to turn heads.

Right then, his vivid green eyes locked on me. "Maya," he greeted in that voice that was all whiskey and smoke. It was like a punch to my gut. Memories of the many things he'd said during sex—some sweet, some dirty, some pure filth—drifted through my brain.

"Hey," I greeted simply.

He slowly stalked past me to greet Cassie and Ava. He had a very steady, confident, purposeful stride. Always moved like he had somewhere to be and something important to do. And I damned every hormone in my body for wishing that one of the things he had to 'do' was me.

Ava directed everyone to their seats. I found myself sat between Cassie and Ryder. Awesome.

"How's it feel to be back?" Stuart asked him while Ava passed out drinks.

"Good, now that I'm free to come and go as I please," replied Ryder.

Max rested an arm over the back of Paige's chair. "You fully settled into your new apartment now?" he asked Ryder.

"It was easy enough," the guy replied. "Fletcher got the place ready for me as a welcome home gesture."

Ava smiled. "Did he give the place any flamboyant touches?"

Ryder grunted. "There was a mermaid vase. I made him take it with him. Which he seemed pretty pleased about, so I think he wanted it for himself anyway."

Between bites of food and swigs of NSTs, we all talked and laughed and joked. It wasn't long before we moved onto desserts. I then helped Ava clear the table, glad to put some physical distance between myself and Ryder. Finished, I reluctantly returned to my seat.

Cassie nudged me with her elbow. "So, you looking forward to your date with Coop?"

I sensed Ryder tense beside me, which was weird, but whatever. I didn't look his way as I replied, "Sure. It's been a while since I've been wined and dined."

Cassie let out a soft snort. "Only because romance makes you uncomfortable. I'm surprised you agreed to go out for a meal."

I shrugged. "Maybe I'm growing up."

"Or maybe you just couldn't say no to Mexican food."

"Yeah, it's more that than anything else."

"You have to let me know how it goes."

I sipped at my drink and nodded. "I will."

"I'm impressed that he worked up the nerve to ask you out. I didn't think he had it in him. Especially since you're sort of scary."

I felt my lips flatten. "I am *not* scary."

She only laughed, the heifer.

More chatting and teasing went on, and then Ava blurted out, "Ooh, we should play Truth or Dare."

Stuart held up one finger. "I am *not* doing a sexy crawl on the floor again."

"But you were so good at it," Max taunted.

"I haven't played that in ages," said Cassie. She glanced at Ava, who was grabbing a small box from one of the kitchen drawers. "Remind me of the rules again."

"They're pretty basic," Ava told her, taking two piles of cards from the box and setting them on the table. "You get the option of whether you want to pick a Truth card or a Dare card. If you pick a Truth card but don't want to answer the question written on it, you have to grab a Dare card and do whatever it says. The penalty for refusing is to … um, let's think of something different from last time … Ooh, you have to remove your top."

Cassie hummed. "Good one. We'll be looking at naked chests in no time. Guys always shy away from the dares."

And so the game began.

"Truth or dare?" Ava asked Stuart, who then picked up a Truth card. But when he didn't want to answer the question of whether he'd ever lied to any person in the room, he had to grab a Dare card.

"Shit," he muttered. "It says I've got to put my hand on the inner thigh of the person on my left, and I've got to keep it there for the rest of the game." He gave Cassie an apologetic look.

She rolled her eyes. "Jesus, Stuart, it says my thigh, not my groin, just do it."

"Fine," he said. "Don't tell Donnie, he'll give me all kinds of shit."

Yeah, her boyfriend totally would, game or not. They'd only been together a couple of months, but Donnie was super possessive of Cassie.

Soon enough, it was my turn. And since I didn't want to answer the question on my Truth card, I took one from the Dare stack. My stomach dropped as I read it aloud, "You have to fake an orgasm for fifteen seconds."

Stuart straightened with a grin. "Oh, this'll be good. Maya never shies away from this shit."

No, generally, I didn't. Purely because I didn't embarrass easily. But when you were conscious that one of the people in the room had in fact seen you come, faking the whole thing felt weirder than it should have.

I couldn't exactly let Ryder sense that, though, could I? So I gave the dare my all—moaning, arching, throwing my head back, almost laughing at Stuart's *'That's it, baby, come.'* Then Ava announced that the fifteen seconds were up, and a laugh bubbled out of me.

(Ryder)

Jesus fucking Christ.

Clenching my hands beneath the table, I drew in a breath through my nose as I silently willed my dick to stand down. There was no chance of that happening. It didn't matter that Maya had been faking the orgasm. Not when the little scene had brought back so many explicit memories. Now X-rated images were dancing around my brain, and I was caught between wanting to claim her mouth and wanting to punch Stuart for calling her 'baby' and ordering her to come.

That was my job.

Except it wasn't.

Fuck, I shouldn't be here. I'd never considered myself masochistic before. But choosing to spend hours around the very thing I was struggling to resist, taking in her scent with every breath … I was just torturing myself really, wasn't I?

Adding to the torture for me, every man at the table now knew what my woman looked like when she came. Okay, so she wasn't *my* woman. But it often felt like she was, which had always been part of the problem.

I could look at a beautiful girl, admire her in my head, and imagine having her beneath me, but I never saw a woman and *had* to have her. There was no surge of crushing need propelling me to take and possess. Until Maya. She took my control from me. And I didn't like it. It made me think of my old man. Made me feel *like* him.

He'd cheated on my mother left, right, and centre. He hadn't cared that it hurt her so badly she left him. I'd always thought it fucked up that he'd whined how she never understood that a man had needs and couldn't always help himself. I'd branded it bullshit. Branded *him* a weak motherfucker. So the relentless, blinding need that struck me the first moment I laid eyes on Maya … it hadn't been welcome. Especially when I hadn't been in an emotional place to offer anything to anyone. I still wasn't in that place. Not fully.

Initially, I'd been set on ignoring the attraction, determined to prove that I could. That resolve had lasted all of a week, at which point I'd felt it better to burn off the chemistry by pretty much fucking us both raw. The plan back then had been simple—enjoy a brief fling with Maya, work off the need she stirred in me, and then move on.

It hadn't quite played out that way.

There'd been no working her out of my system. Being away from her for six months hadn't helped. I still couldn't look at her without wanting to slam her on the closest available surface and shove my cock inside her.

I wanted to hate her for it, but I couldn't. I could, however, keep my distance. That had been my new plan. I was already deviating from it. And now, thanks to that little dare, I was paying for it. But ... well, I'd missed her.

"Okay, Ryder, it's your turn," Ava announced. "Select your fate."

And so we continued the game. Person after person took their turn—answering questions, completing dares, or shedding clothes to pay penalties.

When Maya again reached a point where she had a Dare card in her hand, I tensed. *Fuck, no more fake orgasms.*

She read the inscription aloud, "You have to sit on the lap of the person on your left for the rest of the game."

I blinked. Yeah, that would be me. And there wasn't a chance Maya would want to sit on my ... I blinked again as she stood and turned to me.

"Sorry about this, Ryder, but there's no way I'm stripping," she said, to which Stuart complained.

Asshole.

Thankful my tee covered my hard-on, I pushed the chair backwards. Maya comfortably perched herself on my thigh, like she did it all the time. And fuck if she didn't feel good there. Needing to touch her, I settled my hand on her hip. She didn't tense for even a fraction of a second. Didn't seem stiff or awkward, but I had no doubt she was cursing that Dare card to hell and back.

More truths and dares followed—some simple, some outrageous. And, feeling none-too-friendly toward the guy right now, I gained an awful lot of satisfaction from seeing Stuart reluctantly lay down on the floor and imitate a whale. Karma had my back tonight.

When I later found myself holding a Dare card, I felt my stomach roll as I read, "For ten seconds, you have to make out with the person on your right."

Everyone went quiet. Because the person on my right ... that was Maya, since she was sitting on my thigh.

Ava lifted a brow. "Well, Kingsley, dare or penalty?"

Well that was a no-brainer. "Dare."

"Looks like you two are gonna be making out, then."

I looked at Maya, expecting her to seem nervous or edgy. My mistake. I should have remembered that my girl and 'awkwardness' were pretty much strangers. She fucking straddled me, asking, "Who's doing the countdown?"

"We'll all do it," said Ava. "Start *now.*"

It was no tentative meeting of tongues. I hooked Maya's nape with my palm, pulled her close, and took her mouth like I'd wanted to do for *months*. I couldn't help it. Not when I'd been inhaling her scent all night. Not when I'd missed that goddamn taste. Not when possessiveness pumped through my veins after hearing about her date with Coop, leaving me unable to shake the annoying feeling that someone was trespassing on my territory.

She kissed me back just as hard, digging her fingertips into my chest. There was catcalling and whistling and counting, and then … "Zero. You can stop."

Maya broke the kiss, her eyes dazed, her cheeks flushed. She stared at me for a long moment, swallowing hard. "It would have been better if you hadn't whispered Ava's name," she said.

"*What?*" growled Salem.

Reseating herself on my thigh, Maya burst out laughing. "I'm just yanking your chain, Salem."

And how in the hell did she even have it in her to *joke*? I could barely gather my thoughts. It wasn't at all flattering to know she wasn't going through any such struggle. So when my next dare was to whisper a fantasy into someone's ear, I took the opportunity to make things a little more balanced.

"I might as well use your ear," I told her.

"Please do, I'm intrigued."

She was fucking *screwing* with me was what she was doing.

I put my mouth to her ear and kept my voice too low to carry to the others as I murmured, "Right now, all I can think of doing is stripping you naked and planting you on my cock. I'd make you ride me so fucking hard. I'd keep my hand wrapped around your throat. And when you were close to coming, I'd sink my teeth into your breast and take all the blood I wanted."

I didn't miss the way she swallowed hard again. Or that a little breath stuttered out of her. Good. Now I felt better and—

Maya's nose wrinkled. "I don't think Ava's into that sort of thing."

Salem bristled. "*What?*"

Ava went wide-eyed. "Wait, I was part of the fantasy? Do tell."

"I did *not* mention Ava," I told her growling mate.

Meanwhile, Maya bust a gut laughing again. "I was just joking, Salem, I swear."

This fucking woman would be the death of me.

CHAPTER TWO

(Maya)

Sitting at a table across from Coop, I held back a sigh. It was never a good sign when the person you were dating kept talking about someone else. It didn't take a genius to work out that he was highly attracted to one of the legion members, Arlo. Especially since Coop repeatedly blushed when mentioning him.

I might have been miffed if I thought Coop's interest in me was faked and he was wasting both our times, but I sensed that he *did* like me. He just liked someone else more. Which, to be honest, was a two-way street. I'd much rather be on this date with Ryder.

Really, neither Coop nor I could fully emotionally invest in the other. Not when we had other people on our minds. It was a shame, really, because he sure was cute. Funny, too. Very open and forthcoming. And he *listened*. Really listened. I liked that. Liked that there didn't seem to be a mean bone in his body. Liked that, for once, the guy I was dating wasn't remote or self-contained.

That was my specialty, you see. Attracting emotionally unavailable men. I wasn't sure what it said about me that I had a weakness for them, but it couldn't be anything good.

It wasn't that I wanted to melt or tame them. I believed in accepting people for who they were. Cassie theorised that I was a little *too* accepting; that I made too many allowances for people if they had a lot of personal baggage. Maybe. I truly didn't know.

Setting down my glass of wine-flavoured NST, I spoke, "Can I ask you a question?"

Coop dabbed his mouth with his napkin. "Um, sure."

"How long have you been crushing on Arlo?"

Coop spluttered. "I'm sorry?"

"When you told me about how you recently separated from Derek, you mentioned his friend an awful lot."

Red stained Coop's cheeks. "Only because I'm thankful to Arlo for letting me know that Derek was cheating on me with his ex. I know Derek and Beatrix have a fair amount of history—they were together a long time, and it's no little thing that she followed him to The Hollow when he joined the legion. But that's no excuse for how he betrayed me. And I don't like that he goes back to her again and again. I believe Arlo is right. Derek wants to prevent her from moving on. It couldn't have been easy for Arlo to tell me about this, considering it meant disregarding his loyalty to Derek. If Arlo hadn't … I'm doing it again, aren't I?"

Nodding, I felt my mouth curve. "Arlo *is* pretty hot. Very rugged."

"He is," Coop reluctantly agreed, a smile playing around the edges of his mouth. "But I don't think anything would happen between us. He's close to Derek. Friends don't get involved with their friends' exes."

"Friends also generally keep each other's secrets and don't interfere in their relationships, but Arlo broke those rules for you."

"He said he thought I deserved better than Derek."

"It could be that he has feelings for you."

Coop studied me carefully. "This doesn't make you upset? I mean, you and I *are* on a date."

"And I'm coming to realise something. You like me, but you like Arlo more. That's making you uncomfortable, since he should be off-limits. You want to convince yourself that your attraction to him doesn't matter, that you can move on with someone else just fine, so you asked me out." My voice was empty of judgement.

"No, I don't think it's …" Trailing off, he winced. "Maybe you're right. I'm not using you, though."

"No, you're not. But right now, you're not ready for anything big."

He cocked his head. "You talk like you have some experience with trying to force yourself to move forward." His eyes briefly slid to the side. "Ryder?"

"Ryder," I confirmed. "Here's my idea. You and I keep dating, but not exclusively. If it comes to something, great. If instead Arlo makes a move and you'd prefer to explore things with him, you have the freedom to do so. I think we'll enjoy our dates if for no other reason than it'd be nice for us to have someone to talk to who understands how we're feeling."

Coop gave a slow nod, tension slipping from his shoulders. "I can agree to that. You're right, I'm not ready to commit just yet. And it *will* be nice to talk to someone who understands. You don't have any hope that you and Ryder might—"

"Nope. He's not ready to commit either. I understand that. I don't feel bitter about it. But I kind of wish I did, because that would make it easier to move forward."

"But it's not in your nature to be so caught up in what you're feeling that you'd be blind to what someone else must be feeling."

I sighed. "Such weakness."

He smiled. "Not weakness, goodness."

"Hmm." I took another sip of my NST, again thinking it was a damn shame that he and I couldn't be what the other needed right now. True, I often went for men who were more assertive. Alphas or betas. Coop was neither. I had the feeling I'd be leading in the bedroom, if he and I ever got that far. But maybe I'd like it. Maybe—

"Sorry to interrupt," said a new voice that was, in fact, *empty* of apology.

I tensed. No, he was not here. He was not. But when I looked up, I saw that, yeah, he was. And, as always, my hormones went into hyperdrive. Ugh.

"Something wrong?" I asked Ryder.

"Sam asked me to come get you," he replied, all business.

I stiffened. Something *was* wrong. I looked at Coop. "Excuse me for a sec."

"Of course," my date said.

I walked a few feet away with Ryder. "Okay, what's happening?"

"A group of humans headed out earlier. They haven't returned. The odds are that one or more of them hurt themselves or got lost. Sam wants you, Paige, Alora, Stuart, and me to go search for them."

"You?" The rest of us formed a standard search party, but Ryder never usually came along. Then again, Ryder was never usually here.

He shrugged. "I suppose she wants to see how my tracking skills are coming along."

Well that made sense. "All right." I returned to my table. "I'm sorry, Coop, but I have to go. Legion stuff."

He stood. "Oh, don't apologise. I completely understand."

"Thanks for tonight," I said. "I enjoyed what time we had."

"As did I. I don't know what kind of legion business you're on, but take care."

Aw, he was too sweet. "I will." I kissed his cheek. "I'll see you tomorrow evening."

"Tomorrow," he agreed, since I'd already said I'd be happy to be his plus-one for the party that would celebrate a Bound couple's anniversary.

Ryder and I then walked out of the restaurant. He was a little *too* close. His arm brushed mine with each step, and my brain wandered back to the game last night. If faking the big O in front of him had been hard, sitting on his lap had been harder. And having to kiss him? Shit, all my senses had sprung to life. The words he'd whispered into my ear hadn't helped calm my system down at all.

Shaking off the memories, I asked, "Are the others meeting us at the main gate?"

"Yes," Ryder replied.

From here, I could see that the others hadn't yet arrived. "What do you know about the missing humans?"

"Four went out together. One has lived here for over twenty years, so they're no stranger to the rainforest and are very aware of the dangers. They apparently wanted to check out the hot springs on the eastern side of the forest. You're not going home to change clothes?"

"Why bother?" Sure, a dress and high heels didn't make a good walking outfit, but … "I don't track in this form."

"Ah, yes, you go furry." He paused. "He doesn't seem your type. Coop."

"Hmm."

"You decided to try an omega on for size?"

Well alphas sure left a lot to be desired. Reaching the gate, I said, "We really don't need to make small talk. Silences don't make me uncomfortable."

"I'm not trying to make small talk. I'm curious about why you'd pick a guy who doesn't fit you."

Irritation spiked through my blood. "You don't know me, so you have no idea who'd fit me and who wouldn't."

He stepped into my personal space. "I know what you like in bed," he said, his voice pitched low and deep. "I know what makes you moan. Tremble. Scream. I know what you look like when you come."

"Thanks to the orgasm I faked last night at Ava and Salem's place, quite a few people do."

He hummed, his pupils dilating. "I missed those sounds you make."

Paige appeared in a blur, saving me from having to respond. "You been waiting long?"

"We just got here. Sam sent Ryder to find me," I quickly added, not wanting my friend to think that he and I had already been together. I gestured to an alcove not too far away. "I'm gonna go over there to shift and stash my clothes."

(Ryder)

It was only the awareness that Paige was watching me closely that stopped me from admiring the sexy sway of Maya's ass as she strolled away. An ass I'd bitten, squeezed, spanked … and, shit, I needed to stop my mind from going down that road or I'd be rock hard in seconds.

"I'm guessing by the way she's dressed that she was still on her date when you tracked her down," said Paige, her voice even.

I bit back a growl. "She was," I replied, keeping my expression blank.

"Did it look like it was going well?"

It had actually. She and Coop had been smiling and leaning toward each other, as if they'd wanted their own private bubble to talk. And I hadn't fucking liked it. Jealousy and possessiveness were such pointless emotions, and I hated feeling them, but they'd struck me hard at that restaurant.

I forced a casual shrug. "I can't be sure. You'd have to ask Maya."

Moments of silence ticked by, and I hoped it meant Paige was done. That turned out to be wishful thinking.

"She'd have been good for you, you know," said Paige, her voice soft. "It's a shame that you're not in a place where you could give her a chance to show you that."

Right then, Maya came padding out of the shadows in her jaguar form. All grace and muscle, she was a sight to behold. Her coat was black and sleek with faint rosettes that weren't easy to see at first glance. She went straight to Paige, who gave her a brief stroke. My hand itched to do the same, but I knew Maya wouldn't allow it. That rankled. It felt like I was being deprived of something that was rightfully mine.

Taking the sock Sam had given me from my pocket, I crouched down and held it out to the big cat. She came over and took a long sniff, taking in the scent that belonged to one of the missing humans, and then stepped back with a nod.

Stuart and Alora arrived within moments of each other, and then we all headed out of the gates and toward the portion of the island where the humans had allegedly ventured. Alora stuck close to the jaguar, who instantly took the lead. Stuart and I covered the rear while Paige walked closely behind her squad members.

The humans naturally hadn't tried to conceal their trail, so they wouldn't be difficult to find. Good. Because, as always, the hot air within the vast forest was thick and humid. The further we walked, the more suffocating the oppressive air felt. Sweat beaded my nape, forehead, and upper lip.

Moonlight flashed through the occasional gaps in the lush canopy. The place was nature at its wildest with the overabundance of vegetation and the plentiful wildlife. We sidestepped shrubs, evaded dirty puddles, stepped over protruding tree roots, and ducked under hanging moss or branches.

I was on alert for any calls for help, but it was so damn loud in the forest—especially with the fucking hooting monkeys—that I wasn't so sure any calls would be easily heard.

Maya abruptly stopped, her body tensing. We all halted just the same. Her head whipped around to face Alora.

"What is it?" I asked, stalking forward.

"She's sending me lots of images," said Alora. "Blood. Pain. Death. Someone died here. More than one."

"The trails have separated," I noted. "The humans split into twos. They ran in different directions. Maybe on purpose. Maybe in sheer fright."

"Paige and I will take the left trail," announced Stuart, who then burst into molecules that zoomed away. Paige was hot on his heels in vampiric speed.

The remaining three of us followed the right trail. It was mere moments before we came upon a body.

Alora sucked in a breath. "Jesus Christ."

I had a strong stomach, but even I almost turned away. The male had been savagely attacked. He was covered in vicious rake wounds that ran so deep they revealed bone. Chunks of his flesh had been bitten from his body—particularly from his face and throat. Hell, his bottom lip had been all but ripped away.

"What would do this?" asked Alora, holding the back of her hand against her mouth.

As the jaguar let out a distressed sound that tightened my chest, I took a chance and reached out to stroke her head, thankful she allowed it. "It had to have been an animal. You can see the bite marks. No human or vampire could have done this."

"But animals …"

"Rarely attack humans, especially like this, I know," I finished. "Let's find the other person who came this way."

It didn't take long. They weren't very far away, and they weren't alive. Their body had been just as brutally ravaged.

"Shit," I muttered, scrubbing a hand over my jaw. "This is—"

A blur of golden fur came from our left and landed right on the jaguar with a feral growl.

My heart slammed against my ribs. "What the fuck?"

Maya hissed in pain and shook off the animal. A leopard. She pounced on it in a flash, and it was clear she meant to disable it, not kill it. But the big cat was caught up in a fury. An unnatural fury. Its eyes were crazed, and its fur was coated in blood that didn't appear to be its own. It went for Maya with a roar, the intent to kill clear in its green gaze.

I would have been struck by panic if I didn't know for certain that it stood no chance against her—she was much faster, much stronger, much more explosive.

As I watched them pounce and wrestle and tear into each other, I felt my brow furrow. The leopard should *not* be able to move at such a speed. It was slower than Maya, yes. But it was also *far* too swift for an animal. Surely it shouldn't be that strong either. And wait, how had I not noticed the red glint to its irises until right then?

Was this another shapeshifting vampire? It had to be. Nothing else made sense. And yet, I knew of no other vamps at The Hollow who possessed Maya's ability.

No doubt drawn by the roars and hisses, Paige and Stuart came skidding into view.

Paige gaped. "Mother of all that's holy, what *in the hell?*"

Maya managed to pin the leopard to the ground. In a blur of movement, she'd ripped out its throat. Relief made a breath stutter out of me.

I frowned when the cat didn't turn to ashes. All my kind did so upon their death. Which meant this couldn't be a shapeshifting vampire after all. But it definitely was not an average animal. So what the fuck was it?

Alora blinked. "It's not only me who's thinking that that leopard seemed kind of vampiric, is it?"

"It's not only you," I said.

She nodded. "Good. I just needed to hear that."

Back at The Hollow, I dumped the dead cat on the floor of Sam and Jared's office. The Grand High Pair squatted on either side of the body while myself and the rest of the search party waited for them to examine it.

Jared got a good look at the red irises. "Baby, check these out."

Sam did so and cursed. She briefly looked up at Alora. "You're right, it does seem to be part-vampire. I can't see how that would be possible, though. Vampirism doesn't attach to the cells of animals, it doesn't alter them."

"It's more like the animal has vampiric physical qualities as opposed to being a vampire," said Jared. "But I can't see how that would be possible either."

"I tried communicating with it, but I couldn't," said Alora. "It was like a red haze covered its mind. The kind that comes with bloodlust. It was totally feral. Wanted blood."

Sam pushed to her feet. "Who would attempt to Turn an animal when it's believed to be impossible? The vampire in question wouldn't have done it for shits and giggles. They had to have known it would *sort* of work."

"Maybe they didn't try Turning it in a conventional way," suggested Maya, now back in her normal form and fully dressed. "Maybe someone on the island has the ability to somehow partially convert animals with a touch or something. To sort of trap them in a state of bloodlust that's like a vampiric form of rabies. Infected animals like that would make good … soldiers, for lack of a better word. So this would be a seriously offensive gift."

Rising, Jared pursed his lips. "I've never heard of a vampire having that ability."

"You never heard of a vampire having mine," Paige pointed out.

Jared inclined his head, allowing that. "No one here has reported that they possess such a gift. And if they'd lied—and I can't see why they would—it would have shown when the researchers did their background checks."

"Only if the culprit's Maker is aware of the gift," said Stuart. "I know of vampires who've lied about their abilities to protect themselves. Some

Makers don't want anyone in their nest to have a stronger or more unique ability than they do—it makes them feel threatened—so they banish or kill those that do. There are also plenty of Makers who use those with such power for their own gain."

Sam twisted her mouth. "If I could have hidden what I could do from my old Sire, I would have."

"Some vampires falsely claim that their gift is very weak and purposely don't demonstrate its full potential," Stuart went on. "For example, I knew someone who had visions of the future. They hated their Sire and didn't care to advise him, so they lied that they only saw brief 'flashes' of the future, and they never reported anything useful. They were therefore dismissed as useless."

Alora bit her lip. "Is there someone on the island who can, I don't know, alter DNA or speed up vampiric conversions or something? They could be playing down what they can do."

"I can't think of anyone off-hand," said Jared. "I'll have the researchers look into it." He looked at me. "If they don't uncover anything, I may have to ask you to start scanning people's minds."

Yeah, I'd figured that was coming.

"Do you think there could be more animals out there who were infected like this, if that's even the right word?" asked Maya.

"'Infected' is as good a word as any," said Sam. "I hope there aren't more. For one thing, they don't deserve this. For another, they'll lay waste to the wildlife if they're in a permanent grip of bloodlust."

"We need to put The Hollow on lockdown until we can be sure," Jared declared. "The only people who should be allowed to leave are those we send out to hunt for more of these poor bastards."

Maya folded her arms. "What I'm wondering is … if someone at The Hollow *can* do this, why are they doing it now? Why, if they'd rather not bring attention to their gift, would they use it like this all of a sudden?"

Sam sighed. "I truly have no idea. That's what we need to find out."

CHAPTER THREE

(Maya)

Standing at my side not far from the ballroom dance floor, Cassie leaned into me. "I know we shouldn't really talk about this at a party, but I still can't quite wrap my head around the fact that someone can infect animals with vampiric rabies."

I blew out a breath. "It's totally fucked up. And will leave us no choice but to put the poor animals down, which sucks. I really hate that part." I loathed that I'd been forced to kill the leopard.

"But it would be cruel to them to leave them in a permanent state of bloodlust," said Cassie. "I remember what it was like during my conversion."

"Same here, so I get why it's best to put the animals to rest—*if* there are more out there, that is. I'm hoping like hell that there aren't." Our squad had gone hunting for evidence of more earlier, but we'd so far hadn't discovered any. "The Hollow's researchers claim there are a few vamps here who possess an ability that, if stronger or looked at from a different angle, *could* cause something like this. Ryder will be scanning their minds to find out."

"Speaking of Ryder, he looks damn delicious tonight. Then again, he always does."

She wasn't wrong. I'd purposely kept my back to him as much as possible so that there was no way my eyes could wander to him. I wasn't too proud to admit to myself that I'd otherwise struggle not to ogle the shit out of him.

"That was one hot kiss you guys had the other night."

"We were responding to a dare," I reminded her.

"Uh-huh," said Cassie, all sarcasm.

"He's with Krista anyway." The female vampire was all over him, which was another reason I kept my back to him. The sight of them together made my stomach roll.

"I don't know about that. I mean, she sure is doing her best to wrap herself around him like a victory flag, but he doesn't seem to want her attention. And I heard from someone that he didn't actually sleep with her the night before he left for his trip, nor did he ask her to 'wait' for him. She just said that shit to put other women off. It seems that she's determined to make the guy hers. I don't see that happening."

"It's their business." I truly sounded like I didn't care either way, but Cassie knew me too well to fall for it, so her inelegant snort was not unexpected.

"Did word of the not-really-fake-kiss get back to Coop?"

I nodded. "I explained it was a game. He didn't seem fussed." On the contrary, he'd waggled his eyebrows.

"Really?"

"We're not exclusive or anything."

"So it doesn't worry you that he and Arlo have been very subtly eye-fucking each other all night?"

I smiled. "It's kind of hot."

She chuckled. "It is, but you're supposed to be jealous."

"Why? I barely know him. And like I said, we're not exclusive."

Cassie narrowed her eyes. "You're hoping to spur Arlo into making a move on Coop, aren't you?" She sighed. "Only *you* would help the guy you're dating get together with another person. You know, Derek hasn't failed to notice the eye-fucking either. He doesn't seem happy about it."

I felt my mouth tighten. "I don't like that dude. I *really* don't like how he treats Beatrix."

"Me neither. But she's a sucker for punishment. Forgives him again and again, always sure it'll be different the next time round. It never is." Cassie grinned as her boyfriend approached. "Hey there, handsome."

"Hey there, beautiful," said Donnie. "You promised me a dance."

She hummed. "I did. And I intend to deliver on that promise."

He looked at me. "What about you, Maya? You got any plans to dance tonight?"

"I'm not comfortable doing it without my pole," I replied.

He blinked and then chuckled. "I have nothing to say to that."

"Donnie!" someone called out.

He cursed beneath his breath. "I'll be one sec, Cass." With that, he disappeared.

"You should ask Coop to dance," Cassie told me. "He's too shy to ask you. You're gonna have to take the lead when it comes to him. In pretty much all ways that count."

"I find it refreshing."

"Oh, I believe you. But I also think you'll tire of it fast for the mere reason that you don't like having power over other people. You don't want to control them—it makes you feel uncomfortable. And, well, you're a girl who likes to be *taken*."

"Don't we all like that, at least once in a while?"

Cassie snickered. "That we do."

Reappearing, Donnie held his hand out to her. "Ready, beautiful?"

"Ready," she replied, and then the two headed to the dance floor.

Not interested in standing around like a wet lemon, I headed over to Coop, who was deep in conversation with some legion members. I smiled at him. "Hey, how're you doing?"

"Great," he replied, his eyes bright. "Just talking to these guys."

"Want to dance?"

He winced. "I-I'm not very good at it."

"I am, so we're swell." I took his hand and guided him onto the dance floor. Or I would have, but then Arlo was blocking our path, looking the height of awkward.

Arlo cleared his throat. "Off to dance, I see." It was clear that he didn't want me dancing with Coop but couldn't think of how to stop it happening without coming across as a jealous asshole. How cute.

I smiled. "We are. I'd ask you to join us, but I'm not sure the three of us could make it work when it's a slow ballad."

"I'm going to the bar in any case." He shifted his gaze to Coop. "Drink?"

I stifled a smile. Arlo was basically ensuring that Coop would go straight to him after the dance.

Coop coughed. "Um, a beer-flavoured NST, please."

Arlo nodded and then left.

I pulled my date onto the dance floor and drew him close. "Well that was interesting."

Coop moved a little stiffly as we swayed to the slow song. "Told you I wasn't very good."

I squeezed his shoulder. "You're doing fine."

He cleared his throat. "You look very pretty tonight."

"Thanks. You look kind of dashing." Lowering my voice, I added, "As does Arlo."

A smile pulled at Coop's mouth. "I noticed, though Lord knows I tried not to," he said, his voice just as low.

"I saw you talk to him earlier. What did he say?"

"He was asking how things are going between me and you. He didn't seem too happy when I reported that all was good."

"He's totally into you. In case you weren't aware, he's been eye-fucking you all night."

"Oh, I'm aware."

"Mind if I cut in?" a new voice asked.

Tension seeped into every muscle of my body. He was *not* here. He wasn't.

But oh yeah, the big bastard was.

Coop blinked at Ryder. "Um, no, I-I guess not." Coop gave me a subtle little smirk and then melted away.

Pulling out the acting hat I'd worn during the Truth or Dare game, I turned to Ryder, who hauled me so close I was flush against him. *Not necessary.* But I didn't comment. Nor did I react when I felt his cock begin to harden. I just swayed to the music, rolling my eyes when Cassie gave me a mischievous wink.

Sharp teeth nipped at my earlobe. "Focus."

I frowned at Ryder. "On what?"

"Me."

"Why, you gonna do magic?"

"Smartass." His eyes bore into mine, hot and gleaming with something that made my skin tingle. "I like the dress. Like the heels better. You were wearing those the night I first had you." He flicked up a brow when I blinked. "You thought I'd forget?"

I sighed. "Can we not do this? I don't even know why we are. I don't get why you cut in."

Ryder shrugged. "I didn't like seeing his hands on you," he admitted easily—no hesitation, no embarrassment.

"You're kind of gonna have to get used to it. Or just not look. Anyway, why aren't you dancing with Krista?"

"Why would I?"

Exhaling heavily, I looked away. "Fine. Play dumb."

"Not playing dumb. Just not interested in Krista. I don't waste time pretending I'm into someone when I'm not, unlike certain people I could mention."

I snapped my gaze back to his. "If you're insinuating that I'm not really interested in Coop, you're wrong. He's not my usual type, no, but therein lies his appeal."

"If you say so." Ryder's eyes dipped to my mouth. "Kissing you during the game was a mistake," he said, his voice deeper and thicker than usual.

I swallowed. "Is that so?"

His gaze returned to mine as he lowered his face a little. "It only made me want more."

Same fucking here. But it wouldn't happen, so I had no interest in torturing myself by thinking or speaking of it. He could fuck right off with his games. "I need to use the bathroom," I lied. "Thanks for the dance." I pulled free of his arms and walked away.

Stepping out of the ballroom, I noticed that the rear door of the mansion was open. I headed outside and into the stunning gardens. I loved walking through them. They were beautiful. Serene. Calming. I could really do with something calming right then.

I moseyed along the curving stone path, admiring the exotic flowers, lush green hedges, decorative borders, water features, and flowering trees.

I was just passing a wishing well when I heard a man's voice coming from the octagonal gazebo. His words were muffled, but they lashed like a whip. A lighter voice shakily responded, and then feminine weeping danced along the air.

Feeling my lips thin, I advanced toward the gazebo. Beatrix sat on the stone bench inside it, her face in her hands, her shoulders shaking. Derek leaned over her, telling her to pull herself together. He must have sensed my approach, because he whirled to face me.

"Is everything okay here?" I asked, climbing the two steps.

Beatrix's sobs came to a halt, and she sat staring at the floor.

Derek jutted out his chin. "All is good. You can leave."

I didn't. I leaned against one of the gazebo's posts instead. "I wasn't asking *you*." I slid my gaze to the other vampire. "Beatrix?"

She swiped at the tears on her face and gave me a bright smile that didn't touch her eyes. "I'm okay, thanks."

I didn't move. I just stayed very still, staring at Derek, who eventually stalked off with a hard sigh. I looked at Beatrix again. "You sure you're all right?"

She gave a jerky nod. "I'm fine, I just … I don't understand men sometimes."

I pursed my lips. "I've had that same thought on many occasions."

"I suppose you're wondering why I take him back over and over."

"I am. But I'm not judging you for it."

She blinked back tears. "When we're together, it's just so amazing. He's so attentive. So loving. I guess I've come to live for those moments." She let out a shaky breath and stood upright.

"I'm a good listener, if you ever want to talk," I told her. "Think about it."

"I will." She offered me a weak smile. "Thanks, Maya." Then I was alone.

I didn't continue moseying around the garden. I stayed right there, staring out of the gazebo windows, letting the sounds and smells calm me.

Grass rustling.

I looked to see Ryder prowling purposely toward the gazebo. My heart jumped. My body went stiff. My hormones? They pulled out the party poppers.

His eyes glittering with heat and resolve, he ascended the steps and stalked toward me, not stopping until there were mere inches between us. The air snapped taut. There was no misreading why he was here or what he wanted.

I didn't say anything. Neither did he. It made me think of the first time he'd turned up at my apartment—we'd simply stared at each other for a long moment and then, before I'd thought better of it, I'd stepped aside to let him in. He'd pounced before I even shut the door. We'd spent hours fucking like bunnies, and that evening had birthed our fling.

Right then, he brushed his thumb over my mouth. "I need another taste. Just one more." He dropped to his knees and hiked up my dress.

Oh shit, that hadn't been what I thought he meant. At all. And, although I should have probably at least made a half-hearted objection ... well it turned out I was too weak for that.

(Ryder)

I ripped off her panties, not in the mood to be careful or exercise any patience. I needed this too much. Needed her.

I tossed one slim leg over my shoulder and put my mouth on her. I swiped my tongue between her folds, lapping up the taste of her, and groaned. *Fuck, yeah.*

Gripping two fistfuls of her ass, I licked, probed, and flicked. Not gentle or seductive. I *couldn't* be gentle when so many emotions rode me. Need, jealousy, frustration, possessiveness. It was all there, and it all spurred me on.

I growled as she scratched at my head and pulled at whatever tufts of hair she could reach. I'd missed going down on her. Missed those goddamn moans that were like hot tongues lashing my cock.

All damn night I'd wanted to go to her, touch her, taste her. Maybe it wouldn't have been so hard to resist temptation if it hadn't been for that round of Truth or Dare. Or maybe I'd never stood a chance against her pull. Right then, while I had her with me, I couldn't have fucking cared less.

I drove two fingers inside her, humming in approval as she arched into my hand. I pumped my fingers hard and fast. "That's it, take them." I gently suckled on her clit, knowing exactly how she liked it.

Her thighs trembled. Her inner muscles fluttered. Her breath hitched. And then she came with another one of those goddamn moans, her back arched, her head thrown back.

Now it was my turn.

I shot to my feet and slammed my mouth on hers. I sank my tongue inside and flicked her own. Her response was instant. Wild. Desperate. We greedily ate at each other's mouths, tongues tangling, teeth clicking.

Needing to be in her more than I needed the air in my lungs, I tore open my fly and hoisted her up. Bracing her against the post behind her, I lodged the head of my dick in her entrance. "Who's about to fuck you, Maya?"

Curling her arms and legs tight around me, she nipped at my lower lip. "You."

Not good enough. "What's my name?"

"You don't know? That's weird."

I gave her ass a sharp slap. "Tell me."

Her eyes narrowed. "Just fuck me already."

I gripped her jaw tight. "Don't piss around, Maya. Say my fucking name."

Her upper lip curled. "Ryder," she bit out.

"That's my girl." I punched up my hips, ramming my cock inside her, groaning as her hot inner walls clenched me so tight it should have hurt. I didn't give her a moment to adjust. Couldn't. I was gone.

I pounded into her, filling the air with the sound of skin slapping skin. "Missed this," I gritted out. "So did you." I kissed her before she could deny it. Ravished and plundered and feasted.

She tore her mouth free. "Harder."

"I go harder, you're gonna be sore."

"I don't care."

Taking her at her word, I violently hammered into her. "The next time you're on that dance floor with a man, you'll have my come dripping down your thighs."

She snarled. "Yeah well if a woman kisses you tonight, she'll be tasting me."

"Like I'd ever share your taste with anyone but you." Like I even *wanted* another woman's lips anywhere near me. Maya was all I wanted. All I could think about.

"R-Ryder," she stuttered, her inner walls getting hotter and tighter. I knew what that meant.

"Yes, come for me, sweet girl." Lured by the pulse beating in her neck, I bit down hard. As I drank, she came apart around my cock. Those rippling inner muscles took me with her. I slammed deep as bursts of hot come jetted out of my dick and filled her.

I licked at the bite and then lifted my gaze to hers. Her glassy eyes flickered, a hint of uncertainty in their depths. I could almost see her steeling herself to hear words of regret. How could I regret taking her again? I might loathe how little self-control I had when it came to her, but I'd never once lamented a single thing that happened between us.

Hoping to communicate that somehow, I softly kissed her, sipping from her mouth, in no rush to leave her. But I eventually pulled back and set her on her feet, and then we just stared at each other. We never seemed to know what to say after sex. Or maybe it was that neither of us could say what we wanted, so we opted for nothing at all.

Once we'd righted our clothes, she snatched her ruined panties from the floor and shot me a dark look. Yeah, they weren't the first pair of hers I'd torn. Not even the second. She stuffed the ball of lace in the trash can near the stone bench and then disappeared in a blur of movement. All right.

CHAPTER FOUR

(Ryder)

Leaning against the wall in Sam and Jared's office the next evening, I watched as the vampire sitting in the chair opposite Sam shifted uncomfortably.

"I haven't lied about my gift," he claimed.

"I'm not saying you have," she told him, drumming her fingers on her desk. "I'm saying I need to be sure that you *haven't* lied. Ryder will confirm that after he's scanned your mind. It won't hurt."

The researchers had named six vampires who, based on their abilities, could possibly be responsible for what had happened to the leopard. This guy, for example, could taint people's emotional state—even send them into a fit of blind rage. If an additional aspect of that gift was that George could also send animals into a frenzy of bloodlust, he could be the culprit.

He squirmed again. "I don't like the idea of having someone in my head."

No one ever did, and I couldn't blame them. Especially since, as part of my ability, I could also delete memories.

"Understandable," Jared told him, perched on the edge of Sam's desk. "But this is how it has to go. He's not going to know your every thought or see your every secret. That's not how it works."

George sighed. "All right." As if he had a choice in the matter.

I pushed away from the wall and took a few steps toward him as I carefully delved a psychic hand into his head. He gasped, gripping the arms of the chair. "This won't cause you any pain, it will just feel strange," I told him.

He gave a curt nod. "How long will this take?"

"It will be faster if you think of your gift. Just bring it to the forefront of your mind." Because minds, well, they were trickier to navigate than people might expect. If there were mental boxes for thoughts, secrets, memories, and other such things, it wouldn't be so bad. But it wasn't that simple. Minds were like giant road maps—so many connecting lines, so many intersections, so many points of interest. None were labelled, so finding the correct 'road' could take a long time. But if someone brought up a mental snapshot or concentrated on one specific thing, it would act as a red cross on their personal map.

George did as I asked and then, sure enough, I found the correct 'road.' I explored the entire length of it with my psychic hand, taking my time, carefully checking each offshoot.

Done, I finally pulled back. I turned to the Grand High Pair and shook my head. George here wasn't our boy.

The pair dismissed him and then called in the next potential culprit. I repeated the process with them and then each person who followed. None had lied about their abilities.

Sinking back into her chair, Sam exhaled heavily. "I thought it would be one of them. I *hoped* it would be, because I want this bloody over with. I don't know who else it could be."

"Maybe there's someone on the island who has two gifts but hasn't declared it," I suggested, drinking an NST. "I doubt Antonio is the only vampire on Earth who can aid others in developing additional abilities."

"Maybe," said Jared. "There's only one way we'll know for sure who infected the animals. You're going to need to scan every mind in The Hollow."

"You're talking hundreds of people," I said, taking the seat that each of the suspects had used.

Jared nodded. "I know. I'm aware that using your gift for more than four consecutive hours can psychically tire you, so I understand you'll need breaks and that the process of searching every mind could take a week—maybe even more. But I don't see any other option."

"It may not come to that," I said. "Once they hear that I'll be sweeping each mind, they'll most likely panic and choose to run."

"They might," Sam agreed. "But they won't get far unless they can also teleport. And even if they do, you and Sebastian will find and bring them back."

Well yes, we would.

Claiming he needed to speak with his twin brother, Jared gave Sam a quick kiss and then left.

Looking at me, Sam tilted her head. "Well, are you glad to be home or are you itching to get away again?"

I felt my brow crease. "I wouldn't say I ever *itched* to get away."

She snorted. "Being stuck on the island and isolated from most of its population drove you nuts—and understandably so. It hits a lot of newborns hard, but you struggled with it more than most. That wasn't a criticism. Just an observation."

I shrugged. "I don't like feeling hemmed in. It's different now that I'm a true resident and not in isolation."

"People are glad to have you home. Especially Krista," Sam added, her eyes lit with humour.

"I don't think she's so glad anymore, considering I told her last night that she was knocking on the wrong door." I'd never had any interest in the female. She was too highly strung, too high-maintenance. And I wasn't impressed when I learned she'd spread some bullshit tale that I'd not only slept with her but laid a claim to her.

"I would have thought she'd have been more pissed at hearing the rumour that you and Maya got frisky in the gardens. Does the rumour have any substance?"

Fuck, I hadn't known there was any such rumour. I doubted we'd been seen so it seemed more likely that someone had noticed that Maya and I were missing at the same time. Or maybe Beatrix had commented that I'd passed her as she left the gardens.

Really, it didn't matter where the rumour came from. I had no problem with it being common knowledge, but I wasn't going to confirm it to Sam, because she'd only start firing nosy-ass questions at me. I respected Sam a great deal, but my private business wasn't up for discussion. So I didn't answer. I kept my expression neutral as I stared at her, making it clear that the subject was off-bounds.

Her shoulders sagged. "You're no fun. Come on, you can at least give me a nod or shake of the head."

But I didn't do that either.

"Fine, be that way. But I'm willing to bet that it *did* happen. I've seen the way you look at Maya. She's had your undivided attention since moment one." Sam twisted her mouth. "I wasn't a fan of Jared when I first met him. Thought he was an arsehole, actually. And yet …"

"You wanted him," I finished, happy to lead her away from the prior topic.

"Yeah. It made no sense to me, and I was not at all pleased about it."

Yes, I'd heard all about the pair's rocky start.

"I was ticked off with myself for wanting him. You can bet your arse that I felt like slapping myself a time or two. I went at him with my whip instead." She pointed at me. "I watched you go through a similar struggle with Maya. You wanted her, but you didn't like it. I still can't sense if you've made your peace with it yet." She leaned forward. "Which is why the biggest question on my mind is … did you only have a tumble with her last night because you don't like that she's with Coop?"

I inwardly snorted. Maya wasn't really *with* Coop. Not even close.

"Because if that shag was fuelled by nothing but jealousy, you were a total wanker to seek her out."

Oh, there had been jealousy all right. It was an emotion I hadn't been familiar with until Maya. But I hadn't fucked her merely because the green-eyed monster had made an appearance. I'd taken her because I *needed* it. Needed to have her just once more. I'd told myself I'd keep my hands off her after that.

I'd lied.

More, I'd *known* I was lying to myself.

"And if you're hoping to come between them just because you don't want to see her with someone else, you need to sort your shit out," Sam added.

I honestly didn't feel a need to 'come between' Maya and Coop. Although I hated seeing them together, I didn't feel whatsoever threatened by him. For one thing, the man really was not her type. For another, they weren't exclusive, so it couldn't be serious. Thirdly, they hadn't slept together—something I'd learned from Chico after his mate, Jude, gave up the info while drunk. Really, Coop was more Maya's walk on the not-so-wild side. He was also heavily into Arlo—anyone could see that.

Sam sighed when I remained silent. "You're really going to be tight-lipped about all this?"

Again, I didn't answer. Which was an answer in and of itself.

She huffed. "Fine. But don't hurt her, Ryder. Maya ... she's a hard-arse for sure, but she's all soft and squishy deep down. I'm not ordering you to stay away from her. I'm saying that if all you want is sex, you need to be crystal clear about it. Make sure she knows where she stands to avoid any future issues. Not just for her sake, but for yours. Because you won't get a second chance, Ryder. Maya doesn't hold grudges, but she also doesn't give people an extra opportunity to hurt her. She will cut you out in a heartbeat if you fuck her over. So don't fuck her over."

That was something I'd never do, but I still said nothing. This shit was between me and Maya.

Right then, Jared materialised. "So, when are we starting the process of scanning minds?"

"No time like the present." Sam arched a brow at me. "You need a little longer to recover before we bring in more people?"

I shook my head.

Sam gave a satisfied nod. "Good. Let's start with the legion, then."

(Maya)

In my jaguar form, I stared down at the corpse of yet another dead animal. Me and my squad had found several, and all had been savagely attacked, just like the humans. The kills were too fresh to be from the leopard. Something else had slaughtered them. I couldn't say what kind of beast, though.

"Whoever decided to trap animals in a state of bloodlust has one *hell* of a sadistic streak," said Jude. "I mean, this shit is not only cruel through and through, it's senseless."

Paige made a sound of agreement. "It would be one thing if the vampire was hoping to use the animals for protection or something, but to infect and then abandon them—leaving them crazed and putting all these other animals at risk … there's nothing to achieve by doing any of this."

Looking up at Alora, I sent mental images to her—images of us walking, hunting.

She nodded at me and then turned to the others. "Maya wants us to keep moving. We have to find whatever did this and, sadly, put them out of their misery."

We continued our hunt, finding more and more brutally attacked bodies. My stomach churned when we came upon dead cheetah cubs, and I couldn't help but let out a sound of distress.

"I know, sweetie," said Alora, all choked up. "I know."

We'd only been walking a few more minutes when we heard godawful howling and screechy growls, like two animals fighting. We all took off, tearing through the trees as we followed the sounds. Soon, we came upon a black monkey and a wild boar brawling. No, not brawling. The primate was doing its best to ravage the boar, moving much too fast for an average animal.

"Imani, can you help?" asked Keeley.

"No," replied Imani. "The monkey doesn't have a blood-link to whoever did this."

"I can't control its mind to make it stop," said Cassie. "It's too crazed, there's no rationality there, no thought patterns. Just a red haze."

"Which is the same reason I can't communicate with it," said Alora.

Ava rolled back her shoulders. "Looks like we'll have to take it down the good old fashioned way, then." She whistled loud.

The animals broke apart, their heads whipping to face us. The boar fled, just like any animal in its right mind would do. Not the primate. It glared our way, its irises glowing red, its face a mask of feral rage. Blood matted its black fur and coated the teeth it bared.

Usually, I loved a good fight. But this? No, I was not going to enjoy this.

The monkey howled and, *Jesus*, the sound was horrendous. Then it charged at Ava. It was fucking *fast* as it launched itself in the air. But Ava's gift of muscle memory meant she could replicate any combat move she'd ever observed, so she easily knocked the primate aside. She and I then pounced, hoping to bring it down quickly rather than drag this out.

Unaffected by pain and not giving a flying fuck that it was outnumbered and outmatched, the monkey fought us hard. Not hard enough, though. We swiftly subdued it, and then Jude was there. She snapped its neck in one clean move.

Exhaling a shaky breath, Jude squeezed her eyes shut, pained. I rubbed up against her, wanting to comfort her, and she wrapped her arms around me.

"Let's take it back to The Hollow," said Keeley.

So that was what we did.

Since I had no clothes and didn't fancy strolling into the Grand High Pair's office naked, I ventured there in my jaguar form. Ryder watched me carefully, but I paid him little attention as we all crowded around the dead monkey.

"It behaved exactly like the leopard," said Imani.

"There were a lot of bodies." Alora rubbed at her upper arm. "So much wildlife just … gone."

Paige's nostrils flared. "Whoever infected those animals with bloodlust needs to fucking suffer."

"They will," Sam swore.

"Any luck finding out who they are?" asked Ava.

Jared shook his head. "Not so far, but Ryder's working on it."

Sam swept her gaze over each of us. "All your minds will have to be scanned. It's not a sign of distrust on my part—"

"You can't be seen to play favourites, we get it," Cassie assured her. "It's fine."

Keeley nodded. "Yeah, we totally understand."

"Good." Sam looked back down at the monkey and sighed. "As you can imagine, there'll be no training sessions for a while. We'll need people in the rainforest checking for more infected animals. I want you all out there again tomorrow evening."

"Then that's where we'll be," said Paige.

I made a point of not looking at Ryder as my squad and I left the office.

As we walked down the hallway, Paige sidled up to my shoulder. "So, Maya, I noticed you disappeared from the ballroom last night for a short while. I also noticed that Ryder was nowhere in sight at the time."

I didn't even glance her way, too busy shoving aside the many delicious memories that began flickering through my mind.

"You looked freshly fucked when you got back, so I'm thinking that the rumours are true—you two got down and dirty in the gardens."

I'd known this was coming. The girls had given me pointed looks when I returned from the gardens, but none had questioned me because I'd shot them a 'not fucking now' stare. They probably would have raised the subject before we went hunting tonight if I hadn't arrived at the main gate in my jaguar form.

"Coop didn't fail to notice either."

No, he hadn't. He'd asked about it when he walked me home after the party. I'd told him the truth, and he'd flashed me a smirk. He hadn't been surprised by what happened; said that he'd caught Ryder staring at me several times. Coop wasn't upset. In fact, he'd been more eager to talk about how hard Arlo was finding it to see Coop dating me.

"Know what I think, Maya?" Paige went on. "I think you're dating Coop because you're trying to convince yourself that you're not hung up on Ryder."

Well give the girl a cookie.

"Am I right or not?" Paige pushed.

I wouldn't say I was 'hung up' on Ryder. But there was no denying that I was supremely bad at holding out against him. Still, I had no wish to discuss it with Paige or anyone else, so I let out a chuff.

Paige turned to Alora. "What did she say?"

"She said to mind your own business," Alora replied.

Imani snorted. "Like that would ever happen."

"*None* of us mind our own business," said Paige.

Truer words had never been spoken.

CHAPTER FIVE

(Maya)

Browsing through my collection of dresses later that evening, I frowned on hearing knuckles rapping on my front door. Coop wasn't supposed to be picking me up for our date for another twenty minutes. It wasn't a big deal, though. I only really needed to strip off my sweats and slip on a dress and some heels, so it wouldn't take me long to be ready.

I padded out of my bedroom and through my apartment. I opened the door only to find that it wasn't Coop at all. It was Derek. And just why the fuck would he turn up here?

He cleared his throat. "Hello, Maya. Can we talk? It won't take long."

While I doubted he'd have anything to say that I could possibly want to hear, I was far too curious to send him away. I gestured for him to enter and then closed the door. I didn't invite him into the living area, though. I stayed right there and folded my arms.

"I understand you're dating Coop," he said.

"Most people do. We're going out again tonight. He'll be here soon, so you might want to get whatever this is over with before he appears."

Derek poked the inside of his cheek with his tongue. "I know you don't like me much, but I'm not as much of an asshole as you might think."

I highly doubted that. "Why are you here?"

"I'm not sure if Coop has told you, but I don't feel that he and I are done. I want to fix things between us."

"So, what, you're asking me to back off?" Ballsy.

"No. I just wanted to be upfront with you about the fact that I hope to win him back. I've been trying since we split up, but he rarely even talks to me. I still care for him, Maya. I respect you, but I won't let him go so easily.

If your relationship with him was serious, it would be different."

"You can't be surprised that he's not flinging himself back into your arms. He was made aware that you were cheating on him with Beatrix."

"By Arlo, yeah. Arlo fucking lied." Derek thrust a hand into his tousled chestnut hair. "He wants Coop for himself, so he did what he could to edge me out of the picture. It worked."

Derek was either a very good liar or he was telling the truth. I had a feeling it was the former. "Look, this is all between you, Coop, and Arlo. I don't want to be dragged into it."

"You don't believe me?" It was more of a guess than a question.

"Why would I? You have a long history of keeping Beatrix dangling on a string instead of just letting her go."

"So she says. I haven't slept with her in over a year."

"Not according to her."

"I know. She spreads bullshit stories to get between me and my partners. She wants me to go back to her. I'm not interested—something I *again* told her last night in the gardens."

I frowned. "So what you're saying is that everyone else is lying and that you're the victim here?" I couldn't keep the scepticism out of my voice, but he didn't seem upset. Just resigned.

"I don't expect you to believe me, Maya. Most people don't. I just wanted to give you a heads-up rather than go behind your back trying to win Coop over."

Another knock came at the front door.

Derek sighed. "That's probably him now."

But it wasn't. It was fucking Ryder. Well, wasn't I a popular girl tonight?

His green eyes flicked from me to Derek. "What's going on here?" he asked, stalking inside in that oh so purposeful way he had. Predictably, my body perked right up.

"Nothing at all," said Derek. "I was just leaving. Ryder, good to see you." He nodded at me. "Maya, have a pleasant evening." He sauntered out of the apartment.

Ryder closed the door. "What did he want?"

"Nothing of interest. What do you want?"

"To check on you." He rolled back his shoulders. "You took the death of the monkey hard," he added, his voice softening.

"We all did. Taking down an ill animal was not our idea of a good time." I swallowed, my chest squeezing. "But I'm good."

"No, you're not."

No, I wasn't. I was used to seeing death. I'd fought on a battlefield more than once. But there was something so much more devastating about discovering a string of dead animals, knowing they'd died *hard*—and not even to provide food for other wildlife. And God the cheetah cubs … My stomach rolled, and nausea rose up fast.

Ryder crossed to me and palmed the side of my neck. "Tell me what I can do."

In another life, where he might have been someone I could count on and build something with, I'd have simply asked for a hug. But we weren't a couple. Never would be. And I couldn't afford to let myself rely on him for anything. I'd only get hurt. "You don't need to do any—"

"I know I don't need to, I *want* to. I don't like seeing you hurt. It makes me want to fix it."

Oh, those words were a shot at my fragile defences. "I just want the fucker behind all this to pay for what they've done."

"They will. I'll find out who it is."

"Unless they run."

"If we hear that someone has run, it'll be obvious *why* they've fled. I'll bring them back." He gave the side of my neck a little squeeze. "They *will* pay."

Swallowing, I nodded and inhaled deeply. Stupidly. Now my lungs were full of his scent, and the back of my throat began to burn with thirst. *Hell.* I needed him gone, *not* taking up my space and doodling circles on my skin with his thumb.

I carefully lowered his arm. "Thanks for coming by. I need to get dressed, though, so …"

His brow inched up. "Going somewhere?"

"Yes. And I need to get ready."

"Another date?"

"Yes."

His jaw tightened. "Does Coop know what happened in the gardens?"

I nodded. "I told him."

Ryder edged closer to me, his eyes boring into mine. "All of it? That I ate you out? That you came all over my fingers? That I fed from you while I fucked you?"

"I didn't give him a rundown, no."

"And he doesn't give a shit that I had you last night?"

I frowned. "If you thought he'd pitch a fit and declare that he and I were no longer dating, you thought wrong. He and I aren't exclusive."

"Oh, I didn't expect him to pitch a fit. I don't think he's any more serious about you than you are about him. You're both looking for what you want in the wrong places."

"I'm not even going to ask where you think I should be looking, because my personal life is really not your business. No, don't even *dare* claim I'm wrong on that. You and I had yet another one-time, no-strings fuck. That was it. It was just sex."

Ryder's eyes flared. He put his face closer to mine. "It was fucking great sex."

"It was angry sex." I stepped back. "You don't like that you want me. You never have. And hey, I get it. You have some demons riding you. If I lost someone I loved and then found myself wanting someone else—even if only for a quick fuck—I wouldn't feel too good about it or ... what's funny?"

Scrubbing his hand over the amused smile he wore, Ryder shook his head. "Everyone thinks they know what's going on inside my head. They don't. They don't have a clue, because they don't have the full story."

I crossed my arms over my chest. "Then let's hear it."

Sighing, he looked away.

Yeah, he wasn't going to explain. But then, I hadn't thought he would. I'd learned fast that he wasn't a man who shared easily. He'd reveal bits and pieces about himself here and there, but nothing too personal. His little anecdotes were often so vague that they only left me with *more* questions.

"You should go," I told him. "Like I said, I have to get ready. Thank you for checking on me, but it wasn't necessary. I'm fine."

His eyes drifted over my face, hot and intent. "I never like leaving you, you know," he said, his voice low and soft.

Ignoring the clenching of my stomach, I said, "I have a solution. Stop coming to me."

"I try. Doesn't always work. *That's* what I get angry about. You fuck with my hard-won self-control."

I blinked, taken aback. Did I know that Ryder liked having absolute control over himself? Yes, I did. I could easily imagine him getting pissed about anything that even came close to fracturing that control. But I doubted the situation was really that simple. His anger ran too deep. There had to be more to it.

I didn't push for more details, though, because it would only lead to disappointment—he wouldn't share shit. To be fair to him, he wasn't obliged to. We weren't together. We weren't even bed-buddies. He owed me no explanations.

"Maybe one day you'll stop resenting me for it," I said.

His mouth tightened. "I don't resent you, I resent—"

A knock came at the door.

"That'll be Coop," I said. "And I'm not ready. I don't suppose you could let him in on your way out, could you?" I turned and retreated into my bedroom. I heard the door hinges creak, the low murmur of male voices, and then the *click* of the front door closing. But the talking didn't stop. So, what, Ryder had invited Coop in like it was *his* apartment? Bastard.

I dressed quickly and tracked the voices to the living area. There, I looked from Ryder to Coop. Both were sitting on the sofa, chatting amiably like they were old pals. Coop was so engrossed in Ryder's tale that it took him a moment to realise they were no longer alone.

Coop grinned up at me. "Oh, hey. Ryder's telling me this amazing story about how he and Sebastian tracked a vampire in Egypt." He glanced back at Ryder. "I would love to be a tracker or part of the legion, but that level of danger isn't for me. Being a PA suits me much better." Coop's eyes flew back to me. "You look beautiful, by the way."

By the way. Like I was an afterthought. Nice.

I smiled, hoping it wasn't brittle around the edges. "Thank you."

Ryder raked his gaze over my dress—it was a slow, thorough, blatantly sexual perusal. "Red is definitely your colour, babe."

It'd be the colour of his face if he didn't stop with the 'babe' shit. I looked at Coop. "I'm ready when you are."

If he asked to hear the rest of Ryder's story first, I'd kick his ass. It honestly appeared as if he would, but he must have thought better of it because he stood and said, "Then let's go."

As the three of us left the apartment, Ryder gave him a farewell pat on the back that was a little harder than necessary, missing Coop's amused smile. Turning to me, Ryder kissed my cheek and gave my nape a territorial squeeze. "You really do look beautiful. But then, you always do." The smooth bastard then strode off.

Coop gave me one of his conspiratorial smirks. "He did *not* like that you and I are going out again," he said once Ryder was out of earshot. "Though I don't think he's worried I'll steal you out from under him."

"I'm not his to steal."

"Technically, no. But he's possessive of you. If he thought there was a chance that this date would end with sex, he would have tagged along or done something to ruin it. But he's not taking us dating seriously. I'm not even sure he takes your interest in me seriously."

I was pretty sure Coop was right on that, given Ryder's remarks that Coop wasn't my type and didn't 'fit' me.

As we took the elevator to the first floor, Coop went on, "I'm guessing you two didn't ... you know ... before I got there, because he had the look of a sexually frustrated man."

"We didn't ... you know," I confirmed.

"He asked what my intentions were toward you."

I gaped. "He what?"

"I told him that I thought you were a special person and I wanted to get to know you better. He said you *are* special, and that he'd pound my face into the ground if I stepped a foot wrong," said Coop, grinning. "He had the whole 'don't touch my woman' vibe going on—a guy *always* senses that vibe. Even the kiss and nape-squeeze was all 'yeah, Coop, you can look but no more.'"

"How can you be smiling right now? He threatened you. And he's being ridiculous. You know what, I don't even want to talk about him anymore."

Outside the building, I added, "He wasn't the only person to show at my place tonight. Derek also came."

Coop did a double-take. "Derek? What did he want?"

I relayed all that his ex-boyfriend had told me.

Coop frowned thoughtfully. "Do you believe him?"

I shrugged. "I believe Arlo wants you for himself. As for the rest? I just don't know."

Coop lapsed into silence, not breaking it until we reached the Italian restaurant. "Maybe I should hear Derek out next time he tries to talk to me. Then I can maybe get a feel for how honest he's being. What do you think?"

"I think it's up to you." It was only as we stepped inside the restaurant and saw Beatrix standing at the hostess station that I remembered she worked here.

Coop leaned into me. "You know, Beatrix has tried to talk with me a few times as well," he said quietly. "I've always brushed her off, but maybe I should listen to whatever it is she has to say."

"If you want to," I said.

"Would you mind if we did it now? I know we're on a date—"

"It's fine, we can totally do it now. I'd like to get to the bottom of all this."

Crossing to the hostess station, I smiled. "Hello, Beatrix."

"Hi, Maya." Her smile faltered as she glanced at my date. "Good evening, Coop. Do you have a reservation?"

"It's under my name," he replied. "I booked a private room."

Beatrix glanced at her tablet. "I see, yes." She grabbed two menus and gave us a bright smile that was just a little forced. "Follow me. I'll show you to your room."

We followed her through the restaurant, passing tables and booths and servers. She showed us into our private room, set our menus on the table, and informed us our waitress would be with us shortly.

"Maybe you could stay and talk to us a moment," said Coop when she turned to leave. "You've been trying to speak with me for a while now."

Tensing, she twisted her fingers and cast me a brief look.

"I can leave if you'd like," I offered.

"No, it's fine." She dropped her arms to her sides, straightened to her full height, and turned to face Coop. "I wanted to apologise to you. For the part I played in Derek … betraying you, I mean. I have no excuse. I won't offer up any. I just wanted you to know that I was sorry."

"Derek claims it didn't happen," said Coop. "He said you two haven't slept together in over a year."

Her eyes flashed with hurt. "Yes, it's often his story. He makes me out to be this crazy person who's obsessed with him and can't stand for him to be with anyone else. But if that was true, he would have had me leave The Hollow, wouldn't he? He hasn't asked that I be banished from the island so he can live his life without my interference."

Coop pursed his lips. "I guess so."

"I think he does care for you," she told him. "But Derek … he has to *own* people. It's his thing. And he never releases what he owns. If he believes you belong to him, you'll have trouble shaking him off, Coop."

"I have a question," I cut in. "Why don't *you* want to shake him off?"

She bit her lip. "I should want that, shouldn't I? But I've been at his side since the day he Turned me over two hundred years ago. I don't know how to be without him."

"Because he's made you feel that you can't," I said. "We can help you break free of him."

She grimaced and glanced at the door. "I don't know if I could fit into the world out there. Not after so many years of living here."

I frowned. "No one's saying you have to leave the island."

The sound of dishware shattering split the air.

Beatrix softly cursed. "I have to go," she said, giving us both apologetic looks. "I hope you both enjoy your meal. Your waitress will be here soon." With that, she scampered.

Coop puffed out a breath. "She made a good point. If she was really the bad guy in this scenario, Derek would ask Sam and Jared to relocate her. I mean, *I'd* want someone out of my life if they kept trampling all over it."

"Yes, so would I. Do you still intend to hear Derek out?"

"At least once. If nothing else, it'll give me some closure."

Just then, the waitress entered.

Shaking off external matters, Coop and I turned to enjoying our date.

CHAPTER SIX

(Ryder)

Hiding how weary I felt from the Grand High Pair wasn't easy when I was chugging down NSTs like it was my job. But, whether I liked it or not, overusing my psychic hand always took its toll. The breaks helped, of course. Still, a dull throb assailed the backs of my eyes, and an ache had settled in the base of my skull—it was the same at the end of each evening.

They were necessary pains, though. The culprit *needed* to be caught. Members of the legion had brought back yet more infected animals. Each time, I'd been glad it wasn't Maya's squad who'd discovered one. Killing the creatures hit her too hard. Okay, it hit everyone hard. But I gave few fucks about 'everyone.' My main concern was Maya.

Leaving her last night hadn't been anywhere near as easy as I'd wanted her to believe. But she'd needed a distraction from all that was happening, and I wasn't the kind of distraction that brought her comfort. Not when there was so much history and tension between us. Coop was easier for her to be around, which stung like a motherfucker but was truly my own fault.

Still, I wouldn't have been able to walk away if I hadn't been so certain that the date wouldn't lead to anything. There was no sexual chemistry between them at all. And I knew Maya. Knew she'd never desire someone who would need her to be in control—she just didn't function that way. Finding someone attractive and wanting to sleep with them … the two things didn't always go together.

Sam groaned, pulling me out of my thoughts. "Why can nothing be simple anymore?" she griped, rubbing her temples.

Standing beside her office chair, Jared settled his hand on her shoulder. "Things are rarely simple in the world of vampires."

Sam looked up at me. "I hate how much this is exhausting you. I hate that animals are being savagely ripped apart. I hate that we don't have our culprit yet."

Jared stroked her hair. "That's a lot of hate, baby."

"*Righteous* hate."

"I'm not arguing that."

"God, why couldn't the arsehole have decided to do a runner? I thought they would. I thought they'd flee once they heard that Ryder would be scanning minds. Either they think they can hide the truth from him, or they're not planning to scamper just yet."

Sitting on Jared's desk, I said, "Maybe we should do something to tempt the fucker to give themselves up."

Sam nodded. "Yeah. We could say that they'll get leniency if they fess up."

Jared snorted. "They'd never believe that we'd give them any mercy. They'd definitely never believe it of you."

She exhaled heavily. "I guess I just hoped that luck would give us a helping hand and let us find the culprit fast."

I personally didn't believe in luck. Some would say I should, given how close I'd come to death. If Sebastian hadn't come along exactly when he had, I'd be gone for sure. But I didn't consider that to be a case of luck, because I hadn't been the only person who was attacked that night. Where was 'luck' when Raquel and our unborn child needed help? Nowhere.

Jared looked at me. "You should head on home. Get some rest."

I nodded, said my goodbyes, and left the office. Deciding to take a brief walk along the beach, I exited via the rear of the mansion. The last thing I'd expected to find was Maya sitting on one of the rattan loungers, staring out at the azure blue sea as it gently swept ashore and dissolved into foam.

Surprised she'd be out here alone, I crossed to her. When she glanced my way, my stomach dropped. Something was wrong. Very wrong. Maya always had a sort of ... fire in her eyes. A light. Right then, they were flat. She looked ... lost. Sad. Alone. Like she'd pulled inward.

"You look tired," she said to me, her voice just as flat.

"I am," I admitted, because if I blew her off, she'd likely do the same to me. "Want to tell me what has you sitting out here by yourself?"

"I just wanted to be alone for a little while."

"Has someone upset you?" If they had, I'd smack the piss out of them.

Her brow furrowed slightly. "No."

I heard the ring of truth in her voice. "Then why do you look like you just lost your best friend?"

Her gaze slid back to the ocean. "Nothing you'd find interesting."

"You're wrong there. I find everything about you interesting."

She cast me a sideways look of disbelief. "If you say so."

I did say so. And I meant it. But I couldn't blame her for doubting it.

"Have you eaten yet?"

She shook her head.

I held out my hand. "Come on."

She eyed my hand like she'd never seen one before and was expecting it to bite her or something.

I sighed. "It's a hand, not a grenade. I'm not coaxing you to my home so I can have my wicked way with you. I don't want to leave you on your own. You don't look like you're in a good mental place right now, and I don't like it. Let me take you to my apartment and get some food down you. Then I'll walk you home."

Maya rubbed at her forehead. "I don't know, Ryder. I wouldn't make good company right now."

"I'm not expecting you to entertain me. Honestly, I wouldn't make good company either. My brain's feeling a little fried right now."

She looked up at me, her face lined with concern. "Are you taking enough breaks throughout the evening? You don't want to have some sort of psychic burn out."

Warmed by her concern, I said, "I'm taking enough breaks. Doesn't stop my head from hurting by the time I'm done each night. I'll feel better once I've eaten. But I'm not moving from this spot unless you're coming with me."

She threw me an exasperated look.

"If the situation was reversed and you found me sitting here like this, would you leave me out here alone?"

She hesitated to answer, and then a long sigh slipped out of her. "No."

My chest squeezed. "Then come with me."

She blew out a long breath. "All right." She put her hand in mine.

Hiding my satisfaction, I gently pulled her to her feet. *Good girl.* I didn't speak the words aloud, because I had the distinct feeling she'd have told me to fuck off.

I kept possession of her hand as we walked to our complex. Although I wasn't part of the legion, Sam and Jared had allocated me an apartment in the legion's Residence Hall as I was in the Grand High Pair's service. I lived a few floors above Maya, so we took the elevator up to my level. Inside my apartment, I ushered her into the kitchen and invited her to sit at the small, circular dining table.

Wanting her to relax, I didn't pressure her to talk. I just set a soda-flavoured NST in front of her and then went about making us dinner. Recalling that her favourite comfort food was mac and cheese, I tossed some in the microwave. When I later put two bowls of it on the table, her mouth curved.

"You remembered," she said.

I took the seat opposite her. "Of course I remembered." Not wanting to fuck with her appetite, I waited until she'd finished her meal before asking,

"Want to tell me what's wrong?"

"You'll think I'm cold."

I frowned. "I would never think that of you."

"*I'm* thinking it of me."

"Yeah, I see that. So tell me what's going on up there in your head, and then I can point out that you're wrong to be beating yourself up."

Her head tipped to the side. "You're so sure you'll be able to do the latter?"

"Yes." I lifted my beer-flavoured NST. "But feel free to prove me wrong."

She drew in a long breath. "It was my brother's birthday yesterday. I didn't even remember until an hour ago. *An hour ago.* It's not like we weren't close. We were. Very. And yet, it went right out of my head. How much of a shitty sister am I?"

"You're not a shitty sister. You've done what every one of our kind does when they join the world of vampires and suddenly find themselves unable to be around the people they love most. You started a new life, left the old you behind, and emotionally distanced yourself from those you can no longer be with. That's not wrong. That's not cold. It's the only way to survive this life."

She swallowed hard, staring at her empty bowl. "I miss him. I hate that he must have had a moment where he thought of me, remembered the times I was there for his birthday, and then felt the slice of grief."

I understood. I couldn't relate to it, because there was no one to miss me. No one I missed. But I understood. "Do you have any other siblings?"

"One. Another brother."

"You close to him as well?"

She nodded. "It makes me feel awful that I've had to let them believe I'm dead. They were informed by the authorities that I drowned while white water rafting with a 'friend' I met on my travels."

"Friend?"

"A vampire who was part of my nest. I decided to go on a one-year-round-the-world trip after college. I met a guy who claimed that, like me, he was traveling. One night, we were super drunk—or I was. He said he had a special drink that could make me live forever. I laughed, thought it was a joke. It turned out he meant his blood, which he gave me *after* taking so much of mine I nearly died. And so I became a vampire, and the nest managed to have me presumed dead."

I clenched my fists. *Bastard.* "You said he *was* part of your nest. You killed him?"

"No, the leader of the nest got there first. My Sire had displeased him in some way. The leader was a mean son of a bitch. He had many of his vamps target travellers to boost their numbers. They had a whole operation going where they could provide stories of awful 'accidents.' The kind where no bodies would be simple to find. Many of his vamps didn't want to do that, and even more of them didn't want to stay, but it was tricky to leave."

I frowned. "Why?"

"The leader was *real* good at keeping people close. His gift? His blood was addictive."

I let out a low whistle.

"He used it to keep people in line. Like junkies, we went back for more again and again. My gift was late in fully developing. I could only slice out claws at first. Eventually I'd see ripples of fur. The first time I shifted completely, I attacked everyone around me, killed the leader of the nest, and then fled. I don't think anyone ever pursued me. It took at least three weeks before the cravings for the leader's blood eased away. I was like a recovering junkie, but worse. I wasn't sure I'd live through it."

Pausing, she thrust a hand into her hair. "I hate that my family believes I'm dead, but at least they won't spend their days wondering what happened to me. The not knowing would be harder, I think."

"Probably. They'd be stuck in a strange sort of limbo, hesitant to grieve for you, because it would be giving up on ever finding you alive."

She nodded. "This way they can move on easier." Tensing, she winced. "Not that I'm saying grief is *easy* to move on from—"

"I know what you're trying to say, Maya," I assured her, my voice soft. "I agree with you."

The tension slipped from her muscles. "I just hope my parents won't blame themselves for my 'death.'"

"Why would they?"

She took a swig of her NST. "They were big on ensuring that their kids made their own way in the world. My brothers and I had to leave home once we turned eighteen."

"What?"

"They're not cold people, I swear. They truly were—*are*—devoted parents. They were all about life lessons. Preparing us for the big, bad world. One of those lessons was being sent off to stand on our own two feet. But I wasn't ready to settle. So after college, I went on that trip. And I never made my way home again."

"Why weren't you ready to settle?"

"I wanted to see more of the world and what it had to offer before I anchored myself in one place, that's all." She paused. "I'll bet you saw a lot of the world during your time with Sebastian."

"I did, though I was mostly focused on learning what he taught me."

"Do you think being a tracker will suit you?"

"Yeah." I knocked back the last of my drink. "Each night is different, which is good—I don't like routine. Plus, I like to roam. Being stuck in one place for too long makes me feel suffocated."

"Being isolated must have been hell for you, then."

"I certainly don't miss it."

We talked a little while longer, but we touched no more heavy topics. It was idle chatter, really. She then helped me clear the table and load the dishwasher, despite my assuring her it wasn't necessary. It was such an inane thing, but I liked it. Liked the rhythm we had. It was easy. Comfortable.

"I better head home," she declared once we were done. "Thank you for keeping me occupied and making sure I ate. I have to admit, I probably wouldn't have done otherwise."

"You don't have to thank me." I closed the space between us in two strides. "I want you to do one more thing before you go." Something she probably wouldn't want to do. Something that probably wasn't wise, given how quickly heat could build between us.

"What?"

"Feed from me."

(Maya)

I blinked, startled. "What?"

"You have dark circles under your eyes, Maya. I don't know when the last time was that you drank pure blood, but I don't think it was recent."

Actually, I'd fed from someone last … Fuck, I couldn't even remember. Possibly not since before Ryder returned to The Hollow.

"You've spent night after night hunting and killing. If you try to survive on just solid food and NSTs, you won't be at full-strength. That's not acceptable to me, and I doubt it's acceptable to you."

"I appreciate your concern but—"

"Don't blow this off, baby. We're talking about your health here. Please tell me you're not depriving yourself of what you need out of guilt."

"Guilt?"

"Intellectually, you have to know that it would have been cruel to let those animals live."

I couldn't hold back the wince. I wasn't punishing myself for what I'd had to do by going without pure blood but, yeah, I felt guilty as hell. "Intellectually, I do know that. And I know I need to feed from someone. I will, I—"

"Maya, just drink from me."

He said it like it'd be nothing. No big deal. And to him, maybe that was the case. For me, it wasn't that easy. Not when I'd never fed from him in a nonsexual context before.

He caught my nape and drew me closer. "Don't overthink it. Just do it."

"Ryder—"

"Do it." He tucked my face into the crook of his neck. "You know you want to," he said, all soft and sinful.

I *did* want to. Especially now, when his pulse beat *so close* to my mouth. I could hear his blood pumping through his veins, and it made the back of my throat burn from thirst.

I rested my hands on his upper arms and, without thought, flicked out my tongue to lick the life-giving vein in his throat.

"That's it, baby." He palmed the back of my head, his fingers delving into my hair. "Feed from me. Take what you need."

I shouldn't, but … *Fuck it.* I bit down hard, humming as his warm blood flowed into my mouth.

He groaned. "Fuck yeah, that's it." He held me almost uncomfortably tight, his cock thickening until it dug aggressively into my lower stomach.

My body came to life in a rush. Heated, tightened, ignited. *Hell.* I pulled back and licked over the bite, but he didn't let me go. And I didn't ask him to. Well we'd already established that I was decidedly weak where Ryder Kingsley was concerned.

I lifted my gaze to his, and my stomach did a little flip at the dark glitter of need in those eyes. More, my heartbeat kicked up, and my breathing got a little shaky.

"It shouldn't always be this hard," he said, his voice thick.

"What?"

"To let you go." He briefly squeezed his eyes shut. "I told you I wasn't bringing you here to have my way with you. I meant it."

I knew he had. I wouldn't have come here with him if I'd thought it was all just some plot to get into my panties.

He dropped his forehead to mine and bunched both hands in my hair. "The first time I saw you, I thought you were the most beautiful fucking thing I'd ever seen. I've never wanted a woman the way I want you."

My chest tightened. "Why tell me that?"

"Because then maybe you'll understand."

"Understand what?"

"Why I have to do this." He swooped down and took my mouth with a growl. His tongue boldly sank inside like it had every right. His grip on my hair tightened to the point of pain. And, deciding to ignore that this would be an insanely bad idea, I didn't push him away.

The kiss was hungry and devastating and thrillingly possessive. I wasn't sure who went for whose fly first, but both zippers were soon lowered. Jeans were kicked off, tees were tossed aside, underwear was discarded.

He backed me into the fridge and dropped to his knees. I licked my lips. "You said in the gardens that you only wanted one more taste."

"I fucking lied." His fingertip slid between my folds. "Already soaking wet."

I'd been damp since his blood hit my tongue.

He parted my folds with his thumbs and put his mouth on me. That mouth … oh, it went to work all right. Suckled and nipped and licked. I was a trembling, moaning, needy mess by the time he stood and shoved one finger inside me.

"Has anyone else been in here since I last had you?" he asked.

I thought about telling him that was none of his business, but I didn't want to argue right now. I wanted to get royally fucked. So I shook my head.

A growl rattled his chest. "Good." He added another finger, sucked my nipple into his mouth, and then began pumping his fingers hard and fast. Even better, he used his free hand to expertly play with my clit. Whoever said men couldn't multi-task?

Gripping his shoulders tight, I closed my eyes and let my head fall back. The guy should seriously give a class on foreplay, because *yowza*. With his thumb rolling around my clit, his fingertips rubbing my g-spot, and his hot mouth tugging on my nipple, I had no hope in hell of lasting long. My release hit me out of nowhere, sweeping me up in a hot rush. That was when he set me on the countertop and thrust his cock balls-deep inside me, which only drew the pleasure out.

He fucked me through my orgasm, grunting against my neck. I clung to him, loving the feel of his dick tunnelling into me again and again. He was long and fat, stretching and filling me like no one else ever had.

I sucked in a breath as his teeth grazed my pulse.

"Ask me to feed from you," he rumbled. The sharp nip to my earlobe shot right to my clit. "Ask me. I need to know you want it."

I licked my lips. "Feed from me."

Still fucking me hard, Ryder nicked my flesh and lapped at the blood that dotted the surface. He groaned. "Do you know what you taste like?"

"What?"

"Mine, sweet girl. You taste just like you're mine." His teeth sank down, his cock began to thrust harder, his fingers dug deeper into my thighs … and I freaking imploded. Pleasure violently tore through me. I screamed, arched, scratched, shook, only distantly aware of Ryder's hot come splashing my inner walls as he found his own release.

I sagged forward, breathing hard. Mother of God, I'd needed that. Probably shouldn't have done it, but needed it all the same. I'd give myself a hard time about it tomorrow night.

CHAPTER SEVEN

(Maya)

My eyes closed, I let myself float in the pool, enjoying the drag and pull of the rippling water. The evening had been awful. More hunting. More killing. More dead, ravaged animals. My entire squad had been left feeling so down in the dumps that Cassie had suggested we all come to the private pool behind the mansion—it was often referred to as 'the bat pool,' due to it being the shape of a bat with outstretched wings—and just relax for a little while.

How Fletcher and his boyfriend, Norm, had heard about our little gathering, I wasn't sure. But the cute couple had joined us half an hour ago. Which I was glad of, because they were hilarious. And so now we were all doing our best to chill.

Some people were in the pool with me, lazing or swimming. Others were stretched out on recliners, chatting or just enjoying a little moonbathing. Norm, well, he kept doing belly flops while Fletcher huffed and sent him looks of judgement.

I hadn't been so sure that a dip in the pool would help relax me much. But the tension had left my body little by little as time went by. There was something very calming about listening to the water lapping against the edges of the pool, the waves crashing against the rocks, the palm fronds scraping together in the breeze, and the murmurs and chuckles of my friends. Yeah, we'd needed this.

Keeley made a noise of complaint. "How sad is it that the bubbling push of water from the pool jet is the most action I've had in a while?"

Snickering, I opened my eyes. "Get your kicks where you can."

"It's your own fault that you've had no action," Fletcher told her, standing under the showerhead and letting the spray wash his body and patter against the floor tile. "You're too fussy, my girl. I'm always hearing blokes complain that you turned them down."

"So am I," said Paige, her eyes on Keeley. "I'm starting to think there must be one guy in particular that you want and you're waiting for him to make his play."

Keeley shrugged one shoulder. "Okay so, yeah, there's someone."

I righted myself instantly, placing my feet on the rough pool floor. "Ooh, tell us more. Who is he?"

"Yes, spill all," urged Imani, leaning forward in her recliner.

Keeley sighed. "So maybe I have a little thing for Sebastian. I wouldn't say I'm waiting on him, I'm not a girl who has a problem making the first move. But it's clear that he's not interested, so there's no point. Human and vampire years together, I'm thirty-four. He's been on this Earth for centuries, he sees me as a baby."

Perching himself on a lounger, Fletcher snorted. "Oh no, he doesn't."

She frowned. "Really?"

"Really," he assured her. "A few times now I've been in the same room when you two were stood closely together, I know he's interested." Well, as an Empath, Fletcher truly *would* know for sure. "But he likes you too much to use you for a jump in the sack, so if you're looking for a fling, you won't get one."

"I was hoping for more than a fling."

"It's good that you're all right with making the first move, then, because you'll have to. Sebastian ... he's given up on relationships. As a tracker, he can be away from The Hollow for months at a time. The women in his past told him they could handle it, but they never could. Mostly because couples don't like to feed from other people, but he can't possibly promise that. Like I said, he can be gone for months. He needs pure blood while away. Just the same, his woman would need to feed from others until he returns. You'd need to be good with that."

Keeley double-blinked. "Huh. I never actually thought of that. I wouldn't like that we'd have to regularly feed from others, but I could handle it. I'd prefer that to not being with him at all."

"Then make that clear to him, but don't be offended if he doubts you at first. He's been let down too many times."

It was only right then it occurred to me that any woman who committed to Ryder would be in that same boat. It could be one of the reasons why he wasn't looking for anything serious. Like Keeley, I wouldn't *like* having to share the blood of my partner so often, but I could handle it if necessary. Not that I'd *need* to handle it. Ryder wasn't looking for commitment. I wasn't sure he was looking for anything at all.

Grimacing, Norm reached behind him in the water and wiggled. "I don't think I'll be wearing these shorts again. I've had wedgie after wedgie. If I wanted a G-string, I'd buy one."

"And then I'd bin it, because it wouldn't suit you," said Fletcher.

Norm frowned. "Are you saying I couldn't work a G-string?"

"Luv, don't let it bother you, there are more interesting things to have wedged between your arse cheeks," said Fletcher, a twinkle in his eyes.

Norm chuckled. "That there are."

Fletcher glanced around. "If anyone's interested, I went to see Damien and Lexi earlier."

"Of course we're interested," said Ava. "How is she doing?"

"All right, really," he replied. "Poor Damien was fretting that she was suffering from a case of delayed shock, he kept thinking she'd suddenly lose her mind about now being one of us. But she's rolling with it like a pro. I took her a 'We're Thinking of You' basket and tossed in some muffins, chocolate, bath bombs, lube, and a neon orange dildo.'"

I felt my mouth curve. "A strange combo, but okay. I like Lexi. And I like her for Damien."

Paige smiled. "He's so gone over her."

Ava nodded. "She owns his ass, and I'm not sure if she even knows it."

Norm sighed dreamily. "They're both so sweet together." His gaze cut to me. "How're things going with you and Coop?"

"Okay, thanks," I said.

Fletcher hummed. "So not as thrilling as whatever's going on between you and Ryder, then? You were seen heading to his place last night, and no one will buy that you two sat and played UNO."

Oh, here we go. I just knew I'd get grilled at some point. A few of the girls had earlier tossed probing comments my way, but I'd brushed off each one, not wanting to discuss what was between me and Ryder. Or, more specifically, what *wasn't* between us.

He might have made some sweetly possessive remarks, but they didn't give me hope, because he was seemingly content with just occasionally fucking me. That wasn't what I was looking for from him. But it had become clear that it was essential he and I weren't ever alone in a room, because I couldn't guarantee I'd ever push him away if he made a move.

"Just answer me one thing," said Norm. "Is he hot in bed?"

Fletcher shot him a dark look. "And why, pray tell, would that peak your interest?"

Norm raised his shoulders. "What, *you* don't want to know?"

Fletcher pursed his lips and then looked my way. "Well, *is* he hot in bed?"

"I'm saying nothing," I declared.

"That means yes," Fletcher decided. "She doesn't want to lavish him with praise in case it inspires other lovely ladies to try dragging him into gardens."

I gaped, amused. "I didn't drag him anywhere."

"You thought he'd follow you, though, didn't you? Be honest, it was a trap." Fletcher imitated throwing out a fishing hook and spinning the reel. "You lured him out there."

I chuckled. "Not at all. I just wanted a reprieve, so the gardens seemed a fine idea. I genuinely didn't even imagine he'd come looking for me."

Cassie swam toward me. "If you had *known* he'd follow, would you still have wandered out there?"

I opened my mouth to respond, but I didn't speak ... because I really didn't like my answer.

Cassie grinned. "You *totally* would have."

Yes, I would have. "Which makes me an idiot."

She gently squeezed my arm. "It makes you someone who wants to take a chance on a good guy, even when it doesn't seem like that chance will pay off."

"Further proving that I'm an idiot." The breeze whispered over me, and little bumps rose along my exposed flesh. I dipped down further into the pool so that only my head was above the waterline and then turned to Fletcher. "You're an Empath, so you must have picked up on the resentment he feels."

Fletcher bit his lip. "It creeps in sometimes, like a snake—all slow and sneaky. But it's not directed toward *you*. And it's not as bad as it was before his trip. Like he's close to stomping out whatever's at the source of it."

"Do you think he resents wanting her because he's still grieving his girlfriend?" Keeley asked him. "That wanting Maya makes him feel guilty?"

Fletcher wrung his hands. "I don't like talking about people's feelings, it's like spilling secrets that I haven't even been trusted with. I will say this, Maya. He feels the occasional pang of grief, but he's not swimming in it. He never really was. So I really don't think he's pining for another woman."

I felt my brows draw together. "Why else would he resent wanting me?"

"That's something you'd have to ask him," said Fletcher.

Cassie nudged me. "I'm surprised you haven't already asked him. Are you worried what the answer might be?"

Poking my fingers out of the water, I stared at the wrinkly tips. "I don't want to hear that I, in some way, remind him of this woman he lost." I didn't want to hear that he'd never wanted me for *me*.

"Why do you think it could be that?" asked Alora.

"In his eyes, there must be something different about me, but not in a good way," I said. "None of the women he slept with before me claimed there'd been any angry sex—he and I had some of that. He didn't sleep with any of them more than once. He didn't strike up a fling with anyone other than me, and he demanded exclusivity despite not really knowing me. And since returning here, he hasn't started something with any of the women here. Unless there's something I'm not aware of."

"If he'd had a tumble with any of the women on the island recently, we'd have heard about it," said Fletcher. "The only one he seems to have any interest in right now is you."

I snorted. "He's interested in *fucking* me, which isn't quite the same thing." Done in the pool, I climbed the ladder, shivering as the water drizzled down my body and the cool breeze swept over my wet skin. "I just wonder if the reason he's different with me isn't really about me at all. Like … he sees me as a pale imitation of the woman he actually wants, and he gets angry because I'm not her."

Jude let out a thoughtful hum. "Does he talk much during sex?"

I twisted my rope of wet hair, and water splattered on my feet. "Yeah, he's pretty verbal."

"Does he say your name?" Jude asked.

I shrugged. "Sometimes."

"Then I don't think he's picturing someone else."

I snatched a dry towel from a lounger and wrapped it around me. "No, he definitely doesn't do that. He makes too much eye-contact for me to worry that he's using me that way. But I'm just not so sure I'm the woman he wishes he was looking at, that's all."

"You won't know unless you ask him outright."

I heaved a sigh. "He wouldn't answer. He's locked up tight."

God, what was I doing fooling around with a guy I cared for when said guy could offer me nothing? I couldn't keep this up. And it wasn't fair of me to do so, because I was giving him the impression that I *was* okay with how things were. It was emotional dishonesty, really. That wasn't my style.

"You're going to walk away, aren't you?" asked Cassie.

I blew out a breath. "I think it's best for both me and him that I do."

We hung around the pool a little while longer. For me, the whole thing had lost its relaxing air, though. Because the decision I'd made had left my stomach feeling rock hard. So when Ava suggested we call it a night, I was more than happy to.

We'd come down here in just our swimwear, so I slipped on my beach dress, stepped into my sandals, and balled up my damp towel.

In my apartment, I headed straight for the shower. Generally, I didn't actually *need* to use shampoo or conditioner. Vampirism took care of personal hygiene, so my hair was never greasy or in need of brushing. But, naturally, I would like to wash away the chlorine.

After the shower, I pulled on my towel-robe and used a small microfibre towel to dab at my wet hair. I then left it to airdry, not needing to worry that I'd have some frizz going on. Vampirism kept the strands soft and glossy.

I was grabbing clothes from my drawers when a knock came at the door. Dumping my underwear and sweatpants on the bed, I made my way to the front door. Finding Coop on the other side of it, I blinked. "Oh, hey."

He gave me an apologetic look. "I caught you at a bad time, huh?"

"I was just about to get dressed, but … Is something wrong? You look—"

"Like I've spent the past few hours thinking too much? That would be about right. Are you busy?" he asked, twiddling his fingers. "This won't take long."

"No, come in." I moved aside to let him pass and then shut the door. "Do you want a drink or anything?"

"No, thanks. I'm good."

"Okay, so what's up?"

"I just spoke with Derek," replied Coop, following me into the living area, where we both sat on the sofa. "He gave me the same story he gave you when he came here. I told him about the conversation you and I had with Beatrix at the restaurant. He swore that her word could not be trusted; that she truly *is* the liar here. I asked why he hadn't requested that she be removed from the island if she's spreading false rumours."

"And?"

"He said that they're the last of their nest; that she'd have nowhere to go, no one to turn to, and he doesn't think she'd survive on her own. He said he kept hoping she'd just let him go but, for the first time, he's thinking it might be best to have her relocated."

I hummed. "Do you think he'll really ask that of Sam and Jared?"

Coop shrugged. "I don't know. He was very convincing. But then, so were Arlo and Beatrix."

"Well, at least one of the three is a bullshitter."

Coop rubbed at his nape. "I don't want it to be Arlo. That's why I don't trust my judgment here. I'm too tempted to brand Derek and Beatrix the bad guys. I've been going over it again and again in my head, trying to stay impartial, but it was hopeless."

"What's the gist of what Arlo said to you when he claimed you'd been betrayed by Derek?"

"Well, Arlo came to my apartment one night. He said he'd been arguing with himself about whether or not he should 'do this,' but that he couldn't keep quiet because I deserved better. Then he said that Derek had been sleeping with Beatrix behind my back. Arlo said I really shouldn't take the betrayal personally because 'those two, as a couple, are so old that they don't really see it as cheating on others whenever they get together for a night.' He told me they had a messed up dynamic and that it would be better for me to not be touched by it."

On the outside, that did in fact appear to be the case. "I'm guessing you then confronted Derek."

"I did. He swore it wasn't true, he looked so sincere, but I'd heard from others that he'd allegedly betrayed them with Beatrix, so it was easy to believe he'd done the same to me. And I couldn't see why Arlo would lie about it."

"But now you're not finding it so easy to believe that Derek's the guilty party?"

Coop flapped his hands. "I just don't know. A friend of mine from back home had an ex-girlfriend who lied to his partners that he was still fucking her. She wasn't a bad person, just struggled to let him go. Beatrix isn't bad …"

"But could be having the same struggle."

"Or maybe not. I mean, she was pretty convincing too. And I've met men who have such an unhealthy hold on a woman that she'll stick around hoping he'll come back, almost addicted to the 'good times.' I read somewhere that the effect on the brain is similar to when you play those slot machines at bars or casinos. You keep putting money into the machines because you love that high you get when it sporadically pays off." He sighed. "I really don't know who or what to believe."

Unfortunately, neither did I.

We talked about it a little more but, still unable to reason it all through, we decided to let it go for now. I walked him to the door and opened it wide. Seeing a certain person stood in the hall, their fist raised to knock, Coop and I both went very still.

CHAPTER EIGHT

(Ryder)

I hadn't even had a chance to knock on the door when it swung open. There was Coop, ready to leave. And there was Maya in a *fucking robe*, her hair wet, looking far too beautiful ... and no doubt naked beneath that robe.

I clenched my fists. *Motherfucker.*

Unable to bite back a growl, I stalked forward. No, she owed me no loyalty. No, she didn't officially belong to me. And yeah, this asshole probably had more of a right to her than I did, given they were dating. But none of that stopped a black jealousy from blossoming in the pit of my stomach; none of it put a chokehold on the angry possessiveness that pounded through me.

I didn't realise I was advancing on the little shit until Maya slipped between us and jabbed her finger into my chest. "Don't even," she warned.

Coop raised his hands. "I didn't sleep with her. She'd showered before I got here."

She whirled to face him. "Coop, you don't need to explain anything to—"

"I'll speak to you tomorrow, Maya." Coop quickly skirted around us and hurried out of the apartment, pulling the door closed as did so.

She slowly and stiffly turned back to face me, her mouth tight, her eyes blazing.

I forced my back teeth to unlock. "Was he telling the truth?"

"Just how is that your business?"

"I need to know." It would be worse not to.

"No, you don't. What you *need* is to butt out of—"

"Did he fuck you? Yes or no?" I demanded, my tone clipped.

Her nostrils flared. "You have some goddamn nerve, Kingsley. Where exactly do you get off on thinking I owe you any explanations? I owe you *shit*. He and I are dating—"

"But it's my cock that's been making you come."

"So? That's just physical. He and I might not have slept together yet, but he's giving me more than you are. He talks to me. He shares. He asks me questions. He shows *interest* in me. You don't give a flicker of a shit who I am, what I want, what I need, or anything goddamn else. You only want to fuck me, so don't think that doing it makes you more significant than him. That's just sex."

She couldn't really think I had absolutely no interest in her as a person. No way. "We talked plenty in the past. We talked for fucking hours sometimes."

"Yeah, you talk a lot when you feel like it. But not about the things that matter. Nobody really notices that. They don't notice how you purposely create a situation where you're the main listener. You ask them questions—nothing too personal, because that might invite them to do the same—and flatter them with your 'interest' in them, so they don't often see that you said little about yourself."

I couldn't deny that she was bang on the mark. Very few people had ever called me on it. But I didn't do it on a conscious level. I didn't deliberately set out to control each conversation and contribute so little. Not anymore. It had simply become instinctive after a while.

"I'm not judging you for being so self-contained," she went on. "I'm just making the point that we didn't *really* talk. Not in a way that helped us get to know each other. We talk even less now. And when we do, it's *me* offering up info, not you. And hey, it's okay that you're not looking for us to build anything. I knew that from the start. I can understand it. But you don't get to make out that your using me for sex means *anything* to either of us."

Okay, that remark pissed me off. "I don't fucking use you. I have *never* used you."

"What else would you call banging me to scratch an itch? You don't have to feed me bullshit, Ryder. I'm a big girl. I have no hang-ups about casual sex. I know that's all this was."

I tensed at her use of past tense, and my stomach dropped. She exhaled a tired sigh, and I knew what she was going to say before she said it.

"I'm done, Ryder." The words were shaky. Sad. Firm.

My pulse jumped. "Maya—"

"I don't know why you keep coming back to me. I'm not going to ask, because I have a feeling I won't like the answer. But I need you to go, and I need you not to seek me out again."

My gut tightening, I went to speak, but she slammed up a hand.

"I don't want to hear it. I really don't." Her eyes glistened. "I can't do this anymore. You have to go, you have to stay away."

A dull pain lanced my chest. I couldn't do that. I couldn't. But I got why she thought I so easily could. She thought she knew where my head was at, thought I was grieving Raquel and struggling to move forward. Maya didn't truly understand, she didn't have the facts ... because she was right about one thing: I *hadn't* shared.

I hadn't been honest with her about everything. I'd let her believe the false conclusions she'd come to, just as I had everybody else. And I knew that the only way she'd allow me to stay was if I gave her some honesty.

"Ask me a question," I blurted out. "Any question."

"Ryder—"

"*Any* question. I'll tell you whatever you want to know."

She stared at me for long seconds and then weakly flapped her arms. "Why? Why bother?"

"I haven't held back from you to be a dick. It's just ... reflexive when you grew up around people who weren't interested in who you really were. People who, even as they loved you, wanted you to be someone different."

"I don't understand."

"So ask me to explain." *Let me stay.*

More seconds of staring went by. "Explain what you meant," she finally said, but it was clear that she thought I'd be vague as fuck.

"Can we sit while we talk? The story isn't long, but it also ain't short."

She sighed and then inclined her head.

I followed her into the living area, not feeling any triumph just yet. She was still seconds away from tossing my ass out of here. We both sank onto the sofa, though she kept a respectable distance between us.

"Go on," she urged.

"This isn't a tale of woe. It's pretty boring, really. I had a good life as a human. It was just complicated at times. My dad was the vice president of an MC, so I spent my early years around bikers. I don't remember my mother. She left because he wouldn't stop cheating on her—the man was like a damn nympho, to be fair to her. She took my older sister with her when she left."

Maya cocked her head. "You wanted to stay with him so he wouldn't be alone?"

"No. She left me behind."

"*What?*"

"I didn't even know she was gone until I went to her bedroom to wake her up, thinking she was still sleeping. She apparently told my dad, Mace, that she was leaving. He didn't try to stop her or even particularly give a shit who she took with her. He seemed surprised when he realised I was still there. I don't know why she left me behind, and I can't say I ever felt the need to find her and ask." The hurt had long since faded.

"What she did was *fucked up*," said Maya, an angry flush staining her cheeks.

I shrugged. "Maybe she thought I'd be better off with him, I don't know. Anyway, after Mace got arrested for drug trafficking when I was seven, I ended up living with his parents—people I'd never met until then. They'd had Mace when they were in their early forties, and they were everything the people I'd known before weren't—quiet, conservative, conformers."

"Snobs?"

"No. They weren't narrowminded either. They were tolerant and accepting. They weren't mad at Mace for leaving and joining a MC. But drugs were a hard no for them, and he'd been an addict for years. He'd burned his bridges with them."

"Were they happy to take you in?"

"Oh yeah. They hadn't even known I existed, so I was a surprise, but not unwelcome. For me, though, it felt like going from one extreme to the other. There were no more parties, no more bike rides, no more reckless behaviour, no more bare knuckle fights or gambling or booze. My grandparents drank sherry, went to wine tasting events, and hosted dinner parties. They never swore, never raised their voices, never used slang."

She blinked. "No offence to them, but they sound … really dull."

"I guess they were. I was used to expressive, larger than life people. My grandparents were far from that. And they believed that children should be seen and not heard. So although they were happy to take me in, they wanted to 'get the biker out of me.' Not with violence. But they were pretty strict, and there was constant criticism and punishments.

"I'd never had actual rules before. And these ones … they weren't there to guide you, they were there to box you in and oppress you. I felt suffocated. Wanted to crawl out of my own skin at times. But my grandparents were all I had, and they loved me. Hell, they took more interest in me than anyone else ever had. They just needed me to be someone else. I lived by their rules. Mostly. I never quite 'fit' in their circle, though. No matter how many manners they taught me, I was still rough and edgy beneath it all."

She nibbled on her lower lip. "I'm sorry they made you feel that you didn't belong."

That was exactly how they'd made me feel. "The only person I was ever really angry at was Mace. He was an asshole. Didn't give a shit about anyone. Nothing was ever his fault. And he blamed my mother for how he'd cheated on her. He even implied she was weak for leaving; said she should have understood that sometimes a man just couldn't help himself."

Maya's lips flattened. "You're right, he was an asshole."

"I hated him for pushing her away. In my opinion, *he* was the weak one. I thought it fucked up that he'd ever claim he couldn't control himself around a woman. It was a cop-out, in my mind. And then I met you, and my own control went right out the fucking window."

She went very still. "Ryder—"

"I couldn't stay away from you, so I allowed myself one night. I told myself I'd walk away afterwards. But that one night turned into a fling, because I needed more of you. Six months down the line, after a long-ass trip, I was right back to square one—craving you, needing you, hating the fact that I now needed to cut Mace a fucking break."

Her lips parted. "So all the times you seemed so angry …"

"I was never angry at you, baby. I was never angry that I wanted you. I was pissed that either I was no better than him, or maybe he wasn't so spineless after all—just fucking human."

(Maya)

I really had not expected the conversation to head in this direction. I'd thought we'd end up discussing the woman he lost. Well, maybe not *full-on* discussing her. I'd figured he'd give me a few details or maybe a half-assed story. But no. Right now, he was being more open and honest than he ever had before. And I was seeing that I hadn't understood his motivations as well as I'd thought I had.

I cleared my throat. "You said your father was like a nympho. If he was sleeping with multiple women all the time, I'd say it wasn't a simple case of him being 'just human' *or* of you being like him."

Ryder shrugged. "Maybe, maybe not." He sighed and slid along the sofa so he was next to me. "When I came back here after my trip, I'd intended to keep my distance from you—I won't lie about that."

Okay, yeah, that stung to hear. But it wasn't like I hadn't already known.

"I thought I could do it. I thought wrong." He rested his hand on my thigh and gave it a little squeeze. "I know I haven't been very fair to you. I know you deserve better. And maybe I should do what you asked and let you go, but I wouldn't manage it. I'd end up right back here. Not because I think I have the right to walk in and out of your life whenever it suits me. It's not like that."

"Then what is it like?"

He tucked my hair behind my ear. "I think about you all the time, you know. Worry about you constantly. Wonder where you are, what you're doing, who you're with. I don't think you have any idea how much space you take up in my head. There's no room for anyone else there. Only you." He rested his forehead against mine. "Sometimes, I feel like I'll go insane if I don't make you mine."

Which would have been flattering if I wasn't so worried about *why* I'd caught and kept his attention. "Do I remind you of her?"

He lifted his head with a frown. "Fuck, no. I've never met anyone like you. You have so many layers, and they all cover a super soft centre. I like being in your mind, like its vibe. There's kindness, cunning, sensuality, vulnerability, so much fucking confidence. I want to own all that. Own *you*."

"But you're not ready for someone to be yours again, are you?" He'd lost the last person—well, last *two* people if you included their unborn child—who'd been his. And though the woman's death hadn't affected him to quite the degree I'd thought, it *was* still a factor here.

He palmed the side of my neck. "I want to be ready. Can that not be the important part? Some shit is still fucking with my head, but I'm working through it. I am. I have to, because I can't walk away from you, Maya. Nor do I want to." His grip on my neck tightened a little. "You'd have every right to tell me to leave and not come back until I can swear that I'm *all* in this. But I'm asking you not to do that."

It would be emotionally safer for me if I did, because then there'd be no chance of me falling deeper into something that might later come to nothing—a lot depended on if he *could* truly commit to me at some point. But if I asked him to keep his distance until then, it would be like punishing him for feelings he had no control over. I couldn't do that. Couldn't hurt him that way.

"I wouldn't blame you if you've already given up on me, Maya. I wouldn't. But I need you to give me a chance. I just need a little time. I might not be able to offer you something serious yet, but what we'd have in the meantime … it wouldn't be shallow or casual. It would be real. It would mean something."

"And you'd be honest and open with me from now on? You'd share—"

"I'll tell you anything you want to know. Anything. Just don't send me away."

"I'm not sure I'd be firm about it if I did," I admitted in a mumble. "You're not the only one whose control gets shot to shit."

Something gleamed in his eyes. "Then we're even."

"Yeah, we're even."

"So you won't give up on me just yet?"

"No. But if you start backtracking, pulling away, and blowing hot and cold—"

"Won't happen. I swear that to you."

"If you start finding this hard, you be upfront with me about it. I'm not saying we'd then part ways. We could talk it through and tackle whatever's bugging you. Communication is going to be *key* here."

He nodded. "Agreed. I have a condition, too. You've got to get rid of the omega. I'm done watching him take you out on fucking dates."

I stifled a smile. "I can't keep Coop? But he's cute." I almost squeaked as Ryder snatched me from the sofa and hauled me against his chest.

He bit my lip hard. "You're not allowed to find other men cute."

"I'm not?"

"No. He's got to go. I'm not sharing you."

I pretended to consider it, which made him pinch my ass. "Ow!"

"Maya, he has to go."

"But then who'll take me out on dates?"

"I will, that's fucking who."

"Really? Okay, I can go with that."

"Good." He pressed a quick kiss to my mouth. "Now please tell me we're done talking, because it's been seriously hard to focus when I know you're naked beneath this robe."

"Yes, we're done." Then I found myself flat on my back on the sofa with him kneeling over me. I smiled. "Smooth," I teased. "So what's next?"

He parted my robe and cupped my breasts. "Next I play with these gorgeous tits. Then I go down on you. That might go on for a while. When I'm done—and *only* when I'm done, not before—I'll fuck you into a stupor right here on this couch. I won't stop until you're screaming, and you'll have my teeth buried in your neck when you do."

Well.

CHAPTER NINE

(Ryder)

As the office door closed behind the vampire whose mind I'd just scanned, I turned to Sam and Jared. "For a few seconds there, I thought we might have found our culprit. He might have looked cool and composed, but his mind wasn't so calm."

"It definitely isn't him, though?" asked Jared.

"Definitely not."

"Dion is in our bad books after all that shit with Lexi, so it could be just that he was nervous being around me and Sam."

"Probably." Sam reached over to the phone and lifted the receiver. She pressed a button on the keypad and then said, "Fletch, send the next vamp on the list in, please."

"Derek's not here yet, luv," Fletcher responded from his desk outside the office.

Her mouth flattened. "Is that so? All right. Send in one of the others." She looked up at Jared. "Derek had better be here by the time Ryder is done with this next one."

But Derek didn't show, and Fletcher hadn't been able to get hold of him.

Sam licked her front teeth. "Apparently, Derek thinks he's special and doesn't have to be here on time."

"I'll bring his lazy ass here myself," said Jared, who then teleported out of the office.

I raised a brow at Sam. "Do you think Derek could have fled? That he might be our boy?"

"It's possible. He's never done anything to make me consider him a suspect. But then, he wouldn't, would he?"

He didn't seem an obvious suspect to me either. I couldn't envision him prancing around the rainforest infecting animals with bloodlust. His main focus lately had been the man who'd been dating my woman.

Well Coop wasn't dating my woman anymore. And she *was* officially my woman. Maybe she didn't fully belong to me yet, but I was the only one who had any claim to her now. Something she'd assured me she would inform Coop of later tonight.

I glanced at the clock. She was probably on her lunch break right now and—

Jared returned, his jaw hard. "Derek wasn't home. I teleported into his apartment. He definitely isn't there, and he didn't pack any of his things. It doesn't look like he up and left, but that doesn't mean he hasn't. He could be our boy."

Sam pushed out of her seat. "We'll have to send people out to find him."

"Let me be one of them," I said. "I can track him."

She nodded. "All right." Again, she lifted the phone receiver and spoke into it. "Fletch, something has come up. Send the others home, tell them we'll pick this up later."

"Right, luv," the PA responded.

Jared slid his gaze to me. "Where to first?"

"Derek's apartment," I replied, rolling back my shoulders.

Jared teleported all three of us there. I searched the place but found nothing of interest. After speaking with the neighbours, I learned that Derek had been seen talking to someone in the alley between two of the stores yesterday evening.

Heading into one of the aforementioned stores, I questioned the manager, but he claimed to have seen nothing. The manager of the other store, however, was more helpful.

"Yes, he was out there last night," she told me. "I couldn't hear what was being said, but it seemed like he was arguing with his ex-boyfriend."

I stilled. "Which one?"

"Coop," she replied.

I nodded. "Thank you." Outside the store, I looked from Sam to Jared. "I think we should speak to him."

"He'll be at the Command Centre," said Jared.

Only Coop wasn't there at all. And since the commander he worked for was off on an assignment with his squad, there'd been no one around to notice Coop's absence.

Sam cricked her neck. "I think it's time we paid him a visit."

"I'll get his apartment number from Fletcher—he'll be able to look it up," said Jared, whose eyes then went out of focus, so I assumed he was telepathically contacting the assistant.

I twisted my mouth. "So both Derek and Coop are missing. Think there's a chance one targeted the other?"

"Well Derek allegedly cheated on Coop, so it's possible that Coop wanted revenge," mused Sam. "On the other hand, Derek doesn't seem to be pleased that his attempts to win back Coop aren't working. Derek could have lost his temper or something. That's assuming there's been foul play. We can't know for sure yet."

"How long has Coop been a resident here?" I asked.

It was Jared who replied, "About six years. Derek's lived here for over a century."

"And there have been no cases of—" I cut off as a horrid shrieking sound came from outside. Not from somewhere close by, but from in the near distance. "What the fuck was that?"

Sam frowned. "No clue."

(Maya)

"This is *the best* news," said Ava, linking her arm through mine as—having finished our lunch and required to go on yet another hunt—we walked past cafes and restaurants on our way to the main gate. "I know Ryder still needs time before he can fully commit to you on every level, Maya, but it's major that he's working toward being in an emotional place where he can do that."

Smiling, Cassie nodded. "I knew he had it in him, I just wasn't sure if he'd step up to the plate any time soon. I don't mean that in an insensitive way, I know he has his reasons for struggling to commit. I can understand." She looked at me. "I just felt that you and he would be good together, so it was sad to see him hold back."

"I'm assuming he made this leap because you told him it was time to part ways," guessed Imani. "You said at the pool that you would. I have to admit, I wasn't sure you'd actually do it."

"I *did* announce that I was done," I told them. "That was when he turned into Mr. Sharer. He told me some things—none of which I'll repeat, so don't ask—that made me understand him better. More, he was clear that I don't in any way remind him of the woman he lost. I needed to hear that."

That was the most I'd reveal unless Ryder ever gave me the go ahead to say more—something I doubted he'd ever do. He'd agreed to be more open with me, but I couldn't foresee him extending that courtesy to others. He was too private by nature.

"I'm so happy you guys are gonna take a chance," said Keeley. "Although I'm happier that Sebastian agreed to give things a shot with me."

We all stared at her, stunned.

Paige grabbed her arm. "He did? Seriously?"

Keeley nodded. "I went to see him last night and—"

"Um, Maya?"

Startled by the new voice, I blinked as I pivoted on the spot. "Oh. Arlo. Hi there." I frowned at the sombre look he wore. "Is something wrong?"

He glanced at my squad members and then refocused on me. "Could we talk in private for a moment?"

I shrugged. "Sure." I turned to the others. "I'll just be a sec."

"We'll wait for you at the gate," Cassie told me, casting Arlo a curious glance before walking away.

Once Arlo and I were alone, I asked, "So what's wrong?"

"Nothing at all, as a matter of fact." He lifted his chin, all smugness. "I just thought it would be fair to let you know that, well, Coop and I slept together."

I pursed my lips. "I see." And I was glad to hear it, because it worked out quite nicely that both Coop and I could now move forward with the people we truly wanted.

"He seems to think you are aware that you two are not serious, but I am not so sure," Arlo went on. "So in case you believe you have some prior claim to him, I wished to make it clear that it is no longer just *you* he is dating."

"So, essentially, this is you pissing all over your territory?" Disappointing. I'd thought better of him. Then again, Ryder had acted similarly.

Arlo spluttered. "That is not what this is."

"Oh come on, there's no real reason for you to brag—and you *are* bragging—that you slept with Coop unless you're hoping to get some sort of reaction out of me. You don't want to share him, so you're hoping I'll be so upset that I cut my losses and walk away." Which made me think of something Derek had once said ... '*He wants Coop for himself, so he did what he could to edge me out of the picture.*'

Arlo flushed. "I am not bragging. Nor am I attempting to manipulate you. I just wanted to ensure that you knew where you stood."

"Why? What's it to you? And why bother considering, as you yourself pointed out, that what I have with Coop isn't serious?"

Arlo defensively notched up his chin but didn't answer.

"He won't like that you were the one to tell me, you know. He would have wanted to do that himself. You best have a decent apology ready, because he won't ..." I trailed off as a godawful screech came from not too far away. Then there was another. And another. And another. Each was louder than the one before.

I looked to my left just in time to see a swarm of various birds—toucans, hornbills, vultures, parrots—come flying toward The Hollow. *Flying far too fast.* "Oh, fuck."

They swooped down, heading right for the residents. Some people screamed and ran for safety while others stood still and braced themselves to fight. My girls came running toward me just as I sprinted toward them, intending for us to fight as a unit.

My heart jumped into my throat when a vulture made a beeline for Cassie. *Shit, no.* I leapt and began to shift shape mid-air, just as I'd practiced many times in the training arena. So often I'd been too slow, and I'd worried that I'd fuck up if I ever needed to do this during battle.

I hadn't needed to worry.

I was in my jaguar form as I crashed into the vulture and took it to the ground. Alora was at my side in an instant, and she snapped the bird's neck.

Lifting my head, I shook it hard. The oddest sound seemed to hum in the air. There was no way to properly describe it but—

Fuck. I sidestepped the toucan that dived at me. Again, Alora and I worked together to take it out. And then we disabled another infected bird, and then another. The whole time, sheer mayhem ensued. Many of the legion's squads were hunting in the rainforests, but the other squads were quick to join mine and fight.

Birds screeched and nosedived. People cried out and fell to the ground. Voices yelled orders and urged the injured to rise. Lightning cracked in the sky and—

Lightning. Jared was here, which meant his mate was likely nearby. Just as that thought crossed my mind, a huge bubble of energy seemed to shoot out of the centre of The Hollow. It expanded fast until it encompassed the centre of the gated community, keeping the birds contained and away from the buildings wherein most residents were hiding. *Sam's shield.*

I looked at where the bubble had originated. Yes, Sam and Jared were there. My gut twisted as I saw Ryder stood with them. I wasn't sure how much combat training he'd received, but I doubted his gift would be much help against these animals, so it was good that he was with the Grand High Pair—they could keep him safe better than anyone else.

His eyes locked with mine, and he gave me a look that said, *Stay alive.* I intended to.

Shrieking like banshees, the birds outside the forcefield of energy battered at its walls to no avail. I also heard roars and hissing, and I realised that more animals had come. They must have struggled to bypass the gates and were now stuck outside the shield. I didn't doubt that the squads out there would have heard the cacophony of shrieks and come to investigate; they would take the animals out.

The birds who were trapped inside the shield continued to mindlessly attack. Vampires fought back, filling the night air with telekinetic strikes, psionic blasts, whips of lightning, poisonous darts, bursts of flame, and other notable 'weapons.'

The birds weren't deterred. Nothing stopped them coming for us—not the danger, not the pain, not that they were outnumbered, not panic at being trapped within the shield. All they wanted was blood.

They were so fast that many of them managed to dodge the remote attacks, but not for long. Injured animals fell from the sky, plummeting to the ground or landing in the water of the man-made beach. Whenever their numbers dropped massively, Sam would lower her shield to let more birds inside and then slam it back up to trap them and—

Pain exploded in my head as a hornbill lunged at me hard, its massive beak hitting my skull with such force it was a wonder it didn't burst. There was a nauseating *crack*, and my eyesight blurred. Alora cursed beneath her breath and leapt onto the bird. I helped her neutralise it, but pain still racked my head, and I was dizzy *as fuck*. Then ... it was like I was deflating or something, because the energy seemed to be seeping out of my body—I just felt so damn light and weak all of a sudden.

"Paige!" Alora hollered.

Mere moments later, there was a blur of movement, and then Paige knelt at my side. "Watch out for Imani," she told Alora, splaying her hand on my flank.

There was the strangest sensation inside me as the pain faded, my eyesight returned to normal, the dizziness eased away, and I no longer felt like I'd lose consciousness any second.

I gave Paige a nod of thanks, and then she was gone again. I flinched as the weird-ass sound in the air seemed to intensify. I still couldn't describe it. But it was like some sort of frequency. A *calling*, even. Yes, there was a note of compulsion in it.

As Alora and I wrestled with yet another toucan, I used pictures to ask if she could hear an odd sound that didn't belong.

She shook her head. Maybe I only heard it because I was in my jaguar form; maybe it could only be heard by animals. I looked around, noticing that many of the birds outside the shield occasionally circled one of the Residence Halls before again and again trying to pierce the shield so that they could reach the people within it, their bloodlust too strong to be ignored.

It was pretty easy for me to resist the call, but the animals who'd been infected? They seemed helpless against it. So who or what the fuck was calling them? There was only one way to find out. And now that their numbers had massively dwindled, this seemed as good a time as any to investigate. So when Sam again lowered her shield, I telepathically informed Alora that I'd be back soon and sent her an image of the Residence Hall so that she'd know where I'd be. Then, remaining in my jaguar form, I rushed to the building.

I managed to get there before Sam's shield again slammed up, but I had to shift shape in order to open the front door—that easily, the weird sound was gone. Inside, I returned to my jaguar form and, sure enough, I could hear it again.

I followed it up several flights of stairs and then along a hallway, passing door after door until I finally reached the place where I was sure the call was originating from. And I tensed as I realised that I knew *exactly* who lived at this apartment.

I shifted shape in an instant and knocked on the door. I could pretend I was there to check on them, I didn't have to let them know I'd heard the 'call,' I could bluff—

The door swung open, and I frowned. *What in the fuck?*

CHAPTER TEN

(Maya)

W hy couldn't I move?
Like, seriously, *why couldn't I move*? It felt as if I had ropes curled *super* tight around my body. I couldn't turn, couldn't squirm, couldn't lean forward or backward. And, as I tried to cry out for help, I discovered I also couldn't open my mouth. My heart began to pound in my chest, and a hardness formed in my gut. *Fuck, fuck, fuck.*

I glared daggers at the vampire in front of me, who surely had to be responsible for immobilising me.

"You're not supposed to be here. You're *supposed* to be Arlo. Dammit." Beatrix lifted me, tossed me over her shoulder with that good ole Pagori strength, kicked the door shut, and carried me through the apartment and into the bedroom. She set me down ... and I then noticed Coop standing a few feet away, unnaturally still, his eyes wide. *Oh, hell.*

She smiled at me, all teeth, and there was something very *wrong* about that smile. Something that made my scalp prickle. Something that told me I wasn't facing an emotionally stable person right then. Well wasn't that special.

"There. Stay." She snorted a laugh. "Like you could do anything else. Being able to immobilize people is quite a handy ability at times."

Someone *so* needed to drop kick this bitch.

I tried moving again, but it was useless. A shot of adrenaline spiked through me, and panic wracked my insides. I breathed through it, determined to keep my shit together.

This feeling of being powerless and unable to move was *far* too familiar. It reminded me of the times my Sire had strapped me to a bed whenever the bloodlust became overwhelming, because the asshole hadn't wanted to help me through it. I'd been left there for hours at a time—trapped, alone, frightened. And damn the bitch for bringing it all back.

Being naked only made me feel that much more vulnerable. Something I loathed feeling. I despised her for that alone.

I tried telepathically reaching out to Jared, but I couldn't seem to touch his mind. *Sam's shield.* It must be acting as a psychic barrier—which made sense, given it would have to protect against mind-to-mind attacks. *Shit.*

I took another calming breath. Someone would surely search for me soon, right? Probably not until everything had calmed down outside, but they'd eventually come looking. Someone would surely track me to this apartment. Hopefully not too late to help.

Beatrix looked at Coop, whose eyes glimmered with fear. "It's okay, he'll be here soon. He'll be determined to check on you."

Who? Derek? Was this some sort of trap?

Her gaze slid back to me. "I can see the questions in your eyes, Maya. So much confusion. I do hope you didn't rush on up here to check on Coop because you care for him or anything. He's all about Arlo. Did you not know?" She lifted her hand in my direction and sharply twisted it. "Well, did you?"

Realising she genuinely expected an answer, I experimentally tried flexing my jaw. It worked. Apparently she'd unfrozen the muscles necessary for me to speak. "I know he slept with Arlo, yes," I replied.

"But you came anyway. See, women are the better gender. We're caring. Compassionate. Loyal. We're not cold and cruel."

I wasn't so sure she could truly claim that about herself. "You called the animals here."

Her mouth curved into a fond smile. "Aren't they wonderful?"

Uh, no. "They're rabid. Why would you do that to them?"

Her brows snapped together. "Not rabid, though that word did come to mind the first time the gift manifested. I hadn't expected to develop a second ability when I had another vampire boost my power level. I'd thought it would merely strengthen the ability I already had. I'd wanted to be able to take on my Sire, you see—he was a very bad man. Confined me to his dungeon often. That was when I used my second gift for the first time. By accident, of course. There were rats there. I was horrified by what I'd done to the one that bit me, so I didn't tell my Sire about my ability—he would have had me misuse it."

"You don't think *you* have been misusing it lately?"

"No. I wanted to build my own nest."

"Why? Why all of a sudden utilise an ability you've kept secret for so long?"

An element of vulnerability seeped into her expression. "Animals have always comforted me. They're so much better than people. They don't abandon you. They don't betray you. They don't hurt you. They don't suddenly announce that they're in love with someone else and will win them back by any means." She shot Coop a sour look. "I would have spared Coop, though. It's not *his* fault Derek loved him."

Loved, not loves, I noted. Shit, the bitch had likely killed him.

"But Arlo needs to suffer," she said with a grimace, as if speaking his name left a bad taste in her mouth.

"What do you have against Arlo?"

"Did you know that he and Derek used to share a bed? Derek and I had been together for almost a century when he left me for Arlo. They both sat me down and explained that Derek would always be my 'friend' but could no longer be my lover; that sometimes people drifted apart. It was all very condescending. Like I was clueless and naïve enough to believe they cared what was 'best' for me. Oh yes, they said it would be best if I wasn't tied to someone I was no longer so close to.

"They didn't last long as a couple. Derek came back to me. He always did after his little follies. I used to think of those flings as sort of like masturbating. He was just exploring fantasies that would never lead to anything." Her face hardened. "But then he stopped coming back to me, because Arlo kept *interfering*, whispering in his ear that it was unfair to me."

It was possible that Arlo had meant well, but I didn't say that.

"He convinced Derek to just be my *friend*." Her voice cracked.

I could understand her pain, because I couldn't possibly be only a friend to Ryder—it would be too hard, would hurt too much that he didn't want more. I hadn't known him long whereas she'd known Derek for centuries, so her pain would be so much more acute than what mine could possibly be. "You couldn't let Derek go, could you?"

Her eyes blazed. "He didn't *want* me to. Arlo just wouldn't see that. He wouldn't stay out of it. It can only have been him who put it in Derek's head to get me expelled from The Hollow. My friend works at the Command Centre. She saw the application to have me removed. She warned me about it."

I didn't dare glance at Coop. He'd been the one to pose the question to Derek of *why* he'd never tried to have her removed from the island. Maybe that had put the idea into the guy's head, or maybe Derek had already been considering it. Either way, I saw no need to speculate with her on that. And I was immensely glad that Coop was unable to speak, because it was possible he'd have nobly taken the blame to save Arlo's ass.

"I knew Sam and Jared would easily agree to it," she continued. "Derek is a member of their legion. I serve no purpose here. I came as his partner, and he'd made it clear to one and all that I was no longer that. The Grand High Pair wouldn't care that I have nowhere to go or no one to turn to. Neither did Derek. When I confronted him, he said it would be for the 'best.' Said he'd only kept me round this long because I was too helpless to be alone.

He ridiculed me, laughed at me, called me weak."

So she'd shown him that she wasn't quite as powerless as he'd thought. "Did you always plan to call the animals here?" I asked, ignoring the ache that began to assail the muscles being forced to remain stiff by fucking Beatrix.

"No. I knew the people here wouldn't accept them. They've been hunting and killing them. So have you. I had to keep my nest safe—that's what good leaders do. So I compelled them to stay away."

"But then you heard about Derek's application, and you got pissed."

She shrugged. "Ryder would have scanned my mind at some point anyway. He would have seen that I was guilty. For a while, I thought I might be able to convince Sam and Jared that we could all live in peace with my nest. But that wouldn't have happened, would it?"

No, but Beatrix had believed what brought her comfort. It seemed to be a pattern with her.

"They will kill me," she added. "But not in time to save Arlo or Coop."

"You've already killed Derek, haven't you?"

Her nostrils flared. "He would have thrown me away. *Again*. But for good this time—I saw that. And I've had enough of being thrown away." She whipped out a blade and came toward me. "Now, my plan *was* to slit Coop's throat when Arlo, the man who started it all, arrived. But I'm thinking of revising my plan. I could have you shift into your jaguar form. I could change you with my gift. Then I could immobilise you until Arlo arrives. It would be heart-breaking for him to watch the man he cares for be shredded to pieces. Then he'll know how I felt when he took Derek from me."

Cold fingertips scuttled down my spine. "There's a huge fault with that plan. I'm not going to shift for you. I couldn't even if I wanted to. I can barely move."

"I would release you long enough for you to change forms."

"Yeah, but I still wouldn't do it."

Her mouth tightening, she cast Coop a sideways look. "If you don't shift, I'll kill him."

"And if I do shift, you'll try to make *me* kill him. This is a no-win situation for the guy."

"How about this then?" She advanced on me and pointed the tip of the knife above my heart. "Shift, or I kill *you* right here right now. Then I will shove your body over that balcony for your squad and your friends to find. How about that?"

(Ryder)

"Christ, that was awful," said Chico, rubbing a hand over his face.

The man was right. Dead birds littered the ground, bobbed in the water, and were sprawled in the sand. Now that there were no more birds to beat at the shield, Sam had collapsed it. But no one felt an ounce of triumph at our win, because the animals hadn't been our enemies. They'd been victims.

There were no deaths on our side, and it didn't seem that anyone had suffered any major injuries. Then again, they would have called on Paige long before now if they'd been badly hurt. She tended to hop from one wounded person to another during battles, collecting their wounds to use them as weapons.

"The animals outside the gates are dead, too," said Jared, who must be telepathically in contact with the squad members out there. "There were wildcats, boars, capybaras, and more. A lot more damage would have been done here if they'd managed to get through the gates."

"They probably would have done it eventually," said Max. "Thank God for Coach's shield."

I looked up at one of the Residence Halls. "Did anyone notice how the birds seemed drawn to that building?"

Sam hummed. "Yeah, I noticed." Her gaze locked on something to our left. "Oi, where are you lot going?"

Tracking her gaze, I saw the female squad walking fast.

"To check on Maya," replied Paige.

I tensed. "What about Maya?"

Alora pointed at the Residence Hall I'd just been staring at. "She told me she was heading for this building, and she hasn't come back out yet. She's probably fine, but we just wanted to check."

"I'll reach out to her," said Jared, whose eyes then turned inward. Moments later, his face went tight. "*Fuck.*"

My stomach rolled. "What?"

Jared set his hands on his hips. "She's at Coop's apartment. Beatrix has him and Maya immobilised. She wants Maya to shift into her jaguar form so she can infect her. Beatrix is our culprit, she called the animals here."

My heart slammed against my ribs, and then it was hammering like crazy. Urgency filled me from head to toe. "We have to get to her now."

Jared teleported us all to Coop's front door, having earlier learned his apartment number from Fletcher.

"What's the situation?" Sam asked her mate, all business.

Jared's gaze went unfocused again, and I knew he was talking with Maya. "All three are in the bedroom. Beatrix has her back to the doorway. Coop and Maya still can't move. And Beatrix …" Jared looked at me. "She's currently holding a knife to Maya's heart."

The bottom dropped out of my stomach. "*Motherfucker.*" Nausea rose up fast, and a chilling dread settled over me like a heavy blanket, making me feel like I couldn't suck in enough air. Noting the wary looks the Grand High Pair gave me, I said, "I won't lose it. Just ... don't let her die."

"Oh, that won't happen." Sam puffed out a breath. "Okay, we have to be careful about this, we can't all barge in there. Cassie, Harvey—I want you both to be right behind me and Jared. This is what we're gonna do." She quickly relayed her plan.

"I've told Maya to keep Beatrix distracted." Jared then teleported us into the living area.

My heart jumped as I heard Maya say, "You can threaten me all you want, Beatrix, I won't shift."

"You understand I have a knife pointed at your chest?" Beatrix snarked.

Even though it went against every protective instinct I had, I didn't try to rush to Maya. I waited for Sam, Jared, Cassie, and Harvey to begin walking along the hallway before I moved, stepping in behind them.

"If you don't think I'd prefer to be stabbed in the heart than infected with bloodlust, you're highly mistaken," said Maya.

"Infected?" echoed Beatrix, sounding shocked. "I do not *infect* animals."

"Sure you do. They were rabid, absolutely crazed, lost all sense of who they were, killed indiscriminately. What kind of an existence is that? How could you do that to them?"

"I was building my own nest!"

"You were cursing animals with a fate worse than death, and then they slaughtered whatever they came across—even their own young. The bodies kept on piling up. You're responsible for every one of them."

A few feet away from the open bedroom door, Sam and Jared halted. The rest of us did the same. I glanced ahead of us, and the breath left my lungs. I could see Maya, see how stiffly she stood. And fuck if I didn't want to fist Beatrix's hair and haul her away, but I didn't dare move.

The whole thing was like déjà fucking vu. I'd been forced to watch as Raquel was killed—I'd been too weak and dazed to do a damn thing to help her. It had been agonising to be so helpless. It had destroyed something inside me that would never heal.

I'd never been so fucking angry as I was in this moment. Never felt such debilitating fear that it put a rock in my stomach, tightened my ribs, and stabbed at my chest like an ice-cold blade.

Sam glanced over her shoulder and nodded at Cassie.

"I am done arguing with you, Maya. Shift shape now and—" Beatrix sucked in a sharp breath and went stiff as a board, hopefully now under Cassie's control. My heart beat like a drum as I waited, praying this would work. Finally, Beatrix stiffly backed away from Maya. As per his instructions, Harvey telekinetically snatched the knife from her hand and sent it hurling across the room.

Knowing it was now safe to enter, I rushed through the crowd and went straight to Maya, the metallic taste of fear still in my mouth. I cradled her face with my hands. "Thank fucking Christ you're okay."

She gave me a watery smile. "I knew you'd all come."

"Cassie, make Beatrix release whatever hold she has on Maya and Coop's bodies," Sam ordered.

I caught Maya as she swayed. "I got you, baby." I held her tight, my face in her hair, breathing her in while her squad came over to check on her.

"Ryder," Coop called out. He then tossed me a tee that presumably belonged to him. "For Maya."

I helped her slip it over her naked form. It hit her mid-thigh, so it gave her enough coverage.

"You okay, Coop?" she asked him.

"Yeah." He swallowed hard. "She killed Derek." His eyes glistened. "I was pissed at him, but I didn't want him to die." He swept his gaze over the rest of us. "Thank God Arlo didn't come here, or Beatrix would have killed us before you came."

"Why Arlo?" asked Max.

Maya sighed. "Long story."

"I'll get it out of Beatrix," I said. "A simple scan of her mind will give me the entire story."

Beatrix's face was a mask of rage, her eyes were hard as diamonds, and I had no doubt that she'd be spitting insults if Cassie wasn't keeping her silent.

Beatrix's hateful expression faltered when Sam invaded her personal space.

"I must admit, you weren't on my list of likely suspects," said Sam. Her mouth curved into a smile that was somewhat bloodthirsty. "Let's get you to your new home, shall we?"

Jared swept his gaze over the rest of us. "While Sam and I take Beatrix to a cell, you all help bring some order to The Hollow. Sorry to ask it of you, but there are a lot of dead animals down there."

Maya looked at me, exhaling heavily. "I'm so glad it's all over."

That made two of us.

CHAPTER ELEVEN

(Maya)

Leaning against the doorjamb of the open balcony, I heard footfalls slowly coming my way. Then strong arms slid around my waist from behind, and Ryder pretty much curved his body around mine. It was protective and possessive and comforting.

He nuzzled my neck. "You okay?"

"Yeah." Looking down at the centre of The Hollow, which now looked like no battle had ever taken place, I laid my hand over one of his and asked, "You?"

"No. It might take a while before my blood pressure goes down." His arms tightened around me. "Don't know what I would have done if I'd gotten to Coop's apartment and found you dead."

The torment in his voice punched me in the stomach. Needing to know if my worries were founded, I turned in his arms and said, "Tell me the truth, is this going to make you backtrack for a while?"

His brows drew together. "What?"

"You think I don't know how hard it must have been for you to realise you might have to soon grieve another person?" I couldn't help but fear it would make him put some distance between us to protect himself.

His expression relaxed. "I'm not going to backtrack."

"It would be understandable if you did."

"But I'm not going to. If I'd known your thoughts would take you down this road, I would have made it clear straight away that this isn't the case. Seeing you in danger didn't make me want to pull back. It made me want to pull you closer. To have you as close as two people can emotionally get."

Wait, what? "Ryder—"

"I told you I was working through some shit. I didn't tell you what all of that shit was." He sighed. "I'm used to people wanting me to change. I'm not just talking about my grandparents. I'm talking about every woman I got involved with."

Frowning, I curled my arms around his neck. "Why did they want you to change? There's nothing wrong with you."

"I told you I don't like staying in one place for long. I don't know if it comes from my years with the MC, or if it comes from being boxed in by rules that made me feel oppressed. But for a long time, I couldn't take the feeling of being tied down. Just couldn't. I moved constantly. Always looked for jobs that had no set hours because routines drove me nuts. I avoided relationships because I knew I wouldn't stick around long.

"After a few years, I found myself able to settle in places for longer periods at a time. Eventually, I did pitch a metaphorical tent somewhere. But that's what the shitty apartment essentially was. A tent. I was rarely there. I'd go on outdoor trips on weekends, hiking and shit. Always alone."

My chest hurt. I knew some people preferred their own company over that of others and were perfectly happy to be solitary creatures. Ryder appeared to be one of them. But I still hated the thought of him having no one to share those times with, even if he'd liked it that way.

"I explained to every woman I got involved with that I wasn't looking for anything serious. They'd say it was fine. They'd say they understood. But it was never long before they started complaining that I didn't take them with me when I went camping or that I didn't always come when they called or that I wouldn't commit in any way. They'd say I was cold or immature or that the trips were just 'code' for me being with other women. Even if I was with others, it shouldn't have been an issue, because I'd explained I didn't want exclusivity. Nothing I ever said in advance mattered. Shit always got slung in my face."

"Until the girlfriend you lost?" I asked, my voice soft.

He shrugged. "Maybe Raquel would have been different, I don't know. I wasn't involved with her long enough to find out. A couple of months. We weren't even really together. It was just another fling."

I almost did a double-take. I'd had it in my head that she was the love of his damn life. Which, really, had been my own paranoia at work. He'd never once implied that they'd been a serious couple or that he'd been head over heels for her.

"It was three days after finding out she was pregnant that we were attacked by a vampire. He dazed me with his gift while he fed from her, and then he Turned me and hightailed it out of there, hoping my conversion would slow Sebastian down—he knew the tracker was on his trail. It worked. Sebastian brought me to The Hollow and then went back to tracking my Sire, who is now very dead."

"He deserves to be."

"Regardless of what some think, I didn't love Raquel. I barely knew her. I didn't really grieve her. I grieved the kid she was carrying—that baby was the only person I'd ever really claimed as mine. Three days later, it was dead. That fucked with me. And so it should have. The baby *should* have been grieved by someone. Should have mattered. He/she mattered to me."

And, like everyone else in his life who'd mattered—his mother, his sister, his grandparents—he'd lost that baby. I gave him a soft kiss. "I'm sorry that happened."

"Me, too." He drew in a sharp breath. "The first time I had you in my bed, there was this … I don't know … burst of possessiveness. Similar to the one I had toward that baby. I wasn't ready to claim someone else. I wasn't ready to *lose* someone else."

Skimming my fingertips over his nape, I gave a slow nod. "I get it."

"I don't know if some subconscious part of me figured that holding back from you would spare me pain or some shit. But what went down with Beatrix … it wouldn't have hurt less to lose you tonight just because I wasn't wholly committed to this relationship. In fact, I'd have regretted that I wasn't. I'm not interested in living with more regrets."

My pulse began to quicken. "What are you saying?"

"I'm saying I'm *all* in this. Mind, body, soul. There might be times where I'm gone from months at a time while tracking—"

"But you'll eventually come back to me," I said, warmth filling my chest. "That's all that matters. I'm not going to do what the women in your past did; I'm not going to make you feel that you need to change. But you'd worried I would, hadn't you? That's part of the 'shit' you were working through, isn't it?"

He stroked a hand over my hair. "It didn't hurt when they did it. They didn't have that power over me, because they didn't matter to me. You matter."

"And you matter to me, exactly as you are. I don't want you to change. I get that you'll have to leave sometimes. I get that you'll have to feed from others while you're gone and that I will, too. It's not ideal, but it's also not the end of the world. And we'll get to have lots of 'oh God, I missed you sex,' so there's that. I'll be happy as long as you always come back to me."

He swallowed. "Yeah?"

"Yeah. And you don't have to worry that I'll ever ask you to Bond with me. I'm not sure that's something you could ever do—"

He snorted. "You're wrong there, baby. That's a future I want with you."

I frowned. "The Bond is *super* intense, Ryder. You don't do well with being tied down," I reminded him.

"I wouldn't see it as being tied down. I'd see it as being tied to *you*. That will work for me just fine."

"You sure?" I asked even as I heard the ring of truth in his voice.

His lips curved. "I'm sure. Now kiss me."

(Ryder)

Her face all soft and warm, Maya lifted her mouth to mine and swiped her tongue over my lower lip. She let out a little hum and nipped that same lip. Then she did it a second time but harder.

Growling, I tangled my hand in the back of her hair. "Fucking kiss me."

She did. Her mouth was hot and urgent as it moved against mine. I let her control the kiss for a few seconds, but then I took over and claimed her mouth in a ravenous kiss. She clung to me, scratching at my nape.

Raw hunger whipped through me, inflaming every nerve-ending. My blood pooled low, and my body tightened.

Wanting no audience, I pulled her away from the balcony without breaking the kiss. Intent on having nothing between her skin and mine, I yanked off the robe she'd slipped on after her shower. She shoved down my sweatpants just enough to let my cock spring free.

Then she dropped to her knees.

Hell. My gut clenched as her soft hand curled tight around my dick—it was full and heavy and aching for her. I sank my fingers into her hair and bunched the silky mass in both hands. "Well go on."

She closed her mouth over the broad head and sucked hard.

I groaned. "Take more. Yeah, sweet girl, just like that." I watched as those lips slid up and down my shaft. "Love stretching your mouth with my cock."

She moved faster, her cheeks hollowed, keeping the suction perfectly tight. That tongue of hers wasn't idle. It licked and rubbed and danced around my dick.

"Want to feel your throat, baby." She swallowed more of my cock, and my eyes fell shut as the muscles in her throat contracted around me. "Uh, *fuck.*"

I lost control. Just lost it. I pumped my dick in and out of her mouth again and again, growling as she dragged her nails down my thighs. When I felt my balls tighten, I knew I needed to stop.

With my grip on her hair, I pulled her off my cock. "Stand," I rumbled. Once she rose to her feet, I bit her swollen lower lip hard just because and backed her up. "Now turn around. Good girl. Hands on the wall. Perfect."

Pressing my front to her back, I splayed one hand on her belly and pushed two fingers inside her. "Beautifully slick, just how I like you." I replaced my fingers with the head of my cock and kissed her nape. "My Maya." I slammed home.

She sucked in a breath, her inner muscles squeezing me tight. "Jesus, Ryder."

I slid my hands up her body and cupped her breasts. "Love stuffing you full with my dick." I nipped her earlobe. "Now fuck yourself."

I thought she'd move slowly at first to tease us both. But she was apparently too eager to come because she threw her hips back hard again and again, roughly impaling herself.

"Yeah, use my cock to get yourself off," I said between licks and nips to her neck. "I want to feel you come all over me."

I alternated between squeezing her breasts and working her taut nipples, loving it each time her inner muscles rippled around me. Needing to taste her, I bit into her throat, drank deep … and she came, her head snapping back, her mouth open on a silent scream.

I growled into her ear. "My turn now." Wicked fast, I turned us away from the wall and brought us both to our knees. "On your elbows, sweet girl. Very good." I grabbed her shoulders, reared back, and rammed my cock deep inside her.

"Fuck," she burst out.

I powered into her without mercy, taking and using and claiming her. She was wholly mine now in every way, and I wanted her to know it. *Feel* it. Feel owned and possessed right down to her soul.

I felt my balls draw up and knew my release would hit me any second. I pounded into her harder, faster. "You're gonna come for me again, Maya. Do it. Now." Keeping a tight grip on one of her shoulders, I fisted her hair and snatched her head back hard enough to make her wince. And then she came again, dragging me with her.

Struggling to catch my breath after our orgasms eased away, I leaned over and pressed a kiss to the spot between her shoulder blades. "All mine," I said, curling my arms around her.

She let out a soft chuckle. "Well, yeah. Not to scare you or anything, but I kind of love you. It's okay if you're not there yet—*ow, can't breathe.*"

I loosened my hold on her. "Sorry." I kissed her nape. "I love you, too."

"*Boom.*"

I chuckled. "Boom?"

"Well I'd do a fist pump and stuff, maybe even a happy dance, but I can barely move, so a simple 'boom' will have to do."

"All right. Though I'm curious … what is a happy dance?"

She glanced at me over her shoulder. "What, like, you want me to actually show you?"

"If it'll make your tits jiggle, definitely. Come on, show me. I dare you."

"Dares are what got us into this."

"And aren't we glad of that?"

She smiled softly. "Yeah, we are."

ACKNOWLEDGEMENTS

There are so many people to thank ...

My family for all their support and encouragement. My son for designing the new book covers to revamp - no pun intended - the series. My PA, Melissa, for being so awesome and freeing up time for me to write. My editor, Melody Guy, for her keen eye and the invaluable advice she never fails to deliver. And last but not least to all those who took a chance on CAPTIVATED, I hope you enjoyed it!

Take care

S :)

ABOUT THE AUTHOR

Suzanne Wright lives in England with her husband, two children, and two Bengal cats. When she's not spending time with her family, she's writing, reading, or doing her version of housework—sweeping the house with a look.

TITLES BY SUZANNE WRIGHT

The Deep in Your Veins Series
Here Be Sexist Vampires
The Bite That Binds
Taste of Torment
Consumed
Fractured
Captivated
Touch of Rapture

The Phoenix Pack Series
Feral Sins
Wicked Cravings
Carnal Secrets
Dark Instincts
Savage Urges
Fierce Obsessions
Wild Hunger
Untamed Delights

The Dark in You Series
Burn
Blaze
Ashes
Embers
Shadows
Omens
Fallen
Reaper (Coming 2022)

The Mercury Pack Series
Spiral of Need
Force of Temptation
Lure of Oblivion
Echoes of Fire
Shards of Frost

The Olympus Pride Series
When He's Dark
When He's an Alpha
When He's Sinful (Coming 2022)

The Devil's Cradle Series (Coming 2022)
The Wicked in Me
The Nightmare in Him
The Monsters We Are

Standalones
From Rags
Shiver
The Favor